THE BRONZE HORN
Book One of the Alionian Saga
By
Kelly Washington-McBride

Acknowledgements

In the process of writing this book, there were many people that encouraged and inspired me. To all of my family and friends I say thank you! To Jadeenah, Jada, Kay, Laura and Lillian, my original book crew, thank you for questioning intentions, motives, and decisions of my characters. You made me dig deep. To Debra Spivey and Amelia Ketzle, thank you for keeping me professional. I appreciate and respect your advice. To my father Larry Jones, who is a constant source of inspiration, thank you for reminding me of what I am capable of accomplishing. To my mother, Barbara Jones, I want to say thank you for reading every word and pushing me to finish this book. Without your encouragement I would never have achieved my goal. Thank you to Cassia and Caleb for giving me quiet moments to write. To Aaron McBride, thank you for accompanying me on this literary journey. I know it wasn't easy listening to all of the late night revisions, and the revisions of those revisions, but you listened patiently and responded with enthusiasm. I love you! Thank you for being my muse and my inspiration. Your continued support and interest in this endeavor means the world to me.

Dedication:

To Aaron. My lover. My hero. My friend. I'm your biggest fan.

Chapter 1

Elaina wrung her hands nervously as she paced the floor, bracing for the next wave of screams and muffled noises. It was happening again, only this time it was worse than ever. The sound of pottery crashing to the floor, followed by growls and shouting, filled her ears, causing her to cover them in protest. Elaina was not unaccustomed to such behavior from the rooms above hers. Her father, Gregor Ingleman, would often come to calm the tempest that raged there. Her sister Emona, the elder of the two, was not one known for her gentle temperament. She, a direct opposite from Elaina, would rant and rave and bring those around her to thorough abuse if her slightest demands were not met. Their father would forcefully, yet with a loving hand, compel her to submission.

This time, however, circumstances were different. This time her father was not at Ingleman Hall. He had sailed away some months back on an agricultural mission for the king. *There would be no calming the storm this night,* thought Elaina. The tempest would rage on.

She brushed the black curls away from her face, pinning a few tendrils behind her ear as she did whenever she was nervous. She searched for something to take her mind off of the chaos. She'd been working on a face cloth for her father, embroidered with Kyridian vines that surrounded her mother's initials.

E.I.

Elaina's mother, Ella, had fallen ill during child birth. The knowledge that her entrance into this world had marked her mother's exit had always been a source of pain for her. She was often told that her eyes, those dark brown pools of mysterious beauty, held a keen wisdom that belonged to her Ella. Elaina held tightly to that knowledge, feeling it her only connection to a mother she'd never know.

She began her stitching with shaky fingers. She was in no way an expert at the needle but she produced fine work when she applied herself.

More pottery crashed.

It was not the shouting, angry male voices that gave her a harrowing start. It was a woman's hysterical screams. Those screams pulsed so with terror that before she realized it, she was flying down the corridor to the stairs.

Emona, she thought. *Great One let her be okay*!

The smell of old musky wood ebbed its way into her nostrils, filling her like a memorable lullaby. She used to play games with her sister Emona under these very stairs. They would squeal and giggle and pretend to be a part of the Kings Court. They would adorn themselves with yellow swallow buds from their father's field and wait for their prince to come and find them. Here, under these stairs, their games were harmless. Now, Elaina feared, her sister played a game that might cost her everything.

She ran breathless to the top of the stairwell that led to her sister's dwelling. The Autumn Chamber, as it was called, had been built by Gregor for his bride years ago. Emona, being the first to reach the age of womanhood at twenty and one three years prior, had won the privilege of claiming the luxurious rooms for herself. The door was made of strong cherry wood intricately laid with gold edging. The inside boasted ivory columns in the "King Style" that most royalty had become accustomed to. The floor was fashioned from marble that gleamed its way out to the balcony, overlooking a breathtaking private garden.

Emona had wasted no time putting her own personal touches on her new residence. Rich blue and red silks draped over her couches and beautiful flowers bloomed in numerous vases about the apartment. She loved flowers and demanded that they be delivered fresh to her daily.

Emona, Elaina noted, demanded a great deal from those around her in general. She was born a farmer's daughter of low rank and modest fortune and yet she deemed all others, both noble and serf, beneath her. All were pawns in her grand scheme of life.

As Elaina opened the massive cherry wood door to her sisters flat, she gasped at the scene that lay before her. Broken furniture intertwined with once beautiful tapestries cluttered the floor. A field of broken glass and trampled flowers covered the scuffed marble. Lifting the hem of her skirts, Elaina made her way through the scattered effects and down the hall until she reached the climax of the wreckage. She felt her body grow cold as she stared in horror at what she guessed was the final result of the chaos. A young man lay on the floor, head bloodied and body lifeless. His enemy crouched over him, ready to strike if the body miraculously revived itself.

A soundless scream welled up from her churning stomach, only to be lodged, unmoving in her throat. Frozen by the sight of the deep red blood spreading over the white marble, she was hardly aware of her brother Uman bounding up the stairs behind her.

He stopped short, assessing the damage. "What happened here?" His whispered words piercing the deafening silence. It was an unnecessary question. The truth of it was evident in the crimson stain pooled around the crumpled mass. Regardless, he walked over to the body and knelt beside it to check for signs of life.

Elaina noticed Lai, Emona's personal servant, huddled in a corner, her tear stained face contorted in fear and shock. "Go get Uncle Seth," Uman instructed. Too vexed to move, Lai let out a muffled shriek. "Go get Seth now!" Uman shouted. "He will need to contact the authorities and notify the Earl of Beltrane of this crime." She forced herself to her feet and attempted an unidentifiable curtsey as she hurried out the door.

"That will not be necessary," said Emona who was draped seductively over a chaise in a corner of the lavish room. Even in the midst of the chaos Emona had managed to remain effortlessly regal. She was the raving beauty that evoked desire in even the most chaste of men. Her hazel eyes shimmered against her smooth olive skin. Her mouth was as ruby red as the velvet gown she wore. Her ample bosom was accented by a silver pendant that hung gracefully around her neck. She was the epitome of femininity.

"It was nothing more than a little skirmish," she said dryly. She rose to her feet and let her full mane of jet black curls loosely fall about her waist, framing her body.

"A simple skirmish? There's a dead man on the floor!"

"Even so," Emona said coolly, "If you feel it your noble duty to contact the Earl and make these events known to him, feel free to plead your case to his heir." Emona smirked victoriously as Uman turned his gaze to the crouching figure next to him. The man stood to his full stature and Elaina realized it was Manin Beltrane, son of Warren Beltrane, Earl of The Upper Mantle, proprietor of their province. As she walked further into the wreckage she realized, to her dismay, that the dead man was Farid Galron.

Both Farid and Manin were descendants of near royalty and also cousins. Both men were bound together by blood but even more by loyalty and friendship…or so had been the case as they trained side by side in the King's army. Were they not men of valor and chivalry? Men of both skill and restraint? She looked down at Farid's crumpled body. His mouth held remnants of froth and blood and his open eyes bulged from their sockets. No, this was not the work of a nobleman's hands. This was rage and insanity!

Elaina cautiously turned towards Manin, searching his face for answers. She looked to find signs of regret or sadness over the loss of his one-time brother. If they were indeed there, he kept them well hidden under the cold, conscience-less stare of anger that darkened his chiseled features.

Both Manin and Farid were determined to claim Emona as their bride. It had begun as a genial competition, a challenge between friends. They would woo her and court her until she made her choice. Somehow something had gone terribly wrong!

For the past week Farid had taken it upon himself to camp outside their family's estate, refusing to leave until Emona agreed to marry him. He swore that he'd rather meet some ill fate than concede to his cousin, or to any other man, for that matter. He would win Emona or die trying. *How ironic*, Elaina thought sadly, *that the latter would in fact be his fate.*

Uncle Seth stormed through the entryway in his usual haughty manner with two footmen in tow. At the sight of him Emona swooned, allowing him to catch her just in time.

"What is this?" Seth demanded. "Who dares bring such violence into our home?" He hoisted Emona into his arms and carried her to a nearby couch. He called for a stirring tonic and pressed it to her lips. Emona woke with a gasp, sputtering and choking at the bitter concoction.

She weakly looked up at Seth, all feminine frailty. "Oh Uncle Seth. I am so glad that you are here. It was the most terrible thing." She clung to him like an ocean's victim being pulled under by unforgiving waves. "Farid...he tried to...." Emona collapsed against him sobbing uncontrollably.

"Now, now my little flower. Do not fret so. All will be right. Tell me what happened and I will see you avenged."

"Farid asked for an audience with me. I agreed only because he sent word that he had something very urgent to discuss. But when he arrived here, he became angry and he attacked me. He said if I didn't agree to marry him right now…he….he would kill me."

"I thought that all was lost until Manin arrived." Emona purred, lifting her eyes to her "hero." "He surmised that his cousin's intentions for meeting me were not at all honorable, so he followed him here. He arrived just in time to save me." She lowered her sumptuous lashes, demurely adding, "I shudder to think what might have happened were it not for Lord Beltrane. Through his gallant feat of strength and skill he relieved me of my tormentor."

Elaina did not recall hearing Emona in distress during the battle. She had only considered it possible when she heard a woman's hysterical screams. She was now aware that they belonged to Lai. She should have recognized her girlish shrieks. It was not the first time she had heard them. Once again Elaina felt a knot tighten in her stomach. Emona's tale was surprisingly convincing. Elaina had witnessed her sister's indifference to the entire affair moments prior, and yet, even now she could easily believe that Emona's terror was real.

Seth was aghast at such pronouncements. He believed the noble class to be superior in every way. "How could this have happened?" he said. "He is a nobleman, by God! He comes from one of the best houses in the kingdom. Is our world becoming so devoid of morals that men of stature and means behave like murderers and thieves?"

"I believe it was madness, sir." Manin, seeing the opening that Emona had weaved for him, eagerly stepped into the role of the hero. "Farid had been ill at ease these last few days and I noticed that his behavior had grown strange and perverse. I am sorry for his indiscretion and pray that it does not dampen your outlook on our House."

Seth eyed him coolly. "No, I will not fault all for the folly of one. You, after all, have dealt justice to our enemy. I commend you, my Lord."

Manin made a slight bow at the waist. "It is my honor to serve my House as well as yours, sir."

Seth ordered the footmen to remove the body and have it sent to his family. "They will no doubt want their own time to grieve this matter." As the footmen carried out their orders, Seth conferred with Uman. They talked quietly and Uman sent side long glances at Manin, who had now made his way to the seemingly helpless creature on the couch. Elaina knew that Uman was not pleased with Seth's acceptance of Manin's actions. She could hear him arguing with their uncle, speaking of murder and justice. But there was nothing for it. Seth would hear nothing else on the matter. Manin was nobility and no doubt had the sincerest intentions for Emona's welfare.

"Are you alright, Emona?" Elaina could hear the distress in her own voice. The evening's events had been most upsetting. And given Emona's flippant behavior, she was uncertain how she should proceed. "Did he… hurt you? Is there something that I can do to…?"

"Of course I'm alright," Emona snapped. "And I'll be even better when this mess is cleaned up. Lai, Lai. Oh where is that silly girl? Go retrieve her and tell her to bring several of the house maids with her. I need to have my rooms cleaned immediately. Well…what are you waiting for? Shall I have to fetch her myself?" She turned an annoyed glare at Manin. "It's a wonder how I manage in this household with such incompetence!"

Elaina was beginning to lose all sisterly concern for Emona. Obviously she was not in distress and the likelihood that she had been threatened by Farid was dwindling more and more by the moment. She thought to protest, but just as she opened her mouth to speak, Seth called for everyone's attention.

"It has been a troublesome day. I know that had your father been here, he would be grief-stricken at an attack on one so precious to him. He would also be grateful to one so noble of character and virtue, stepping in to right the wrongs of a lecherous cur. Since your father is not here," he said to Emona with arrogance aplenty, "I will stand in his stead to offer my sincerest thanks and gratitude for Lord Beltrane's actions."

Elaina could not help but see the personal satisfaction on her uncle's face. Seth, the eldest of the two children born to Leros Ingleman, had never been willing to learn the family trade. He concerned himself with matters of station and breeding, longing for the life of a nobleman. He cared little for the land that Gregor and their father Leros cherished so richly. Intent on living a life of ease, Seth spent much of his time vying for a position amongst the social elite.

Seth was angry when their father passed and entailed everything to Gregor. Seth was the eldest son. The land was his birthright to possess. But feeling that responsibility to one's future generations was more important than the hurt feelings of one shiftless individual, Leros left the Estate to the offspring that he thought would cherish it the most. So it was that Gregor inherited the land on which his family lived.

He cultivated and multiplied the yields that were produced there and became a prosperous man in his trade. He was not a nobleman. He cared little for such titles but his family was well provided for. He even allowed Seth to live in the house that he built upon the announcement of his engagement. Seth was permitted to live at Ingleman Hall as long as life flowed within him, but he could never inherit the land. Such pronouncement was bittersweet for Seth, who had no way to support himself. His brother was his livelihood, a notion that always left a festering aggravation between them.

Seth rarely received the opportunity to exert his elderly authority and wisdom over his brother's household. Whenever the opportunity did present itself, he grasped the reins and steered events to his favor.

"My heart is heavy for your family's loss," he continued. "And for the burden you must bear for righting this wrong." Manin made a slight incline of his head as if to humbly accept his words. "However, in the face of such tragedy I believe we can find joy. Joy that there are still good men in this world, ready to spring into action and save the weak and helpless."

Elaina chuckled slightly at the thought of Emona being weak and helpless. She had witnessed her ferociously beat the stable boy for not saddling her horse properly. She could manipulate men with the slightest of ease. One wink of an eye or a simple coy smile and she had them in the palm of her hand. She even seemed to hold an uncanny power over most women. She would fight for whatever she wanted and she always won. She also controlled Seth, even though he would never admit it. The only two people that Elaina deemed immune to her charms were herself and her father. No, there was nothing weak and helpless about Emona.

"So it is my humble pleasure to reward you with the greatest gift that I can bestow upon one as noble and prosperous as you. We have not much, but that which we have, we offer to you freely. May I present my niece's hand to you as a symbol of our esteem and sincerest thanks? She is of low birth, but she possesses great beauty and vitality. If she finds favor with you, accept her hand as a token of my, nay, her father's, gratitude. I know that you will care for and defend her for the rest of your life in as much as you have done so today."

The gleam in Manin's eye was unmistakable. He was being offered what he desired above all else. Shielding his excitement he took Emona's hand in his. "It was but my duty to protect your fair niece. She is a rose among weeds, too delicate to be trampled under wolves' paws. Though she is of low birth, she is a rare jewel. I would be a fool to deny myself such a gift. Yes, I will accept your most generous offer and take her as my bride."

Jubilation spread through the flat and to the remaining inhabitants of the estate. There was to be a wedding between a farmer's daughter and a nobleman's son. Could a better thing have happened to their family? Even the servants were bustling about in celebration. "God has smiled on the house of Gregor," she heard one of the maids say as they tidied the apartment. "Indeed," beamed her elated companion.

Elaina did not share in their happiness. The knot in her stomach grew tighter as a sense of foreboding overwhelmed her. She noted the look on her sister's face as her uncle announced her betrothal. It was not a look of joy and acceptance. It was one of defiance.

Time seemed to slow down considerably as Elaina watched Seth clasp arms with Manin. The latter displayed a wolfish grin that sent a shiver down her spine. The room grew dark and her ears filled with a crackling sound like the crushing of leaves. Out of the darkness a scene emerged, hazy at first, then clear and crisp. Smoke billowed around her, syphoning the air from her lungs. A great house was in flames and its inhabitants cried out to her to save them. She stumbled through the wreckage, drawn to the voices, searching for their owners. In the distance she saw a small lacquered box that pulsed and beat with an unnatural cadence. She reached for it but was hindered by the recognition of her name being called.

"Elaina...Elaina! What is wrong with you, child? Do you not hear me calling you?" Uncle Seth frowned down at her. "Tell the cook that we will celebrate in grand style tonight. She is to prepare a feast fit for a king!"

Shaking herself from her vision, Elaina turned to obey her uncle's orders. In doing so she caught a glimpse of Emona, a defiant gleam in her eye, smiling placidly at her intended. At that moment Elaina was sure that the engagement would result in the destruction of her family.

Their father was a well-respected man in their community, but he was not immune to the law. The Nobles held the ear of the King. If this agreement was not met, then Gregor would pay the price. She was saddened to think that anything could harm her father but she understood Emona's determination to have things her way, and the fact that she cared very little about whom she hurt in the process. *"Oh Great One be merciful,"* she moaned, clutching her stomach.

She quit the apartment, flew down the stairs, and ran out of the main door into the light of the moon. Several concerned maids scrambled after her, stopping in the entryway long enough to see the tiny figure in the distance, emptying her worry on the front lawn.

Chapter 2

Elaina navigated her way through the great room and down the corridor that led to the kitchen. The smell of savory dumplings and tea cakes called to her. She hadn't eaten all morning and her stomach growled in protest. Seamstresses, tailors, and makers of other finery had descended upon the house in force, holding her hostage for hours.

"Freedom," she declared, when they finally decided to break for a brief intermission. It had been three months since Emona's engagement to Manin and since that time the house had been a carnival of preparation. Emona wanted the best of everything for her special day. Flowers were to be brought in from Ingaria and Ilemans Plains. Expensive silks and lace were acquired from merchants across the sea. The best musicians the kingdom had to offer were hired to entertain the guests. Family and friends from both houses had to be notified in the "proper" manner, so Manin's formidable mother, Countess Cynthia Beltrane, arranged for a wedding planner, Lady Winthrop, to handle all of the formalities. She was a short, stout woman with a constant look of disapproval on her face.

"Sit up straight. Tuck in your stomach. You don't want to look like a puffer fish on the greatest day of your sister's life. Walk like a lady, not a scullery maid!" It was enough to set one's nerves on edge. As soon as the round faced little woman announced that there would be a break in their work, Elaina sprang from her chair and ran through the great room. This was her chance to escape and she intended on doing just that! A few of the tradesmen laughed as she fled the room. The planner shot them her signature glare and called out behind Elaina, "Don't stray too far. We will convene again shortly and your presence will be required."

"Oh bother," she said as she entered the kitchen. The ladies that made up the highly praised team of cooks smiled warmly at her from their stations. Elaina could smell the works of their hands. Roasted duck with apricots, potatoes seasoned with herbs from the garden, vegetables full of life and color. Pies of varying flavors lined the cooling racks surrounded by a myriad of other delicacies. "Sweet heavens! Cooks are the most wonderful people in this world." She reached for a savory dumpling only to recoil in pain when Welda, the head cook, slapped her hand, frowning sternly.

"Don't touch that! Countess Beltrane has arranged a formal meeting between our house and theirs. They are coming to dine with us tonight. Your uncle has ordered more food than necessary but it will indeed be a grand feast." She pulled out a loaf of fresh bread and cheese and sliced a few pieces off for Elaina.

"He wants everything to be perfect for tonight." She placed two dumplings on Elaina's plate and coaxed her to sit and eat. Welda was one of Elaina's favorite people. She was wild at heart but full of wisdom. She had been a cook in her mother's house and accompanied her when she married Gregor. Her face was wrinkled with time and care and her hair gray with worry for the ones she loved. She had no children but she had loved Elaina's mother as her own. Now her devotion extended to Ella's children.

"I can't wait until all of this is over," Elaina whined.

"Events like these are a part of life. And now that your sister will be joined with one of the Noble Houses, you had better start getting used to attending them. Besides, you have always been so fond of weddings. Why do you despise them now?"

Elaina knew her answer but could not put it to words. Those feelings of dread and despair had never truly left her. She felt strong enough to lock them away in a dark corner of her heart, but she could not eliminate them completely. She felt her stomach start to tighten again and resisted the ever-growing sense of foreboding that raged inside of her. How could she explain her feelings to Welda when she did not fully understand the cause of them herself?

"I… I don't despise them. It's just..." she swallowed hard. "There is so much preparation that it makes me dizzy." She shoved a dumpling in her mouth and felt a twinge of regret when she realized that she had eaten without really enjoying any of it. Welda was one of the best cooks in the entire kingdom. Elaina never took for granted anything that she made.

"Well, I am sure you are just tired. Go on to your room and take a rest. You have a long evening ahead of you."

"But what about the tradesmen and that ill-tempered Lady Windbag? She will likely advise Uncle Seth to beat me for not returning."

Welda gave a little chuckle. "Not that your Uncle has a stomach for that sort of thing. But maybe that's not a bad idea." At this they both laughed and Welda shooed her upstairs.

"Don't worry about Lady Winthrop. I'll take care of her."

Once in the safety of her own room, Elaina stared up at the ceiling, her mind whirling. Why was she so fearful? Emona had participated in every step of the planning of her nuptials thus far. She even showed some excitement over the materials bought for her gown and made a fuss over the dinner menu. She appeared to be the perfect bride, hopeful and full of wonder. She even seemed calmer in nature. Early in the morning she would often rise and take a long ride out in the country. Her affection for nature was not great but she loved her horse and would go riding for hours.

Maybe she's happy. Maybe she loves Manin and truly wants to be his bride.

She curled herself up into a little ball as she looked out of her window. The sun had taken on a golden hue and splashed the sky with bright pinks and purples.

Maybe...

She slipped from consciousness into the world of dreams. Even still, the cold fingers of despair sent an icy current down her spine. She pushed it away and settled deeper into her dream. It was warm and inviting and she let it embrace her completely. Worry would have to wait. It was time for rest. Their guests would soon be arriving and she would have to greet them with a radiant and refreshed face. Little did she know that no amount of sleep could prepare her for what was to come.

She arose to the sound of hooves beating on the cobblestone road. The guests were arriving. She found a wash bowl and towel that one of the maids left for her while she slept. The water was still warm and felt nice on her skin. She picked out a gown of deep blue with lace around the neckline. Glittering sapphires dripped from her ears and neck. They had once belonged to her mother and she wore them with pride on special occasions. Elaina had never been one to flaunt her beauty. She was a modest girl who enjoyed modest things, yet she couldn't help admiring the reflection in her mirror. Her long black curls were pinned back with a sapphire clip that had been fashioned into a butterfly. She let a few tendrils fall to frame her face and the rest she let flow down her back like a satin curtain. She smiled at herself. She knew she'd never be Emona, but today she felt beautiful. She sauntered down the stairwell trying to look as graceful as possible. The room was filled with the essence of Krydian flowers. It was customary to use this flower at weddings because the Krydian itself released a light and airy aroma that made one euphoric. It was said that it symbolized the love and bliss of a newly wedded couple.

Elaina gave a quick curtsey to her guests as she passed them on the way to the kitchen. Most were strangers; however, she did notice a few familiar faces. There were several nobles, people of great importance that often visited the estate to conduct business with her father.

The cooks were bustling about at a dizzying speed. Elaina could hear Welda shouting orders before she had crossed the threshold. She smiled to herself. Welda had a strength about her that was peculiar. When she spoke, people listened. Even her Uncle seemed to have respect for her.

"What are you doing in here?" she demanded. "You are supposed to be entertaining your guests."

"I know," Elaina murmured, "but I don't know many of them. I was nervous." She picked up a tart from a serving tray. "And besides, I wanted you to see how I look."
She stood up and twirled around letting Welda see the expanse of her dress.

"How lovely, Elaina. You're the very image of your mother. It's a wonder if Emona is not the only one that walks away betrothed tonight."

Elaina gave a hearty snort. "When I marry it will be for love, not money or title. I could care less if he is a nobleman or the King himself. He must love me and I him. That will be the way of it."

Welda's smile was tight and far from amused. "From what slumber tale did this bit of logic come, my dear? At some point you may find that your dreams can hardly become reality. The choice of a husband for love is not even guaranteed to the rich. The only thing that you can hope for is to marry well and pray that he is kind."

Elaina shuddered at her words. *Is that what really awaits me?* She shook her head.

"Mother and father married for love."

Welda's eyes grew sad. "Yes, my dear, they did. Your mother...she was...well, a special kind of woman."

"And you all say that I am just like her. Maybe my choice of marriage will be also."

Welda gave up the fight and said, "Yes, maybe it will be." She turned away from Elaina to check a tray of tarts that a young scullery maid had just pulled from the oven. "No, these have not browned enough. Return them for five more minutes. Sarah, make sure that you do not forget the......"

Gregor had always teased that Welda's ability to strategically execute a feast to perfection made her a wonder in her own right. She commanded her crew with precision and determination.

Like a general to her soldiers, Elaina chuckled.

"Enough with your daydreaming." Welda shouted over her shoulder. "Get in there and entertain your guests."

The evening had gone as planned thus far and Elaina was starting to breathe a sigh of relief. Nothing wayward had happened and they were more than half way through the event, though it did strike her odd that Emona had not ventured from her apartment. It was almost time for dinner to begin and the groom had advised everyone to take their seats. Elaina found her place between Uman and one of Manin's uncles. General Patesh was a kind old man who had fought for the King in his younger days. Now he was an advisor to his army and one of the Kings closest friends. "You look lovely my dear. Why, if I was a young man I would ask you for your hand," he mused.

"General Patesh, you are yet in your prime," she cooed. "But I am afraid that if I agreed to the match, many a young lady would fall into despair at losing a chance with so distinguished a gentleman as yourself."

"If I weren't old enough to have known your grandfather, stout upstanding fellow that he was, I would take my chances with the despair. But some young man will no doubt offer for you and my heart will be broken," he teased.

"Yes, and I am sure that Lady Patesh would be there to pick up the pieces."

"Quite right, my dear," he winked. "Quite right."

Elaina continued in their light conversation while watching the stairs. She knew that Emona loved to make a grand entrance. She smiled at the General and mindlessly continued her flattering praises. At last she heard footsteps coming from the stairwell. *Emona*, she thought. But it was only Lai. The small figure stopped at the entryway and looked about the room and focused at the head of the table. She made a slight bow as she headed towards Seth with a weathered look on her face. She whispered in his ear and his face turned stony and pale. Elaina's heart sank. She felt the lump tighten in her stomach. She sharply inhaled to keep from doubling over from the pain. Seth signaled for the groom and gave instruction for the dinner to begin immediately. He admonished his guests to eat and drink to their hearts content, and then, flashing his warmest smile, quickly excused himself from the table. The servants poured out from the kitchen right on cue, filling every goblet with red currant wine.

They were into the third course when the guests started to inquire about Seth and the bride to be. Hushed whispers spread around the dining hall. "I wonder what's wrong?" said a tall slender woman across from Elaina. "She must be ill."

Sensing that something had gone awry, Countess Beltrane offered a reasonable explanation. "I was so nervous during my betrothal to Warren that I took ill. I find that it happens to many brides as their wedding day approaches."

Elaina nodded to her gratefully, "She was a little feverish this morning. Maybe I should go and check on her." With unfeigned concern etched into her features, she excused herself and made her way to the stairs.

She rounded the corner to the main room and realized that Uman had escaped the onslaught of inquiries from eager guests. Upon seeing her, he quickly dropped his eyes and turned questioningly to Seth, who had stationed himself on the balcony that overlooked the garden. He glanced over his shoulder, noticing her presence, but remained silent. Elaina turned towards Emona, who was standing in a glittering silver gown that looked as if it had been gleamed from the stars themselves. Her arms crossed at her breast and she wore a look of sheer defiance.

"What's wrong? Emona, are you sick? Shall I send for a physician?" Elaina tried to remain calm but their silence was unnerving.

"Has something happened? Uncle? Will someone tell me what's-" Elaina's inquiries were cut short by a sudden commotion rising from the stairwell.

"Out of my way! I demand to see what is wrong with my bride!" Manin and his mother had forced their way past a protesting footman and straight into the apartment.

"Ah, Emona, my darling, what a vision you are," he said, overcome with love. "It pains me to know that our guests have not been afforded the opportunity to revel in your beauty as much as I." His golden hair fell smartly over his ears and ended in a brown speckled cut at the nape of his neck. His chiseled features always made Elaina think of one of the statues that graced the halls of The Citadel. He was a handsome man from a well-respected family and she could understand why Emona would choose him as her mate.

"Come, we should not keep our guests waiting." He turned and headed for the door but halted when he saw that Emona made no move to follow.

"I will not be attending tonight's festivities," said Emona. Manin looked shocked. He moved closer to her, not fully understanding her protest.

"You need not be nervous, my love. The house of Warren welcomes you with open arms. There is no one who will refuse you honor. Just take my hand and I will escort you to our guests...."

Manin held out his hand and Emona recoiled at the sight of it. He looked from Emona to his mother and back to Emona again.

"What...what is this? Are you ill?"

"No, I am not ill," snapped Emona. "I will not accompany you because I do not wish to marry you."

The Countess eased herself into a plush high-backed chair. The color had drained from her face and hysteria took over. "What is the meaning of this? I demand answers! The House of Warren will not be mocked."

"My intentions, my lady, are simply to free myself from a claim that I never agreed to. My hand was given to your son without my consent. I have already promised myself to another and will be married four days hence."

Upon hearing this news, Manin leapt at Emona. Grabbing hold of her shoulders, he shook her and screamed, "No! You are mine! You have been promised to me! You love me! How can you say that you want another?" He gazed into Emona's eyes, searching, silently pleading with his own. He found no compassion in them, only the cold stare of a woman dead set against his claim.

Emona shook free of him and spat, "I belong to no one. I give myself to whomever I please and it will not be you."

Elaina couldn't believe what she was hearing. Emona had never protested the marriage and neither did she refuse the gifts that Manin and his family had sent her. She had participated in all of the planning and betrothal events up until this point. A sense of panic spread through her. *What will this mean for our family? For father?* Gregor had sailed to Lanier Isles on business three months prior to the announcement of their betrothal and had not yet returned.

"How dare you! Do you think that you can so easily break your engagement contract? Your insolence will not be tolerated! You have brought shame upon our house with your scandal!" Lady Beltrane raged. Her face turned red and distorted with disgust. "I claim full right of lineage and will bring this matter before the King!" she threatened.

Seth, who had remained silent through the entire exchange, spread his arms in a gesture of friendship and flashed a boyish grin. "Dearest Countess, if I may," he stepped forward not waiting for her reply. "I am sure we can come to some sort of agreement that will be beneficial to everyone. There is no need for legal recourse. Let us settle this here and now."

"What do you have in mind?" barked the countess, unmoved by the cordiality of Seth's speech.

"There can still be a joining of houses. I have another niece of marrying age. She is comely and smart and very respectful. She is pure and in good health and should bear your son many children."

Elaina heard a sharp inhale and a smothered cry. It took her a moment to realize that it had come from her.

The Noblewoman's attention turned towards Elaina and she eyed her coolly. "Hmm," she said, "Maybe. She is pure enough in aspect to at least belie the look of virtue. But she has no formal training in the ways of nobility. I will not suffer shame upon our house due to some insolent trollop!"

Seth moved in to satiate the chance for an agreement. "Of course, my Lady, but who better to teach her the ways of nobility and virtue than you? Take her as your son's wife and mold her into the image that best pleases you."

For a moment the world went silent. Elaina saw the exchange of offers between the two guardians but the only sound she heard was the rush of blood flowing through her veins, stopping at her heart, coaxing it to beat, making it continue to function. It was as if she was standing outside of her body, witnessing the barter of her life for the sake another's happiness. She looked to Emona. Surely her sister would not agree to this madness. She did not want to marry Manin. *Emona will not let this happen*, she assured herself. But to her despair her sister said nothing. She stood there, stony and defiant, ensuring that her demands were met.

Elaina felt the icy fingers of desperation envelop her once more. In her heart she screamed for help. In her mind she pleaded with herself to run. But she remained hopelessly anchored to the floor.

"No, I will not have her." Manin stood in the corner like a lowly school boy, dejected and angry. "I will have Emona or no one else!"

"It is I who will decide who you will have!" shouted Lady Beltrane. "You have chosen poorly by electing to mingle our noble line with one that is obviously morally inferior. You would squander our good name over a harlot's bed? I think not."

She rose from her chair and strode over to Elaina. She circled her, examining every inch of her petite frame. "He will have her," she nodded. "But she will stay at our Manor for a year to learn proper etiquette and decorum. The wedding shall be postponed until further notice." She looked at Emona, seething with hatred. "I take it that you can pretend to love my son for one more evening. Our guests need not know what has transpired here. I demand this recompense for the pain you have caused my family."

"It shall be so," Seth said quickly, wanting desperately to seal the deal.

"This is hardly the greeting that we expected from your family" said the Noblewoman. "But I feel that we have reached a suitable arrangement. I will send for her things in the morning."

"Wonderful!" beamed Seth. "Now let us join our guests and share in the celebration of young love."

The atmosphere was strained, but strangely enough everyone, with the exception of Manin and Elaina, seemed a bit relieved that the crisis had been averted. Everyone filed from the room and down the stairs. Only Elaina remained. Confused and dismayed, she desperately struggled to understand what had just taken place. In a matter of moments, her, life had changed, and she was powerless to stop it. A bundle of emotions smoldered inside of her until she could hold them no longer. Falling to the floor she let go of her anguish. She pulled her knees up to her chin and sobbed into her dress. Her tears became a storm, unrelenting and torrential, siphoning every ounce of strength she owned. Too weak to move, there was nothing left to do but wait for the darkness to come and swallow her up into an ever-looming void of nothingness.

Chapter 3

"Elaina. Elaina, wake up."

She opened her eyes to the blurry recollection of her room. The familiarity of her surroundings lulled her momentarily into a false sense of normalcy. She sat up slowly. Every inch of her was stiff with pain. Every muscle screamed in protest. *Was it all a dream?*

"Good morning dear." Welda stood before her with a breakfast tray. "I brought you something to eat. You will need your strength if you are to journey to the Upper Mantle today. Here, drink this." She handed her of mug of spiced tea. "It will put some color in your face." Suddenly the events of the preceding night came rushing back to her. She was being shipped to an unknown place to satisfy the ire of nobility. Tears welled up in her eyes and involuntarily spilled over.

"Oh, come now, my lamb. Don't spend your strength on tears," Welda said, hugging her about the shoulders. "Your uncle and sister are waiting for you downstairs. We must get you dressed so you can meet them."

Elaina had little desire to see Seth or Emona. She had many things to say to them, but she did not think that she would be able to muster the strength to do so. She hastily dressed, and at Welda's insistence, gobbled down her breakfast. She gave Welda a quick hug and took to the stairs.

Seth and Emona seemed to be in high spirits that early morning hour. "Ah, there she is," he said. "The bride to be." He embraced her and planted a kiss on her forehead. "What an honor to have both of my nieces married to the King's bloodline."

"Yes, congratulations, sister. You have done well for yourself." Emona sat at the heavy oak table, stirring her tea and smiling. "You will make a most beautiful bride."

Elaina felt a flood of anger surge through her. How could they be relaxed and content when they had just given her away as if she was nothing more than a child's rag doll?

"I have done nothing for myself. It is you who have brought me to this end." Her words became an angry torrent, hard and unforgiving. "You have traded me away like some child's plaything, or a shop keeper's wares, given to the highest bidder. To you my life is no more than a tool for barter."

Emona pushed her chair from the table and indignantly answered, "He is nobility. In his house you will live in wealth and splendor. He is handsome and well respected. What more can a girl of your station ask for? You should be more grateful. He is a good choice for you."

"Why should I be grateful for that which you did not want nor could appreciate? He was not my choice, he was yours, and you rejected him for another. Why must I pay the price for your flippant ways? Why should I be forced to marry a man that I do not love?"

"Silence child! You know the law," snapped Seth. "We have made an agreement with their House and it must be met. Furthermore, Emona is to be wed to a Nobleman from Ingaria. He is very wealthy and a cousin to King Arilian himself. An alliance of such magnitude could spell many good things for our family. Would you have me throw all of that away for some childish notion of love?"

"I would have you to consider me, Uncle! To think of my feelings before you so easily gave me away."

"But I did consider you." He said in an affronted tone. "I thought you to be a respectful, dutiful daughter who would hold her family's needs above her own. I see that I was wrong."

His words cut through her indignant armor. Elaina was fiercely loyal to her family. She loved them all, especially Emona, but this was a lot for them to ask of her.

"You hold our reputation in your hands Elaina," Emona said as she approached her, gentled and humble. "You hold my reputation in your hands." She grabbed her sister's hand and placed it on her abdomen. Elaina's eyes grew wide, realizing Emona's secret.

"I hold his child."

Now everything was clear. Elaina had noticed a change in Emona lately. She was a calmer, gentler form of herself, quiet and removed. Elaina thought this change had come because of her marriage to Manin. She would be numbered among the elite. Power and prestige would be hers. However in the process of securing her position in the Upper Mantle, she met a more worthy benefactor. She beguiled him and he took her to his bed. Now, intoxicated by her love and elated at the news of an heir, he arranged an intimate and immediate wedding as not to call attention to her delicate situation.

"Do this for me," Emona pleaded. "Do this for my unborn child."

"But...so you are..." What was she to do? If she refused, the family would be brought before the King on charges of fraud. Emona would be labeled a harlot and so would end her marriage to the Ingarian Noble. Her child would be disgraced before it even took its first breath. Her father's good name would be besmirched and he would be imprisoned.

Father.

Elaina searched her sister's face and glimpsed a trace of apprehension in her eyes. She knew there was no way around it. She would surrender to the marriage to save her family.

"Yes. I will marry him."

Seth exploded in laughter and relief. "That's my girl. We always knew you would. Do not worry about preparations for your journey. I have already had Welda pack your things. The Countess of Beltrane is sending transport to take you to the Upper Mantle. They should be here shortly. There are fresh clothes laid out for you in your room. Hurry along and change. You must look your best when you arrive at the Manor."

His reaction was a little startling, but Elaina concluded that, though the decision for her to marry Manin was a shock to her, it was a well thought out plan to Seth. He knew that Emona was pregnant well before the evening of the dinner and had feigned surprise at the table for her benefit. She also surmised that it had been Emona that suggested the union between Elaina and Manin and, as usual, their uncle agreed. Everyone already knew. Even Uman had been a part of the scheme. That must have been why he had left her alone with the guests that night. They were no more than actors taking their places, waiting for the curtain to go up. Elaina nodded at Seth's orders and headed in the direction of her room. She suddenly felt tired. All of the energy and the fight that had fueled her fury this morning had left her.

Father, where are you?

He was still in Lanier Isles. He was not scheduled to return for some time. He could not come to her rescue and there was no one left to support her cause. She drew her feet up to her chin and stared out the window. Spring had come to Inglemans Landing. Soon the trees would bloom with varying arrays of flowers and produce. The gardens would glow with new life. It would be breathtaking, but she would not be there to see it. This had been her world. Here she had her family and friends and all of those she loved. Now they were lost to her. She closed her eyes and enveloped the darkness that they held. Now, she was alone.

It was early evening when a she found herself in the coach yard preparing to board the carriage that would take her to the Upper Mantle. Elaina looked at the estate, memories of her childhood flitting through her mind. A gentle hand lay on her shoulder and she turned to see Emona trying not to look concerned. It was not like her to show emotion toward anyone else's plight. Her face was filled with unease, and for the first time, Elaina felt that her sister actually cared. Tears welled up in her eyes as she embraced her. "I will miss you, little one," she said, her voice quivering with emotion. "I- I wanted... everything will work out. You will see. You will be happy there." The footman stepped down from the carriage, placed Elaina's luggage in a hidden compartment, and took up a position at the door. He was a wiry old man who smelled of horses and nature. He gave her a toothy grin and removed his hat while he attempted a halfhearted bow. "Is my Lady ready for her journey?"

Elaina nodded and stepped into the carriage. She remained silent and lifeless until the image of her home faded from view. It wasn't until then that she cried. She sobbed loud enough for all of heaven to hear her.

The carriage moved at a steady pace and she figured that they were making good time. The driver rarely made stops, so Elaina took every opportunity to stretch her legs. They traveled until they reached the vast expanse that separated the "haves" from the "have-nots." Desolate Way. Here there were no houses, shops, or bustling streets. It was the place where cobblestone met dirt and only nature made its presence known. Here at this juncture Elaina crossed into a land unknown to her. She had never ventured this far from home, a fact that filled her with both excitement and terror. While she could not be considered fearful, she was not the adventurous type. She preferred the familiarity of home as opposed to a life of discovery abroad. But now she had no choice. She would have to make a new life for herself in a new land. The idea was daunting but inescapable.

The sun soon fell from its perch and the moon rose to take its place. They had traveled all day and Elaina was famished. She reached for the little basket that Welda packed for her. It was filled with her favorites - cheese, apples from the orchard, and date bread as only Welda could make it. An involuntary tear escaped beneath closed lashes. Welda had been waiting for her when she returned from her meeting with Seth and Emona. She had held her while she cried and then wiped her tears away.

"This is not the time for tears, my lamb," she said. "This is the making of you, Elaina. Wherever your journey takes you, you must traverse it with courage. Remember the essence of your mother lives inside of you. Look to it for strength. You have the blood of your ancestors in your veins. You will endure this."

The thought of her old friend made her smile. She would miss her the most. She took out a piece of date bread and offered it to the driver through the wooden shutter that separated them. He looked surprised by her generosity but mumbled something about being content with his snuff and graciously declined. She ate as she watched the last golden rays of the sun tuck behind shadowy silhouettes of mountains and trees. She welcomed the night. Stars shimmered into view, twinkling some unheard melody, lulling her to sleep.

"It's time to wake, Miss" the driver said through the wooden shutter. "We should be arriving in the Upper Mantle shortly. I take it you will want to be prepared when we reach the Manor."

Grateful for his warning, Elaina roused herself, smoothed down her hair and wiped the sleep from her eyes.

She felt the carriage wheels hit the cobblestone road and tried to quiet the nest of butterflies that began to flutter in her stomach. The city was alive with movement. The streets were filled with merchants laying out their wares, beckoning to passersby to come and indulge in them. The smell of fresh bread filled the air, wafting out of the bakeries nearby. A rather large inn called Prominence Hall, stood at the end of the street. It looked to be a comfortable establishment where, Elaina concluded, many strangers would lodge to ease the weariness of their travel. They passed the inn and turned onto a winding road that continued for several miles. As they approached the manor, Elaina's mouth fell agape in wonder. She understood that her father's estate had been one of the largest in Inglemans Plains but it looked like a pauper's shanty compared to Warren Manor. The drive to the estate was lined by sculptured trees against a perfectly manicured sea of green grass. Its red brick surface was littered with glittering fragments that suggested it to be made of material that was not native to their land. It was breathtaking.

The carriage came to a stop at the front door and a guard helped her out. Without speaking a word, he motioned for her to follow him into the massive abode. The anteroom was as grand as the outside of the Manor had been. Its white walls where were adorned with lush draperies and golden framed seating. A small, round-faced maid gingerly crossed the room to greet Elaina.

"Hello. My name is Sinta. I am head maid over all of Warren Manor." She instructed the guards to retrieve Elaina's belongings from the carriage. "I take it that your trip was a pleasant one." Elaina moved to respond but was cut off by the woman's continued introduction. "If you need anything, anything at all, I am the one to ask." She motioned for Elaina to follow her as she made her way down a corridor and up a marbled flight of stairs. "I will escort you to your room. You should take some time to rest; I am sure that your journey has left you quite withered. You may wander the grounds if you like but you are to attend a formal dinner held in your honor tonight. Make sure that you are dressed and ready when you are called for. Lady Beltrane does not like to be kept waiting."

"Will Manin be here tonight?" Elaina asked sheepishly. Sinta turned to her sharply and said, "Lord Beltrane will be in attendance." She eyed her a moment and took a step closer. "It would do you well to maintain a formal relationship with Lord Beltrane and the Countess. While you are to be married to Master Beltrane, you are not yet nobility. It will be best to show restraint and respect when addressing them."

A bit put off by her curt reply, Elaina silently nodded and followed Sinta to her room. It was as large as the greatroom had been in Inglemans Landing. The curtains were made of a billowy blue material that made Elaina think of a cloudless sky. The chairs were constructed of plush velvet and golden gilded oak wood. The bed was hewn from heavy cherry wood, framed with ribbed columns at each corner. It was covered in ruffles and lace that could have easily been mistaken for a sea of white foam.

Elaina surveyed her surroundings, "Is this my room? It's beautiful."
Sinta's eyes filled with pride. "Yes, I personally see to it that all of the rooms here at Warren Hall are outfitted with the best that the Upper Mantle has to offer." With a sweep of her skirts she sauntered over to the fireplace where a dark-haired maid knelt, stoking the fire, coaxing warmth into the room.

"This is Andira; she will be your chamber maid. She will report to you every morning to help you begin your day. She is at your beck and call until you release her." She made another grand strut to the door and said.

"Remember, I will call on you for dinner. Do not keep Her Ladyship waiting." And with that she closed the door.

Elaina stood looking at the door for a moment, not knowing quite what to do next. She recalled Sinta's warning about her not becoming too familiar with Manin and Lady Beltrane. She felt a slight pang of desperation. How would she get to know the man she was to marry if she could not be allowed the opportunity to be herself around him?

"Shall I unpack your things, Miss?"

"What?"

"Your things. May I unpack your things?" Andira's face was beaming with kindness and comfort. She was a bit shorter than Elaina with bright blue eyes. Her skin was kissed by the sun, as was her personality.

"Oh, yes please." Andira set about putting away her effects as Elaina acquainted herself with her surroundings.

"How long have you worked here at Warren Manor, Andira?"

"I've been here seven years, Miss. My father was the head groomsman for Master Warren. We were farmers on the outskirts of Lingear Village. We had a couple of hard winters that produced no harvest, so papa decided to forget farming and take up a simpler life."

Elaina couldn't believe that farming was something that one could just give up when the mood struck them. Sure there would be hard times, but it took patience and perseverance to work the land. It became your mistress; you became one with it, knowing every curve and line of its makeup, every secret that it held. You could love it or loathe it, but you could never leave it. She had understood this of so many others. She knew the same to be true of her father.

"So how did he come to be in the Beltranes' employ?"

"My mother was a midwife who had delivered one of the maid's children. She heard that Master Warren needed good workers so my father inquired about it and that was that."

"Well, it is good to have family around you. I would like to meet your parents, Andira. I am sure they are as inviting as you are."

"Thank you kindly, Miss," Andira said with downcast eyes, "but I don't suppose that's possible. Both my mother and father have passed from this world."

Elaina saw the sadness in the young maid's eyes and felt uncomfortable at having been the cause of it.

"They both caught fever and died two summers ago. I believe my father was really the one who suffered from the illness. My mother never left his side the entire time he lay dying. She died one week later. Doctor said it was fever but I think she couldn't bear to be without him. It is better that they are together in heaven." Shrugging off the heavy details of her life, she lightened her tone. "Anyway, the Beltranes allowed me to stay and work, giving me a job as a chambermaid."

Elaina felt an instant closeness with Andira. She couldn't imagine what it must have been like to witness both of her parents waste away from illness and heartbreak. While her mother had died when she was a baby, she had not witnessed a loss of one so close to her. But now that she had been sent away from her home and the life she knew, she felt as if a death had occurred, leaving her to face this frightening new world alone. She considered the sun-kissed maid and figured her to be about the same age. She settled within herself to make her a fast friend. By Sinta's no nonsense demeanor she could tell that she would need an ally.

Andira finished her duties and then appeared in front of Elaina, giving her a short curtsey. "All finished. Is there anything else I can do for you, Miss?"

"No, thank you, Andira. That will be all."

When the chambermaid advanced to the door Elaina had a wonderful idea. "As a matter of fact, there is something that you could do for me. There is to be a celebration tonight, given by Lady Beltrane, in my honor. I would like it very much if you would return and help me to prepare. I am not accustomed to the ways of nobility and I feel that I must learn quickly if I am to be accepted as Lord Beltrane's wife."

"Yes, Miss. I will help you." She put a slender finger up to her cheek, formulating a plan to best serve her new mistress. "I will send for refreshments to be brought down from the kitchen and will return after you've had enough time to rest." Andira flashed a warm smile and left Elaina to herself.

She felt the slightest ember of hope come to life inside of her. *Maybe things won't be so bad here after all. Maybe I will enjoy my new role as wife and Lady at Warren Manor.* She changed from her travel clothes into a comfortable nightgown. The trip had been long and grueling and she knew that she would need to be rested if she were to make a good impression tonight. She tied her long hair into a braid and placed a ribbon at the end to secure it. True to her word, Andira had the cook send a healthy tray to Elaina to restore her strength. She ate heartily, knowing that she would probably be too nervous to eat much later that night. All eyes would be on her, judging her every move.

Feeling satisfied and groggy, she retired to the mound of wood and sea foam that passed for a bed. *Ahhh...It was like sleeping on clouds themselves.* She snuggled in and let her mind wander.

Manin is a good man, she thought. *He will make a good husband. I must try to be a good wife to him.* She hoped for the best but admitted to herself that she knew little of such things and had no example to follow. After her mother died, her father was so stricken with grief that he never took another bride.

She thought about Andira's parents. She wondered what it must be like to love someone so much that she would perish without them. Would her relationship with Manin reach such heights? Would their love blossom like the field lilies at new spring?

Love...

Would he ever really love her?

The tiny ember of hope that had burned so clearly in her started to falter, but she quickly coaxed it back to life with a kindling of faith and determination. She would win him over and he would fall in love with her. She was sure of it. She drifted off to the familiar plains of sleep until a gentle hand roused her to awareness.

It was Andira. Beaming and fresh she whispered, "Wake up, Miss, it's time to get ready."

Chapter 4

Elaina stretched like a lazy cat in the afternoon sun. "Hello, Andira. Thank you for waking me. I just wish I had more time to sleep." She let out an exaggerated yawn. "I feel like I haven't slept at all." She swung her feet onto the floor and examined her toes.

Andira had taken the liberty of having a bath delivered while Elaina slept. It was hot and ready for use. She'd even placed up a screen for privacy. The water was warm and inviting. She submerged herself completely, wanting to wash away the fear that stained her emotions. *Get a hold of yourself Elaina*; she heard her inner voice say. *You are here now, so present yourself as worthy of such a betrothal. Beguile him.*

"I brought jasmine and chamomile oil to scent your skin, Miss. Would you like the chamomile now?"

"Yes, please." Andira was certainly a farmer's daughter. It was tradition that before a bride was introduced to her intended's family, she bathe in Chamomile to calm her nerves and then oil her body with the scent of Jasmine. Not only was it a delicate perfume but it also brought an alluring glow to the skin.

After she had bathed and oiled she slipped into the dress that Andira had set out for her. It was a lilac gown with a silver hand-beaded train. Elaina looked in wonderment at her reflection in the mirror. Andira had done very good work resizing the dress for her. It clung to her body just enough to give the look of full womanhood while remaining demure enough to project innocence and chastity. Andira was a Godsend!

"May I brush your hair, Miss?"

Elaina nodded. "Yes, please." She chuckled to herself a little. Andira was supposed to be her maid but it seemed clear as to who held the power at this moment.

Andira knew the Beltrane family. She understood their customs and expectations. Elaina was more than happy to fall in line with her demands and gain as much advantage as she could.

"Do you know who will be at the dinner tonight? Will anyone be joining Lord Manin and Countess Beltrane?" She had no idea how the Countess planned to explain the change in brides to the rest of the Beltrane family. She was certain that anyone who had attended the feast at Inglemans Hall would not be there to ask questions that night. Still, she figured if she had to be scrutinized all evening, then she wanted to know who and what she was up against.

"Yes, Miss. Viscount Welford and his wife, Lady Welford, will be attending. They have three children, all of marrying age. They are pleasant enough, but Lady Welford is obsessed with beauty. She loathes getting older and won't let her children tell their ages for fear of looking old herself. It is rumored that she had hoped to unite one of her daughters with Master Manin. General Briston will attend. He arrived last night from the palace. He is gruff and only speaks of war and politics. Lord Rone Mosenvelt is also attending. He is captain of his Majesty's private army and also his nephew."

As Andira continued with the guest list, Elaina tried to take in all of the information given to her. It was a lot to remember but she would do her best. "What about the Earl of Beltrane? Will he be here?"

Andira gave a muted smile. "No, Miss. Master Warren is away on business. He won't return for some time." Elaina sighed, a little disappointed. She had met Warren Beltrane when she was a little girl at her father's estate. He was a kind man, with an agreeable nature. She had hoped that he would be an ally for her tonight.

"There, all finished. You look very lovely, Miss."

Elaina had to agree. She looked ravishing. Her jet black hair fell down her back like a silken cape. "Thank you," she said, embracing the young maid. "I am grateful for your kindness."

"It is but my duty," she retorted, but her eyes held a sense of pride that her labors had been acknowledged.

There was a knock at the door. Before she could answer, Sinta stormed in, bellowing orders. "Good, you are ready. You are required in the Main Hall. All of the guests have arrived and you are to appear before Lady Beltrane at this time. Come along." She rushed out of the door, barely giving Elaina a chance to follow her.

"Good luck, Miss," Andira called after. "Thank you! Oh, and Andira...call me Elaina."

Sinta was halfway down the stairwell when Elaina finally caught view of her. She stopped at the bottom and waited for Elaina to catch up. "Hurry up, now. Don't dawdle." Sinta circled her, taking a final audit of her appearance.

"Very lovely. Now, I will have you announced. Wait here until I return." As she turned to the main hall and disappeared from sight, Elaina felt a little faint. As she had so many times before, she thought about turning and running. She could get a horse and ride all night back to Inglemans Landing. She could catch a boat and go to find her father. She could...but she realized that there was no chance for any of that now. She had agreed to come and she must keep her promise. She hated being the dutiful daughter at times. Emona greatly lacked integrity and yet she managed to have things fall right into her hands.

Sinta returned and drew her to the Hall entrance. "Oh Sinta," she whispered, "I'm so nervous."

Surprisingly, the staunch maid gave her a warm, reassuring smile and said, "You are a lovely young woman.

I know of your father, Gregor. He is a great man. I also happen to know that you come from an upstanding family. You are well-afforded a chance for happiness. Have courage my dear. They are announcing you now."

Elaina never heard her name called. Everything went silent as Sinta pushed her though the entryway. The gentlemen at the table stood and all gave her a slight bow. She gave the daintiest curtsey possible, being careful not to collapse from fear. Her legs felt like wet cloth, ready to curl up at any moment. Manin offered an arm to walk her to her seat. She took it gingerly and looked up at his smooth countenance. He was handsome in his powder blue vest and silk cream trousers. "Miss Elaina, may I introduce you to Viscount Welford and Viscountess Welford."

"A pleasure to meet you Miss Elaina," the Viscount retorted. He was a stout man with gray balding hair that stuck out in tufts behind his ears. His wife was a bit taller than him with a slender frame. The lines around her eyes had been powdered in a failed attempt to hide their existence. She was a woman of no young age and yet Lady Welford held a strong exquisite beauty. Elaina thought of her as an aging enchantress, holding on to the last vestiges of her power.

"The pleasure is all mine, your Lordship," she said with a graceful bow. Manin gave her a slight tug and moved to the next guest.

"General Briston, may I introduce Miss Elaina."

"Very nice to meet you, my dear," he said flatly. Elaina felt a little relieved at his indifference. She would not have to worry about making conversation with him because he cared very little about meeting her.

"Thank you, General."

This time she didn't wait for the tug from Manin. She quickly stepped beyond the General and on to the next guest. She looked to Manin for reassurance, but found none from her intended. They moved forward with urgency. Manin seemed pressed to end his rounds with her and take his seat.

"Lord Mosenvelt, allow me to introduce to you Miss Elaina."

Rone Mosenvelt bowed deeply before Elaina. "My Lady," he said, his voice as smooth as velvet. "Manin, where have you been hiding this delicate flower?" he said with a grin, never taking his eye off Elaina. "Surely I would have known one of such beauty here in The Upper Mantle."

"No, my Lord. She is from Inglemans Landing. An agricultural state to the south."

"Ah,"said Rone. "They must have fertile soil to yield such lovely produce." He gazed at her intently and she felt her face flush with heat.

Manin escorted her to her chair, to the left of his, and then took his seat. Lady Beltrane called for the servers and at once dinner began.

The evening proceeded well in Elaina's eyes. The conversation focused mainly on politics and a possible vassus uprising. General Briston dominated the discussion for most of the evening, giving a report on which city-states he felt would fall into disarray if the uprising took place.

"Ingaria would stand for the King, of course," said the General. "But it is overrun by land-hungry vassals. If it cannot be united, I believe that it will be the first to fall."

"We should not presume defeat for Lord Regas this soon, General," interjected Lady Beltrane. "Remember that it was his land alone that remained unscathed in the Preon War. We should not underestimate his abilities."

"That may very well be true, Cynthia," retorted General Briston, "but Ingaria is about to change hands. Regas is old and worn. He is not the man he was in the Preon war. He has grown complacent in his tower."

"And recent gossip says that the Duke has designated his upstart nephew to rule in his place," chimed

Viscount Welford. "Will he be adequate to lead? He is young with little experience. Can Regas really think that he chooses wisely?"

Elaina was quite relieved that everyone was too immersed in the matters of war and land to pay her much attention. She settled into herself, musing over the beauty of her surroundings. The main hall was a visual delight. Its gold-flecked walls held grand reliefs that were stationed at every arch and adorned each column. Elaina studied a garden nymph that appeared to spring from the arch above the entryway as though it were alive. It held a whimsical smile and a certain look of mischief. She let her mind explore the possible devilment that it might perform. Free and willful, she could think of no better life. She had delved so deep into her musings that she did not realize that she was being addressed.

"What do you think of all of this, *Miss* Elaina? I am sure that you have some concern for the state of your home." Welford stared at her expectantly. She was to give a response without knowing the source of the question. She cursed herself inwardly for letting her mind wander.

Her face flushed with heat as she scrambled for an answer. "I am not very knowledgeable in such matters, Lord Welford. I fear that my answer would be less than adequate."

"But I am sure that you have some answers to the claim of your father's alliances."

"My father?" Elaina questioned. What did her father have to do with this droll conversation? He was a loyal servant to the king.

"Regardless of Beltrane's title, it is a well-known fact that your father has the allegiance of every vassal in your province. And he has not been seen since this mess began. One could almost say that he is in hiding." He lifted his shoulders in a non-affected shrug. "You surely must know the truth of the matter."

Elaina glanced about the room and found everyone's attention on her. She was trapped in unfamiliar territory. Surely he wasn't insinuating that Gregor was the leader of the vassal uprising. But he had done just that, and all the while reminding her of her inferior station. She was not one of them. She was of the lower class and could not be trusted. It would serve her to remember her place.

"I – I don't think...." She stumbled, not sure what to say.

"If you will excuse my interruption, Lady Elaina," Rone Mosenvelt interjected. "I believe that the question should be more to the fact of where these allegations originated. There seem to be threads of untruth spreading through Alionia regarding its most loyal subjects. It is my understanding that the purpose of such slander is to set all parties involved at odds and fling the less fortunate into the arms of injustice."

Welford shook his head in agreement as if this suggestion satisfied his interrogation.

Elaina breathed a sigh of relief that the moment was over, but remained attentive to the conversation in the event that she was called upon again to speak. She would be ready next time, she told herself, but the opportunity never came. The hour was late and the guests began to retire to their rooms.

Manin, without verbally addressing her, led her to the entryway of the hall to speak their final farewells to their visitors.

"It was a wonderful evening, Lord Beltrane," gushed Lady Welford. She turned to Elaina and looked down the bridge of her very fine nose. All of the warmth that she had heaped upon Manin only a moment ago had been reduced to a bone-chilling disdain. "And what a beautiful guest you have brought us. I look forward to further meetings with you, my dear. You can tell me all about your cows, pigs, chickens, and other farm animals,

no doubt turned family pets, that you have at your home."
She placed a hand on Elaina's cheek and smiled
humorlessly. "You do so remind me of my youngest child
Selena. Only she is younger and slighter of figure than you,
and far fairer in complexion. You really must wear a
bonnet to shade yourself from the sun or such beauty will
never last." She removed her hand and sneered at her
before returning to converse with Manin one final time.

Elaina felt heat rise in her cheeks. She knew the
Viscountess was belittling her but to respond as she would
have liked would endanger her standing in the Beltrane
home. She was their guest. She would soon be Manin's
wife. She might be thought to be of inferior birth at the
present time, but surely they would accept her when she
and Manin were wed. Wouldn't they? She blinked back the
burning sting of tears that she felt pool behind her eyes. She
put forth her most dazzling smile to Lady Welford, gave
her a dutiful bow and wished her good night.

The last guest to retire was Rone Mosenvelt. He
stood at the table lost in thought. Manin remained
stationed by the entryway, patiently waiting for his visitor
to approach. Rone made his way somewhat hesitantly to
the couple and offered a formal bow.

"It was a most splendid evening, my friend. As
usual, Lady Beltrane has outdone herself." He was a
handsome man with bold features. His eyes were bright,
exciting, full of mischief, and somewhat familiar. They
reminded Elaina of the garden nymph from the relief. His
black hair was pulled back into a neat bundle. The shadow
of his freshly shaven beard gave the illusion of rugged
wildness and yet he maintained an air of dignity that befit
his station.

"I would enjoy the benefit of your company
tomorrow. I have been at Warren Manor on very few
occasions but I find it quite appealing." He gazed intently
at Elaina. "I would like the opportunity to see more. Shall I

call on the two of you for a walk of the grounds?" Manin graciously accepted. Elaina, feverish under his burning gaze, curtsied in agreement.

With that he bid them good night and retired to his room. Manin, as silent as he had been all evening, motioned her forward and escorted her to her chambers. As they made their way up the marble stairs she searched for the right words that could ease the discomfort of the situation. Finding none she remained silent until they reached their destination.

Talk to him, she told herself. *He will be your husband.* Gathering her courage she said, "Thank you for the lovely dinner. I am grateful for your hospitality." He gave no response so she continued, "My room is also lovely. I feel that I will be happy here." Believing her attempt at conversation had failed and feeling a bit silly for having tried, she turned to enter her room.

"Elaina."

"Yes."

"I will send for you tomorrow to accompany Lord Mosenvelt and myself on a walk of the estate. I take it you will be ready when I call?" His voice was firm and lacking warmth.

"Yes, I will be ready," she retorted.

"Good."

He took a few steps towards the stairs before turning to address her one final time. He stood there, examining her, and for a moment his expression softened. "You do look lovely tonight, Elaina." Then he flew down the stairs and out of sight.

Elaina looked after him in bewilderment. He had praised her. She threw another log on the fire of hope. *I must prepare for tomorrow,* she thought.

Andira had a hot cup of spiced tea and a warm fire waiting for her when she entered her room. "How was your evening Miss...err...Elaina?" she asked. Her eyes were full of excitement and Elaina was happy to have someone to share the evening's events with. She told her every detail, even of her inattentive blunder. Andira was on the edge of her seat, reliving the entire ordeal vicariously through her tale.

"So now Lord Mosenvelt wants to take a tour of the Manor," she said. She felt a rush of heat surge through her as she remembered his intense stare. If Andira noticed, she never inquired about it. She simply continued to listen with friendly interest. At last she told her of her conversation with Manin. They stared at each other wondering how to decipher his actions. A smile spread across Andira's face and they both exploded into girlish giggles.

"This is a good sign Miss, err, Elaina." She was not used to calling her Mistress by her first name and it would take some getting used to, but Elaina seemed pleased with the change so she resolved herself to comply. "Well," she said jumping to her feet, "we have much to do to prepare for tomorrow." She rushed to the chest where she had arranged Elaina's belongings and began setting out clothes. "Tomorrow you must be as ravishing as you were today."

Elaina was a ball of excitement trying on one outfit after another, searching for just the right one to catch a man's eye. She felt the familiar rush of heat surge through her and it made her wonder, just whose eye was she attempting to catch? Manin's? Or Rone Mosenvelt's?

Chapter 5

The sun shone brightly through the powder blue curtains of Elaina's room. Its rays warmed the floor boards and traveled up her legs, resonating through her body. *It's a beautiful day for a walk,* she thought. She let the sun caress her skin as she dreamed of her afternoon with Manin. Maybe today they would receive a chance to hold a meaningful conversation.

She sipped her warm cup of tea and began her preparations for the afternoon events. Andira arranged for a bath to be drawn for her and she lounged in it, feeling the chamomile vapors diffuse into her skin. The relaxing aroma of fresh picked flowers wafted by and she exhaled in delight at her surroundings. She admitted to herself that she loathed the idea of coming here at first. The circumstances that thrust her into this position were less than favorable, but at this juncture, she could not understand why she had protested so much. She knew that the task of making a man fall in love with her would be no simple feat. *But to live in such grandeur*, she thought surprisingly, *just might be worth it.*

She oiled in lavender this time. It was a more overt scent, easily captivating and enthralling. Andira, as usual, had set out her clothes. She had picked a white silk blouse with colorful embroidery on its sleeves. She had paired it with a red tunic and a heavy skirt in case the afternoon spring air held a chill. Elaina allowed Andira to braid her hair and pin it into a smart bun before eating the breakfast that the kitchen cooks had brought up for her. She reminded herself to go by the kitchen later and thank them for their hard labors. "It is always better to have the cooks on your side," Welda once told her. "That way you can be sure that you never go hungry."

The sun had reached its full strength when Sinta arrived to escort her to the West Hall gate. Manin and Rone Mosenvelt were immersed in a jovial conversation when she met them.

"Miss Elaina," they both said with a bow.

"I take it the morning sun finds you refreshed and in good health," said Rone.

"Oh yes, it is a beautiful day." She beamed. "I am very excited to see the grounds of Warren Manor. I hear you have a beautiful garden of tree sculptures." She turned to Manin and flashed him a dazzling smile. "Will we be able to see it?"

"If you'd like." He stared at her, his eyes covering every inch of her face as if he were memorizing it for some later meditation.

"Yes, I would like that very much." She lifted her eyes to meet his constant gaze and felt a tingle run down her spine. The night of the engagement he had openly rejected her. Had his attitude toward her softened so quickly?

Rone uncomfortably shuffled his feet and cleared his throat. "Shall we be off, then?"

He started towards the gate and like two flustered school children, they followed.

Even with the heat of the sun, the air held a crispness that rustled through her cape. She inhaled the aroma of spring foliage as they approached the sculpture garden.

"How magnificent," she called, running ahead of them to get a better look at the lush oasis. "Is it a maze?"

"Yes. It was constructed on the order of my great grandfather. His mother's ancestors were from a heavily forested region. She was often homesick and longed for the surroundings of her youth. So he had a small forest planted in her honor. When she died he wanted his children to appreciate the wonders of nature, so he had the trees constructed into whimsical figures. Each generation has made an addition to it. My grandfather added the maze. My father added the fountain in the middle of the maze." Manin looked at the garden in pride. This was part of his birthright. It would be up to him to add the next addition.

"And what will you add to this priceless heirloom?" interjected Rone.

"Perhaps a statue of my wife."

Elaina felt her breath catch in her lungs as she turned to see him staring at her intently. She tried to calm the delightful chaos that was whirling through her mind. *He is accepting me as his wife.* Her breath quickened and she turned towards the maze in embarrassment.

"How thoughtful of you," Rone said dryly. "I would like to see the fountain inside the maze. Have we time for a little adventure?"

"Certainly, my friend," said Manin, and they all filed into the structure.

The maze was lovely in construct but not difficult to maneuver. Elaina took notice of the systematic course of rights and lefts that led them to the extravagant fountain. It was hewn from dark marble. It boasted three layers with bronze horns jutting from the stone, spilling out water like liquid music.

"Magnificent indeed," Rone said, quite moved by its opulence. As he and Manin discussed its construction, Elaina moved closer. There was something about this fountain. Something that called to her, captivated her. She reached her hand out to touch it and immediately the rest of the world disappeared. A black void swallowed both her and the fountain. In the distance she could hear a faint cry of music. It was haunting yet peaceful. It called to her, spoke her name in some unknown language, and filled her heart with longing. A light shimmered into view, blinding at first and then dimmed into an opaque scene. She was standing on a beach of black sand. The wind whirled around her like the notes of a song. She noticed that her hand still remained fixed to the marble fountain. She tried desperately to remove it but found that she was bound to it by some unseen force. The music reached a crescendo, pulling her, calling her name in chords she had never heard before. In the distance she saw a shadowy figure approaching. It stretched out its hand and called, "Elaina."

A longing to be joined with the hazy specter became difficult to resist. But just as she stepped forward in dazed confusion to meet it, she was flooded with an unnatural fear. Overcome with terror she wrenched her hand from the marble and let out a blood curdling scream as pain ripped through her. The shadow and the beach drifted from sight, leaving only searing pain in their wake.

Rone was the first one at her side. He'd smiled as he watched her sway rhythmically while she caressed the fine marble. Her eyes closed, her pink lips slightly parted. His amusement turned to panic as he noticed the color ebb from her cheeks and witnessed her collapse to the ground.

"Elaina!"

He flew to her side and cupped her head in his hands. "Elaina, are you alright?"

Within seconds, Manin was beside him looking anxious. "What happened?" he demanded.

"I only know that she fainted. Is she hurt?"

They searched her as decorously as possible for any visible signs of injury. Finding nothing, Manin scooped her up in his arms and carried her back to the manor.

When Elaina came to, she was in her room in bed. She sat up with a start and pain rang through her head. She found Andira sitting beside her, busy at her mending.

"What...what happened?" she asked. She felt weak and exhausted, like she had just run a great distance.

"Miss, you are awake." Andira looked relieved and immediately began to fuss over her, fixing her pillows and begging her to drink some warm tea.

"Andira, how did I get here? The last thing I remember was being in the garden at the fountain and…" All at once, the vision of the shadowy figure - if she could call it a vision - came back to her. The swell of unknown music filled her ears and she steadied her mind to hush it into silence. She wasn't sure what happened to her, but she figured that she shouldn't tell anyone until she sorted everything out.

"We aren't exactly sure what happened Miss, but you gave us a terrible fright."

Elaina looked at the maid, a little bewildered. "Why so formal, Andira?" She had stopped calling her Miss shortly after her arrival.

Andira motioned in the direction of the fireplace. There stood a male figure with his back to her.

"Manin?" she asked.

"No, Miss. It's Master Mosenvelt. He hasn't left your room much since the incident. Master Manin has been here too, of course. He comes in along with Lady Beltrane to check on your progress."

Elaina became suddenly aware that she was dressed in her night gown with nothing but her bed sheets to cover her.

"Andira, hand me my robe, please. And a comb - I must look a mess."

Elaina made herself as presentable as possible, and then motioned for Andira to notify everyone that she was now alert. "I will go to Master Manin and Lady Beltrane at once and give them the good news." Elaina watched her leave the room, stopping to tell Rone on her way out.

He turned toward the bed and looked at her. Elaina couldn't name the expression on his face. It was a mixture of anger and relief. He crossed the room in a few great strides and knelt beside her bed.

"Elaina. Thank the heavens you're alright." He grabbed her hand and pressed it to his lips.

"I didn't know what to do. I...I couldn't..." He looked up at her and his eyes spoke words that his mouth could not form.

Without thinking she reached out and caressed his hair. His once tidy locks now fell loosely about his shoulders and he looked as if he had slept in his clothes for a week.

"Lord Mosenvelt, have you been here all night?" She knew the answer but she wanted to hear it from him.

"Yes my lady. A night, maybe more. You were ill for several days. I could not leave until I knew that you were alright. I watched you – saw you swaying at the fountain. You appeared in good health until you collapsed," he said, rising to pace anxiously. "What affected you so greatly? The physician found nothing and yet you trembled with fever. At one point I feared the worst." He dropped his head, reliving each horrible moment.

"I am well now, Master Mosenvelt..."

"Rone, call me Rone. Please." He looked at her intently, pleading in his eyes.

"Rone," she nodded.

He walked towards the bed once more and studied her.

"Elaina, I- I need to tell you something. Something very important. When I was but a youth, we...."

In an instant the room became a bustle of excitement. "Good heavens child, you're awake. What were you thinking, giving us a fright like that?" Lady Beltrane rushed to Elaina and placed a hand on her forehead. "Fever's gone. Great One be praised," she said, and started ordering the servants to bring broth and fresh tea at once. Elaina tried to refuse. She wasn't hungry in the least bit, but the Noblewoman insisted. "You must eat to get your strength back. We can't have you fainting all over the place."

In the midst of the commotion Manin rushed to Elaina's bedside. "Elaina, you're alright," he said with a pant. He pulled her into his arms and kissed her gingerly on the mouth.

"Manin, really," Lady Beltrane gasped.

"Mother, I believe that I am entitled to kiss my future bride, particularly one that I am very glad to see in good health."

Elaina blushed at the fact that the first kiss she received from her soon-to-be-husband was in front of so many witnesses.

"When you are better we shall finish our walk," he gushed. "But I fear that we must steer clear of the garden until we find the source of your ailment."

Lady Beltrane set the maids about the room cleaning and arranging for Elaina's recovery. It was only then that she noticed Rone gazing at her from a quiet corner of the room. He clasped his fist over his chest, gave a deep bow and exited the room. A lump grew in her throat as she watched him leave. She wanted to call out for him and ask him to stay but she knew that would be seen as inappropriate behavior for a lady, especially one that was betrothed to another.

Besides, Manin was there, giving her his undivided attention. He lavished her with affection and she accepted it fully. It seemed to her that this frightening incident turned out to be a blessing in disguise.

The night was far spent when Lady Beltrane allowed the maids to seek out their own rooms. She convinced Manin that Elaina would be alright without him for a few hours and they all retired to bed. Elaina woke the next morning in high spirits, feeling that a greater measure of her strength had returned. She was very interested to learn what had taken place while she was unconscious, so Andira unraveled the story over date bread and warm milk.

"Master Manin and Lord Rone brought you in from the garden and carried you up to your room. Madam Beltrane sent for the doctor when nothing we did could revive you." She nibbled at her date bread like a little field mouse, enjoying every morsel. "Master Manin yelled at the doctors when your fever started to rise. I think he was nervous because he retreated to his study for a while."

"And Rone Mosenvelt? What did he do?"

"He stayed here with you the entire time you were ill, except when I dressed you, of course. He was very helpful. He tracked your fever and washed your arms and head with cool water. He is a very kind man."

"Yes, he is." Elaina thought about the strange conversation they had before the others had come in. He seemed genuinely concerned about her. She recalled the feeling of her fingers running through his hair, his lips softly caressing her hand, his eyes burning into her soul. That flame rose to consume her now but she squelched it under the knowledge that Manin was to be her husband. He might not have stayed with her all night but he was just as concerned for her safety and openly showed it. Elaina imagined being carried in Manin's strong arms through the manor and up to her bed chamber. Oh, how she wished she had been awake to experience it!

"He was in good spirits until your fever spiked and the doctors could do nothing about it. He and Master Manin then exchanged heated words and Master Manin retreated to his study once again," Andira exclaimed.

Elaina was shocked. "An argument? What was it about?"

"I'm not sure," Andira admitted. "I was helping the physician, but it didn't last long. Master Manin left soon after it started."

Elaina tried to put it all together. Why had the two men argued? She knew that Rone had tried to tell her something before everyone entered the room. Was that the source of their disagreement?

"My mother always said that when trouble comes around, fear can threaten friendships but for a moment," Andira replied.

Elaina nodded in agreement. "No doubt they were just worried over my failing health. Maybe today we can all have tea and mend any hurt feelings."

"I don't think so," Andira exclaimed, "Master Rone left early this morning. He said he had an urgent matter that he had to attend to. He and Master Manin appeared agreeable when he left."

Elaina was annoyed by her unhappiness at Rone's departure, especially since he hadn't come to see her before he left. She shifted in her bed, ruffling the covers, trying to hide her disappointment. *He is a good friend*, she told herself. *I hate to see good friends leave.* She forced herself to accept this affirmation as a viable reason for her sadness, allowing her to miss him without feeling guilty. She would like to finish their conversation. But, unfortunately, that would have to wait.

Chapter 6

The days went by quickly after the incident in the garden. Elaina had fully regained her strength and had begun a daily regimen at Warren Hall. Manin showed an increased interest in forging a relationship with her. They enjoyed tea together every mid-day and often took long walks on the Manor grounds. Realizing the steady progression of their relationship, Lady Beltrane demanded that Elaina meet with her every day to receive lessons on proper etiquette. If Elaina was going to be a part of their family she would have to behave like a Beltrane. At times she felt a twinge of anger rise when the Countess made disparaging comments about her family. She wanted to speak up, defend their honor. But she knew it was better to keep silent. She would have to suffer the pompous woman's insults until her marriage with Manin was cemented.

One evening Manin took her for a walk in the garden. The swallow buds were in full bloom and radiated the essence of sunshine into the air. Manin remained silent for most of the walk, only responding when Elaina posed a question. They stopped at a marble bench and he invited her to sit with him. He held a nervous energy that, Elaina noticed, was quite infectious.

"Lord Beltrane….you've been rather distant in our conversation today. Has something upset you…have I upset you?" She looked to him with wide eyes, searching for an explanation.

"Do call me Manin. And no, my darling, you have done nothing wrong. It is….well, I know that you have taken lessons from my mother for months now. It is my understanding that you are well versed in the ways of our family."

He turned towards her and grabbed her by the shoulders. "I have grown quite fond of you during your stay here and I think that it is time that we marry. Will you have me?"

Elaina could barely speak. She was sent here for this very purpose and yet she was still surprised by his offer.

"Yes, Manin. Yes, I will marry you."

He pulled her to him and kissed her urgently. His mouth was like a ravenous inferno, burning everything it touched, siphoning air from its environment, allowing only the flame to exist. Elaina wanted desperately to envelope that fire. She accepted the idea of marriage to Manin at first because she had no choice. After she arrived at Warren Hall and started to spend time with him, she realized that she now wanted to be his bride. She would be a lady of means and status. She would live at Warren Manor with a man of noble heritage and continue that line through her own children. She knew the importance of cementing this union and she had succeeded. Yet in the midst of her triumph a wave of desperation flooded through her. No! she heard a voice in her say. *No, run Elaina, run now!* The old familiar pain that had once haunted her returned in force. It pulled and tightened so viciously in her stomach that she staggered under its spasms. Manin realized she was stumbling and tightened his hold, believing that she was swooning in his passionate embrace.

No, I will not run, she told herself. *I am tired of being afraid. This is my destiny and I have a right to be happy.* Pushing aside her fear, she relaxed, melting in his arms, surrendering to his flame.

When Elaina returned to the manor she told Andira the good news. The two women shared their joy as she prepared for a dinner in the Main hall. Lady Beltrane had invited many of the Nobles from the surrounding provinces. It was a political dinner. Rumors of war and uprising had spread throughout the kingdom. The nobles now rallied to ensure order and preserve their way of life.

Elaina often felt torn between the two worlds. She was not born into nobility like most of the people who would be attending tonight's dinner. No, she was merely a farmer's daughter. Her family was blessed to be able to afford servants, who to her were more like family, and hired hands to work the fields. But even with her father's success, he was not nobility. He was a vassal. He worked hard to preserve and prosper his land only to give a portion of his yield to a governing lord. Elaina never questioned her family's loyalty to the King. But now she considered the significance of this vassus rebellion. If, in fact, the lands went to war, nobles against vassals, the elite would no doubt win. They had the backing of the King. King Arilian would send his army and quickly squelch the coup. Many innocent lives would be lost in the process.

The guests spilled into the hall, chattering about the weather and other trivial matters. Elaina tried to look stately as she greeted each one in her golden silk gown. She did not know many of the gentry, a fact that only heightened her interest at seeing them arrive, each with their own entourage, championing their province with a proceeding banner.

After each statesman was announced, they took their seats and the dinner began. Lady Beltrane took her usual spot at the head of the table. Though she was a woman, and considered by nature to be a fragile being, she had a commanding presence. She was a Countess who held as much power as her husband. In fact many of the vassals that had sworn fealty to her husband had made the same pledge to her.

From where did she glean her strength, thought Elaina. It was obvious that the woman ran Warren Hall and handled most of the social and economic responsibility of their House.

It occurred to her that she had not seen the Earl of Beltrane since she arrived. She was often told that he was "away" on business. What kind of business would keep him away this long?

A fair-haired servant waddled over to the Countess. He bent uncomfortably in his fleece tunic. It appeared to be a size too small and swelled flesh poured out from both sides, concealed only by the servants' tunic that he tucked inside his britches. He whispered in her ear and she said, "Ah, good, have him announced."

He waddled back to his post and signaled the attending guard. His strong voice rang through the air, "Lord Rone Mosenvelt."

The air that sustained her evaporated from her lungs and her heart played an unnatural rhythm. She hadn't seen him since their conversation in her room. He greeted everyone as he walked in.

"Please excuse me for lateness, Countess. I was detained at the palace. My apologies."

"No apologies are need from such a man as yourself, attending to the welfare of us all," gushed Lady Beltrane.

He bowed at her praise and looked for a seat. A servant brought him a chair and placed it right across the table and only one guest away from Elaina. *What devilment is this?* Elaina thought? She looked up at the garden nymph springing from the arched entryway. It was smiling at her discomfort, mocking her and the feelings she did not wish to acknowledge. *"You did that, didn't you?"* she accused. His smile appeared to deepen, amused by her aggravation.

"We are glad that you could join us, Lord Mosenvelt. We have much to discuss," exclaimed Viscount Welford. He and Lady Welford had been two of the first guests to arrive because, Elaina assumed, they wanted to get seats closest to the Countess. She was baffled by the logic of the nobles. How could the location of your seat detail your station? But, then again, there was a lot that she did not understand about their ways.

"I am pleased to be among you," he smiled ruefully. "I longed for the company of old friends," he said looking at Elaina, "so I was compelled to come."

Elaina took a draw from her peach wine, trying to cool the burning in her body. His words, his stare, his every move always had a profound effect on her. She must learn to control her feelings.

"So what news do you bring us from His Majesty, the King?" asked Welford. "What does he suggest we do with these ruffians?"

"He suggests we do nothing," Rone said flatly.

"Nothing?" Welford shouted, "What do you mean nothing? King Arilian sits nestled in his fortress while these dogs lap at our heels! He neglects his duty to protect his most loyal subjects!"

"Caution Landon," warned Lady Beltrane. "You speak too much against our king. Remember that it is not he who is against us. Arilian is a wise man. I am sure there is reasoning behind this course of action."

"As usual your foresight is admirable, Madam." Rone turned to address the Viscount. "King Arilian feels it best to try to negotiate with the leaders of the rebellion. We must first weed out the source of the problem before we plot a course of action."

"The source of the problem, my dear boy, are vassals who have forgotten their place." He bared his teeth as he looked at Elaina. Lady Welford sat next to him, a vision in blue, their province's noble color. She suppressed a gentle laugh and cut her eye at Elaina.

Welford continued, "They have sworn their oaths before God and country and now they wish to renege on the basis of misuse. It is slander, I say." The Viscount's face turned bright red in anger as he shook his fist in defiance at

Rone. "The vassals have become insufferable and I will not sit by and watch my province succumb to these dogs of war!"

"These 'dogs' as you call them have remained loyal to the nobles and to the King for centuries. There are many, if not most, who still remain so. How will we decipher the true from the false, sir? Do you suggest that we arrest every vassal in the kingdom and punish them for treason?" Rone's demeanor was calm but his words held a ferocity that silenced the Viscount. "It is unwise to strike at shadows in the dark. That is why we must first put a face on our enemy."

A bejeweled duchess from Marna interjected. "All of this talk of war...it is unsettling. If some of the vassals are unhappy why don't they just form their own province somewhere and leave the rest of us to ourselves?"

Rone's lips curved in a humorless smile. "An honorable notion, my lady. However, it would set a bad precedent for the rest of the kingdom. We need to remain unified, not fractioned off for individual rule. The truth of the matter is that some are meant to lead and some are meant to follow. If the leaders act honorably towards their subjects then the balance remains stable. If the rulers are unjust to their servants," he said glaring at Lord Welford, "taxing them more than they can afford and depleting the regions' resources for their own greedy purposes, then yes, there will be an uprising. More importantly, there have been reports of outside influences stirring up the ire of unhappy vassals."

Whispered surprise spread through the hall.

"Outside forces?" Lady Beltrane asked. "Who would do such a thing? We are at peace with the surrounding kingdoms."

"That is what we intend to find out. But in any case I must convey the importance of peace with the vassals until we find out who is really behind the upheaval. You can rest assured that when we discover the source we will move with swift justice."

The conversation went on much the same for the rest of the dinner. Elaina held silent, listening intently to the concerns of all present. This matter was important to everyone, even her.

When dinner finally concluded the guests milled around the hall, seeking out new courses of conversation, hoping to lift their spirits. Manin and Elaina stood watching the crowd when a baron from Segnara requested a word with him.

Manin excused himself and joined the baron. Elaina surveyed the crowd. She didn't want to admit to herself that she was looking for Rone. She simply entertained the idea that she enjoyed looking at the crowd of nobles. Manin was in deep discussion with the Barons and Elaina smiled to see him meld so well with his older counterparts.

A gentle hand touched her arm and sent a delightful shiver up her spine and back down again. She whirled around to discover the culprit. It was Rone. They stood holding each other's gaze, conversing with their eyes. Rone bowed low before her and reverently cooed, "Your highness."

Elaina let out a delighted laugh and said, "Your highness? That's preposterous, Rone. Have you been away for so long that you have forgotten me and my station? I am but a simple farm girl sent to serve my betters." Her statement was in jest, but at times that was how she really felt.

"What service do your hands need perform? A woman of your beauty should be hailed as a queen, not a servant," he said.

"You stated earlier that some are meant to lead and some are meant to follow." She continued coyly, relishing their innocent flirtation.

He stepped closer and replied, "Then you lead and I will follow." His tone was fierce with longing.   The temperature in the room seemed to change from a cool spring evening into a sweltering summer night.

Elaina wasn't sure how to respond. Their simple flirtation had turned into something more serious. She knew that encouraging his advances could lead them down a terrible path and yet she didn't quite know if she wanted to turn back.

"Master Rone, I….," she felt dizzy from his intoxicating stare and forced her eyes to the floor. "You flatter me, Sir."

"No, I speak only of that which my heart feels."

"Rone…there is something….Manin has…" Before she could finish, Manin was at her side. He put his arm around her waist and pulled her close to him.

"Hello, my darling. I hope I didn't keep you waiting too long."

"No, Manin, you didn't. Besides, Master Mosenvelt has been keeping me company."

Manin eyed him coolly. "Yes, what good friends we have. And since we have such good friends around, I would like to make an announcement." Everyone focused their attention on him and he continued. "I have asked Lady Elaina for her hand and she has accepted. We will be married within a month."

The hall exploded in cheers and congratulatory greetings. Elaina and Manin were assaulted by a mob of well-wishers, all wanting to touch the engaged couple, each wanting to give advice on new love. Elaina scanned the room for Rone. They had been separated when the crowd advanced upon them. When she finally located him, her heart nearly broke. He wore a look of devastation. His usual straight, elegant demeanor had been replaced by a defeated slump. Elaina wanted to run to him and explain everything. She wanted to tell him about Emona and her

Uncle, and the deal they had made with the Countess to keep their family from losing everything. She wanted to let him know that she was doing this to save her father from ruin. She wanted to hear the words that only his eyes had spoken. She took a step forward and realized it was a hopeless endeavor. She had no future with this man. It was a silly girl's fascination with something she could not have. She was lucky to have been accepted into the Beltrane family, seeing that she was not from a noble line.

Rone was the nephew of King Arilian. If, Great One forbid, tragedy stuck their kingdom, and Arilian and his immediate family were killed, Rone would be in line for the throne. Who was she to think that someone of such importance could…would have any real interest in her? She stepped back beside Manin, who was lost in a nest of cackling hens, discussing wedding plans and nursery furniture.

She looked at Manin and then back at Rone. He called to her in silence, sending his heart to her ears. The desire to run to him was overwhelming. *No!* she said to herself. *My duty is here.* She lowered her head remorsefully, giving him her answer. His shoulders slumped a little farther. Then he clasped a tight fist over his heart, gave a deep bow, and left the hall. Elaina gasped for air, feeling that all that was in the room had left on the heels of Rone's boots. She cried inwardly for a brief moment and then turned her attention to the wedding "planners." *I must focus on Manin,* she chided. *He is my life now. He is my destiny.*

Chapter 7

"I believe rose blooms are best," Lady Beltrane decided. The preparations for the wedding were in full swing and she took an account of everything, right down to the smallest detail. Elaina never received the honor of participating in the planning of her own wedding. Everything was decided for her. Being of inferior birth and breeding, a fact that Lady Beltrane reminded her of often, she was told she lacked the foresight to properly prepare for an event as grand as the wedding of a baron. Secretly she supposed her exclusion was also due to her sister's betrayal of Manin. Lady Beltrane could not control her son's decision to pursue Emona, but she would control the relationship between Manin and Elaina as long as was reasonably possible, and that control would start with their wedding. As far as Elaina knew, every detail up to her wedding night had been decided for her and she could do nothing but happily go along with it. She maintained that it might be better to offer her opinion when she had fully achieved a station in the House. Being a Beltrane did have its advantages, after all.

Elaina knew that every province in the kingdom was run by a group of noble Houses. The lords of these houses were said to be some extension of the royal line. It was well known that the higher one's position in the House, the more royal blood was presumed to flow through their veins. Warren Beltrane, however, was bestowed the title of Earl of Beltrane, Land Warden over the entire Upper Mantle province. While noble-born, he began his life as the son of a simple nobleman. His actions alone had risen him to lofty heights within the commonwealth. Next to the King, his word was law in their region. Even Lady Beltrane wielded more power than most men in the province just because she was his wife. Elaina thought about her role in the governing of her homeland. Would she be able to command as much power and respect as the current countess did? She would cross that bridge when she came to it. Right now she focused her mind on the task at hand, that of surviving Lady Beltrane and getting through the wedding.

It was the day before the wedding and guests had already begun to arrive. The usually quiet manor was filled to the brim with noise and jubilation. Lady Beltrane ordered Elaina to her rooms, saying it was not proper for Manin or any of the guests to see her before her vows were exchanged. Following orders, she retreated to her chambers, a little relieved to be shed of the dizzying fray. Her nerves bubbled inside of her so much that she wanted to jump out of her skin. Come tomorrow morning she would be Lady Beltrane, wife to a baron and, if succession had its way upon his father's passing, the next Earl of Alionia.

This knowledge only heightened her anxiety. She decided that she needed some fresh air. She wound her way through the manor and around to the west gate. A few groundskeepers were attending to the flowers that lined the walkway there. They tipped their hats in tribute as she ventured into the bright sunshine.

She walked, lost in thought, paying little attention to where her feet were taking her. The birds composed new song from the high perch of the trees and all at once Elaina wished she could be one of them, swirling through the air, choosing her own path, inhaling freedom. She realized that she had wandered toward the garden maze and debated whether to enter it. The last time she was here she had a disastrous experience. She appealed to the practical side of her mind and assured herself that if she did not approach the fountain, she would be safe. She moved through the maze with ease, studying each sculpture with admiration. The wind blew a strong gust and she pulled her cloak tighter. She lifted her face to the sun and drew in its warmth.

"The sunlight becomes you."

The voice was smooth velvet. She turned to see Rone standing before her. Her heartbeat quickened.

"Rone….where did you…how did you know I was here?" She feigned anger at his intrusion on her solitude.

"I knew your love for nature would call to you. When I didn't see you in the manor I sought for you here." He stepped forward, stopping just before he was close enough to touch her.

"Manin and I are to be married tomorrow," she blurted out. She saw him grimace at her words and wished she could retrieve them. Lowering her eyes she asked, "Will you attend the wedding?"

He could take the distance between them no longer and rushed forward, taking her hands in his. "No, I will not be there. War has broken in Marna. The king has ordered troops to invade in the morning. I shall lead my men in an effort to secure order and guarantee as few casualties as possible."

Elaina reeled at the idea of war in Alionia. If it had already started in Marna then it would no doubt spread throughout the entire kingdom.

"I am sorry you have to go," she cooed.

"As am I. I would have welcomed the opportunity to further our acquaintance."
Elaina felt a shiver run down her spine, only this time it wasn't the cool spring air that chilled her. It was his intense heat, his burning gaze that made her tremble.

"You are a very special woman, Elaina," he said, taking her by the shoulders.

"Rone…you are mistaken. I am no one special. I am a little farm girl sent here to do my family a service."

"No, you are special. From the moment I saw you I knew that our destinies were intertwined." He paced back and forth spilling his thoughts before them both. "I am a man of rational thought. But from our first meeting, I have thought of nothing but you. My mind is consumed with you day and night. Tell me that you feel the attraction between us."

She turned her back to him and considered her answer. It is true that she felt an undeniable attraction, but it would be scandalous to admit it.

"I am fond of you as well, Lord Mosenvelt," she started slowly. "However, I must remind you of my engagement to Manin. We will be married tomorrow and my service to him and my family will be complete."

"Your service? You make your union to him sound like a tradesman's work order." He considered her for a moment and hope shone in his eyes. "So you are not happy in your arrangement?"

"It is not always about happiness," she said recalling Welda's words. "Women of my station are not usually presented with opportunities for such a fortunate marriage. I am lucky to have gotten this far."

"So you marry for wealth and power. I did not take you for a woman of such character." His demeanor was stolid but Elaina knew better. She felt both angry and anxious at his assumption. She was not an opportunist. That was Emona's position. She had merely stepped in to keep her family from ruin.

"I care very little about wealth and power, sir. I do, however, care about the well-being of my family, and this union will ensure that they continue to thrive. It must be difficult for you to understand these issues, seeing that you are of noble blood and not subject to the chastisements of your superiors." She moved away from him and found a cluster of doon flowers growing out from the maze wall. She plucked them from their bindings and nuzzled the petals with her finger.

"I understand more about these things than you know." Rone eyed her a moment and then asked, "Do you love him?"

"What?"

"Do you love him? If you tell me you love him I shall leave and never speak of my feelings for you again."

Elaina was caught in a whirlwind of emotions. She knew that she did not love Manin, but if she confessed her true feelings, she would betray her betrothed. She strengthened her resolve and, lifting her chin said, "I will grow to love him."

The look on her face let Rone know that he was fighting a losing battle. He decided to concede. "Very well then, my lady. I shall trouble you no longer." Taking her hand he delved into the dark pools of her eyes. "But grant me one request?"

"Yes, my lord."

"My duty presses my return. I will lead my men into battle in the morning. Accept my blessing of your marriage with a kiss."

Speechless, Elaina nodded her consent.

He reached around her waist, pulling her into his strong embrace and kissed her softly. His lips were soft but urgent and she swooned inwardly with delight. She had been kissed by Manin, but this was different. This was fire and ice, enthralling and captivating. It was a force bigger than either one of them, drawing, pulling them under wave after wave of passion. Elaina fought wildly against her own desire, using her circumstances as armor. She was locked in a heated embrace with another man the day before her wedding. She felt guilt rise to overtake her, only to have it swept away by their forbidden...love? passion? desire? She knew not what to call it. All she could think of when her resolve finally broke was giving in to her true feelings. With wild abandon she returned his affections and kissed him back.

After what seemed like an eternity in heaven's arms, they released each other. Panting and dazed, their eyes opened to the truth. Theirs was a love that would never be fulfilled. She looked into his eyes and saw his anguish. He knew she would never be his. In a voice barely above a whisper he said, "Love will always watch over you, Elaina." Broken from his loss, he turned and left the maze.

Go after him, Elaina. He loves you - go with him. Her inner voice pleaded with her, but as usual, the dutiful, responsible side of her drowned it out. *No.* She had a commitment to keep. She was not prone to flights of fancy like her sister Emona. She was dependable. She was loyal. She was….not in love with her soon to be husband. *No matter, she told herself. I will grow to love him.*

She made a slow march back to the manor, wishing she could believe her own lies.

The day had finally come. Today she would pledge her life and love to one man and would forever be under the protection of his name.

The Countess sent a band of servants to help Elaina prepare for the ceremony. Under Andira's direction they scrubbed her with olive oil and sea salt, bathed her in rose water, and oiled her in white rose oil. They dressed her in a silk gown made by the finest seamstress in Alionia. It was a creamy white delicacy with iridescent pearls on the bodice that matched the pearls on her elbow length gloves. Her hair was combed into an attractive up-do that made her look regal and mature.

When the maids finished their work they gushed with nostalgic admiration. "The wedding day is the height of a woman's life," one misty eyed maid mused.

"And the wedding night is the height of a man's," chuckled another. The other maids clucked similar sentiments, giving advice on what to expect on the night she became his in body as well as in name. Elaina blushed at their advice but was also grateful for their frankness. She had not given much consideration to her wifely duties, and thought of only making it through the wedding. She felt a little dizzy knowing that Manin would soon know her in a way that no other man ever had. But he was strong and handsome and respectful. He would no doubt be gentle with her as they explored their way through their first night together as husband and wife.

Andira shooed away the cackling hens and pressed an embroidered handkerchief into Elaina's hand. "Open it," she ordered.

Elaina pulled open the sides of the delicate material to find a pair of exquisite pearl earrings. "They were my mother's," said Andira. "She wore them the day she married my father. They brought her luck so I thought.....well, maybe they will bring you luck today as well."

Elaina's eyes filled with tears at the little maid's kindness. "But these are precious heirlooms. They should stay in your family. You should wear them on your wedding day."

Andira closed her hands over the pearls and pressed them on Elaina. "I have felt close to you since you came to Warren Manor. You have treated me not as your servant but as your friend, or even a sister. I am grateful for your kindness and wish to repay you with a little of my own. Besides, I have no need as of yet." Andira smiled wryly, "I shall borrow them back when I find a suitable prospect."

Elaina embraced her and wept tears of joy. Andira had become a good friend to her. She'd been cast from her family and sent to an unknown place and Andira had been there with an extended hand and a welcoming heart. For that she would always be grateful.

Wiping her eyes Elaina laughed, "I guess in a way we are both orphans, you by illness and I by circumstance. I shall consider you my sister from this day forward."

Andira beamed. "Thank you. Now, the first thing your sister will tell you to do is to stop crying. You don't want puffy eyes on your wedding day." They both laughed and proceeded to the West Gate. It was time for Elaina to take her wedding vows.

The carriage bounced along the cobblestone road on the way to the chapel. Countess Beltrane thought it best to have them marry at the family church on Hillendale Mount. Elaina had never been there, but she heard it was a beautiful old chapel and rather large. Why one family would need their own chapel was beyond her range of reasoning. Come to think of it, she had never seen them attend a service since she had come to live with them. Elaina's family worshiped at the community chapel in Inglemans Plains. Most of the families there attended worship regularly, all giving their time and reverence to the Great One. The One God.

As they approached the chapel she felt a sharp pain form a knot in her side. Perspiration formed lightly on her brow as she labored to breathe. Feeling as though she would faint, she grabbed Andira's hand for support.

"It is just wedding day frights. They will soon pass. Here, drink this." She handed her a flask of hard liquor. "This will calm your nerves." Elaina, a little surprised at the easy production of such an item, took a slight draw from the flask and handed it back to her maid.

"Thank you, Andira. I'm fine now." She stepped out of the carriage and up to the church steps. It was a massive structure made of foreboding grey stone. The doors of the church opened, and Elaina could see that it was filled to the brim with nobles from every corner of Alionia.

Manin stood with the priest at the altar. He was arrayed in the regalia of the Upper Mantilian nobility. His eyes lit up at the sight of his beautiful bride. She was exquisite in her creamy white hand-beaded silk gown. The sunlight caught the sheen of her pearls and illuminated the room. The line of her long neck was graced only by long silken wisps that dangled perilously from her meticulously sculptured confection of curls. The sensuality of her bare shoulders were muted by an intricately hand-stitched silk train that flowed from her bodice, a river of white fabric, heralding its Goddess. She carried a small bouquet of rosettes. The Countess believed that anything more would have been too ostentatious for "the girl," so rosettes in white ribbon it would be.

She was a vision to behold, true loveliness, beauty personified. Her groom's chest swelled with pride as the congregation cooed their approval.

Excitement whirled through her as she walked down the aisle to Manin. The closer she came to reaching him, the more she realized that everyone was watching her, reviewing her, judging her worthiness to be added to the ranks of the noble elite. She would now be a part of a much larger and more vicious world. She suddenly felt very small.

When she reached the front altar, Manin took her hand and the ceremony began. The priest spoke slowly and deliberately to allow the magnitude of the vows to sink in. "There is much to consider of love," he said. "You must love each other wholly, forsaking all others."

All others. That would include Rone. He would be in Marna by now. What if he was in battle at that very moment? Would he be safe? He was Commander of the Tumult Knights. They were the King's personal guardians and the best military force in the kingdom. If he could

~ 76 ~

command such a fierce group, then he would certainly survive the uprising in Marna. She felt guilty thinking of him during her wedding ceremony. Her cheeks blushed red and she silently scolded herself.

Rone had professed his affection for her, but had he ever actually said love? Even if he had, could she have believed his words after such a brief acquaintance? No, her affection for him could not be real. Manin was her life now. She looked into Manin's eyes, forcing her heart to accept him as her love. She recited her vows with solemn resolve and in return was given a sizable ring with a princess-cut stone the color of blue reef water. It glittered brilliantly on Elaina's dainty finger, and she couldn't help but smile at Manin's generosity.

When the final pronouncement was made, Manin kissed his bride and escorted her from the chapel to the church steps. The crowd emptied the church behind them, many piling into carriages which would carry them to the Manor for the regal dinner celebration that was soon to come. A few stayed behind to congratulate the newlyweds as they awaited their carriage. When it arrived, Manin helped her in and then climbed in behind her. She was sure that she had never seen this particular carriage before. Manin explained that it was used only when the occasion was worthy of it. It was the Earl's transport when he ventured to the Royal Palace or when he acted as ambassador to other Provinces. Its cab was black with a lustrous sheen that drew the eye. The plush seats were lined in red velvet for extreme comfort. Two large greys were adorned with rosettes and vinery and large silver plumes. The sound of their hooves played a dizzying tune in Elaina's head.

She smiled shyly at her husband. They were alone at last. As they bounced toward the Manor, Manin took her dainty hand in his.

"You are ravishing, my sweet." His eyes hungrily devoured her. "I made a good choice by taking one so pleasing to the eyes as my bride. I believe you will enjoy being my wife." He leaned a little closer and caressed her cheek with his gloved hand, "And I have no doubt that I will enjoy you."

Elaina flushed with heat and looked out of the window. She felt uneasy under his gaze and did not want to consider at that moment what "enjoy" meant. She had made it through the wedding. It was supposed to be a happy event and yet all she felt was despair. Manin, sensing her anxiety, lightened his tone and asked, "What's wrong, my darling? Are you not happy to be wed?"

"No....yes, I am," she said. "It is just...well, I had always dreamed of my father or even my brother giving me away. I....I just wanted them to be here." She could admit that she hadn't wanted to see them after they had bartered her away, but today things were different. Today she wanted the care and reassurance that only one's own family could provide. Lady Beltrane informed her that she sent a declaration of engagement to Elaina's family. When she inquired about it a second time, she was told that a wedding invitation had been sent to them but she had gotten no reply. Maybe now that the arrangement was complete, they had no more need of her. Her heart was broken. Surely her father was back from Lanier Isles by now. Why had he not come to see about her?

"I should have journeyed home to deliver the news myself. Maybe they believed that I was still angry with them for...well...the way things came about. They must believe that I did not want them to come..."

"Elaina," Manin said, caressing her soft shoulders, "we did everything we could to reach them, but we received no response. Perhaps now it is time that you leave that part of your life behind you. You are a Beltrane now. We shall be all the family that you surely will ever need."

At that moment the carriage came to a stop and the footman helped them out. As they entered Warren Manor, Elaina could hear the roar of voices and the tingle of music coming from the Hall. Manin sent for the head groom to have them announced, and then turned to Elaina. "Uplift your countenance, my sweet. I want my bride looking her best today!" She complied willingly. This was a day of celebration, after all. With or without her family, she would be merry on such a joyous occasion.

A boisterous cheer went up when the trumpeter announced the couple. "Lord and Lady Beltrane." Elaina glided gracefully across the room on the arm of her handsome husband. They took their seats at the honored table and dinner began. The meal was delicious. Cooks from every province were hired to assuage the palates of everyone in attendance. This decision was made to suggest hospitality towards the guest, but really, Elaina knew, it was meant to demonstrate the wealth and prestige of the Beltrane House. Who else, besides Ingaria, would be able to accomplish such a feat?

There was sliced pork roasted in plum sauce from Segnara, stuffed capon - a Mantilian delicacy - and creamed fish from the waters of Marna. Roasted vegetables, meat pies made from succulent pheasant, and cheese tarts glazed with apricot jam met the expectations of every guest. It was said that wine flowed in the veins of Ingaria's winemakers, for their vineyards were the finest in Alionia. The Countess had made certain to order an abundance of Ingarian wine. She would have only the best for this grand occasion.

After the meal, came the dancing. This was by far Elaina's favorite part of the evening. Many gentlemen, old and young alike, sought a chance to dance with the beauteous young bride. Elaina kindly obliged them the honor, but longed for the moments when she was reunited with her husband. She liked the way he took her in his strong arms and guided her around the dance floor.

The rhythm of the music was slow and sweet as she gazed into his eyes. She saw something in them. Something warm, compassionate, and vulnerable. Her heart softened and all of the resistance that she had ever held towards him melted away. She would love him and give all of herself to him, mind, body, and soul.

A man about Manin's height tapped him on the shoulder and breathed a light excuse. "Pardon my intrusion, Lord Beltrane," the young man said. "But I believe it is my right to dance with the bride."

Manin gave him a tight bow and said, "Lord Jantus, allow me to introduce my wife, Lady Elaina Beltrane."

Jantus bowed and kissed Elaina's hand. "My lady, the tales of your virtues do you no justice. Truly, I am honored to meet you."

"Thank you, my Lord, but I'm afraid that you have me at a disadvantage." *Who is this dashing young man?* thought Elaina.

His eyebrows rose as he looked at Manin for an explanation.

"She is young and still learning the world of the nobles," called a voice from behind them. It was the Countess. She made her way over to Jantus and gave a deep curtsey. "Marquees, it is wonderful for you to join us on such a joyous occasion. You honor us with your presence."

"Countess Beltrane, it is good to see you again. I must say that today's festivities have been superb. I have always been delighted with the concept of marriage and would urge anyone to do so, especially since I myself have taken a bride." The countess's eyes lit up with surprise.

"A wife? I had heard no such news, my Lord."

"Yes. It remained a secret until I was named regent of Ingaria. That is why we are here. To wish our beloved Elaina well."

Everyone looked at Elaina for answers, but she was as lost as they were. "I'm sorry, my Lord, have we met? Maybe you know my father. He has conducted business with nobles from every province in Alionia."

"No, my dove," said a sweet, alluring voice. "He is my husband."

The entire hall turned to watch the voluptuous beauty glide cross the room in a crystal-adorned emerald green velvet gown. Her curled black tresses swayed about her waist. Her full pouty lips were painted crimson and her smooth olive colored skin appeared as soft as silk. Her sculpted breasts were perfectly perched above a swelling belly full with child. Even in her delicate condition, she was a goddess.

"Please allow me the honor of introducing you to my wife, Lady Emona, Marchioness of Ingaria."

Great One be praised, it is Emona, thought Elaina.

Lady Beltrane curtseyed and murmured an unintelligible greeting. Manin clenched his jaw and grumbled perfunctory congratulations. His back became rigid with indignation as he looked at Emona's swollen belly. "You are with child..."

Before he could finish, Elaina broke in. "And what a wonderful surprise this is." She embraced her whole-heartedly. "I am so glad that you came, Emona. I was worried when no one replied to the messages we sent."

"Messages? What messages?" Emona inquired.

"The messages about our engagement and wedding date. Countess Beltrane sent them to Inglemans Landing but we received no response from you. It saddened me to think that my own family would not be here with me to celebrate such a wonderful event."

"I am sorry, little one, but I know nothing of these mysterious messages that you speak of. I have been in Ingaria with my husband. He received an invitation, and that is how I learned of your wedding. I did, however, speak with Welda, and she says that no invitation reached the gates of Inglemans Landing."

Elaina blinked in disbelief. "Surely that can't be correct. Lady Beltrane saw to it personally that you all were notified." She turned inquisitively to the Countess, but she remained silent. "Certainly there has to be some explanation."

"I'm sure there is," Emona said, glaring at the countess. "Uncle Seth is living with me now, so perhaps Uman misplaced the announcement."

"Or perhaps it was intercepted due to the uprising," interjected Jantus. "I hear the insurgence is spreading. It may soon hit our doors, Lord Beltrane. We must remain vigilant in these trying times. But for now let us leave it in the capable hands of the Tumults. I believe Rone and his knights are more than capable of dealing with these rabble-rousers. Today, enjoy yourself and the company of your lovely wife. I have come to find there is no better place to be than in the arms of the one you love." He wrapped his arm protectively around Emona's waist and placed his hand on her rounded abdomen. His face beamed with pride in the presence of his little family. Emona smiled at him, and for the first time that Elaina could remember, she truly looked happy.

Unable to endure the sight of Emona any longer, Countess Beltrane excused herself and stormed away. Manin mumbled something about needing a drink and stalked off to find one. Jantus, wanting to offer a toast to the groom, followed him, leaving the two sisters alone to talk. Elaina found two chairs in a quiet corner of the hall and motioned for Emona to sit.

"Emona, I did not know that the man you were betrothed to was the regent of Ingaria. He is handsome and he seems to be quite taken with you. You have done well for yourself."

"Yes, he is the acting regent of Ingaria. He is wealthy and handsome. Any woman of good sense would love to be in my place." Emona looked at her with sad eyes. Tears welled up and spilled over. Elaina was surprised at her sister's sorrow. She hadn't seen her cry since they were children.

"Emona, what's wrong? I thought this is what you wanted. Aren't you happy?"

"That's just it," Emona sniffled. "He is everything that I could have ever wanted and more. I am very happy, but there is something that always taints that happiness."

"What might that be?"

"You. I think of how you traded your happiness for mine. I…I have dreams. Frightening dreams of you being in danger. It's all my fault. At times I am so consumed with sorrow that I fear for my life and that of my child's. Please, help me Elaina!"

"What would you have me to do, 'Mona? I know no magic spells to release you from this curse." Elaina could feel her anger rising. Had her sister come here to witness her wedding or to ease her own conscious conscience? It was just like Emona to make everything about herself. She looked down at the pregnant woman's hands and noticed they were shaking. She looked at her face and found her once-vibrant eyes to be dulled by guilt and shame. She released her anger and sought to soothe her sister's affliction.

"Emona, it is enough that you have come here today. Let go of your worry. I am fine as, you can clearly see."

"No, little one. I have acted wickedly towards you. Please forgive me."

"Of course I forgive you, especially now that I am happy with the arrangement," she chuckled. "Manin is a good man and he will make a fine husband. Rest well, sister. Everything is coming along splendidly." Emona smiled and the worry seemed to melt away like a winter frost.

"Come, now," Elaina demanded. "No more tears on my wedding day. Let us speak of happier things."

The conversation changed to talk of family and friends and soon the women were laughing. Emona told her how quickly Seth had chosen to move to Ingaria after she was married. He enjoyed rubbing elbows with the elite and now counted himself as one of them. Uman decided to stay behind and run Inglemans Landing. Welda agreed to stay with him and so did many of their servants.

"And what of father? He also chose to stay in Inglemans Landing?"

Emona swallowed hard. "We have heard nothing from him, Elaina. He hasn't yet returned from Lanier Isle."

Elaina's heart stood still. It wasn't like him to stay away for so long. "I had wondered why he did not come to the wedding," she exclaimed. "What should we do?"

"Jantus has hired someone to search for him. We should learn of his whereabouts shortly."

"Good," breathed Elaina. "Please send word when you have found him. I shall say a prayer for him until then."

Chapter 8

The hour was drawing late and most of the guests had said their farewells. Jantus returned to collect Emona, so the sisters said their goodbyes.

"It was so good to see you, Emona. Thank you for coming. I shall write to you and tell you how I am enjoying married life."

"Please do. I will send word to you once the baby is born. I would like nothing better than for you to come and visit." Elaina walked them to the Hall entrance. "Little one, thank you for...everything. I am in your debt. If you need anything please let me know. My husband is the regent of Ingaria, you know!"

"Yes, I know. But I will be fine. I have the love of a wonderful husband - what more do I need?" At that Emona and Jantus climbed into the carriage and headed for home.

Elaina looked for Manin and found him surrounded by a group of inebriated noblemen. Many of them still held glasses of ale and were loudly toasting their nuptials and wedding night.

"It is good to wed..." said one drunk baron, trying to hold up his cup, "and even better to bed. May you be blessed in both, my boy." He tried to get the goblet to his mouth, but in doing so he spilled its contents all over his jacket. His companions only laughed and began another toast. Elaina said a quick farewell to a few more guests and headed to her room. She wanted to prepare herself before Manin came to call on her.

Andira, perceptive as usual, was already setting out her eveningwear. She helped her out of her bridal dress and into a peach colored nightgown made of soft chiffon and lace. She let her silken mane fall loosely about her shoulders and then anointed her from head to toe with the scent of rose water. Upon exiting the chamber, Andira hugged her and gave her a sly wink and smiled. "Good luck."

Elaina was a jumble of nerves. She tried to remember everything that Welda and the maids from earlier that morning had told her. Her stomach bubbled and knotted as she paced the floor, waiting for her new husband. *What if he doesn't come?* The hour was late and when she had left the hall he was still in the company of many of the province's noblemen.

What if he is too tired to come to me after the guests leave? She moved towards the bed and sat down, a little breathless. Then the thought hit her. *What will I do when he does come?* The idea of that was a little too much for her. She decided that it would be best for her to lie down for a moment. She assured herself that she wouldn't go to sleep, just rest a bit. She positioned herself comfortably on the bed and imagined what her life would be like from this moment on. She was now the wife of a prominent man and though she never cared much about wealth or position, she knew that she would indeed enjoy the best of life. She looked at the ring on her finger and smiled. Certainly a token of such elegant beauty was an expression of the love that would grow between them. Her eyelids grew heavy and she surrendered to sleep, tired from the day's happy festivities.

She awakened to the jostling of the latch on her chamber door. She sat upright and called out, thinking perhaps her maid had come to check on her. She stood and surveyed the room. The candles she had lit to light her husband's entrance had burned down to stumps. By the look of things, she had slept a great deal longer than she had intended. The door latch shuddered once again and finally gave way, allowing her beloved husband to burst into the room. Her heart pounded with anticipation at what was to come. He closed the door and remained there, hands fixed to the wooden panels as if holding it in place. Elaina fixed her hair and smoothed her gown and tried to exude sensual grace. Manin turned to his eager bride and sneered, "What are you looking at?"

His words startled her and she felt a cold shiver run down her spine. She took a few steps forward and stammered, not sure how the wooing process should begin. "I....I just thought...."

"You thought what? You thought I wouldn't find out? That I wouldn't catch on to your little scheme?" He spat his words at her and they smelled of ale and rage.

"Manin, husband....what do you mean? Find out what?"

"Do you think I am such a fool over a pretty face? I realized your plan when that tart of a sister of yours showed up at *my* wedding." He stumbled towards her and lifted an accusing finger. "This was all a very clever plan to gain a place in noble society. She never loved me. She used me to get what she wanted and you helped her. You helped her so that you could gain a place for yourself!" His words were slurred and froth gathered at the corners of his downturned mouth. Elaina knew that this would be a night to remember, but it was now turning into something she had never imagined. Or something that she would rather forget.

"No, my love. There was no plan. If she had one I knew not of it until I was given to you the night of the banquet."

"Given to me? You forced yourself into my house using your beauty as a cushion. You are just like her. You have no regard for me. You are not honorable and you will have no place as my honored wife."

Elaina's head spun so that she leaned against the bedpost for support. What was he saying? He seemed happy to make her his bride earlier that day, but now on their first night together, he was rejecting her.

"Husband, you have had too much to drink this night. Perhaps you would feel more yourself in the morning. We could discuss this a…"

"Don't tell me what I need do. Your tactics of manipulation will not stand here," he shouted.

"What manipulation? I have done nothing wrong! My sister may have been wrong in her dealings with you but I assure you I had no knowledge of her plans. I didn't even know that she was with child until the day your mother sent for me." Manin's eyes grew wide and darkness shadowed his face. Elaina knew she had said too much and fear rose in her throat, threatening to choke out every ounce of her breath.

"You knew that she was with child?" He stepped toward her, menacing and violent. "She would humiliate me while carrying another man's seed!" He shook his head, trying to make sense of this revelation in his ale-soaked brain. "She lured me to her apartment, bade me kill my own cousin, for her love, my own blood brother…"

His hands shook as he buried his face in them. He cried like a mother who had lost her only child. Elaina moved to console him only to be stopped short by his vengeful expression. "She manipulated and deceived me. She told me she loved me when she knew another man's bed and carried his child. She mocks me still, sitting in her high tower, Mistress of Ingaria. She has become another man's prize when she was rightfully mine!"

He peered at Elaina through blood-shot eyes. "You are just like her, aren't you? You will give yourself to another as soon as the opportunity presents itself."

"Manin, no," she said, her voice barely above a whisper. "I love you, my husband. I will be true."

"Liar!" he screamed. Half between tears and anger he grabbed her by the arm and roughly swung her close to him. "Do you think I don't know of your precious Rone? I know he came to see you on the eve of our nuptials. You gave yourself to him, didn't you?"

"No! I most assuredly did not. Manin, I am true."

"He wishes to take what is mine, rightfully mine! Well, he will not have you. No man will. You are my wife and only I will possess you." He lunged at her, ripping the fabric of her gown, exposing supple skin. The sight of her flesh only excited him into frenzy and he roughly forced her towards the bed. Elaina realized that she was being forced against her will and wildly fought him. She bit and clawed at him until he became tired of her struggling and landed a hard blow on her temple. Blinding pain exploded in her head and she slipped from consciousness.

Feeling her body go limp, Manin tore the fabric of her garment to completion, exposing all of her. She was his, he said to himself. She was his wife, his property. It was his right! In a drunken rage he forcefully took what he wanted from her, calling her Emona all the while. It was Emona who needed to pay. She was the cause of his turmoil. She needed to be punished and he was the one to do so. When all of his energy had been spent, he rolled over, feeling that he would wretch if the room did not cease to spin. He looked at his unconscious bride and horror bit his soul. What had he done? She lay there bloodied and bruised like a delicate flower, crumpled under the gardener's foot. How could he have done such a thing?

In a panic to make circumstances appear less vile then they were, he gently settled her in the bed and pulled the covers on top of her. He grabbed the ripped garment she had worn and tucked it down inside an overflowing chest that held most of her personal things. Nervously he straightened his clothes and headed to the door. As he looked back at her "sleeping" form he felt a pang of regret, but he forced the remorse to fade. This was not his fault. She was in on Emona's plan. He was sure of it. Had she dealt honorably with him, maybe he would have been able to trust her. He would keep her at a distance to watch her until he deemed her a worthy wife. *For now*, he thought, *she got just what she deserved.*

    Elaina woke to the song of a red lark singing sweetly outside of her window. The sun showered her room with prism-like shafts of light, escaping through the slits in the curtains. She attempted to sit up only to be met with a protest of stabbing pain. She placed a hand on her temple and yelped at the tenderness of the area. She looked down at herself and realized that she was naked. With trembling hands she drew back the covers to reveal bruises and blood stained sheets. Immediately the previous night's events came rushing back to her. She sat in disbelief, not really sure of what to do. There was a light rapping on the door but she made no move to answer it. The latch gave way and Andira gingerly entered, carrying a breakfast tray and a pitcher of goat's milk.

    "So how is the blushing bride this morning?" she began. She opened the curtains to let the heat of the sun warm them both.

    She reached for the pitcher of goat's milk and poured a generous amount into a glass for her mistress. "I thought that I shouldn't come too early. I didn't want to interrupt anything," she said with a giggle. "I waited until I saw Master Manin about the manor before I came in." She turned on her heels and asked, "Would you like some cold goa...?"

    Andira looked in horror at Elaina's face. She stood silent and frozen, her mind racing, her heart breaking. Elaina peered at her through sad eyes, unable to speak. Their silence was broken by the glass of goats' milk shattering on the floor. Startled into action, Andira grabbed the robe that she had draped on a chaise the night before and wrapped it around Elaina's shoulders. She felt her friend's body tense under her touch, but she made no moves to refuse her. She sat vexed, holding her mistress, whose low moan had now turned into a gut-wrenching wail. Rocking her and whispering soft words of comfort, she could hold back the torrent of her own tears no longer. What could have happened to have such a special night turn into one of violence? She let her own tears fall freely as she grieved with her heart-bound sister. "Oh Elaina," she sobbed as she stroked her black tresses. "I'm so sorry."

After soothing the weary bride to sleep, Andira ordered a bath to be drawn and new linens to be brought for the bed. To maintain Elaina's dignity, she enlisted the help of Sinta to see about her wounds. The older maid looked at the sleeping girl regretfully. She had seen many things in her life time but nothing struck her heart as much as this.

After having sent the water-bearers from the room, she enlisted? Andira's help to rouse Elaina, and together they helped her into the tub. The water was warm and laced with salt to ease the pain and tension in her body. While she soaked, Sinta applied a salve to her temple. "This will ease your pain and help the bruise to heal faster," she said. Elaina nodded her silent thanks.

Sinta approached Andira with an inquisitive look. "Has she said anything to you about what happened?"

"No," Andira replied. "She has said nothing since I found her."

"The poor dear is in shock, and for good reason too," said the head maid.

"But I don't understand," Andira whispered. "Master Manin seemed perfectly happy with her. She was a willing bride. Why would he treat her so?"

Sinta gazed in Elaina's direction. "Who knows the evils of a man's heart? She is not the first to be treated so and unfortunately she will not be the last. What matters now is how she deals with what has happened to her. Many young women never get over a tragedy like this. Some have even died of a broken heart." She walked towards the door with Andira at her heels. "We have done what we can by attending to her wounds. It is up to her to allow the Great One to heal her spirit. Stay with her," she instructed. "I will personally see to it that she is not disturbed."

Sinta sent word to the kitchen that Lady Elaina would be taking her dinner in her room for several days. She notified them that only she would carry the tray up to the chamber until further notice. She approached the small dining hall where the noble family usually broke their fast. The Countess was sitting at the table with Manin, quietly conversing on what seemed a serious topic. Manin saw the fury in the old maid's eyes as she studied him. Realizing that she'd seen Elaina, he desperately searched for something else on which to place his attention.

"Excuse me, My Lady," she said with a curtsey. "Lady Elaina will not be able to join you for breakfast."

Lady Beltrane looked at her son, inquiring as to why. Manin concentrated on his breakfast, never looking up from his plate.

"If I may, my Lady," Sinta said stepping forward. "I believe that all the excitement of the past days' activities has left her drained and weak. She has a considerable headache and the beginnings of a fever."

"A fever?" said the Countess. "Shall I send for a physician?"

"No, Madam. She is resting quite comfortably now. I do not think that a healer will be necessary. If there is any change in her condition I shall inform you." Sinta turned to leave just as Lady Beltrane called after her. "Maybe I should come with you and check on her. She seems to be rather fragile. This is the second time she has taken ill since she has been with us." She waved her hands in a frenzied fashion, irritated by her daughter-in-law's delicate state. "What if she is unable to bear children?" she said to Manin. "How will you carry on our family line? That is of the utmost importance."

"I'm sure she will survive the birthing," sighed Manin.

"That's not what is important. My concern is whether or not she will be able to conceive and hold a child. If she cannot, then she is of no use to us."

Sinta could hardly believe what she was hearing. She understood Lady Beltrane to be a hard, and at times, ruthless woman, but her lack of compassion towards Elaina was inconceivable. It would seem that the girl had been brought to Warren Manor just to continue the family line. There was little concern given to her life or welfare. In all the time that she had been in the Beltrane's service, never had she been more ashamed to call herself a faithful servant. There must be more to the Countess's fears and she intended to find out just what it was. For now she would play the role of the dutiful servant to her mistress, all while playing protector to Elaina.

"I shall go and check on her," Lady Beltrane decided, starting to rise from her seat.

"No," demanded Manin, sending a quick look at Sinta. "I am her husband. I shall check on her. Please inform me when she has recovered enough for me to visit with her."

Sinta's lips curled into a tight smile, "As you wish, my Lord."

The rain pelted his shoulders as he stood in the deep brush, hidden from sight. He had led his men to Mallant Cove and so far they remained undetected. A storm that raged off the coast had finally edged its way onto land, and though most of its ferocity had subsided, it still darkened the sky, allowing this covert scouting on what would otherwise have been a sunny day.

"Lord Mosenvelt," a well-muscled soldier beckoned, "We have received a report of movement just south of the cove. A convoy has been spotted taking the Grime road about a quarter day's light from here."

"A convoy," said Rone thoughtfully. "An aristocrat from Marna, perhaps?"

"I don't know, my Lord," said the soldier.

"Well, it is best we find out."

Rone took several men around to the south side of the cove, and they traveled quickly through the heavily-wooded area. Staying within the shading of the trees, the men took note of the incoming convoy. Several men in black armor guarded a silver-gilded carriage. Before the procession flew a banner adorned with a silver moon and a viper. Rone's eyes grew wide at the sight of it.

"My Lord?" said a soldier inquisitively.

"This is no Alionian aristocrat. That banner is from Nanshar. But what are they doing here? The King spoke nothing of visiting dignitaries." Rone stood up, judging the distance between the convoy and the surrounding caves. Remaining out of sight, he motioned for his men to follow as he tracked the carriage.

After some time the transport came to a halt at the edge of Mallant Cove's biggest cave. One of the dark-clad soldiers blew a bronze horn. It reminded Rone of the horns from the fountain on the Beltrane's estate; the fountain at which the raven-haired beauty had stopped the beating of his heart due to her sudden illness. He cursed himself for letting his mind wander into the trap he'd been trying hard to avoid all day. He was grateful for the suspense of the moment. He had to concentrate on his surroundings, strategize, look out and care for his men. He would do whatever he could to keep from thinking about her.

Elaina.

For a light moment he allowed himself to think of her face, her lovely smile that shone like sunlight, her smooth dark skin that smelled of roses, her laugh that sprang wells of joy in his heart. From all that he knew of her, all that he had remembered, she still hadn't changed. She was still the same sweet creature that she was when he'd first met her, only now she belonged to another man. She was Manin's wife now and he must respect that. He cleared his mind of her and focused on his mission.

Only moments after the horn had sounded, a group of men arrayed in Marna livery emerged from the rocky shelter. They looked around nervously, surveying the area before nodding towards the mouth of the cave. Feeling it was safe, a man of no small stature sauntered from his hiding place. He took a soldier's stance that made Rone uneasy. Not many vassals could boast the physical make up and warrior aura that this man held. His face was obscured by the hood that complemented his disguise. He wore the same livery as the others and yet he was different. As he stood awaiting his guests, the carriage door opened and two cloaked figures stepped out. One was tall and robust, with a heavy gate that suggested a body of spent years. The other, he deduced, was female. Rone made out the line of her slender figure through her cape. There was an unmistakable hint of elegance that surrounded her as she glided gracefully forward. The mystery man in livery bowed deeply to the new arrivals and they began to converse in muffled tones. The woman removed a pouch from the folds of her cape and handed it to her robust counterpart. He offered it to the man in livery. After examining its contents, he nodded his approval and escorted his guest into the cave.

Rone motioned for his men to recede into the brush so he could collect his thoughts. *So the rumors are true,* he thought. The Nanshar were in league with the vassal defectors. Upon reaching the camp he ordered his men to pack their belongings. He must get this news to the King at once.

Chapter 9

Three days had passed since her wedding night and Elaina still had not left the sanctity of her chamber. Sinta delivered her meals to her as promised, and Andira did the best she could to coax her to eat. Most of her bruises had started to vanish due to the powerful healing properties of Sinta's salves. However, Andira noticed that though her physical wounds were healing, her emotional wounds continued to fester. Sinta assured her that matters of such delicate nature took time to sort out. Still, she could not help but worry. What if she never recovered? What if she remained a shell of herself forever? Andira could not bear the thought of that, so she prayed every night for a miracle that would bring Elaina safely back to her.

Night brought little relief to Elaina as she tossed fitfully in her bed. Sleep eluded her at every hand, and yet she could never stop her pursuit of it. She would fall asleep only to wake shrieking at shadows that Andira could not see. On the third night, Sinta eased her distress by brewing a tea made with herbs that Andira had never seen before.

"Have her to drink this," Sinta ordered. "But make sure she drinks every drop. She will rest soundly until morning."

Andira followed the older maid's orders and was delighted to see Elaina settle into a peaceful slumber. Bright colors swirled in a hazy fog as Elaina maneuvered her way through the land of dreams. Darkness covered it all, leaving her alone in a place with no time or reason. *Where am I?* Elaina thought. *Where did everyone go?*

She heard the distant whisper of voices, unintelligible, but familiar. *Hello. Is anyone there?* She walked a step further into the black void, straining to see the slightest glimpse of light. The voices grew slightly louder. *Hello. Oh, someone...please help me. I'm here all alone. I...I'm lost. Please help me get home.* Just then, in the midst of the stifling darkness, stood a table with a bronze horn sitting fixed in a marble stand. She walked toward it slowly, admiring the intricate design on the bell of the instrument. She picked it up, not quite sure of the reason for its appearance, but somehow feeling an innate compulsion to blow it. It was necessary to blow the horn, vital even.

She pushed her breath through the instrument and was rewarded with a resounding aria, bright and captivating. Its melodious chiming illuminated her surroundings, melting away the gross darkness. When the bright light subsided, she noted her familiar location. She was on a beach of black sand lined by a sea of blue water. Jagged black mountains loomed like angry guards in the background of a lush tropical environment. It was breathtaking. She ran to the shore line and waded in the clear blue water, allowing it to splash about her waist. The warm salt air whipped through her hair and circled her body. A voice whispered her name softly but with purpose.

"Yes, I am here," she called. *"Who are you? Where are you?"* She ran onto the black sand and let the warmth of it ease the chill that now ran down her spine. More voices added to the one that had already spoken to her. They spoke in unison, giving her instruction.

"Elaina," the voices said. *"You must recover from your sorrow and rejoin the world of the living."*

"Living," said Elaina. *"I am alive."*

"No," said the voices, *"You are not. You have retreated from a world that needs you. A world that is in grave danger. You are the key to saving your world and all those you love."*

"But, what can I do? I am no more than a farm girl who couldn't save myself from my own husband's brutality. How can I save anyone else?"

~ 97 ~

"The power lies within you Elaina. You have hidden it deep inside yourself. Call upon its strength whenever you need it. Listen to the voice inside you. It will guide you to wisdom's door. Release anger and embrace compassion - it will give you courage in the face of fear. But most importantly, embrace the warrior's heart; you will need it in the trying days ahead."

"The warrior's heart? But...what about my husband? My life is no longer my own. He will enslave me in his anger. How can I live in his house?" she cried.

"Courage, Elaina. You are wisdom's child. You will stand in the face of danger and prevail. Always remember you have a choice."

"A choice....a choice in what?" The black sand under her feet illuminated into an orb of white light, blinding her and then receding once again into the familiar surroundings of her bed chamber. She sat straight up in her bed, wanting to make sure that her vision was clear. Yes, this was her bedroom, and there, sleeping soundly on the chaise, was Andira, keeping her vigil, as she had the last few days. Elaina moved the covers and placed her feet on the cool tile floor. Something bumped against her ankle and she knelt to see what it was. She stared in amazement as her hand caressed the whimsical designs on the bronze horn. For the first time in days she spoke aloud. "It wasn't a dream! It was real!"

"Andira, Andira wake up. I have something to tell you." The tiny maid leapt to her feet and stood in amazement at her babbling mistress. Elaina excitedly tried to explain her experience but found it difficult to express. Andira called for another maid to find Sinta and bring her to Elaina's chamber at once. She eyed Elaina fearfully, hoping that her mind wasn't failing her. She pressed her hands to her mouth to stifle a cry as she watched Elaina pace back and forth, babbling about sand and voices. When Sinta reached the bedroom, she was still dressed in her robe and night cap.

"What is it? What's wrong?" she asked, breathless from her rapid ascent of the stairs.

"It's Elaina," said Andira. "She's ....well she...I don't know. Look at her."

Surprised to see her standing and alert, she approached Elaina warily. "Elaina. Are you well? Why aren't you in bed? You need your rest." Feeling as though she might burst from excitement, Elaina flew into a much too exuberant explanation of her vivid dream.

Sinta studied Elaina and her strange behavior. She listened to her raving in slight amusement until her eyes settled on the little bronze horn that she was wildly waving in the air. She grabbed Elaina and set her down abruptly in a chair. She ordered Andira to lock the door and not to open it for any reason. She pulled up a chair in front of Elaina and then calmly smoothed the folds of her robe.

"Mistress, you must calm down. I see that something important has happened to you. Please start over and tell me everything from the beginning. Can you do that for me?"

Sobering, Elaina nodded, and began her tale. She explained how her Uncle had bartered her life for Emona's chance at happiness and how unhappy Manin had been the night of the engagement banquet when he realized that Emona wouldn't be his. She was duty-bound to save her family from the courts and she had done so by coming to Warren Manor. She told of Manin's apparent acceptance of her and the horrible experience at the fountain and her first encounter on the beach of black sand. Both maids were stunned to learn that Elaina's sister was now wife to the regent of Ingaria. But they realized the revelation came at a heavy price for Elaina. Seeing Emona had enraged Manin, sending him on a drunken rampage.

"He said that Emona had a plan that I was involved in. I tried to tell him that it was not so, but he didn't believe me. He said that she wasn't true and that I wouldn't be true to him either," Elaina said.

"Why ever would he think that?" asked Andira. "You have shown no interest in anyone other than your husband."

"Well," Elaina said slowly, "the day before the wedding Rone Mosenvelt came to see me. We talked in the garden."

"Surely he doesn't believe that Master Rone had any ill intentions towards your marriage. I always thought him to be a kind and upstanding gentleman," protested Andira.

"He is kind and upstanding and Manin had no right to accuse him of taking advantage of my virtue," Elaina growled.

"You mean he had no right to accuse *you* of wrongdoing, my dove. It was your virtue in question, I believe, not Master Rone's," said Sinta. "Unfortunately you bore the ire of this brazen fool in complete innocence." She looked at Elaina intently and saw the fire glow in her cheeks. The young bride dropped her eyes searching for fault within herself. She had enjoyed their kiss in the garden, perhaps a little too much, and couldn't explain her reaction to it. His lips were soft and warm and tasted of honey. She could have stayed in his arms forever if fate had been less cruel to her. But she knew the course her life was taking led her away from this passionate man and straight into the arms of her now estranged husband.

Sinta laid a caring hand on her knee and said, "You have done nothing wrong, my dear. There is no excuse for how he has treated you."

"For that matter," spat Andira, "I would have rather seen you with the likes of Lord Mosenvelt than…than this monster." Her face flushed red and she looked as though she would cry.

"Andira, mind your tongue," snapped Sinta. "It is not yet decided how Elaina chooses to deal with this situation. We as loyal servants must continue to do our duty as though nothing has happened. Where did you get that horn?"

Elaina explained her dream and that upon waking she found the horn at her feet.

"I know it was not here before. And it is identical to the one in my dream…if it was a dream. Oh, it's too difficult to explain."

"Whether it was a dream or not is hardly of any consequence. I am relieved to see you restored to us," Sinta said. "May I see it, the horn from your travels?"

Elaina held it out to her and watched something flash in her eyes as she grasped the bronze horn. Sinta closed her eyes and caressed its smooth surface. Elaina could almost hear sultry notes playing in the distance, soft and low, mournful and exuberant all at once. Sinta's eyes opened and she gazed at Elaina with a look of recognition and something else that she did not quite understand. She handed the horn back to her and instructed her to hide it.

"It is not to be made common knowledge that you have this horn. Not until we can sort out the meaning of it all. Hide it away with your things. You may never know when you will have need of it."

Elaina dressed quickly for breakfast. The cook would have donned her post by now, and she knew that she must make an appearance before the course was complete. Manin wouldn't be expecting her to break her fast in the breakfast nook. She had taken her meals in her room since their wedding night and he had not yet once come to see her. She felt nervous at the thought of seeing him again. How could she look him in the face after what he had done to her? Would he receive her, beg her forgiveness, or would he attack her again? She could not be sure, but she knew one thing. She must face him no matter the outcome. Besides, Lady Beltrane had already inquired why she had not yet joined them. Sinta had told her that it was sickness that kept her concealed but she did not tell her that it was a sickness of the heart that afflicted her. No doctor could heal the pain that loomed inside her.

She held her bronze horn as Andira brushed her hair. She would draw on her vision for strength. The voices that spoke to her told her that she must face her fear. They also said that she was the key to saving the ones she loved. Saving them from what? From ruin, from the wrath of the nobles? She had been sent here to do just that and look how it had all turned out. She still could not make sense of it all. She'd spent her entire life being controlled by others. How could she save anyone? She sighed and laughed to herself, *I guess today is a good day to start, and I'll do so by taking charge of my own life!*

She hurried down the hall until she reached the breakfast nook. She said a short prayer for strength before cheerfully bursting through the entryway.

"Good morning, everyone. What a beautiful day this is." She crossed the room to the table where Lady Beltrane and Manin sat ingesting their morning meal.

"Elaina, it is good of you to join us," quipped Countess Beltrane. "I was beginning to wonder whether I should send for the physician." Her words were said in jest; however, Elaina could feel the bite of her indifference.

"I am afraid that I am not accustomed to such grand conviviality as those of the noble class, Madam. I apologize for my absence these few days, and I assure you that I am in good health. I am also very hungry," she said, sitting directly across from Manin.

"Good morning, Husband," she said with a dazzling smile. "I pray the morning finds you well."

Manin looked at her dumbfounded. Was this some kind of joke? He had not seen her since the assault on their wedding night and yet now she was acting like the loving bride.

"Manin, don't just sit there gawking at her, have some manners for once in your life," Lady Beltrane snapped. "My heavens. You are Lord of this house now. Whether in love or lust, the sight of your wife should not render you speechless. What would the lords of this province think if they saw you carrying on so? Furthermore, what would your father say? I'll tell you what he would say......"

The sound of her voice was drowned out by the silent conversation between Elaina and Manin. He looked her over and tried to deduce her plan. Something wasn't right. On the outside Elaina appeared to be the perfect figure of beauty and grace to all who would look upon her. But when his eyes met hers he could not help but shudder at what he found in them. There, across from him, sat a beautiful woman, seething with rage. He could see the fire of hatred burn uncontrollably in her eyes and yet she remained completely composed. A chill ran up his spine, making the hairs on his neck stand on end. It was then that he realized the inevitable truth. His vile actions would cost him!

He had let his passion lead him in choosing to court Emona. He knew she was fickle and manipulative, and yet he wanted her anyway. He was accustomed to getting what he wanted. Why should Emona have been any different? Unfortunately things had not turned out as he'd planned. He had lost Emona and had to settle for the consolation prize. She was sweet and docile and pretty. He thought she could easily be bent to his will. After seeing what he had lost, he gave in to his anger and committed an unpardonable act. Now, by Elaina's actions and demeanor, he knew he would pay for it dearly.

Elaina smiled sweetly at her husband. She could see the turmoil raging inside of him. His reaction to her unexpected appearance gave her a boost of confidence. The cook set a healthy meal before them and Elaina ate heartily. She felt better than she had in days. She complimented the servants and made small talk with Lady Beltrane. When she felt she had accomplished enough for that morning, she excused herself from the table. Before leaving the nook entirely, she turned to Manin and said, "Dear Husband, I would be most pleased if you would accompany me on a walk of the grounds today. It has been days since we have been able to spend some time together and I must admit that I miss your company." She fluttered her eyelids and gave him a suggestive look that made the Countess fluster with indignation.

Gritting his teeth, he stood and bowed to his new bride. "I would be delighted."

"Good," said Elaina. "Shall I meet you at the West gate at midday?"

Manin nodded his consent grudgingly. Delighted to have the upper hand, Elaina retreated to her room. She wasn't sure what she would say to him during their walk, but she was sure that she had ruffled him. She smothered her elation with sobering determination. Now was not the time for cocky posturing. For the moment, she would remain calm until she figured out the best way to execute her next move.

Chapter 10

The vibrant sun shone over the garden as Elaina and Manin made their way to the maze. Neither had spoken since they'd left the manor, a fact that made the summer air feel even more oppressive. Elaina walked a few steps ahead of her forlorn husband at all times. It is better to appear distant than to be mistaken for a cowering whelp, chasing behind him, she reasoned.

When they reached the center of the maze, Manin, clearly agitated, moved to confront her. "So, what trickery is this?" he snapped. "What is it that you want?"

"All I wanted," Elaina said coldly, "was the love of my husband, but that has been lost to me. Now I want something very different."

"And what might that be?" sneered Manin.

"Justice. I want justice."

"Justice?" laughed Manin. "For what? For a husband taking what was rightfully his to begin with? I think not."

"You have wronged me, Sir. You have slandered my virtue and demeaned my body. You forced what I would have willingly given out of love."

"Love means nothing amongst liars," shouted Manin. He set his jaw arrogantly. "You come from a family of liars. You are skilled in the art of deception. I care very little about your talk of virtue or feelings. You are my wife. You said your vows before God and country. By my divine right you are now mine to control."

Manin stepped angrily toward Elaina to tower over her. Her heart beat a frenzied rhythm as she attempted to step away from his menacing presence. She tried to appear undaunted by his methods of intimidation. To give in would be to lose any ground that she believed she had gained at breakfast that morning.

"I am your wife, but you do not own me and you will never control me. I am a lady and I deserved to be treated with respect. We have entered into this arrangement and now we must come to some understanding as to how we will live amicably together under your father's roof. I do not wish to bring him shame by our open disagreement."

"We have no open disagreement," snapped Manin. "Do you think the opinion of a few chamber maids are of any concern to me or my father?"

"I speak not of the maids, Manin," Elaina retorted. "I am referring to the other Lords of this province. I will make known your conduct on our wedding night as well as on any other occasion if you persist with your violence. You must agree that you will not take from me that which I do not willingly offer. You must also treat me as your wife, and if you cannot love me then you must respect me. That is the way of it."

Elaina had given him the extent of her demands. If he conceded to her request then she still had a chance for a comfortable life and a civil marriage. More than one noble house had survived two opposing participants. Appearances were kept, children were made, and social and financial obligations were fulfilled. Their relationship would be no different than the many others that had come before them.

Manin stood facing the foliage wall that blocked his sight of the Manor. He felt a warm tingle tickle his feet and then rise through his legs. It was a curiously delightful sensation at first, but by the time it reached his shoulders he realized that it was not a beautiful feeling of elation that was building in him. It was rage. A cold, callous, unreasonable rage that he could not control.

"How dare you threaten me in my own home? You ungrateful wretch." He advanced towards her, driving her further into the center of the maze. "Do you really think that anyone of noble blood will stand for you? You are nothing. Your family sold you to me to save themselves from ruin. You do belong to me. I paid for you, so now you are mine, and I shall do whatever I like with my property." Elaina looked around her for a way to escape. Things were not turning out as she had planned, and now she had begun to regret her impulsive decision to meet with him in a secluded area.

"As a matter of fact," snorted Manin, "you are no more than a servant in my house. You will come when I call and do what I command. I shall bed you when I choose and you will bear my children. You will do as I see fit or I will still have your family brought up on charges of fraud based on the fact that you were not pure when I married you."

"But, Manin, that's not true!" cried Elaina.

"Who do you think the courts will believe?" sneered Manin. "Me or you?"

Elaina understood the validity of his words. She did not have a place in his noble society. Lady Beltrane might have been able to sway the Mantilian lords, but Elaina was new to them and the promise of help carried little weight in her argument. She would be labeled a harlot and her family would be shamed.

"Would you be so cruel as to continue to handle me this way? I have done nothing to deserve this." Elaina dropped to her knees. Tears of frustration rolled down her cheeks. Manin's threats were real and she knew it. There would be little she could do to protect herself from him.

Rising in defeat, she braced herself on shaky legs and faced her husband. "It will be as you wish. I will do what is required of me, just leave my family alone." Her head hung low as she walked back to the exit of the maze. Just then, Manin, feeling a surge of victory, grabbed her arm and swung her around. "And just where do you think you're going," he growled. "I have not yet given you permission to leave." His grasp on her arm was excruciating.

"Manin, you're hurting me. Please let me go."

He laughed as she vainly tried to free herself from his grip. He had her secluded in the middle of the maze, well away from the prying eyes or ears of anyone that might think to save her.

"Manin, please."

Her feeble cries excited him to arousal. "Let you go?" he asked calmly. "Now why would I do that? As I said before, you are my property and I will do with you whatever I choose, when and wherever I choose."

Pulling her to him he kissed her roughly on the mouth and tore at her dress. *Oh no*, thought Elaina. *Not again. I cannot bear this again.* Visions of that horrible night came flooding back to her and she was filled with terror. *Surely, if he takes me again I shall not survive it.* She must find a way to escape. She pushed away from her captor but the more she struggled the more intense his advance became. Finally, finding no other alternative, she dug her long, sculptured nails into the flesh of his face. Clawing and raking his skin she fought for her dignity and her life.

Manin felt blood run down his face and recoiled momentarily. He placed his hand on the open wounds that had now begun to sting in the warm summer air. She had gouged him deeply. Manin considered himself to be a prince among men where his looks were concerned. He had charmed his way into many hearts and even more beds with his beautiful face. Now this lowly wretch dared to scar him! Rage increasing, he quickly moved to bar the exit of the maze. He would not let her go that easily. She would pay for what she had done to him.

Seeing that she could not reach the exit, Elaina turned and ran in the only direction available to her, to the center of the maze, to the fountain. She stumbled up the stairs that led to the massive structure, praying that someone would rescue her from this nightmare. Why did she bring him here in the shadow of the maze? What had compelled her to talk to him here of all places? She looked over her shoulder and found, to her dismay, that Manin was right behind her. He reached for her arm but lost his grip only to find her hair as a reasonable replacement. Manin pulled her to an about-face using her hair as his instrument of restraint. He showed her the lacerations that she had inflicted upon his face.

"You will pay for this insult," he said, pulling her hair tighter with every syllable. "Did you think that you could get away without punishment?" His voice dripped with hatred and venom. "First I will have my way with you, and then I think I shall seek out your chambermaid. She shall be lashed for her mistress' insolence."

Andira.

"No, she has nothing to do with this!" cried Elaina.

"From now on, she does. Every time you defy me, your little maid will pay, and so will that old crone Sinta." Manin placed a hand around his wife's delicate neck and scrambled to lift her dress with the other.

Elaina tried to scream, but he was restricting her air flow, making it impossible to breathe, let alone scream. *This is it,* thought Elaina. *He will kill me after he has had his way with me, and then he will punish Andira and Sinta.* Despair surrounded her like a black cloud as she began to slip from consciousness. As she gave in to the black void she heard a collection of voices faintly call to her like the whisper of wind through grass. The voices were calling her, pulling her, guiding her to her inner strength. Elaina reached out to touch the source of those words and felt smooth marble under her palm. Her hand clamped on to the cold stone and she realized that she grasped the fountain.

Help me, she cried. *Help me to save myself. Help me to be strong.* Instantly a whirlwind of energy flowed from the fountain, tingling its way up her arm, wrapping itself around her body. She felt a warm sensation, as if being bathed in liquid music. It engulfed her, tightening and squeezing her so completely that she thought surely she would be snapped in two. Finally it plunged inside of her body filling her lungs with air. She inhaled sharply at first then steady and silent, feeling and hearing nothing but the sound of her own heartbeat.

I am ready. Slowly her eyesight returned and she found herself in the clutches of her horrible husband. He had managed to keep his hand around her throat while he wrestled with his britches. When he had accomplished his goal he sneered at his once trembling bride.

"I think I will enjoy this, my sweet." He hiked up her dress, thrust her knees apart and pushed her against the fountain. He had the power. This was a lesson that she would learn this day and carry with her forever. He would be her life-giver and sustainer, and he could take away that life when he so chose. Smiling, he positioned himself to take his prize, but was stopped short by a thunderous sound that radiated through his body, sending him flying through the air toward the maze wall. He bounced off its foliage and landed head first on the stone walkway, rendering him deaf and blind for a brief moment. He groped around in visual impotence, trying to find relief.

"What is happening? Elaina, where are you? I am ill. Come, help me to the Manor." He called out again but heard nothing in response. When the black scales fell from his eyes he found a very entranced Elaina floating over him with eyes of white fire. She pointed at him and spoke in an ethereal voice.

"You will not touch me again. Nor will you touch Sinta, nor Andira. If you do, you will suffer a pain like no other." The wind whirled around her, lashing about her hair and clothing. The sight of this supernal being frightened him to his core and he nodded his compliance, ignorant of his previous anger.

The wind subsided and Elaina was slowly lowered to the ground. She sat quietly, impassive. She had witnessed every moment of their interaction, and yet she was powerless to do anything about it. It was as if she stood outside of her body and watched as she raised her hands to meet Manin's chest. A force of energy shot from her palm into his body, sending him flying through the air. She saw herself glide gracefully toward him, heard herself speak the words. And when her heart and mind had been satisfied, she felt the flame of her soul dampen into a slow blaze. She could feel the warm energy continue to flow through her, but it was now a small ember glowing in a hollow cave.

She looked at Manin, who peered up at her dumbfounded and silent. His face was smeared with blood and dirt and his clothes were rumpled and torn. She reached for him, certain he had sustained major injuries, but he shirked back from her touch, fearing that he might be "blasted" again.

"Manin," she said calmly. "Are you alright? Can you stand?" She held out a hand to help him.

"Get away from me. You...you... What are you, anyway?" He scrambled to his feet and stumbled awkwardly as he backed his way to the exit of the maze.

"I am Elaina. The same woman you married," she called after him. But somehow deep inside, she knew that wasn't true. Something within had changed. A new strength had awakened in her. She recalled the words from her vision the night before. *The power lies within you, Elaina. You have hidden it deep inside yourself. Call upon its strength whenever you need it.* Call upon it she did, and by doing so she had saved herself from a terrible fate.

Chapter 11

The Countess paced the floor, nervously wringing
her hands. A courier had brought news from the
surrounding Lords that a meeting of the Houses was in
order. News had broken of Warren Beltrane's whereabouts
and the Lords of the Upper Mantle were eager to vie for
position. She ordered Sinta to find Manin and bring him to
her at once. Plans must be made to solidify their hold on
the Estate.

Sinta scurried out towards the garden. Elaina had
told them of her plans to speak with Manin in the maze.
The maids felt that she risked much by being alone with
him so far away from protective eyes, but Elaina had set
her mind on her mission. She felt that she could draw
emotional strength from the fountain. Its bronze horns
reminded her of the horn that was gifted to her by the
voices in her vision. As Sinta approached the maze, she
saw a terrified Manin running towards her. Her heart sank
when she considered what terrible plight might have
befallen her mistress. But much to her relief, Elaina came
running out after him.

"Master Manin," she called. "Master Manin.
Madam has told me to come for you at once. It is urgent,
my Lord." Sinta eyed him curiously, noting the scars on
his face and his severely disheveled appearance. "Lord
Manin, are you alright? Shall I call for assistance?"

"I need no assistance," he growled. "Now out of
my way. I have urgent business to attend to." He pushed
past her, not stopping to look back at Elaina, who was just
then making her way across the lawn.

"What happened?" asked Sinta. "He looks like he
tangled with a bantra tiger."

Elaina smirked to herself. "He might as well have."
She saw Sinta's questioning look but she chose not to

divulge any more information out in the open. She would tell her later, in the privacy of her bedchamber.

"What brings you out here? Surely you weren't concerned and decided to come and check on me? I told you that I would manage everything alright." She smoothed her dress and fluffed the sleeves of her summer blouse. She was putting on a brave face. She was sure that Sinta was aware of this by the look of her ripped clothing but she stood staunch and collected. She had expected anger from Manin but she had hoped that they would be able to come to some sort of agreement. Yet, dashing any faith she had left in him, he attacked her. He had attempted to force her into submission and he was quite willing to use those around her to do so. What would have become of her if she had not reached the fountain? The thought of that violent end made her tremble. It was a good idea for her to choose the maze as their meeting destination after all. Without the fountain and the power she derived from it, she might not have been able to free herself.

"I was concerned for you, my dear, but that is not why I have come. The countess is very worried. She ordered me to find Lord Manin at once. She said it was urgent news."

"Urgent news?" Elaina questioned. "I wonder what it is about. Sinta, is there any way you can find out what is going on?"

A sly grin spread across Sinta's weathered face. "Why, Elaina, are you asking me to eavesdrop?"

"No, I would never do that," she gasped. "Merely gather information." The two women laughed as they walked arm in arm across the sea of grass.

"I am sure I can find out something. As head maid I am privy to most of the happenings in the Manor." A whimsical look overtook her determined expression. "I will do this for you on one condition."

"Anything, just name your price."

"I must know how Lord Manin received all of those cuts and bruises, and spare me no detail."

Elaina let out a girlish giggle. "Gladly, though you may find the story hard to believe."

"You might very well be right," said Sinta, "but indulge an old woman anyway."

Manin stormed into the manor, angry and frightened. He could not explain what had just happened at the maze. He was sure he had the upper hand at first, but somehow she had bested him. He had thought her to be like so many other girls he had held in his grasp. They were young and docile, ready for submission. He could easily bend them to his will and when he was done with them he would move on to another conquest. However, this lovely creature was different. Yes, he had taken from her the choice to give him her physical love. But wasn't it his to take anyway?

He stopped to look in the gilded mirror fastened to the West Gate interior wall and grimaced at the sight of himself. "Horrid she-devil," he hissed as he fingered the scars on his face. "She will pay for this!" He hobbled to the stairs and found new pain resonating from every muscle in his body. The foliage of the maze wall had cushioned the impact of his body hitting its stone skeleton, but its branches tore at his clothing and skin and left him full of splinters and scrapes. The ground had not been as giving when his face abruptly found it. There was nothing there to cushion him and his head still throbbed its reminder. He cursed with every step as he made his ascent to his chamber. His mother had called for an audience with him and he knew that he could not meet her like this. There would be questions…none of which he wanted to answer. He called for his chamber maid and ordered a bath to be drawn. He would soak away his pains, but not his anger. No, he needed that to decide what he would do next. He would teach his young wife to submit, or he would be forced to kill her.

By the time Manin reached his mother's sitting room, she was completely irate. "Where have you been?" she screamed. "I have been waiting for you for hours." She paced the floor, letting her agitation guide her. "You were with that little light skirt, weren't you? Does she hold your attention so completely that you cannot attend to more important matters?"

She walked over to him and eyed the marks on his face. Softening into a motherly tone, she asked, "What happened to you? What have you done to your face?" She reached to touch him but he turned away.

"Nothing. I tried to climb the maze, but got caught in the bramble." Manin inwardly cringed at how effortlessly he could lie to her. He did not relish doing so, but he had learned early that usually a lie was better than the truth when it came to the Countess. She had the ability to take the simplest situation where he was concerned and turn it into a spectacle of regret. He was quite sure that she would not understand or believe the incident with Elaina, so it was best to lay the blame on his own frivolous and childish behavior. His mother never really saw him as a man anyway, in his opinion. She doted and fussed over him like a mother hen would her baby chicks. She expected such behavior from him; why should he disappoint her with the truth?

Lady Beltrane threw up her hands, clearly exasperated with her son. "What were you doing climbing the maze wall? Honestly, Manin! You act as if you came from some common wench's line. You are a Beltrane. You must act like one. You might have married beneath you but you do not have to act like her kind." She flounced to her bronze-handled bell and rang for the maid. "Julia, please find Sinta and tell her to bring a salve for Master Manin."

This was the opportunity that Sinta had been waiting for. She would be in the midst of the conversation between Manin and his mother, and she could report back everything she learned. She was well aware that the Countess viewed her servants like most of the nobility did. She believed they were too simple-minded to understand the complexities of aristocratic life and would divulge scandalous details in front of them as if they were invisible. Sinta grabbed her bag of medicinal wares and clambered to the sitting room. There she found Lady Beltrane still pacing the floor, wringing her hands. Manin sat, head down, like a child that had just been chastised for wayward acts. He had washed and changed his clothes, but he was still bruised. Sinta set to work, cleaning his wounds and applying salve as slowly as possible while mother and son conversed.

"I received a message from the Lords of the Mantilian houses today. They now know the truth about your father's demise. I assume that weak-minded fool of a king could hold his tongue no longer. A courier brought the Call of Rights to me this morning. The meeting is to be held five days from today." She wrung her hands and continued, "We must act quickly. You are married now. You have fulfilled your part of the law on all accounts. You have the right to take your father's place as the head of the Mantilian court. If we seize the reins of power now, no one will stand against us. I have requested an audience with the King. I sent my courier to Arilian's Palace right after I received the Call of Rights. If he will appoint you as ambassador to the throne in your father's place, then our lives will be made easy."

"And if he does not grant your request, what shall we do then, mother?" Manin asked. He hated the intrigue of it all. He was content to let his father do the work of the

Earldom while he, the privileged son, enjoyed the benefits of his labors. Now that his father had died in some remote land, the responsibility of the household had been thrust upon him. He resented his mother's prodding to elevate herself in the ranks of the house by using her own son; however, the idea of power excited him. He knew that just as it was with Warren Beltrane, his mother could do nothing without the backing of an influential male. When he was appointed as ambassador and advisor, she would no longer be able to treat him like a child.

"Well, what shall we do then, mother?" he snapped.

"He will grant my request. I know Arilian and his kind. He believes in valor and honor and all of that nonsense. He will believe that Warren's service deserves some compensation. I will remind him that he was often away from home on errands of His Majesty's choosing. His son hardly knew him. I will tell him that now that you are a man, you wish to honor his memory by following in his footsteps. The old fool will be hard-pressed not to grant you the position."

Manin moved away from the careful stitching and salve application that Sinta was trying to complete. She felt that their conversation was coming to an end and she did not want to be left alone with him if the countess decided to leave the sitting room.

"Then when shall we leave for the palace?"

"In two days. Arilian will hold court then, so he will be able to grant us an audience. Sleep well tonight and leave that strumpet of a wife of yours alone. There will be plenty of time for production when you have secured your place as head of our Court."

Lady Beltrane turned to Sinta, who was collecting her medicinal instruments. "Sinta, I want you to lay out appropriate attire for Elaina. No doubt the King will want to meet Manin's new wife. Make sure she is presentable and is versed on the ways of Arilian's Court." Sinta curtsied at her tight-faced mistress and scurried from the sitting room.

When she returned to Elaina's bed-chamber she found both Elaina and Andira to be an eager audience.

"Well," she began, "the first news that I will report is sad news indeed. Warren Beltrane is dead. He died on a special assignment for King Arilian." Silence passed between the women as the declaration of his demise sunk in. "I remember some time ago, the King summoned the Countess to the palace. It was rumored among the servants that she was given news about her husband's whereabouts." Sinta stopped, not sure how to proceed. "It was noised abroad that he had a Mistress in Lanier Isle that he went to "confer" with quite often, but that was merely speculation." Waving her hands to dismiss idle gossip she continued, "Lady Beltrane returned from her private audience with King Arilian a little...well..."

"Flushed," interjected Andira. "She was red as a beet and mean as a Siphon hornet! She yelled at all of the servants for days and even had Havor, the carriage driver, replaced because she misstepped while exiting the carriage.

"Come to think of it, Master Manin returned from the army abruptly and was acting rather odd as well. The air of the Manor was very tense, almost stifling."

"I believe I know why." Elaina and Andira listened in earnest as Sinta unfolded the shocking truth.

"Apparently Lord Beltrane died on Lanier Isles months ago. The details are vague but nevertheless, news of his death was ushered to the King some months ago. Seeing that he was a faithful servant to the kingdom, King Arilian summoned Lady Beltrane to the palace and held a private audience with her. He was fond of Warren and wanted to deliver the news to his widow personally. Being the shrewd businesswoman that she was, the Countess set aside her grief and set about devising a way to ensure that she and her son could maintain their position in the Commonwealth.

"She begged the King to keep the news of her husband's death a secret until her son was married. Under Mantilian law, any man holding an office of importance must be married. And while Lady Beltrane is a woman of power and influence, she still needs the backing of a male figure to maintain her position lawfully. She was well aware that now, with her husband gone, she would be reduced to a widow of little means. When word reached the Upper Mantle that the Earl had met an untimely demise, the key players in the province's political arena would no doubt position themselves to take the reins of the region. But if Manin took headship of the estate, then she would be able to keep her home, her power, and her influence over the Commonwealth. Knowing that their seat would be in jeopardy, Lady Beltrane insisted that Manin find a wife immediately. The King had granted her request of secrecy, but not without limitation. She had only four months to see her son married. After that he would have to adhere to the law of the province."

Sinta had waited around the corner to hear the remainder of Manin and his mother's conversation. She collected as much information as she could from them. The rest she filled in on her own, using what she knew of Mantilian law.

Manin had displayed little interest in any of the noble daughters of marrying age, finding them vapid and annoying. Then he met Emona. To him, she was the very essence of excitement and temptation. She was beautiful, brazen, and full of mystery. She excited passions in him that he had never known. He decided that if he must marry, he would choose her as his bride. In any other situation, the Countess would have condemned the betrothal of a farm girl to her son, but she knew that time was of the essence. If she was to ensure the position of her family, she couldn't be too particular. Also, it provided the opportunity to move quickly without any of the probable girl's family's catching wind of her plot. When Emona had rejected Manin and Elaina had been offered in her place, Lady Beltrane agreed for the simple fact that she believed that Elaina was a docile creature who wouldn't ask too many questions or bring attention to the family's plight. She secretly beseeched the King for a few more months. She needed the extra time to prepare Elaina for her new role and to settle Manin into the idea of this new bride. The King reluctantly granted her request, fearing that the nobles of the Upper Mantle province would accuse him of showing favor to one House over the others.

Now that Manin was married, the King no longer felt obligated to hold her secret. The lords of the Mantilian Houses had long respected and revered Warren Beltrane, but it was no secret that, given the opportunity, any one of them would jump at the chance to rein over the fertile province. It was well known that it was an agricultural gem, rich with nutrient-laden soil, healthy livestock, sumptuous fields and orchards, and open trade relations with Lanier and Nanshar. The land had been inhabited by his family for generations; the Deed of Rights had been gifted to Warren Beltrane after the previous land lord, a wayward relative, was sentenced to death for his involvement in a plot against the King and his family. Beltrane was instrumental in the capture of this traitorous dog and was thus rewarded with the title of Earl, Ambassador to the King, and proprietor of the Upper Mantle. Now that he was no longer a barrier, it would be possible for the next appointed leader to uproot Manin and the Countess and not only take the title but their grand estate, as well.

Elaina rubbed her temples and tried her best to wade through this ocean of information.

"So, Lady Beltrane wants the title for her son and the honor for herself," she mused. "How admirable of her."

"Yes, she wants these things for herself, and understandably so, my dear," replied Sinta. "She has given much to her marriage and gotten little in return. Warren was a good land owner and a good master to all of his servants, but he was not a good husband. He was hardly ever home and all those rumors of his infidelity…

"She felt that she deserved something in return. If she can get the King to grant her request one final time then she will be satisfied of the debt that she felt Warren owed her."

So the truth was out. She had married a selfish brute, believing herself to be the savior of her family, when in reality she was no more than a pawn in a political scheme, an insignificant character in the play for power. Now she was trapped in a marriage with a man who did not love her and held little regard for her well-being. If Manin gained even more power, there would be no one to save her from his brutality. His word, save for that of the King, would be law. No one would dare oppose him for the sake of a vassal-bred wench. Elaina became enraged when she realized what her life had been reduced to. She mulled over the revelation in silence, letting it all sink in. Manin had accused her and her sister of duping him into marriage to gain power and station. She found the irony of the situation nauseating. How could he accuse her of something that he had clearly done himself, and at the prodding of his mother? Elaina shuddered, cursing her Uncle for having agreed to the marriage arrangement.

Chapter 12

The journey to the palace was laborious and everyone, including the carriage driver, was glad to see it end. There were so many people heading to the palace that soldiers were stationed at strategic checkpoints along the road to assure the safety of the passengers and, more importantly, the members of the palace. Every so often, a carriage was searched and its inhabitants questioned.

Elaina surveyed her fellow travelers. Some of the carriages were arrayed in fine colors, with banners of the surrounding provinces boasting nobility. Others were simple but clean, gleaming in the noonday sun. She leaned closer to the window, hoping to spot another carriage from the Upper Mantle. Maybe an opposing House in the province thought to beseech the king for position and title as well. Who was to say that Lady Beltrane's assumption would be correct, that the Noblemen would wait until after the Call of Rights to petition the King? She held out hope that Manin would not be given the title. If someone else received it first, then there was still a chance that she could be saved from her husband.

The carriage came to a stop, and two obviously irritated soldiers opened the carriage door.

"What is your name, Sir?" said the dark-haired serviceman. He looked about the carriage but addressed only Manin.

"I am Lord Beltrane. I escort my mother, the Countess of Beltrane, and my wife, Lady Elaina. We have been granted an audience with the King." Manin stuck out his chin and puffed his chest so that his back stood rigid as a board. For a fleeting moment, Elaina admired his tenacity. The soldier looked over the carriage once more and waved them on. Manin's arrogance had gotten them into the palace with little difficulty.

The entrance into the royal estate was a complete wonder to Elaina. Never in her life had she seen ceilings so high, columns so wide, or arches so fanciful and grand. Opulence flowed from every golden silk drapery to every jewel-encrusted chair. She stared bright-eyed at a relief of a father in snow-white robes playing with his children among the clouds. The Countess beside her nodded at its beauty. The painting was full of life and gaiety.

"How lovely," said Elaina. "It is so peaceful and bright."

"It is King Arilian I and his children," Lady Beltrane said flatly. "There are many more around the palace. Come now, don't stand there with your mouth agape. Or shall I tell His Majesty that we are late because you found an old painting more important than his company?"

Elaina, noting the Countess' bitter tone, nodded and followed her silently to a room appointed for visitors of the palace.

Manin sat quietly, deep in thought, oblivious to the existence of everyone else in the room. If he was nervous, Elaina could not tell. He appeared absolutely resolved to the outcome of this meeting. He always got what he wanted and today would be no different. His mother sat emotionless and sterile. She focused on the task at hand. She must make the King agree to her demands. It was the only chance she had to preserve her way of life.

Elaina stationed herself beside a window overlooking the royal garden. It was lushly filled with exotic flowers of every color imaginable. A green carpet of manicured grass surrounding islands of grey stone were sporadically positioned about the grounds. Each island held an epochal statue of a knight, head bowed, sword in hand, kneeling in fealty to his Lord and Master, the King.

A cool breeze wafted through the window, chased by the aromatic presence of flowers. The heat of the carriage ride had been so oppressive that at times she felt she faint. The checkpoints along the road only added to her agony as the humid summer air drew out beads of perspiration from her brow. But here, now, at the garden window, she felt renewed. She embraced the light scent of roses that sailed past her and let the current run through her hair.

Brodriek, the King's steward, appeared to escort them to their meeting. The King was holding court in the Summer Chamber. Its travertine walls and open windows allowed cool air to flow freely into the room while its deliberate placement in the back of the palace brought in sunlight without the oppressive heat. The walls were painted white with flecks of gold sprinkled here and there, giving an illusion that the walls themselves were glistening in the sunlight. The hall was lined with palm trees that shaded the crowd of capable men making up the King's court. Whispers milled through the room as Elaina and her companions approached the throne.

"Your Majesty," said the steward. "Lord Beltrane, the Countess of Beltrane, and Lady Elaina Beltrane." Accepting the reverential bows and curtsies from his visitors, Arilian called them forward.

At first glance Arilian looked to be a kind old man. Yet there was something in his manner that spoke of youth and vitality. His wrinkles unmasked themselves with every turn of emotion, disclosing the expanse of his years and his responsibility. His eyes however, were shrewd and vibrant. He had seen much from his life and looked forward to seeing much more. He was a man of justice and honor, ruled by his passions but tempered by integrity and stability.

"Good day, my friends," he said gingerly. There was a glint of gaiety in his eyes. The wrinkled lines that surrounded his dark blue pools played peek-a-boo with his guest. "You have requested an audience with me, have you not? State your case and I shall regard it as justly as possible."

The Countess moved forward and curtsied a bit deeper than before.

"Your Majesty, as you know I am the humble widow to one of your most dedicated servants. Warren Beltrane worked in your service for many years. In that time he remained loyal to the throne and all of Alionia. My House shares the same regard for the kingdom as that of the Earl. The news of my husband's death has spread abroad and sadness fills our home. We pray one thing to be granted to us to lift this heavy burden from our hearts. Name my son, Manin, as Earl, Ambassador to the King, and proprietor of the Upper Mantle. Bestow upon him that honor so that he may follow in his father's footsteps." Another ripple of whispers spread through the court. Arilian held up his hand for silence.

"Is it not the law of your province that unless appointed by the King the court decides who will succeed the previous magistrate? It would be more appropriate for one of the members of your court to nominate your son for the position. If he is deemed worthy by the Commonwealth, he will be appointed with my blessing."

The color began to drain from Lady Beltrane's face. This was not going the way she had planned. He had granted her first two requests out of pity. It would seem that that ship had now sailed and she would have to rely on other means to accomplish her goal. She prodded Manin to step forward and speak.

"Sire, you speak true, as always. That is the Law of our province. However, it is also stated in the Law that in times of unrest, the King shall appoint a magistrate to govern." Manin stepped forward slightly and puffed out his chest. "I would certainly say, Your Majesty, that we are in an age of turmoil and unrest. If time is spent following the usual principles of appointing a leader for our province, then it will surely fall. Already several Houses have succumbed to the malicious nature of this rebellion. Panic will spread through the Commonwealth and there will be anarchy. Appoint me, Sire, and I will ensure peace and safety to those in our province."

"Those are very strong implications, young man," said the King. "While I applaud your fervor and commitment to your province and to your father's legacy, I hardly believe that deems you worthy to lead. You are right to say that these are times of unrest; however, statements of anarchy and panic are not words often used by leaders in the earshot of the public. Your father was a man of wisdom and decorum. It would do you well to learn from his good example."

The King looked at Manin, expressionless. The room remained quiet until he began to speak once again.

"I am quite aware of the upheaval in fair Alionia. My heart feels for my people, all of them, noble and common. It is for that reason that I am willing to hear your request. Have you brought a willing party to stand for you?"

Manin looked at his mother who stepped forward proudly. "I will stand for him, Your Majesty."

"Surely your request is enough, Countess. I see it as a conflict of interest to stand for him while being attached personally by parentage. Is there no one else who will stand for him?"

Silence numbed the room as the Beltrane's dreams slowly slipped through their fingers. Elaina, who had stood tense since the start of their visit, began to relax. It appeared that no one would be willing to stand as nominator to the seat, thus negating the appointment. Someone else would get the seat and Manin and the Countess's power over her would be limited.

A voice rang from the far end of the throne room.

"I will stand for him Your Honor." All eyes turned to see a dark man with broad shoulders approaching the throne. He bowed deeply before the King and announced himself. "Your humble servant, Simon Levee, Your Honor. I am a member of your military advisement. I have the honor of knowing Lord Beltrane. We served together in Your Majesty's army. He has always been a courageous and upstanding gentleman. He served as leader and confidant to many of the new recruits that joined our forces. It was unfortunate for us that he had to return home to attend to family matters, but I see now that it was with great reason and honor that he has done so. I implore you, Sire, to consider this nomination."

More whispers rustled through the hall. Manin cast a sideways glance to his one-time acquaintance. He had served in the same company as Simon, just not in the capacity that he alluded to. Actually, Simon was several ranks above Manin and made that fact known at every given opportunity. He was large and brash and cared very little for anyone ranking lower then himself. He had caused much strife in Manin's life as a cadet. He had cost him several beatings and severe punishments. His disdain for Simon double as Simon grew in favor with their military officials. Manin wanted to make a name for himself in the army. He wanted to make his father proud of him, of his accomplishments. Yet Simon always stood in the way of that by making his superiors see his flaws and not his strengths. When Manin was called home due to his father's death, he was relieved to be shed of the massive brute. He sold his commission and returned home, glad to be free from the whole horrifying ordeal. Simon seemed equally eager to see Manin, who he referred to as a weak-minded simpleton not cut out for military life, leave, never to return.

Why did he stand for him now? Manin looked at his mother's relieved face. She knew nothing of Simon's treatment of her son. At this point, Manin realized, it would not have mattered. If his nomination would help to ensure her goal, then she would accept his help, regardless of his past indiscretions.

"Very well, then," said King Arilian. "Have you fulfilled the other requirements of the Law?"

"Yes, my King. I have studied the Law extensively and I have recently taken a wife."

"Present her to me," he commanded.

Manin turned to Elaina and held his hand out to her in florid gallantry. She stared at him, momentarily fixed in her position. Manin reached out and took her hand, squeezing it harder than necessary, and, in the eyes of the court, "lovingly" brought her before the King.

"Your Majesty, may I present to you my wife, Lady Elaina Beltrane." Elaina shuddered at the look in his eyes. It was a look that dared her to make any error that would cause him his appointment. He would most assuredly kill her if she did. He silently made sure she understood his intentions. A shiver ran down her spine as she turned to face the King. She curtsied deeply and gracefully.

"Your Grace," she said in a smooth low tone. She focused on the barouche carpet that lined the expanse of the hall from the entryway to the throne. It was a dizzying pattern of deep reds and blues.

"Lady Beltrane, it is an honor to have you join us at court. From where do you hail?"

"I...I am from Inglemans Landing, your Majesty. South of the Upper Mantle."

"So you are not noble born?" the King raised his eyebrows inquisitively.

Elaina could hear the sound of her heart beating. No, she was not born of nobility. This fact may very well be the single flaw in Lady Beltrane's plan. Manin could possibly be denied his desperately desired appointment because his wife was not of noble blood. Elaina thought quickly. This might be her last chance to save herself from a terrible fate. She knew that Manin would be infuriated with her. He would accuse that he had lost the appointment because of her. He might try to kill her. She knew, however, in her heart of hearts, that their marriage would be a different kind of death, slow and arduous.

"No Sire, I am not noble born. My father, Gregor Ingleman, has a farm there not far from the coast."

"So your father is a farmer? Would you say that is a respectable occupation?" The King's eyes shone brightly and there was levity in his voice.

"I would say it is, Your Honor," Elaina snapped. "My father is a very respectable man. He makes an honest living and provides generously for his family. I am proud to be his daughter."

"This one has a bit of fire in her, does she not?" the King asked Manin.

"Forgive her impertinence, my King," Manin begged, placing a grip so firm on her shoulder that she collapsed to her knees, giving the appearance that she was kneeling before the King. "She, being of common birth, knows not yet the formal ways of nobility. I assure you she will be taught better conduct in the future."

The Countess scrambled forward to add, "And I can assure you that she will not be a blight on the province. She will follow Manin's flawless example of how a responsible leader should behave."

The King rose from his seat and walked to where Elaina knelt. Looking down at her, clearly amused, he said, "No need for forgiveness, Master Beltrane. There is no harm in having pride in one's family, especially when it is one so deserving of the honor."

"Rise, child," said the King, holding his hand out to lift her bowed head. "I am well acquainted with your father. He is a good man. Very loyal in service. And if I remember correctly, he spoke quite highly of his youngest daughter. I take it you are that very child." He looked at her and the wrinkles appeared around his eyes once more as he smiled. "Of course, the term "child" would not be appropriate to describe you. She is very beautiful, Beltrane, and full of spirit. Be sure not to quench the fire in her."

Arilian faced the crowd and projected his voice so that every ear in the hall would hear his words.

"See here," he began, "This union between noble and common must serve as a representation of the blending of minds and hearts that must be evident in the people of our land. It is imperative that we that are of noble class enable ourselves to see the beauty and vitality that is in our brother, the common man. Manin, you have chosen well, and because of that choice, I will grant your request. I will appoint you as Earl, Ambassador to the King, and proprietor of the Upper Mantle. May your wife serve as a constant reminder of the responsibility that you have to the people of your province, noble and vassal."

The hall exploded with applause for the newly appointed Earl. Lady Beltrane, the former, thanked the King profusely as she victoriously made her exit from the throne room. She was followed by a solemn Manin, and a very devastated Elaina. When they reached the receiving room that overlooked the garden, Elaina flew to a breezy open window and gripped the seal tightly to keep from fainting. She had hoped to be Manin's undoing, but instead became his biggest asset. She cursed herself for having married him. She cursed him for having brought her here and she cursed the King for using their union as a representation of inclusion for the kingdom. Theirs was a relationship of neither inclusion nor civility. She knew now that there was no escape for her. No one would stand against what the King approved and supported. She would have to live in misery with Manin until the end of his wretched life or hers.

She labored to breathe, willing the air in and out of her lungs. The old familiar pain in the pit of her stomach had returned. She took a seat and waited quietly for the invitation to return to the carriage for the slow ride home.

Lady Beltrane was aglow with motherly pride. "Well done, Manin," she praised. "We have accomplished that which we set out to do. Now there is much more in store for us. First, we must make our announcement at the Call of Rights. Those old sour-faced farts will have no recourse against us. They must accept the King's decree." She giggled with delight. "Then we must prepare to return to the palace. There will no doubt be a ball to celebrate your good fortune. And to think we owe it all to your young friend who was sensible enough to nominate you."

"Yes, I am indebted to him. But let us not forget," he said turning a furious glare towards Elaina, "my young bride. It was mainly due to her presence here that I gained my position." His nose flared with anger as he stroked her smooth pale cheek. "I will have to find some way to repay her."

Chapter 13

The induction ceremony was a solemn affair. The royal chorus sang in empyreal reverence as the King bestowed the title on Manin. He had suffered the onslaught of threats and bitter feelings set upon him by the Lords of the Mantilian court. They accused him of being a usurper. They would not see such a young upstart revel in what his father had built, not having participated in its governing. However, their protests were quickly silenced when a written edict from the King himself was produced, granting Manin full headship of the Upper Mantle.

Now that the ceremony had reached its end and the delegation was final, the induction ball could begin. There were many high-ranking officials at the soirée. Elaina could hardly believe that all the pomp and grandeur of the evening was merely meant for Manin's benefit. She had learned on the way home from their previous visit to the palace that many noble families had ventured to the capital to seek help and refuge from the skirmishes arising in their provinces. No doubt the royal court wanted to assure its affluent subjects that the Kingdom was not in danger of collapse, but that it thrived more now than ever. Arilian wanted everyone to know that he held tightly the reins of the nation.

The dowager Countess Beltrane, as she was now being called, was elated at the majesty of it all. She had accomplished more in the life of her son than Warren Beltrane could ever be credited for. He had committed great feats of bravery to earn his title, but he never took the time to teach their son to become worthy of it. She took chances that should never have been offered to a woman, even one of her position in society. She had risked everything and won. Now, as she looked around the room of nobles, all here to celebrate her son, she savored the sweet taste of triumph.

Elaina stood amongst the ladies of the court and listened to their sprightly chatter. They were aglow with gossip and intrigue. Elaina engaged in light conversation, smiling here and there, nodding in agreement to trivial matters. She felt like a prisoner to these dainty captors and was relieved when Simon Levee asked her to dance. She took his arm and he escorted her to the floor. Simon was tall and husky with a dark bronze glow. He swept her across the floor with less grace than was required of a man of his importance. Stumbling clumsily over her, he begged her pardon.

"I am afraid that I am not much for dancing, Countess Beltrane. I have training in many areas, mastering them all with ease. Unfortunately, dancing is not to be listed among my many accomplishments.

Elaina smiled politely and reassured him. "It's no matter. We all have special talents and gifts. I commend your courage. You have tried where some would shrink away. Your actions speak for themselves."

"Thank you, Countess. I hope that the nobles in your province feel the same way about your husband in the coming days."

"My Lord?" said Elaina, surprised by the shift in conversation.

"I only mean that it will be difficult to sway the Mantilian Commonwealth to believe that he is fit to lead. Especially after all of those death threats…" His voice trailed off, leaving her to fill in the missing words.

"Death threats!" exclaimed Elaina. "Surely you jest, sir. The Mantilian Court is comprised of honorable and just men who have the good of the province in mind. I understand that they were not happy with the way that Manin was appointed, but surely they cannot intend any violence against his person."

"Him or his family?" Levee said flatly. "I see that he hasn't spoken with you concerning this matter. I believe it is better that you are aware of the turmoil that is well on its way to reaching your doorstep. What would happen if he were to have a son? Would that child succeed him as he did his father? The nobles of the Upper Mantle will not take kindly to the ideal of dynastic rule becoming the norm in your province."

"Master Levee, I hardly think tha…"

"It would be a shame for such a young couple to lose their children in some horrible plot to forgo a dynastic rule." He eyed her ruefully as he talked. He seemed to derive a perverse joy in the distress she displayed at his words. He pulled her closer and whispered in her ear.

"Of course," he said. "It would be a shame if you became a widow so soon after your recent nuptials. You are such a beautiful woman." His hand slid down her back and ended dangerously low, just above the rising swell of her backside. "Someone will definitely have to take care of you in the event of Manin's untimely demise."

"That is quite enough, Master Levee," Elaina exclaimed, breaking free of his grasp and backing away from him. She noticed that several couples had stopped dancing and were now focusing their attention on her and Simon. She nervously tucked a tendril of her hair behind her ear as she tried to compose herself, barely managing to give him a slight curtsey.

"Thank you for the dance, my Lord. I feel a bit faint. I shall take some air immediately. Excuse me."

"It was my pleasure," he said bowing with gallant perfection. "I can only hope that I am granted an opportunity to do so again in the near future." He smiled maliciously at her as she made her escape.

Elaina rushed to the opposite side of the hall, intent on putting as much distance between him and herself as possible. *Impudent cur!* He was the same man who had stood for Manin in the presence of the King and His court. Now he was insinuating that a coup d'état might be in order!

As she walked the perimeter of the ballroom, she searched for Manin, who, since his induction, had remained in the presence of the King. He had saddled himself to the good-natured monarch and for the time, Arilian seemed to welcome his company. Manin's marriage to a vassal was a bold statement to the Commonwealth. It represented tolerance and uniformity, concepts that he would openly promote to prompt the blending of social classes. Arilian never liked the barrier placed between them. He had witnessed firsthand the exceptions made for those of noble class that at times were less worthy then those of their common counterparts. If everyone could see each other based on their heart and merit and not based on their lineage or wealth, then Alionia would be a far better place. He was well aware that this was a fleeting hope. The nobles of each province would fight endlessly to retain their privileged lives.

Arilian smiled as the lovely Countess approached his throne and reverenced him with a curtsey.

"Your Majesty."

"Countess, you look quite lovely this evening. Manin, you are indeed a lucky man. I believe there are many men here tonight that envy your good fortune for more than one reason."

Manin stuck out his chest in agreement with the King's statement. Yes. He was the man of the hour. He'd stood in the shadow of his father's image far too long. Now it was time for him to make a name for himself. Perhaps a better name than that of his father.

"Manin, I have kept you from your bride for far too long." Arilian stood and raised his hand and suddenly the animation of the hall came to a complete stand still.

"It is with much joy that we honor our new Earl. He is the son of a good man who shall be greatly missed. But rejoice we must in the knowledge that his legacy lives on in the life and actions of his son. We also rejoice for the union between this young man and his beautiful new bride. She as well comes from a line endowed with all the virtues that could ever be bestowed upon a man by the Great One Himself. Though he was of common birth, he made every good use of his value to this kingdom. Let us honor family's legacies through this young couple."

Resounding applause rang from every corner of the hall. Arilian commanded music to be played so that the new earl could dance with his wife. Manin haughtily took Elaina's hand and led her to the floor. He gave her a flourishing bow before taking her in his arms and leading her gracefully around the room.

"Well, my wife, it would seem that the entire kingdom cheers our union. I have made an advantageous decision after all. With your beauty and my power we shall be a force to reckon with."

"Manin, I wish not for power. I only wish for us to live amicably in our home. If this promotion from the King brings it to fruition, then so be it. Just please say that we can…."

"Hush now. There are eyes and ears all around us, hungry for gossip. I will have none of your simpering here. While we are in His Majesty's presence, you will act as my devoted companion. Is that clear?"

His false smile made her stomach turn. He was content to make the King believe that he wanted this marriage. He wanted everyone to believe this farce. How could she in good conscience go along with his scheme? She had no choice but to adhere to his demands until, Great One willing, she was presented with an opportunity to do otherwise.

"Do not think for a moment that I have forgotten what you did at the fountain. Did you think that I would now cower in fear of you? That I would let you control me? If you in any way give me the impression that you intend to threaten me again I shall have you taken before the King and declared a witch. I will report your entire family and anyone that associates with them as conspirators against the Crown." He twirled her with a flourish before bringing her close to him again. "I hold the reins of your life, and it will serve you well to remember that! Is that clear, Countess?" His lips turned up in a dazzling smile that made him look beautifully demonic.

"Yes, you have made yourself perfectly clear." They finished their dance in silence. Elaina wanted to break free from his grasp, but knew that eyebrows would be raised and Manin would be infuriated. She waited until the music changed from its romantic melody to a lighthearted tune.

She curtsied to him as she had her previously offensive partner and addressed him in the same manner. "If you will excuse me, my Lord, I do believe that I find myself a bit faint. I shall take some air immediately. Thank you for the lovely dance." She turned in the direction of the terrace doors, ready to make her escape, only to be thwarted by his crushing grip on her elbow.

"Perhaps," he said with cold disdain, "a little time in the company of your husband will revive your spirit. Come, we shall dance for a little while longer." She reluctantly allowed herself to be led back onto the floor just as a new dance was beginning. The tempo was quite swift and she worked diligently to keep up with its pace. With the end of each dance she sought to make her escape, citing physical instability as the culprit. However, just as diligent in his scheme, Manin always found some reason to keep her on the floor. It was only when the King silenced the music and called for all the noblemen to meet him in the advisors' assembly hall, that she found some relief.

After some time, the King and his courtiers returned and the festivities were quickly brought to an end.

"It is with deep sadness that we must bring this glorious day to an end. It has been brought to my attention that the insurgence has grown to a dreadful level. Many noble Houses across Alionia were burned and some of their occupants killed."

Gasps of horror and disbelief were heard all over the hall. "Please do not panic. This abominable act will not go unpunished. We shall strike back." Arilian's words were laced with finality. "I have ordered each Governing House to return to his province to rally his people. Each House must settle their affairs and collect their belongings. You will return within a week to The Citadel for protection. Any House that has not returned by that time will not be admitted." At that a host of questions arose. How could he assure safe passage between the provinces and the Citadel? Had the problem grown so great that they would have to leave their homes? What would become of their belongings? Arilian hushed the crowed once more and did his best to reassure his subjects.

"My most loyal friends. This is but a temporary exodus from the life that you know. The threat that rages against you will be stopped and you will return to your world just as you left it. However, to put your hearts at ease, I have assigned a small military force to accompany each leader to his designated land. They will stand ready to defend you with their lives while you settle your affairs and make your way back to the Citadel. Treat them as honored guest in your homes. Your very lives could depend on their bravery and fortitude."

The King was quickly escorted to his study while the guests gathered their belongings for the frightening trek home. Brodriek brought word to Manin that he and his family were to follow him at once. The King wanted a word with them. As they walked down the corridor to the royal study, Elaina felt her stomach flip. Her life had once been so simple, boring even. Now there was both excitement and tragedy at every turn. How she wished she could go back to her simple little life in her simple little room. But there was no chance of that now.

The King rose from his seat, looking weathered with concern. His smile was faint. "Lord Beltrane. Your celebration has been shortened by the reality of the world we live in." He walked around his desk to face them with natural familiarity. "I hope that this war we face does not dampen your enthusiasm in the effort to unite the classes. Your vision is needed even now more than ever."

Vision? Unite the classes?

"Your Majesty, I assure you that I am as firm in my convictions as ever. There is a great need for the unification of our people. Let us hope that it can be so before it is too late."

"Good. Very well said, my boy. That is why I have taken it upon myself to reserve the best soldiers in my army to escort and defend you and the people of your province." He motioned to Brodriek and the white-faced steward exited the study, obviously in pursuit of the King's unspoken request.

"I also took into account, my dear," he said, addressing Elaina, "that the safety of you and your husband is no doubt of the utmost importance to you. You will prize his company for many years to come. Young love is a wondrous thing and must be protected at all costs, so I have selected my best man to see to it personally."

Brodriek burst through the door, short of breath, and somehow still managed to conduct a most perfect bow.

"Ah yes, Brodriek, please show him in."

Elaina's heart jumped from her chest to her throat. Standing before them was the well-regarded and ruggedly handsome Rone Mosenvelt. Rone greeted the king with friendly fervor. He bowed to Manin, Dowager Beltrane, and then, much lower than he did for the others, to Elaina.

"Thank you for your assistance in this matter, Mosenvelt. I trust that you will see to the safe return of my guests, as well as that of their people," said Arilian.

"It is my honor to serve your Majesty. I will welcome the time to see you again, but I fear that the hour is far spent and we must be on our way."

"Yes. You are quite right. You must leave at once." Arilian ordered the carriage to be brought around to the Southwest entrance. All of the Mantilian nobles that attended the ball had filed into their carriages and were awaiting departure. The driver stepped down to open the carriage door. He reached for the dowager's hand, but was pushed aside by an impatient Manin, who leapt inside the carriage without thought for the women, who should have been secured first. Slightly embarrassed, his mother called in after him, "Thank you, my son. It is good of you to prepare my seat for me as usual." She waved an approving smile to the King as she was handed in by the driver.

Rone stood beside the King as he witnessed the nauseating scene. "Are you sure about him, Sire? That he is the right man to lead his people? He is young and brash and cares little more for others then for himself. Plainly speaking, he's an obnoxious brat."

"He may be all of those things, Rone, but oftentimes beautiful flowers grow out of dung heaps." The King smiled at him and clasped one arm in his. "If he proves harmful to our nation then we shall deal with him according to the nature of his offense. For now we will give this bird a chance to fly. Guard him with your life. He is useful to us yet."

Rone nodded in compliance.

"Godspeed, my boy. Blessings go with you!" said Arilian.

"Godspeed, Uncle," Rone said. "May the light of the Great One shine on you always."

He made sure that the carriages were secure and that all of the nobles were present before he ordered the convoy to begin its journey. He led the party through the gate and several miles down the road before pulling the reins of his horse to an about-face to watch while the convoy went by. He had placed the Earl's carriage in the middle of the party. If, Great One forbid, they were ambushed, the Earl's would be neither the first nor the last carriage in the party, enabling the soldiers to rally to their defense with more ease. When Manin's carriage came into view, Rone ordered the procession to halt. He rode up to the carriage and jumped down from his horse and opened the door.

"My Lord," he said addressing Manin, "We have cleared the gate. We shall ride without interruption until we reach the manor. Is there anything that you need before we begin?" He looked to Dowager Beltrane and then to Elaina. Her white ball gown was a radiant contrast to her beautiful raven hair. Her arms were folded about her chest and she rubbed her elbow nervously when their eyes met.

"Your foresight does you credit, Mosenvelt," Manin said smugly. "Is he not a good soldier, Mother, to cater to the welfare of those he is sworn to protect?" He gave Rone a mocking smile. "I believe that we are content at the moment. However, we will not fail to call upon you when you are needed. You may carry on." With a flick of his wrist Manin dismissed him, ending their exchange and sighing over the boredom of it all.

"Very well, then," said Rone through clenched teeth. He mounted his horse and the procession resumed its march. He rode beside the carriage, intent on keeping his word. He did not need to ask Manin's permission to continue the journey. He had done so to cater to his arrogant nature. It was well worth it to get one more glimpse of the woman who haunted his dreams. He focused his mind and sharpened his senses. He would have no surprises rise to face them tonight. And while he was promised to guard the Earl, only one person in that carriage was of any value to him. For her he would give his life if necessary.

As they rode from the palace to the manor, Elaina felt an eerie calm overtake her. She was well aware that Rone rode outside of the carriage, protecting them from possible danger. She could hear the sound of each hoofbeat striking the ground, but dared not look out the window.

Rone, she thought.

He had come at the King's bidding to keep her safe. She knew that she was not his sole responsibility, but at that moment nothing else mattered. He had come. Immediately, she felt the tension of the day melt away. She closed her eyes and matched the strike of his horse's hooves with the beating of her heart.

Rone.

Chapter 14

After arriving at the manor, dowager Beltrane ordered the servants to ready the house for a brief holiday. She busied the servants with packing and cleaning, taking inventory of every item known to be hers. This was an opportunity for a secretly resentful serf to execute her vengeance by mishandling or even stealing something of value from her mistress. Servants were often morose in their dealings with nobles, she thought. They were bitter for their plight and wished to take out their angst upon whomever they could. They sulked about, blaming their betters for their shortcomings. She huffed at the idea. They should be grateful that they were allowed to retain the positions that they were given.

Her bones creaked as she moved along the candlelit manor, inspecting the work of her peons. Her body ached. All the energy and effort she had used to strategize and execute her master plan had physically and emotionally exhausted her.

She called Sinta and laid the responsibility for oversight on her shoulders. "I have had a busy week and today was the most taxing day of all," she said. "I must rest now. Make sure that everything is completed by morning. Work through the night if you must, but have all of the work finished when I arise to take my morning tea."

Sinta nodded humbly but didn't speak. She was in for a long night; it was best to conserve her energy. "Oh, and Sinta, make sure that everything is accounted for. If anything is missing I will hold you personally accountable."

She understood the dowager's meaning. She would have her demoted and beaten if she failed to execute her orders. Sinta had been saved from her mistress's ire many times by Warren Beltrane. She had become his favorite when she was brought to Warren Manor as a young maid. She had covered for him when Lady Beltrane, who, at that time, was known as Lady Cynthia Calloway, inquired as to his whereabouts. He was later caught in his lie and forced to make amends. Lady Cynthia Calloway soon after became Lady Beltrane and Countess to the Mantilian Court. She allowed Sinta to remain in their employ, but vowed that she would never fully trust her. It was a vow that she held faithfully to even now. She knew that she was a capable maid but she despised her close friendship with her husband. With Warren dead and buried there would be no one to stand between Cynthia and her ability to administer what she deemed an appropriate form of justice.

"Yes, Madam," Sinta replied a bit too curtly. Lady Beltrane gave her an incredulous look, but continued in her climb of the stairs. She waited until the old woman was secured soundly in her chambers before running to Elaina's. She found Elaina and Andira hovering over her chests, filling them with her most coveted possessions. She found it easy to pack, seeing that Andira never removed more than two items at a time. Also, Lady Beltrane had ordered Andira to dress Elaina in new clothing, believing most of the pieces she had brought with her to be trash. "It is no longer acceptable for her to dress like a vagabond. If she is to be a Beltrane, then she is to dress like a Beltrane." Andira couldn't bring herself to throw out Elaina's belongings, so she kept them packed away, and out of the clutches of Lady Beltrane.

The servants hadn't been given an explanation as to why they were to pack, but they knew that something important was happening. They had friends in other Houses that sent word that trouble had come to their door. When a Noble house was set upon, the servants were often left unharmed. Only the Nobles were killed or taken.

Elaina explained everything that had happened at the ball. She told of the King's fascination with their relationship, and the misconception that Manin actually wanted her as his wife. She explained her dance with Simon Levee, as well as her equally unpleasant dance with Manin and the King's speech afterwards. She even told of their private meeting with the King and the protection that he ordered for them. Sinta frowned as she considered what it all meant.

"If the King is taking these precautions, then something terrible must be coming. People haven't been called to the Citadel since the Preon War. That was a bloody battle. Many lives were lost."

"So, what will become of you when we leave?" Elaina asked. She never considered that they would be left behind. "I will petition the King for the two of you to accompany me to the Citadel. He seems to be fond of me and I am sure that he will say yes." She rose to her feet and made her way to the door. "I shall ask Manin this very instant. If I have to be his happy companion in the eyes of the King, it would behoove him to make my happiness of utmost importance." She sauntered down the hall to Manin's room, a wave of boldness spearing her on. She had gained the favor of the King and was willing to use it as leverage. *Besides,* she thought, *he will not strike out at me with so many people here to see him. What better time to ask than now?*

She knocked on his door, but received no answer. She knocked again. Still no answer. More fervently she knocked until the latch creaked open and Manin swung the door wide. She pushed past him, not giving him a chance to refuse her.

"Manin, I must speak with you. It is a matter of utmost importance. Since the King has ordered us to the Citadel I think it best…"

Elaina stopped short when she realized something was wrong. Manin had never closed the door. He remained fastened to the handle, his usual look of indifference in place. She noticed that he had removed his boots and that he was naked from the waist up. She turned in the direction of his bed and found it to be occupied by Lily, the buxom servant girl that Elaina had seen wandering the Manor. She was clearly naked but huddled under the covers so as to hide that revelation. The boldness that had once fueled her vanished. She looked at Manin with a questioning eye.

"I found you to be unworthy of my bed. I have needs to fulfill, so I found someone who could fulfill them. Now, if you will excuse me," he said, motioning her towards the door. "I have my evening to enjoy. We can discuss whatever you deemed so important in the morning."

Shattered, Elaina rushed out of the room and found Sinta and Andira waiting for her in the hall. They looked at her remorsefully. "I am so sorry you had to see that, Elaina," Andira said sadly. "It is one thing to be mistreated. It is an altogether different matter to break the bonds of marriage so callously. He has added insult to an already gaping wound."

Sinta wrapped her arms about Elaina's shoulders and led her back to her room. "He has bedded her since your wedding night. I had not the heart to tell you. He is no gentleman, Elaina. He has never been. At this point, I can scarcely call him a man at all." She poured Elaina a hot cup of tea and laid out her bedclothes. "You have had a long day. Come now. It is high time that you get some rest. We will discuss this more tomorrow."

After her tea and a thorough grooming, Elaina settled into bed. She wanted to forget everything that she had learned during the expanse of the day. She wanted to forget the war and the packing and the promise of a better tomorrow. She wanted to forget the heartache resulting from her husband's infidelity. He had treated her horribly thus far. Why should she feel surprised or hurt by these egregious actions? Still, she felt a pain that she could not put into words. Willing herself to sleep, she tried to forget.

The stench of burning bodies filled the air as she ran through the carnage that surrounded her. The air was thick with death. Screams rose like smoke from the ashes that had once been living forms. Their souls cried out for help. She stooped to pick them up but they blew away in the wind. She ran into the manor and up the stairs, searching for help. No one was there. No one could save her. She ran to Manin's door and flung it open only to be pushed back by an explosion of flames and smoke. Through the inferno she could see Manin and Lily in his bed locked in a heated embrace. Flames leapt up around them and yet they seemed oblivious to their fate. The flames spread throughout the house. She ran as fast as her legs could carry her, scratching and clawing her way out of the burning building. The ground shook as the roar of the tumbling house sent her flying through the air. "No. They are all gone. I could not help them." Despair rocked her to the core as she searched through the rubble of the fallen house. She wailed in silence.

She tried to scream.

Silence.

Then a low rhythmic pulse could be felt surging through the wreckage. She searched for its source, pushing aside broken furniture and the charred remains of what had once been her life. On her hands and knees she waded through the chaos until she found her destiny. There amongst the ashes was a small lacquered box with glowing glyphs. The box throbbed in her hands and the rhythmic drum beat grew louder. She stood, enraptured by the beauty of the box and its seductive cadence. She opened the lid to find a beating human heart inside. At once she thought to throw it away. What could she do with it? How had it survived such destruction? She removed it from the box. Held it in her hand. Felt it beat. Watched it thrive. She needed this heart. She must connect with it. Pain pierced her body as her chest ripped open, exposing a hollow cavern. She pushed the beating heart inside and was instantly consumed by a swirl of emotions. Joy, pain, turmoil, peace, hope, love, and fear all came crashing in on her at once, overwhelming and consuming her. She opened her mouth, gasping for air. The sound of the beating heart grew louder until it exploded in her ears, causing her to breathe in for the first time with new life.....

Elaina sat up with a jolt. It was the second time that a dream had broken her sleep that night. She felt her chest to make sure she was intact. Much to her relief, her heart remained where it had rested all her life. She threw the covers back and walked to her window. The moon shone brightly in its jewel-encrusted sky. The trees below swayed whimsically in the breeze, flapping their limbs as if paying homage to the moon in dance. The grounds were quiet. When she had first retreated to the safety of her bed, the maids were bustling through the manor, making ready for the Beltranes' departure. Now all life had come to a standstill, all but the swaying trees beneath her window. Suddenly the walls of the manor closed in on her. She needed to escape. She donned her shawl and slippers and tiptoed down the stairs.

Everything that could not be packed or stored away had been covered in white linen. She turned into the west gate exit and was surprised to find two uniform-clad soldiers standing guard by the door. They nodded respectfully, acknowledging her presence but did not move to stop her. She gave them a pleasant smile and walked past them into the moonlight. She pulled her shawl around her as she made her way down the red brick path and onto the sea of grass. She removed her slippers before wading ankle deep in the soft verdure. It was cool from the fresh dew that dripped from each blade. A breeze caught her shawl and she lifted it into the current, giving the appearance of wings. Removing all inhibition she closed her eyes and let the draft whip through her hair and clothing.

"Incredible," she heard a voice say. "The moonlight becomes you as much as the sun does." She opened her eyes and was amazed to find Rone standing before her looking quite amused. Her cheeks flushed red to know that he had discovered her in a less then proper position.

A gust of wind swirled around her, tussling her hair, sending her shawl spiraling to the ground.

Rone released a hearty laugh. "It would seem the wind agrees with me." He swept up the shawl and placed it on her shoulders, curling it around her bare arms.

"Thank you," she said readjusting her covering so he would not see her tremble under his touch. She folded her arms in front of her chest. She realized that she was dressed only in her nightgown, and the shawl made a feeble cloak in the moonlight. She had thought that she would be alone and hadn't taken precaution to dress more appropriately.

"Are you in good health, Countess?" he asked after a few moments of heavy silence.

She shuddered at the formality of his manner. He was different just a moment ago, before he returned her shawl. She could even call him warm. Now he was cool and restrained. Every bit the gentleman. "Yes, I...I am quite well. You have rescued my shawl for me. I am in your debt."

"You needn't thank me for my duty," he said taking a step closer, "It is my pleasure to serve you, Madam."

"You speak so formally, sir. I believed our friendship to be beyond the bounds of such protocol. Have your feelings of friendship changed towards me so much that such propriety is needed?"

"Madam, my feelings of friendship changed towards you long ago." Elaina felt as if she'd been hit in the stomach. Her mouth went dry and she tried to appear unmoved by his words.

"Well, you needn't waste social grace on me, sir. I have no need of it."

Rone searched her expression. He had wounded her. "It was not my intention to offend you, Countess. I merely see you as my better. I am here to serve you in any way you see fit."

And now he was mocking her!

"You are the King's nephew. You are of royal lineage. I am a farmer's daughter."

"You are a countess and I am a soldier. Farmer or countess, my vision of you is the same." He took her hand in his. "There is more to a man then than his parentage. There is his heart, his mind, and his soul. All three he wishes to give to the cause that matters most to him."

"And what cause, Lord Mosenvelt, do you feel so passionately about, that you would give all of yourself to it?"

"I have several causes to live for. I live for my King. I swear undying loyalty to him. I live for Alionia. I will defend it until the end of my days." He lifted her chin to stare intensely into her eyes. "And I live and breathe for the one I love. I would die for her if fate required it." His voice was but a whisper.

Love!

Had he just told her that he loved her? Could she really be the woman that he could and would live for? Die for? Elaina swallowed hard to clear the lump in her throat. She fought the undeniable urge to fall into his arms and pledge herself to him. There seemed to be an unnatural tether between the two of them. She could not explain it but she…wanted…no…needed to be with him. She wanted to be his love. She needed to live for him. Why had life been so cruel to her? She would be happy with Rone. He would fulfill her dreams in every way. She need only say the word and he would take her away from the hell that she knew. But it could not be so. She had said her vows with Manin, and no matter his infidelity, she could not bring herself to be untrue.

"I hope that when you find her she is appreciative of your devotion."

The fire in his eyes instantly cooled. He backed away from her, releasing her hand in the process. Elaina felt the absence of his warmth, but she knew it must be so. She had hurt him, but surely it was the right thing to do. He looked wounded for a moment, but quickly composed himself, returning once again to the restrained soldier.

"As do I."

"It is almost morning. I should go recover what is left of my rest time." She turned to go back to the manor when he noticed a bruise on her elbow.

"Elaina," he asked, "what happened to your arm? I saw you nurse it at the palace, but thought you to be nervous. Now I see you are bruised."

She pulled the shawl over her elbow and looked across the lawn, avoiding his gaze.

"Nothing," she said, "I am quite clumsy at times. I must have bumped up against something, that's all. Good night, Rone."

She ran towards the manor, stooping to collect her slippers on the way. The moonlight danced off her silken mane as she bounced out of sight.

Rone stood looking after her. He was still fixed in the memory of her beauty when Sinta grabbed his arm.

"Evening, Master Rone."

His usual smile returned as she looped her arm through his. "Sinta? Now what on earth are you doing up at this hour?"

"Everything that can be done with only a few hours of sleep," she chuckled.

"What a lovely night to look at the stars. It's a wonder that more people do not take time out of their sleep to enjoy them."

Rone cleared his throat nervously. He did not wish to discuss his true reason for walking the grounds this night. He had tried to sleep, but found that he was too restless. He was under the same roof with Elaina, but he could not talk to her or touch her. He longed for her, but knew that his wanting was pointless. He had relieved the night watch and strolled around the grounds hoping to take his mind off of her. But to his delight she had been plagued by the same sleepless spirit, and had taken to the night wind for comfort. His heart beat faster as the image of her, arms spread, chin up and eyes closed as the wind whirled around her, came into view. He had seen a shimmering white aura around her. She looked... celestial. He was lost in thought for so long that he didn't realize that the conversation had stalled and that Sinta was staring at him, clearly amused.

"Well I will leave you to your watch. Who knows what *beautiful* danger might be lurking in the shadows."

They walked towards the manor. "Sinta," he asked a bit soberly. "What happened to Elaina's elbow? She has an ugly bruise."

Sinta shrugged and walked to the gate. "Who knows," she said, not turning to face him. "However," she called over her shoulder, "I can tell you that is not the only injury the poor girl has received since she has come here. In fact, it's probably the smallest one yet." With that she entered the gate and left him to his thoughts.

Rone was a jumble of emotions. Elaina had made it quite clear that her marriage was not a love match. It was a contractual agreement like many noble unions. Even still, Manin wouldn't be fool enough to abuse her. Would he?

He noticed that neither Manin nor the dowager really ever acknowledge Elaina's presence. Manin and his bride did not even share the same room like most newlyweds. She seemed very unhappy, and now she had bruises! What was Manin playing at? If he hurt her then he would have to answer to Rone. He had sworn an oath to his King to protect the very man that he now wanted to kill.

He ran through the entrance of the gate and to the main hall where the majority of his soldiers were lodging. He ordered a guard to be stationed at her door at all times. If anything happened to her, he would know about it.

Chapter 15

Simon Levee made frequent visits to the manor. After his gallant assistance of Manin at the palace, his previous folly was forgotten and he and Manin became fast friends. He was treated like a hero by Dowager Beltrane. She had refused to believe that Manin's appointment had anything to do with Elaina. In the dowager's mind, the only factor that aided in the victory of their quest was the helpful nomination by Simon Levee. He, against the wishes of Rone Mosenvelt, was granted full access to the Manor.

Rone had never cared much for Simon. He was much too loud and quite full of himself. They had had a brief encounter in the military when Rone was first promoted to captain of the Tumult Knights. The Tumults, a group of expertly trained knights that performed highly dangerous and secretive tasks for the king, were known for their bravery as well as for their efficiency in the areas of combat, surveillance, and retrieval. When Rone rose gracefully through the ranks in his military career, Arilian took notice. Rone had an undying loyalty to his King and country and understood the intricacies of combat. He displayed bravery in the face of fear and matched his courage with an unflinching sense of integrity. Arilian, seeing the potential in him, not only chose him for this division, but made him the leader of these brave men.

Simon Levee had made his own assent through the ranks of the King's army. He had started out as a lowly ensign when fate smiled on him and Captain Wayland Briston had taken notice of his hard work and had him promoted to lieutenant. Years later, under the direct supervision of Briston, Simon had found his way into the military chambers of the King's palace as one of his respected advisors.

Simon was content to hold his position. Though he did not have direct access to the King, he was still seen as an important man in the eyes of his peers. He used his title as often as he could to gain whatever advantage that was available to him. When he wanted personal information on a particular baron and his household, he sought to enlist Rone and his Knights. When Rone refused to aide him, he flew into a rage, citing his denial as insubordination. But since the Tumult Knights had been hailed as the King's personal guard, military officials had no power over them. They answered to the King alone. Having no recourse against him, Simon thought to undermine his authority by questioning him in front of his subordinates. Rone dealt him a sharp rebuke and had his inquiry into the personal life of his intended target made known to his superiors. The two men had been at odds ever since.

When Levee called on the Earl this particular morning, Manin seemed to be in very high spirits. They talked at length in his study, and when Levee made his departure, Manin seemed more excited than ever.

Elaina tried her best to stay clear of Simon whenever he came to call. She remembered the words he had spoken to her at the ball. She wearied of him and wished to tell Manin about his actions that night, but knew that he would not believe her. She decided that under the circumstances, it was best to stay close to her rooms.

She noticed that a guard was posted outside her door day and night. It was no doubt Rone's doing and she was grateful for his kindness.

About four days after their return from the palace, Mantilian nobles began to arrive at the manor. They would be leaving the Upper Mantle the next morning so they thought it best to have all the formalities in place to make a smooth transition to the Citadel. Elaina and a few choice maids kept the men occupied while they waited for everyone to arrive. Pouring herself into her role, she portrayed the image of a gracious hostess in every way. She engaged them in light conversation while serving them tea and spiced cakes. She enjoyed her visit with them so much that she was surprised to see them burst from the meeting room flushed and angry.

"How can you make that decision for all of us?" said one angry gentleman. "You have not the power to say whether we live or die."

"Your Father would not deal with us so foolishly," said an older gentleman, wagging his finger in protest.

"My Father isn't here!" Manin shouted. "I am the law in the Upper Mantle now. I advise that you respect me as your superior. And as for whether you live or die..." Manin laughed haughtily and perched himself in a high-backed chair, looking devilishly austere. "Live if you may or die if you must, but I will not be moved from my position."

The noblemen expressed their outrage, but their protests fell on deaf ears.

"I believe," said Manin, rising to his full stature, "that you know the way to your carriages." He turned his back to the furious crowd. "Good day, gentlemen."

Shouts of anger and the promise of revenge were heard spilling from the manor steps as each party member piled into his carriage. Manin lifted a glass of peach wine in salute to himself. He had challenged the Mantilian court and won. They could not by law stand against his decision. They would have to cater to his demands if they wanted to live.

Lady Beltrane bristled as she charged through the meeting hall doors with Rone at her heels.

"Manin. What is the meaning of this? I was told that you do not plan to escort the Nobles to the Citadel. Please tell me that this nonsense is only a rumor."

"It is no rumor, mother. You have heard correctly. I have no intentions of escorting them anywhere."

"Manin!" dowager Beltrane exclaimed. "You cannot leave these people here to die while you hide behind the safety of the Citadel walls. What will the leaders of the other provinces say about you? They will believe you to be an inadequate governor who was unable to lead his people to safety. They will label you a coward." She brought her hands to her chest to calm her palpitations. "What will the King say? You will be in direct violation of his decree."

Manin smiled reassuringly. "The King will be proud of my decision. He has already seen me for the visionary that I am. He will no doubt understand that what I do, I do for the good of the kingdom."

"What are you getting at, Beltrane," snapped Rone. "The King already gave you his orders. All you need to do is follow them."

Manin laughed again, challenging Rone with a sneer. "You see, Mother? That is the difference between pure-blood nobles and half-breeds. We know how to lead and all they know how to do is follow."

Rone clenched his teeth. He was growing increasingly irritated with Manin's arrogance. He had a firm desire to land him a hard knuckle to the jaw.

"The problem is that you have no vision, Rone. But I do. No, I will not escort the people of this province to the Citadel. We will stand and fight our attackers."

"What? Don't be absurd. We haven't the means to fight any one. We don't even know who we are up against." Dowager Beltrane flopped in a chair and placed her head in her hands. She could hardly believe what she was hearing.

"But we do know who we are fighting. Simon Levee has informed me that the rabble is not quite as large as the King expected. They are a small, inexperienced band of ruffians whose main purpose is to loot the homes of nobles after they leave for safer territory. If I call upon the troops that are already stationed here in the Upper

Mantle, we will be able to defeat them without the help of any other military assistance. We will make our glorious stand just as Regas did during the Preon war. Only we shall come out of it more victorious." He stood resolute in his decision.

"You are wrong," Rone said flatly. "Simon Levee has misled you. This force we face is not some infantile rebellion. It is an army from a land that is not our own. I have seen them with my own eyes. You need to lead your people to safety. Forget these dreams of grandeur."

"At least send the women and children, Manin. War is always harder on them. When I was a girl in the Preon War I-"

"I have not the time for your incessant babbling, Mother. The women will stay as well as the children. It will be good for them to witness first-hand my cunning mastery of the art of war."

"I will not sit by and watch these people become casualties to your insanity. In the morning I will send a cavalcade to the Citadel and with it a message to his majesty the King that you are in direct violation of his orders. I will go tonight and make ready as many Houses as possible. Be prepared to leave when I call in the morning."

The dowager nodded, relieved that Rone had taken action.

"You will go nowhere. We must stay united in our victory. No one in this house shall leave. If I have to stand alone as a representation of our noble spirit then I will do so. But any one that holds my father's name will remain at my side."

"So you would leave them to die with you?" Rone asked angrily.

"I hardly think it will come to that, but if that is our destiny, then so be it. What a glorious end it will be for the House of Beltrane. We shall be known through the ages as the lone House that stood victorious. We shall be the new Ingaria."

"Manin! What has gotten into you? What are you saying?" Lady Beltrane motioned to Elaina for a glass of wine. She needed a cool drink to calm her frazzled nerves.

Elaina spied the glasses on the small maplewood table on the opposite side of the room. She tripped over the carpet as she passed Manin, spilling the contents of his glass over his vest and onto the floor.

"You imbecile! Look what you've done!" He raised his hand, intent on making contact with her face. She braced herself for the impact, but never received the blow. She turned around slowly to see Rone holding Manin's arm, with danger in his eyes.

"Understand one thing, Beltrane. The next time you raise your hand to the Countess will be the last time that you will ever be able to use it." Manin understood the intensity of his threat. To save face he pulled his arm away and swatted at his clothes with a kerchief his mother was now offering him. He called for his newly-appointed chambermaid, Lily, to come help him out of his soiled attire. She bounced around the corner, looking excessively buxom and carefree. She sneered at Elaina as she looped her arm through Manin's.

"May I assist you, Lord Beltrane," she said invitingly.
Elaina's stomach turned. Manin had not been able to hit her physically, but he wounded her far deeper by this grotesque display. She fixed her eyes on the floor to keep from seeing the pitying eyes of the maids around her.

"Ah, it is so good to find the competent help that one so desperately needs. Come, Lily." She flashed him a toothy grin as he led her to the door. "Clean this mess up," he ordered. The maids rushed to the spilled wine in an effort to quench the ire of their master. Each one of them had come to like Elaina. Their hearts ached for her and the injustice she suffered at the hands of this merciless tyrant.

"No!" Manin shouted. "You clean it up." He threw the soiled kerchief at Elaina and ordered all of the maids out of the room, lest they try to help her when he left. He turned to Rone triumphantly. "Since you care so much for her, you can help clean it up." He strode from the room, mother in tow, preening like a peacock and reveling in his power.

Slowly, Elaina knelt and picked up the kerchief that lay at her feet. She promised herself that she wouldn't cry as she mopped up the spilled contents.

Rone looked at her, horrified at the scene that had just unfolded in front of him. How could Manin treat her this way? He stooped to aide her only to be rejected by her avid refusal of help.

"Elaina," he said softly. His heart broke at the sight of this wilting flower.

"Rone, please don't," she said, never meeting his gaze. She did not want him to see her cry. Her face burned red as she held in a torrent of tears.

"Elaina, let me help you."

"There is no help for me," she sobbed. She was no longer able to push back the tide of her tears. She leapt to her feet and ran from the room.

Rone paced the floor. He could not let Manin get away with his behavior. He wanted to call him out and challenge him to a duel that he knew he would not lose. His uncle had ordered him to protect Manin and his people. He had to get them to the Citadel before the close of the week. Too much time had already lapsed since the King had called him to the palace to undergo this task.

He decided that he would place duty before vengeance. He would go and rally the nobles and send word to the King of Manin's folly. Then he would return to settle his score with Manin and take Elaina away from this dreadful existence.

Chapter 16

Dowager Beltrane ordered her servants to collect all of their belongings and put them in the carriage that would be taking them to The Citadel. She called Lily into her sitting room and demanded that she pack for Manin as well. She would encourage Manin to leave one way or another. The dowager walked down the hall to Elaina's room, where she found her whimpering daughter-in-law crying on her bed. She was being comforted by Andira and Sinta. Immediately anger rose in her at the sight of the crying girl.

"Am I the only one in the house who has not lost their senses? Why are you just standing about? Get these chests packed and placed in the carriage immediately."

"Pardon our folly, Madam," curtsied Andira. "It's just that Lady Elaina was upset. We sought only to help…"

"She is upset. Does that mean that the whole world should cease to function? Stand up, child." Elaina turned to the dowager with blood-shot eyes and a red nose. Her cheeks were damp with tears and she looked a frightful mess.

"Stop your sniveling this instant! Do you believe that you are the only woman to suffer through an unhappy marriage? You have brought this upon yourself by seeking to marry above your station. Manin would never see you or your sister as anything more than what you are common! Look at you now. You whimper and cry like a spoiled brat. Control yourself. Act with dignity, for heaven's sake. You are a Beltrane in name at least."

Elaina wiped at her tears. She could take no more of their misguided superiority. "Your family name is not such a prize, Madam."

Sinta reached out to calm her but she pushed her away. She would have her say, no matter the cost.

"You speak so much of honor and dignity, but neither you nor your son possesses any of those qualities. You use your prejudice for others as a cloak to shield your foul hearts."

"Mind your tongue, girl. You forget who you are talking to," snipped the dowager.

"I have forgotten nothing. And I will say what I please. Manin has no right to treat me as his servant, nor does he deserve to be absolved of his infidelity."

The older mistress laughed, enticing her to rage. "He could bed a thousand maids and that still will not change the fact that he is an Earl of noble blood and you are nothing more than street trash, just like your mother before you. She thought she was higher than her station, but where is she now?" she acidly spat. "Dead, rotting in the ground. I knew that bringing the likes of you and your sister into our good name would tear at the fabric of our morals. If Manin has become base it is because you and your family have caused him to lower his standards."

"I have caused it?" Elaina clenched her fist as she spit her anger out at the old woman. "You as his mother have failed him. He is an insolent brute who has no feelings for anyone but himself. He would leave you to die here with him in some horrendous plot of self-aggrandizement and yet you still defend him!" Elaina felt a strange tingle spread through her body. Her anger had become so great that she felt as if the atmosphere around her would fold in on itself, crushing her and everyone else in the room.

"How dare you accuse me for your failings!" She pointed a trembling finger at dowager Beltrane. The room around her began to shake as she felt the anger in her soul give way to wrath.

Cynthia Beltrane must pay for her wrongdoings. Justice must be swift.

"Elaina. Elaina you must calm down. This is neither the time nor the place. You must control yourself." Elaina felt a pressure push her offending hand to her side. Her anger receded as Sinta flickered into view.

Lady Beltrane, frozen with fear, tried to recover with dignity.

"Never in my life have I seen such an ungrateful, wretched girl. When we arrive at The Citadel I shall report you to the King. He will deal with your impertinence there." She flounced from the room, more frightened than angry. She wasn't sure what Sinta had saved her from, but she knew it would not have been pleasant. She had witnessed a similar display from Elaina's mother long ago. Its outcome had been disturbing, to say the least. She had threatened to take her before the authorities, but thought better of it afterwards. The whole room had shaken when Elaina had confronted her. *Maybe it was best*, she thought, *that I do not stir her anger.*

Manin called everyone into the dining hall for a celebratory dinner, to commemorate the dawning of a new era. The servants were also ordered to attend to witness his triumph over his enemies, lest they have any doubts as to where their allegiance should lie. He raised his glass to victory, good fortune, and long life.

Out of all the servants that lined the walls of the dining hall, Lily was the only one allowed to sit at the table. It was apparent that Manin was championing her as his mistress. She was dressed in finer clothing than her usual livery and wore a large turquoise broach on her ruffled blouse. Manin had bought it months ago with the hopes of giving it to Emona on their first anniversary. Now his saucy maid wore it on her ample bosom.

They ate in silence for most of the meal. Only Lily's sporadic chatter broke through the melancholy of the evening. Finally dowager Beltrane ended the horrid celebration by ordering everyone to bed.

"It has been an exhausting day. Tomorrow promises to be just as strenuous. Let us all retire to our beds. We shall see what the day brings come sunrise."

Relieved, the servants retreated to their rooms to discuss the fate of the manor amongst themselves.

Elaina fell fast asleep only to be awakened hours later by Andira's frantic pleading.

"Elaina, please wake up. We must go now." She pulled the covers back and shook her. "Elaina, please hurry."

Elaina sleepily rose from the bed and Andira shoved a heavy robe into her hands. They ran into the corridor that joined the master rooms and right into chaos. The hall was filled with smoke and screams of frightened servants filtered from every corner of the manor. The guard that stood outside of Elaina's door appeared to be relieved to see the two women exit the room and motioned for them to follow him. He led them through the smoke-filled hall and down into the south gate entrance. There, awaiting them in a room three steps from the gate, was Manin, dowager Beltrane, and Lily. They looked terrified.

"What is going on?" Elaina asked.
"The manor has been attacked by angry noblemen, Countess," the soldier offered. "Earlier this evening, several Noble Houses were set upon by members of the rebellion. Everyone was killed and their houses burned to the ground."

They were angry at Manin for leaving them to die in his pursuit of glory. Elaina felt pity for their loss. She felt the same as if it had been her own friends or family.

"So what do we do now? Is it possible for us to escape with our lives?"

The room was silent for a moment. No one wanted to speak the inevitable truth. They would all die that night at the hands of an angry mob.

There was a knock at the door and everyone held their breath. The soldier drew his sword and opened the door slowly. Relief swept through them as Sinta and the soldier that escorted her entered the tiny alcove.

"I have come to help you escape. Quickly, put these on." She handed each one of them a parcel of linen.

"And what is this," snapped Lady Beltrane.

"These are your servants' clothing," Sinta snapped back, "and they will save your life."

"I will not wear servants' clothes even to save my life. Are you insane? A woman of my station does not cower in serfs' rags," she balked.

"Your station means little if you are dead, Madam," the soldier replied.

"I shall wear the cloak and nothing else. I must retain some form of my nature if by chance, someone comes to our aide. They must know who I am."

Elaina had already changed as discreetly as possible. Lily stood beside Manin, not sure what to do.

"I think that is a splendid idea," he said to Sinta. He gave Lily a cloak to wrap around her fine clothing. Her hair was disheveled and her makeup smeared. It was apparent to Elaina that she had never received a chance to dress in her nightgown but had put on the only clothing available to her when the guards came to Manin's door to retrieve him.

"I will stay here to see about the manor," Manin said gravely. He had planned to have a more glorious end to the insurgence. He would not let a few vengeful aristocrats steal this victory from him.

"But Manin, if you stay you will be killed," pleaded Lily.

"Courage my dove, I have a plan. I want you to go with my mother and these two soldiers to the Citadel. The carriage, to my knowledge, and against my wishes," he said glaring at his mother, "has already been prepared. Take it through the wooded exit on the far side of the estate. If someone sees you tell them you are servants fleeing from an estate that was set upon by thieves.

"Tell the guards to round up several servants and dress them in fine clothes and send them out of the front exit. When the mob gives chase I will retreat to the hidden chambers under the manor." He turned to the soldier next to him. "Send a message to your captain informing him that the house is under siege. We need reinforcements now."

The screams of frightened women rang through the air as windows were broken to release smoke from the building. The soldiers that were guarding the manor were now engaged in hand to hand combat with Manin's enemies. As stealthily as possible, they made their way to the loaded carriage. Lady Beltrane and Lily climbed in first, securing their position. Andira and Elaina climbed in after them.

Elaina had simply refused to leave without the two women that had been her confidants and friends from the time she had come to Warren Hall until now. Not wanting to lose time in their escape, Lady Beltrane agreed to bring them along.

Sinta climbed in next to the soldier who now wore the driver's livery. It was much too snug a fit to be convincing, but it would have to do. The second soldier climbed onto the back of the carriage. As they pulled out of the gate, a third soldier on horseback, carrying the news of the attack, shot past them, disappearing into the night.

Elaina said a prayer for safety. They were going to need the help of the Great One if they were to make it through the night.

When Rone received the news of the attack he was
ten miles away from the estate. After his tour of the Noble
Houses he realized the extent of Manin's grave mistake.
Several homes were burned to the ground and the bodies of
their inhabitants were placed on display for all to see.
Dozens of spikes lined the road with mutilated bodies
hanging off them like rag dolls. It was a horrible sight to
behold. No wonder the Mantilian nobles were out for
Manin's blood. Who could blame them? His anger
swelled against the pompous dim-wit. I *should surrender
him to their wrath,* he thought. However, he knew he had
made a vow to save the blaggard and he must remain true
to his word.

Rone would have reached Warren Hall much sooner
if a wave of troops from Nanshar hadn't marched onto the
path that was needed to get back to the Manor. He and his
men were forced to hide in the brush while the Nanshar
soldiers made camp. Usually Rone and his Tumults would
hide from no one, but wisdom dictated a retreat. There
were too many opposing soldiers for even Rone and his
knights to handle. At daybreak, the Nanshar soldiers broke
camp and the Tumults were able to resume their trek back
to Warren Hall.

When they had almost reached the manor they were
met by a lone rider. He relayed the message to his leader in
detail. Immediately, the party set off to the house at
breakneck speed. When Rone reached his destination, he
was horrified at what he saw. The house was charred and
ashen. The beautiful windows that once adorned the
massive structure had all been broken and shards of
colorful glass lay everywhere. Aside from a few servants,
the house seemed to be empty. He had witnessed the
carnage of the previous manors. Women and children had

paid the price for their heritage right along with the men. His pulse quickened as he earnestly looked for signs of noble existence. After questioning the remaining servants, Rone was led to an underground passage that produced several secret rooms. There he found Manin, curled up on a plush mattress, sound asleep. He kicked him with the hard tip of his boot.

"Wake up!" he demanded. "Get yourself up and account for what you have done!" He kicked the mattress so hard that Manin fell head first off of the bed and landed on his face with a thud.

"That is not necessary. I am capable of getting up myself." He rose to his feet, rubbing the ache from his nose.

"Ah, Rone, I am glad you have come. Have you brought reinforcements?" Manin exited the hidden passageway, leaving Rone and his men in furious astonishment. "Come. There is much to be done."

Rone took the stairs with livid alacrity. He looked at Manin incredulously. "Where is everyone? Why are you the only one here?"

"Everyone is gone," Manin said in a nonchalant manner. "Look at this place. They have ruined my fortress. They shall pay for this injustice. The King will hear about their treason. When I have emerged victorious they shall…"

Rone could take no more of his grandstanding. "You complain about smoke and a few broken windows when the people of your province, the people you were sworn to protect, mourn the loss of so much more. I have seen the carnage that your madness has caused."

He shuddered at the abominable destruction he had witnessed. Rone was a soldier. He knew the harsh realities of war. He had seen his fellow comrades killed in battle and he had taken more lives than he cared to count, but he always believed that there was a reason for such violence.

He performed his task out of dedication for all of Alionia, not for himself. What he had glimpsed on his tour was the atrocious slaying of women and children because of their leader's weakness. This was not an honorable battlefield but a massacre.

"There is often a price for greatness. Everyone will see that in the end," Manin shot defensively.

"This *is* the end. There are no reinforcements coming to help you. They are at this moment escorting the nobles to The Citadel. What's left of them. The only men that remain are those that stand before you now. I have returned only to take you, the Dowager, and the Countess to the Citadel. We shall collect them and be on our way."

Manin shuffled angrily. "You cannot deny me my victory, Rone. It is my right to have protection. I choose not to leave so you must leave me with a way to protect myself."

"You may stay if you like but I will not leave my men to save your worthless life. Now tell me where the others are hidden so we may leave."

"You cannot do this!" shouted Manin. "You are to protect me. The King has ordered you to do so!" He flailed about like a mad man, throwing pieces of broken furniture around the room. "You have to follow his orders," he demanded. "It is your duty!"

"I guess I don't know that much about following after all." Eyebrows raised, Rone looked around the room. He had lost all patience with the earl. "Where are the women?"

"They are gone. I sent them to the Citadel last night during the chaos."

"You did what? You sent them without an escort? Manin, Nanshar soldiers are everywhere! They could be in real danger!"

Manin hardly looked moved by this revelation. "That was merely speculation. Simon Levee has informed me…"

"Simon Levee has misled you. It has been known for some time now that Nanshar has been the source of the rebellion. This rabble, as you call them, is no little matter."

Manin stood bemused by Rone's words. Would Simon really mislead him? Surely he would not have done so purposely. He had stood for him at the palace and he had come to the manor to make amends for his previous mistreatment of him. He bristled inside. It had all been a ruse to make Manin the fool. He had fallen into his trap and possibly lost the favor of the King in the process. Charges would be filed against him and he would be stripped of his title. Worse still, the Nobles of the region would kill him if given the chance. He cursed his father for having died, leaving him to take the reins of the power. "I never asked for this," he said to himself. "This is not my fault. My father should have directed me better in these matters."

"Do you think they will come here? It is no matter," he decided. "I sent my mother and the servants out in the carriage. The nobles believe that we have fled the estate. If the Nansharian army search the house, they will believe that we have fled as well. I shall remain in the hidden pass. There is enough food stored there to last me for a while."

"Where is Elaina?" Rone asked. "Where have you sent her?"

"I sent her with my mother and Lily. She took those meddling servants with her as well."

Rone was beside himself with anger. He shot a dangerous glance at Manin. "You sent her with maids as her only guards?"

"Of course not. Two soldiers accompanied them. And if I do say so," he said, a bit flippant, "your men seem bad-tempered and ill-prepared. I had to think quickly and come up with a plan to save the manor and our victory. I suggested that two carriages be sent from the property. My finest carriage would hold several well-dressed servants. The other would carry the nobles and their servants. With the finer carriage leaving the manor it distracted the crowd enough to allow the other party to steal away." He was very proud of his plan. "Not to worry, Rone. If the carriage is found by Nanshar's soldiers, they will tell them that I was killed in the uprising. They will let them go because they are just women. They pose no threat to an army."

Rone thought about the massacred women and children that lined the main road of the Upper Mantle. They posed no threat to the enemy as well and yet they were still murdered. Lashing out he struck Manin square in the jaw.

"You impudent cur," he growled. "You would use her as a diversion to secure your own head?" Enraged he struck Manin again and sent him tumbling to the floor.

"She has no money and no power of her own. She is worth very little," Manin said coolly. "If they do find her they will think her some noblewoman's chamber maid. I sent her out in servants' clothes."

Rone could hardly believe what he was hearing. Suddenly, fear for Elaina's safety swept over him and he lost control. Grabbing his sword he swung it dangerously close to Manin's head, stopping only a hairs length from his nose.

"If it weren't for the vow I made to the King to protect you with my life, then I would kill you here and now." The impulse to strike was so strong that his hand trembled with indecision. Composing himself, he sheathed his sword and walked to the door. Incensed, he turned to Manin and spat, "If one hair on her head is harmed, no oath will stand between you and the punishment that I inflict!"

Rone quit the manor, leaving a very frightened Manin cowering on the floor.

Chapter 17

The sun blazed down on them as they pulled back onto the road. The little band of refugees had undergone quite an ordeal in their effort to escape the attack. When the carriage had pulled out of the gate and into the woods, they all held their breath. The idea that they might escape undetected was foolish at best, but somehow they managed to get clear of the estate.

The road to the Citadel was a terrifying nightmare. They proceeded at a steady pace, trying not to draw unwanted attention. As they drove down the countryside, they saw the destruction of the land they once called home. Burned houses stood as monuments to a mad man's lust for glory. The smell of burned flesh filled the air, swirling their stomachs into an uneasy churn. In the distance they could make out the faint outline of gangly poles lining the road. As they drew closer they realized that the misshapen poles held the bodies of mutilated nobles. There were women and children, all dressed in their once-grand attire, now tattered and filthy. Their faces were twisted in grotesque expressions, testifying to the horror of their demise.

The driver drove the horses a little faster than before. When they reached beyond the stench of death the carriage stopped and the riders spilled out. Feeling sick from grief and fear, Elaina ran to the nearest tree and retched.

When she returned to the carriage, the soldier in the driver's livery was checking the horses. Elaina had learned that his name was Chaney. He had enlisted in the King's army when he was only sixteen. He had lied about his age to gain entry because he had nowhere else to go. He was a rebellious lad who had lost the sympathy of his father, who was considered an upstanding man amongst his peers. He was not quite as privileged as the upper levels of aristocratic society but he maintained his standing in the Commonwealth. He had reluctantly set his wayward son out onto the street when he felt that he could do no more to dissuade his abhorrent behavior. Chaney found his way into the ranks of the military and then, by nomination from Rone, into the Tumults. He told Elaina that he held no ill will against his father for his actions.

"It was just the push I needed to enable me to find my destiny. My father is proud of me now and what is more, I am proud of myself."

"We should move out now while it is still dark," Chaney had advised. "We must get as close to the Citadel as possible."

Dowager Beltrane had other plans. "I say that we camp here. It has been a horrendous day. I do not think that I can go on."

"But Madam," said Jothan, the soldier that rode on the back of the carriage, "we will be sitting sport for anyone who would wish to fall upon us. We should leave." Jothan was a bit taller than Chaney. He was leaner too, but he held a fierce determination in his eyes that led Elaina to believe that he would be a terrible opponent to meet in battle.

"I can go nowhere tonight," the dowager demanded. She motioned to Lily. "We will stay here and camp by the road. I am sure we will be alright for several hours."

"Madam," Elaina said respectfully, "perhaps they are correct. They know more about this sort of thing than we do. It would be in our best interest to follow their lead. And besides, you can sleep in the carriage on the way. You have done so on occasion since we left the manor."

The older countess looked angrily at Elaina. "You may not care about your appearance, my dear, but I will not arrive at the Citadel looking like a derelict before King and country. I am tired and I will go no further. Since you agree with them so much you can sleep outside on the ground just like the rest of the servants. Come Lily, we shall sleep in the carriage."

She ushered Lily in before her and slammed the door before pulling the shades down. They had no choice but to stay and make camp for the night.

When morning arrived, dowager Beltrane was in better spirits. She had slept on the padded seating of the carriage across from Lily and woke looking quite refreshed. The rest of the travelers were matted with dust and dirt. Their lips were parched from the rough wind and dry air. The soldiers looked strong and alert, though they had not slept much that night. They had taken turns circling the perimeter of the camp, watching for any possible interference.

Elaina shook the dirt from her hair, thinking of how she must look. As she and Andira piled into the carriage, the dowager looked disdainfully at them. Lily had followed the dowager's lead and had removed her servants' cloak and changed into one of Elaina's garments. She had combed her dark hair into a fetching style and donned the broach Manin had given her on her lapel. She haughtily looked at Elaina. Her eyes spoke her silent words. *I have won. I have your husband's bed and your mother-in-law's respect. You are obsolete.*

Elaina felt her ire rise against the girl, but quickly squelched it. Why should she fight for something that she never really wanted anyway? She could content herself to live amongst the likes of Sinta and Andira. They seemed happier in all of their lack and servitude than any of the Nobles that she had met.

As they rode closer to their destination Jothan signaled to Chaney that a group of riders were closing in on them fast. Chaney shifted the carriage off to the side of the rode but it became apparent that the oncoming riders had no intentions of going around them.

Chaney maneuvered the carriage back onto the road and quickened his pace. To their dismay another group of riders sprang from a hidden alcove in the foliage below. They quickly moved into position, cutting off the path and driving the carriage off of the road. They were surrounded on all sides.

The riders were dressed in clothing resembling the style of Alionian livery. In aspect they resembled work-worn serfs intent upon theft. But Chaney knew better. He nursed the hilt of his sword, eyeing his captors warily. There were twenty men, at least, surrounding them. Each one held a warrior's stature. The man at the forefront of the division shouted a command in a tongue that was not known to Elaina. Immediately, two men jumped down from their horses and surveyed the carriage. They removed several chests that held the Beltranes' fine clothing. The leader of the group yelled another command, and soon after, Chaney and Sinta were being pulled down from the driver's platform. When the carriage door opened, Lily began to scream. Her screams continued until the man in charge laid a hard hand across her face. He had gracefully vaulted from his horse so that he could inspect his captives. He looked the dowager over, circling her and Lily. He pulled off Lily's broach and put it in his pocket.

"You are privileged, are you not?" His accent was thick and seductive. "And yet you ride with no guards. Where are you going?"

The dowager said nothing. She held her head high to exert her superiority.

"You remain silent." He walked over to Jothan and drew his sword. "Maybe I can persuade you to loosen your tongue." With a strike too quick to combat he plunged the sword deep into Jothan's chest. Jothan stared in amazement at the sword jutting from his body. Blood filled his lungs and spilled out of his mouth. He fell slowly, his spirit gone before his body hit the ground.

The captain pulled his sword from his victim's chest and wiped the blood across the lifeless body. "Who shall be my next example?" He stood before Lily. He rubbed his hand against her cheek softly. "What is your name, my pet?"

Stuttering, the frightened girl replied, "L...Lily."

The man smiled, pleased with her quick response. "And where have you come from, Lily?"

"We are from the Upper Mantle. I travel with my mistress and her daughter-in-law."

The dowager looked at her in outrage. She had shared Manin's bed on more than one occasion. She was allowed to sit at her table. She had even been allowed to sleep in the carriage while the real countess slept on the ground. Lily, in an effort to save herself, had given away their secret. Now they would all surely die.

"So, you are not born to privilege, eh? You surely look fine, doesn't she, men?"

The soldiers jeered and shouted lewd comments to their leader. He only smiled at the frightened, white-faced Lily. "I have never seen servants dressed in such fine attire."

"It was my master's plan," shouted Lily. "We were to dress in servants' clothing to convince you that we were common."

"And yet you are dressed in fine clothes. Your plan has many flaws. Who is your mistress, then, and where is her kin?"

Lily pointed to Lady Beltrane. "She is my mistress." She turned to Elaina, "And that is her kin."

He looked at Lady Beltrane. "She is noble. Her haughty stench offended me before she stepped from the carriage." He moved to Elaina. Her hair had been matted and tangled from her night on the hard ground. Her face was smudged with dirt and her clothing was torn and packed with dust. Her full beautiful lips were cracked from her night in the dry air.

The captain turned to Lily. "I say you are lying. Her skin is too dark to be noble. She looks as if she has worked in the sun. She is disheveled and slightly offensive." He placed a handkerchief over his nose. He walked to Andira and Sinta. "And who might they be? Aunts, cousins, all made to look like peasants while you, a serf, strut in your mistress's clothing? You take me for a fool?" he yelled.

"The gentleman on the end, who is he?" he said, motioning to Chaney.

"He is a soldier," she sobbed. "I speak the truth. I am a servant and she is the noble."

"Captain, if that is your rank. You seem like an intuitive individual. She speaks true. I am a soldier," said Chaney. Lily looked relieved. "But she lies to save her life. She is the mistress of these three servants. She has enjoyed a life of ease and privilege. It was my job to protect my Lady. That is why I am in their company."

"And you tell me this, because…" said the man.

"Because I am bound by a code of honor. These three women have lived a life of work and turmoil. It would be wrong for them to suffer the injustice meant for another. I believe that right is right. Besides, you will kill us all anyway. There is no room for deception."

"You are correct about one thing, my friend. I will not let you live. You have dealt honorably, so I will make it quick and painless.

He stood before Lily. "It is just like your kind to expect those lower then you to pay the price for your vanity. In seeking to gain your life you will lose it. And since you would forfeit your servants' lives, I will let them go." He ordered his men to return the chests to the carriage. Andira and Elaina were placed inside the carriage while Sinta regained her post on the driver's platform.

"Remember this day, that you have been saved at the hands of the Nanshar. May you return our kindness by swearing your loyalty to our new regime."

The soldiers opened a path to enable the carriage to roll through. Elaina looked back at the three captured individuals with mixed emotions. She felt an undeniable sorrow for their fate, especially for Chaney. He had saved her from certain death. It was a debt she would never get a chance to repay. Dowager Beltrane held her head high. She had resigned herself to the inevitable. She had lived as a noble, enjoying all of its comforts. Now she would die as a noble, with dignity and honor. Lily stood trembling, sobbing uncontrollably. Elaina felt a pang of pity for her.

Andira reached out and touched her hand as the carriage turned onto the road. "She wanted to take your place in every way. Now she has her wish. She will die as the wife of an Earl."

The women made their journey in silence. There were no words that could be spoken to heal their hearts. The sun had reached its peak when Elaina glanced out of the window and realized that they were going in the opposite direction of the Citadel. They had bypassed the road that led to the estate some time ago and were now making their way to the city entrance. As they pulled onto the main street, they found that Nanshar soldiers were everywhere. The streets were crowded with serfs, drinking, carousing and cheering their liberators. They stopped at Prominence Inn in hopes of finding a place to eat and regroup.

The innkeeper was a short, portly man with balding brown hair. He was kind enough to give them a room in which to bathe and refresh themselves.

"Sinta, where are we headed?" asked Elaina once they had reached the sanctity of their room.

"We are heading south to Inglemans Landing."

"Inglemans Landing? That is my father's estate. Why are we going there? Why didn't we head towards the Citadel?" Elaina liked the idea of seeing her childhood home again, but she wasn't sure she was ready to endure the challenges that they would have to face. What if they were attacked again? What if the soldiers didn't let them go this time? There were too many possible outcomes to such an action.

"We could not go to the Citadel. When the soldiers let us go, they were watching the direction that our carriage would turn. If we had proceeded on to the Citadel, they would have known that you were noble and fleeing to safety. They would have followed us for a while and then overtaken us and killed us all. It was best to do what any liberated serf would do. Head south." As usual, Sinta had thought the situation through and had come up with the best solution.

"What do we do now? No one will know where we are or what has become of us."

"Who cares if we are lost to them," said Andira. "There is no one left to search for us. I say that we make a new life for ourselves as best we can."

"But surely someone will look for us. Don't you think so, Sinta?" Elaina was filled with despair.

"I am sure he will look for you, my dove," she said, placing a reassuring hand on her shoulder.

"I am not sure that Master Manin will look for us. Who knows if he is still alive? I didn't think that you would care one way or another if he did or not." Andira brushed Elaina's hair to a soft sheen. She was no longer her maid but she was used to doing so after every bath her mistress had taken. It would be hard to break old habits.

"I do not believe that it is Manin that she waits for," Sinta chuckled.

"Then who…" Andira stopped short realizing for the first time what Sinta had known all along.

"Oh!" she said. "Oh, I am sure he will come."

Sinta exploded into laughter as Elaina's cheeks flushed bright red. Her companions had not spoken his name aloud but she had spoken it over and over again in her heart. She had called to him with her soul. She lay down on the bed, exhausted from the day's events. They would resume their journey in a few hours, so it was best to rest while they could. Her eyelids became heavy with the promise of sleep. She allowed herself to be swallowed up into the black void of her dreams. Dreams that contained only one image. Her soldier, her protector. Her…Rone.

Chapter 18

Dust flew through the air, stirred by the stride of
Yelmet, Rone's faithful steed. He had ridden with his men
for most of the day, frenzied in his search. He had to find
her. When Manin belittled her in front of a room full of
people, he had wanted to avenge her then. But being the
faithful soldier that he was sworn to be, he put duty before
love and left to secure the others in his care.

He cursed himself. Why had he left her there?
Why had he not assured her safety before leaving to see
about the other nobles? Manin was an obvious fool and
held very little regard for her life. He dug his heels deeper
into his horse's side. He stopped abruptly and marked the
trail that he was following. Rone was an excellent tracker.
He was prized by the King as one of his best search and
rescue officers. He could not explain why he was so
successful at this skill. The only explanation that he could
give was that the ground spoke to him. It told him the
secrets that it held. It opened his vision to things that
others never took note of.

He reached a spot on the road that looked as if a
carriage had pulled off the path. The tracks continued
along the grass for a bit until they resumed their spot once
again on the paved trail. Not long after, one of his men
called to him. They had found something.

A circle of soldiers surrounded their discovery.
Rone stepped through the crowd and looked in dismay. It
was the body of Jothan, his fearless soldier. He had
suffered a fatal wound through the chest. He said a silent
prayer over the body and saluted his fallen comrade. Then
he stepped from the circle, allowing his soldiers to mourn
their loss.

"If Jothan was killed on the way to the Citadel, that
would mean the carriage we are tracking probably belonged

to the Beltranes. They were set upon and Jothan was killed in the battle. So what became of the others?" he wondered out loud.

In the distance, he could make out two small mounds surrounded by huge, sharp-beaked buzzards. He led his horse across the road to survey the area better. As he approached the congregation of birds, his heart sank.

"No," he whispered. "It can't be." There, in the dirt, were two half-naked mutilated bodies. Their hands and feet had been cut off and their throats slit. He looked to the first victim and found that his estimation of who the carriage belonged to was correct. It was Lady Beltrane. She had been stripped down to her undergarments and apparently beaten before her throat was cut. He stood and prayed for the strength to continue. If they had killed Lady Beltrane, then surely Elaina was the mangled body next to her. A sob rose in his throat. He looked up into the sky, his vision hazy. He could not bring himself to look upon the decimated form. Finally, after much coercion from his inner voice, he approached the second body. She was face down in the dirt, several yards away from dowager Beltrane. Her dark hair was jaggedly cut and her clothing was removed. Her naked flesh evidenced a brutal lashing. Rone knelt and turned the body over.

It wasn't Elaina. It was Lily, the servant girl who Manin had flaunted in his wife's face. Somehow she had been killed instead of her mistress. Her face was bruised and her eyes were open. The last face she probably saw was the one who took her life, he thought. He breathed in a guilty sigh of relief, relief that Lily had died instead of Elaina.

"Great One, pardon my selfish heart," he murmured. He ordered his men to wrap the bodies and place them on a horse to be transported to the Citadel. They would be given a proper burial. He surveyed the area one last time before fully giving in to the idea that Elaina had survived. The only evidence of her existence were tracks from a carriage heading in the opposite direction of The Citadel.

"There is no sign of Chaney or the women, sir," said one of his knights warily. He was aware of Rone's mounting concern and did not want to distress him. "Perhaps he was able to assist them in their escape," said the soldier.

"Perhaps," Rone replied.

He mounted his horse and directed his men as to take the bodies to the Citadel. He also sent word to the King of Nanshar's involvement in their deaths and reiterated his disapproval of Manin's actions. He had already sent word with the nobles that morning, detailing the events at Warren Hall and throughout the entire Upper Mantle region. Still, it was necessary now to relay his recent findings. The bodies of the women that he found had their hands and feet cut off and their throats slit, just like the bodies of the murdered nobles from his tour. This style of execution was common among the Nanshar. It represented an act of elimination from society. By removing their hands, they removed the victim from the wealth of the land. By cutting off the feet, they removed their freedom, and by slitting their throats, they severed the lifeline between the head of a nation from the body, or its people. They, in this brutal act, were announcing their intentions. They were removing the nobles from Alionia in hopes to sever the prominent head from the common body. Their plan was to overthrow the government and take the nation as their own.

Rone turned his horse south and rode as swiftly as Yelmet's strong legs would allow. The King would want a full analysis of the situation from him. He would report back to him as soon as he could, but first he would find Elaina and take her to safety. He laughed to himself at the thought of the word.

Safety. In truth that was something he could not really offer her. The time of peace that Alionia had taken for granted was over. They must now prepare for war. Many would fight and die. Only the Great One knew if he would be numbered among the fallen. If that were to happen…

No, he could not guarantee her safety, but he would do whatever was in his power to try.

"I'm thirsty," whined Andira. "And I think my skin is baking." After taking a much-needed rest at the inn, the three women climbed back into the carriage and set off for Inglemans Landing. The carriage trotted along uneventfully until they reached the treacherous terrain of Desolate Way. The vehicle rolled quite smoothly at first. But, much to their dismay, the weather had taken a terrible turn while they were resting, making the dirt road muddy and slick. The carriage pitched and wobbled as they warily journeyed forward.

"Maybe we should stop here. The sun is burning brightly now. The roads will dry and soon we will be on our way again." Andira and Elaina murmured their agreements as Sinta pulled the carriage to a halt. When the horses stalled their canter, the left side wheels lost their hold of the road, causing the entire carriage to slide and dip. The coach fell to its side, jostling the women in the cab and sending Sinta flying from the driver's platform. The carriage slid several feet from the road on a downward slope, pieces of the frame detaching in its descent. The screams of its occupants were muffled by the sound of cracking wheels and the feverish whinny of the horses.

When the worst of it was over, Elaina pulled the latch on the door and climbed out to assess the damage. She offered a hand to Andira, pulling her from the toppled cab, and found to her dismay that the carriage was beyond repair. The horses frantically tried to free themselves from the wreckage. Elaina approached the frightened animals carefully.

While working on her father's farm, she learned a great deal about horses. If she did not release them soon, they would be no good to them and would have to be put down. She climbed up the side of the carriage and slid down in between the platform and the trapped animals. She made sure to stay clear of the powerful hind legs that were now kicking in a feeble fruitless attempt to gain solid footing. She noticed that one of the horses was able to stand, but it was attached tightly to the second horse, which seemed to be having trouble rising on its front leg.

Elaina eased her way over to the first horse's side, being careful to keep her feet firmly planted in the mud beneath her. If she were to slip, or make a sudden move that startled the horses, she would be crushed beneath their weight. When she reached the horse's neck, she patted him softly, speaking kind, reassuring words as she unlatched his bridle. When she had finally freed him from his prison, he leapt up with a start and whinnied and huffed about.

"Wait, wait a minute. Shhhh…" Elaina reassured. "It's going to be alright. We are safe now. All is well." She approached him slowly, stroking his flaring nostrils with her calming touch.

Now that he was secure, she turned her attention to the second horse, not yet on his feet. She circled around him to find his front legs. Her fear of being kicked paled in comparison to the knowledge of the horse's leg. It was broken. He would not be able to continue the journey. She released him from his bonds and set about doing as much for him as she possibly could.

"Look who I found?" called Andira. While Elaina was rescuing the horses, she had gone on a rescue mission of her own. When she climbed out of the carriage, Sinta was nowhere to be found. She stumbled down the muddy hill that had become the carriage's final resting place, and spotted Sinta, crumpled at the bottom of a large rotting oak tree. She cautiously maneuvered down the slope, but lost her footing and slid to the bottom, landing breathless right next to Sinta.

"Are you hurt?" Sinta mumbled. She sat up and grimaced at her pain.

" No broken bones or major injuries." Andira chuckled to herself. "I fear my pride is more wounded then anything. When I was a little girl I would have been able to take a hill like that most easily."

"I fear that I did not fare so well," said Sinta, rubbing her left arm. Andira looked at her forearm. It was turning horrible colors and had doubled in size.

"Are you well enough to stand?"

"Yes, I think I can," rasped Sinta.

Andira helped her to her feet. Getting up the hill was going to be a cumbersome task. Taking one step at a time, she led her injured companion back up the muddy incline.

When they finally reached the top, they found Elaina huddled over the injured horse. She had taken a few pieces of the fruit that they had acquired at the inn and was feeding it to the animal.

"Is he hurt badly? Can you save him?" Sinta asked.

"I am afraid not," she replied. "But I don't have the heart to kill him. I wish there was more that I could do for him."

She stroked the animal's lame leg with sorrow. She had witnessed several horses being put down after injuries had claimed their sturdy legs. Infection set into their hooves and her father had no choice but to put them out of their misery.

Sinta placed her good hand on Elaina's shoulder. "Maybe there is something that you can do for him."

"But how?" she asked.

"There is power in you. Use it. Have you not noticed the energy that has awakened in you? It saved you from Manin at the fountain. It almost put an end to the dowager the night before our departure from the manor. I have watched you and I see it flowing inside of you. Tell me that you feel it."

Elaina starred at her in stark disbelief. "Yes, but, I don't know how to use it. I don't even know if it's me or the maze. What if it doesn't work away from the fountain?" But Sinta was right. She knew that she had some kind of power inside of her. She had told the maids about what had happened at the fountain with Manin. Andira was surprised and elated. She was grateful to the Great One for allowing Elaina to save herself from another brutal attack. She wasn't sure how to make sense of it all, but she was happy nonetheless. That was Andira. Happy for any good outcome. Sinta, she noticed, was very quiet about the entire incident. She never commented on the events of that day. Her only reaction was one raised eyebrow and the faintest glimmer of something else that Elaina could not decipher.

"Trust me, Elaina. You can do this. You have to try."

"Try what, Sinta? I do not know what to do," she retorted.

She paced in front of the crippled animal. He seemed to plead with her with sad liquid eyes. Maybe Sinta knew something that she did not. It was Sinta who had given her the tea that caused her to sleep the night she was transported to the island of black sand. It was Sinta who noticed the bronze horn when she returned from the island. It was also Sinta who had stopped her from doing something dreadful to dowager Beltrane when her anger caused the manor to shake. Sinta seemed to know more about her abilities then she knew herself.

She eyed the maid coolly. Sinta returned with the same cold stare. "I guess it wouldn't hurt to try," Elaina said, giving in.

"Good. We must begin at once." Sinta instructed Elaina to place her hand over the horses wound, and probe inside her own mind to find her center. Once there she slowed her breathing and listened to Sinta's instructions.

"Calm your mind, and focus on the horse. Feel his pain. Take it into yourself. Relieve him of his trouble…"

Everything faded to black. The only two entities present were Elaina and the horse. He was hurting. He cried to her, begged her for mercy.

Will you release me? he questioned.

Yes, she answered.

She pressed her hands deeper into the wound and felt his hard shattered bone. Placing the broken pieces together, she let a burning heat rise to fuse the bone together. She held the leg until muscle and flesh found each other and sealed over the gaping wound. When the work was finished she released him with a gasp.

Andira stared in amazement at what she'd just witnessed. "How…how did you do that? How is that possible?"

Elaina looked up at Sinta's smiling face. "How did you know that I could do it?"

"Because your people can do a great many things," she said wryly.

"My people? What do you mean, my people?"

It was beginning to be a little too much for Elaina. She stood, mouth agape, looking at Sinta questioningly. Her life seemed to be riddled with questions and intrigue at every turn and she had yet to receive any answers. Why had this newfound power awakened in her, and where did it come from? Why had no one spoken of it until now? Whatever the answer, she was determined to learn more about it, and Sinta was going to help her.

"You have another limb to fix. Sinta's arm is broken," Andira pointed out. "Maybe you can use some of your power to heal her."

Elaina stood on wobbly legs and placed her hand on Sinta's forearm. She noticed how tired she had grown all of a sudden. She was drenched in sweat and her hands trembled so much that Sinta stepped away from her touch.

"Maybe you shouldn't try just yet. The horse was a large animal. He took a lot of your energy." She pointed to the horse who was shuffling around them, testing out his newly healed leg.

"I would like to try," demanded Elaina. "Your break would be smaller, I could..." the world twirled like a spinning top. "I could...uh...." She tried to blink away the haze that surrounded her. She felt so very tired. She stumbled, trying to catch the ground that had risen up to find her. She closed her eyes, fighting the sensation of being pushed to the ground.

She heard Sinta say very curtly, "Stop fighting, Elaina. You need rest. Give in." Having no other recourse, Elaina did just that. She gave in to her urge to rest and fell immediately to sleep.

"What happened to her?" Andira asked amazed. "She was talking and then she just...collapsed. Is that a result of her using her abilities?"

Sinta shrugged. "Perhaps fatigue got the best of her. I'm sure it's nothing to be concerned about."

"Well, I may not have Elaina's powers, but I can help you with that arm."

She found a loose board that had ripped from the side of the carriage. She tore the hem of her dress and wrapped it around the board and Sinta's forearm. Using the remainder of her hem, she placed the boarded hand in the middle of the cloth and then tied the ends around Sinta's neck. "There, I'm afraid that that will have to do until we find a physician, or Elaina wakes up, whichever one comes first. We should be on our way now."

Andira gathered a few chests, being sure to leave behind Manin's and dowager Beltrane's. They would have no need of their clothing where they were going. She did, however, keep the chest carrying Elaina's belongings and other items that they could sell along the road. She and Sinta managed to push the sleeping Elaina up on a horse, which was not an easy task. At Andira's insistence Sinta climbed onto the back of the other horse, holding the reins with her good hand. After tying the chest to a makeshift pull that she designed out of broken carriage pieces, Andira took the reins of Elaina's horse and led them to the road.

After a while, she looked at the sleeping woman. "When do you think she will wake up?" she asked Sinta.

"Who knows? She must have been very tired."

She also looked at the sleeping figure. She knew that Elaina would be refreshed when she woke up, but she also would be full of questions. Yes, they would have to talk about a great many things. "But for now," she thought, a smile spreading across her face, "I will let her sleep."

Chapter 19

"It's about time you woke up. I thought you were going to sleep forever." Elaina woke to the torpid swaying of the chestnut horse. Dusk had fallen and the nocturnal wood life had begun their night of play. Andira was smiling at her wearily. She led the horse farther down the dark path, mumbling something of hunger and fatigue.

"Where are we? How long have I been asleep?"

"We have almost reached the end of Desolate Way," Sinta replied. Her eyes danced with amusement. "Do you feel rested, dear?"

"Yes…I think so. I was having the most wonderful dream." She stretched lazily, still covered in a comfortable haze.

"Well, I am certainly glad you got a good rest, because I feel positively dreadful," Andira yawned. Elaina noticed the horses were pulling two of the chests they had lost during the accident. Sinta sat on the horse next to her with her arm bandaged, looking tired and worn.

"We should camp for the night," she said, a command rather than a suggestion. "You both have journeyed far while I have slept. Let me take a watch over the camp."

Too tired to protest, Andira led the horses off the road toward a collection of large boulders. They tethered the horses to the remnants of a rotting tree. The sun had done its job, just like Sinta had predicted. There was no trace of the rain that thwarted their journey previously. The ground greedily soaked up whatever the sun had not, leaving the soil dry and barren. The two exhausted women rolled up their cloaks to use them as cushions before settling into a sound sleep. Elaina walked the perimeter of the camp. She had noticed that Chaney and Jothan had often done this when they kept watch over their small company. Her heart shuddered with guilt and pain for her fallen companions. She was supposed to be numbered among the dead or captured. She had been spared by the careful words and honorable intentions of a brave soldier, and by the ignorant ravings of a manipulative turncoat. No matter their position, she mourned all who had fallen.

She looked up at the stars. They twinkled in their celestial casing. She had been through so much within the last few months, but this was the first time that she had ever felt free. Here under the stars, covered in dust and mud, unsure of what awaited her, she felt peace and reassurance. Reassurance that her life had purpose. She had escaped her husband, for the time being. She had even escaped death. She was given a chance to follow the destiny that had been mapped out for her from her first breath. She must save her people.

Elaina looked at her sleeping companions. They had shown her friendship and compassion from the time that they'd taken her into their care. Now, she realized, it was time for her to care for them. The voices on the island told her of her power, and alluded to her destiny. Elaina walked over to the once-lame horse that she had affectionately named Chestnut, and patted his side. His leg showed no signs of the trauma that it had incurred.

She heard the voices swirling 'round in her head:

"You are the key to saving your world and all those you love."

She would do just that. She would save them all. Here under the stars, her destiny was clearer than ever.

The sun flew to its normal haunt, rousing early birds from their nests. The travelers collected their belongings, desperate to resume their journey. If things went as planned, they would make it to Inglemans Plains before night fall. When everything was packed and they finished their meager breakfast of bread and apples, Elaina approached Sinta about her broken arm.

"I am feeling quite refreshed. Maybe I can look at your arm now."

Sinta studied her for a moment. She leaned forward, staring hard into her eyes. "Yes," she nodded. "You are ready. You may try now."

Elaina placed a steady hand on Sinta's forearm and delved deep into the "darkness" that surrounded her once before. There she saw Sinta, felt her pain, knew her thoughts. She felt the heat rise and the bones mend. When the healing was completed, she noticed a glimmer of something off in the distance. She maneuvered her way through the dark void until the object came into view. It looked like a small bronze horn, similar to the one that she acquired during her dream. She moved closer to it to get a better look. Suddenly a wall of fire leapt to block her path. She reached out, impulsively wanting to remove the offending obstacle. When her hand reached the fire, an agonizing pain ran through her fingers. She yelped as she quickly withdrew to suck her fingers, releasing Sinta's arm.

"Ouch. What did you do that for? That hurt."

"You should not snoop in places that you were not invited to explore. Lesson two, respect others. Never let your powers lead you where others have not given you permission to go, except in extreme cases."

"So, this was a lesson. You burned me to teach me a lesson?" She looked at her incredulously. "I never knew that you had taken me on as a pupil."

"Is there a problem with that?" snapped Sinta.

Elaina remained silent, nursing her sore fingers.

"Well, don't you want to learn how to use your talents?"

"Of course I do…but…I have some questions that I need answered first."

"You will have your chance to ask as many questions as you like. Right now we are wasting time. We must reach Inglemans Plains before dawn. We can talk on the way."

Sinta unwound the bandages that held her arm to the board. She removed the wooden plank and tested her range of motion. She smiled to her brooding companion.

"It feels much better now. Thank you."

Elaina grumbled and huffed her way over to Chestnut. She pulled his reins in the direction of the road. "A lot of thanks I get," she mumbled. "I attempt to help and I get injured in the process. All because I was a little curious."

"Elaina," Sinta pleaded, "It's a matter of integrity. Come now, really. Don't you believe that you're behaving like a child?"

"No," she pouted.

"Come here," Sinta ordered.

Elaina obeyed respectfully, like a child to her mother. Sinta grabbed the top of her fingers and closed her eyes. The stabbing pain subsided into a slight tingle and then melted completely away.

"There. Now can we be on our way?" Sinta turned away from her astonished friends. They were aware that Elaina had some unnatural talents, but Sinta had never shown an outward sign of any such abilities. Andira moved closer to inspect the newly healed fingers. The dark blisters were gone, leaving pink flesh in its place. They exchanged wondering glances.

"Are you coming?" chuckled Sinta, "or do I have to go by myself?" She led her horse to the road and trudged down the path. Elaina and Andira collected their wits and hurried after her.

Andira was allowed to ride Elaina's horse for much of the morning. She had walked for most of the previous day, so Elaina felt that she owed her that privilege. She walked beside Sinta in silence. She couldn't help lifting her fingers and examining them periodically. It fascinated her that Sinta had healed her with a mere touch. She had performed a more complicated feat on both Sinta and the horse prior to her own affliction, and yet having it performed on her was an ethereal experience.

On the other hand, it was also disturbing. Why did Sinta keep her abilities a secret? Even when Elaina had explained her strange experience at the maze when Manin attacked her, Sinta offered no explanation. While it was wonderful to witness Sinta use her power to heal, hadn't she also used it also to hurt her?

She stole a few sidelong glances at the maid. There was more to Sinta than she originally expected, that was for certain. Elaina was eager to discover those mysterious facets; however, she was not sure that Sinta would be forthcoming with the information.

"Sinta…I," she hesitated. Her behavior over the burn was deplorable and she was deeply ashamed for it. She was frustrated by the barrier that Sinta had set up against her, and the blisters administered to her fingers had not helped her disposition. At the time, she had deemed her reaction worthy of such a painful onslaught, but regretted it now. She was not a child after all. She could not go about pouting and throwing tantrums.

"I am sorry for the way I behaved just now. I am still getting used to my new abilities. The fact that I am not the only one who has them is quite alarming."

Sinta nodded her forgiveness.

"I believe you had some questions for me. I am ready to answer whatever you might ask."

"Alright. Um…what was lesson one?"

"What?" Sinta asked puzzled.

"You know, lesson number one. You said that lesson two was that I should never let my powers take me where I wasn't invited. So what was lesson one?"

~ 197 ~

"Oh, yes. An important lesson indeed."

Elaina blinked. "So what is it?"

"Do you remember how tired you felt after healing the horse's leg? You were exhausted, and yet you still wanted to heal my arm. Even after I protested."

"Yes, I remember."

"Well, you should know that when you are first learning how to perform any new feat, it is important to rest afterward. If you push too hard you can cause yourself great damage. You must always stop and rest."

"But I did rest," Elaina insisted. "So I passed the test. I learned the lesson." She beamed with pride.

"Well," Sinta hesitated, "not exactly. You fell asleep, but with assistance."

"What do you mean?" Elaina protested.

"Do you actually remember lying down, Elaina?"

She could recall being tired and dizzy. The sky had started to spin and the earth came up to meet her...

"Well, I don't actually remember lying down, but I do remember waking up."

"I know," Sinta grinned mischievously.

Elaina eyed her thoughtfully.

"It was you. You made me fall asleep, didn't you? How did you do it?"

"It is an ability I have used for as long as I can remember. When I was but a youngling, my Nana would want me to rest when I wanted to play. She did not believe that girls should play with boys, even before the age of womanhood. She believed that there should be clear boundaries between them. I liked the games my brothers and their friends would play. I found them much more exciting than the games of my feminine peers," she chuckled. "I would put Nana into a deep sleep and run and play until my heart's content. She never did understand how I came to be so incredibly dirty playing with my dolls."

~ 198 ~

"So you learned that you had this ability when you were young?" Elaina mused. "Why was I not aware that I had my abilities? Did I not have them then?"

"They were always there. You were born with them, as are all of our kind." Sinta lifted her head proudly. The sun glinted off her up-turned nose. Pellets of sweat dotted her forehead, adding a subtle glow to her bronzed skin.

"So we are of the same people? Who are they? Tell me about them."

"I am from Lanier Isles, as was your mother, and her mother. I knew Ella; she was a lovely woman."

Elaina's eyes brimmed with tears. It was the first time she had heard her mother's name used in years. Though Gregor spoke of her often, he would only refer to her as "his love." To speak her name brought too much despair to his heart.

"What was she like, my mother?" asked Elaina.

"She was innocence and light itself. She had a strong inner beauty that matched her physical beauty. Many men wanted her, but only your father could hold her heart." She looked at Elaina and smiled. "In a lot of ways, you are very much like her."

The tears spilled from her eyes as she thought on Sinta's words. She dreamed of her mother as a little child. She dreamed of her face and her voice, her soft hands coming to comfort her amidst the terrors of night. Uman and Emona were both given the opportunity to know her. But she had been excluded from that privilege. Ella, after twelve grueling hours in labor, died holding her newly-delivered daughter in her arms. As a young girl, desperate for knowledge of a mother that she would never know, Gregor told Elaina the story many, many times.

"She held you in her arms and smiled. 'She will be called Elaina, because she will bring light to this world,'" Gregor would tell her. *"But soon after that she became ill.*

She was weak from the labor, having lost a lot of blood. I help her hold you." This was always Elaina's favorite part of the story. She would reenact the scene with her dolls so that she could get a better understanding of her mother's actions. "I held you up to her; she kissed you on the forehead and spoke several words over you. Then into your tiny body she blew her very essence." At those words Elaina would take a deep breath in as if she were at that very moment in her mother's arms, taking in her life force. "After that she was gone."

"Where did she go Papa?" she would always ask.

"Back to the stars, my little dove. Back to the stars where all heavenly beings belong."

When the tale was finished, Elaina would squeal with delight and beg Gregor to tell it again. When she reached the age of eight, Emona chastised her for her bedtime ritual. "You silly, inconsiderate child," she would say. Emona wanted to be sure Elaina understood that she was the older sister and that that fact awarded her the distinction of being the wiser of the two. "Can't you see that every time you ask father to tell you that story, you only make him more sad and lonely? He blames himself for Mother's death. If you care for him at all you will never ask him to tell you that horrible story ever again."

Elaina didn't quite understand what Emona meant by her father blaming himself. How could he have had anything to do with her mother dying? After all, it wasn't some horrible accident or tragedy that had befallen Ella. It was her birth, her entrance into the world that dictated her mother's exit.

Was it possible that her father blamed himself for her mother being pregnant with her? If she had never been born, perhaps her mother would still be alive today. She decided that the answer to that was without a doubt the right one and willed herself to never ask her father to retell the story. She also decided to be as little of a bother to her father as possible. She had already taken the one thing from him that he loved most in the world. She would not add insult to his injury. From that day on she was the model child, obedient and respectful. She strove for the love of her father, hoping that someday he would forgive himself for conceiving her.

Chapter 20

The stifling stench of heat and death that was
known to Desolate Way was cut by a sweet west wind.
Sinta could tell they were near the border. She estimated
they were approximately a half day's journey from their
destination. If their trek remained uneventful, they would
reach Ingleman's Plains by nightfall.

The women walked, discussing the history of their
ancestry and life on Lanier Isles.

"It is a beautiful place. It was said to have been
given to us by the Great One Himself." Sinta led the horses
over to a small patch of dying grass. There she placed two
apples and a few hard sweet pieces she had acquired at the
Inn before they left town. She poured water into her hand
and let her horse drink. He lapped up the water
appreciatively before turning his attention to the apple
before him. She repeated this action for Chestnut and then
returned to Elaina, taking up a spot next to her on one of
the chests that was tethered to the horses. Andira, after
enjoying an apple of her own, positioned herself as
comfortably as possible and listened to Sinta's story.

"When the Great One created this world, he made
men and women to live in peace and harmony. There were
no classes or stations back then. Every man had equal
rights, and was judged only by his deeds. But for some
reason the people wanted a ruler of flesh and bone to lead
them. After a time, The Great One obliged them and
appointed one man to rule over the people. He was a good
leader, just and fair, but he was alone, not having found a
mate amongst his kind. Every night he would climb to the
top of his Mountain and look into the heavens. He would
marvel at the stars and their beauty. He cried out to the
Great One and asked for a bride hewn from the stars
themselves. The Great one refused, saying that he did not

know what he asked for. He told him that no man could tame the stars from the heavens, and if he tried, it would bring an end to his world as he knew it. The man begged and pleaded with his master. He swore that he would cherish and love the star maiden if only the Great One would grant him his request. It would be on his head forever if he brought harm to his land because of the love he had for this special woman.

The Great One agreed to his request, knowing what the outcome would be. He plucked a star from the heavens and made from it the most beautiful woman that this world has ever seen. Her hair was as black as a night sky. Her eyes were silver orbs that shone thru to the soul. She held beauty in every word and action. When the man saw her, he loved her instantly. She was what he had wanted in a bride. However, the man had not understood what the Great One had meant in his warning. As soon as he saw her, he covered her in a thick linen drapery, afraid that another man would see her and want her for himself. He brought her home to live with him and refused to let her leave the house. She became sad and lonely. She had been removed from her family in the sky and now she was not allowed to meet anyone else because of her husband's fears. One night while her husband was sleeping, the beautiful star maiden rose from her bed and quietly left the house. She did not mean to disobey her husband. She only wanted to see more of the world around her, and to meet the people in that world.

As she was walking, she came upon a group of men herding sheep. They were beguiled by her beauty. Each one of them offered her everything he owned if she would marry him. She, already having a husband, declined them all and continued her journey. Soon after meeting the shepherds, she came upon a group of seafaring men by the great waters. When they saw her they all fell in love with her. They promised her everything they owned and more if she would only marry them. She declined them, as well, and continued walking. After a while she came to a field of golden wheat. The gatherers of the field had risen early to begin their toil. They, too, saw her, professed their love, and offered her the world. When she refused them, they let out a loud wail, stirring every one within the land. The shepherds as well as the seafarers joined them in their lament. Soon, every man that laid eyes on her pleaded for her hand. Her husband was stirred from his sleep at the sound of such great anguish. When he realized that she was not asleep beside him, he ran to find her. He pressed through the crowd of men, trying to get to his star maiden. But by the time he reached her it was too late. The women of the land had become jealous and angry. They resented the fact that their husbands, brothers, sons, and fathers, were moved so greatly by one woman's beauty, a beauty and elegance that outshined them all. They were so enraged that they surrounded the maiden, stoned her and chopped her into a thousand pieces. When the husband reached his mutilated wife, he was overcome with grief. He tore his clothes and plucked his eyes from his face, never wanting to see the stars again, never to be reminded of the great love he had lost.

The Great One looked down from his holy perch and saw the abomination that the people had committed. He asked the husband where his wife was.

"She is dead, my Lord," he replied.

"Who has done this thing?" the Great One asked.

"The women," all the men shouted.

The Great and Mighty Creator of all Things looked at the women, and they were frightened and ashamed.

"You have killed one of my most precious creations. I fashioned her from the stars themselves. But you have destroyed the beauty that I have gifted to this world. Because of your jealousy and anger, you will forever be enslaved to your husbands. You will strive for his love, toiling forever for that which you could have easily had."

He looked at the men who longed to possess the fallen maiden. "You men of the field, sea, and land, you coveted that which did not belong to you, driving the women of your land to wrath. You have known peace until this day. From this day forward you will be at odds with your fathers, neighbors, and wives because you were not satisfied with what you already had."

The Great One gathered the tattered pieces that were once his beautiful star and turned them to dust. He then fashioned an island with high mountains and black sand, and sprinkled the star dust over it. He gave the island his blessing and then out of the dust sprang the first of our ancestors. They were the children of the star maiden, fashioned from the dust that was once her body. We are their descendants, Elaina. We call ourselves the People of the Stars."

"I have heard this story before," said Andira. "My neighbor would tell this story to her daughters before they went to sleep back when I was a child. My father and mother would rise early at times to tend the land so I would stay with my neighbor and her daughters until my parents' work was completed. I believed it to be a tall story, you know, pure nonsense, nothing more than a fantasy to lull little children to sleep, or better yet, to make them behave."

"It is no tale, I assure you," Sinta replied. "It is our legacy and our birthright. Because we were from the heavens we were blessed with certain abilities that mere men do not possess."

"We brought with us all of the qualities of the stars, wisdom and foresight, health and longevity, persuasion and beauty. All of the most vibrant characteristics of our celestial beings were brought down and divided among us. There are some who can charm and persuade any man or woman to do her bidding. Others can see through the shadows of time and understand what will be. Some can heal and others can enchant and bewitch with beauty that is blinding. All of our women, we that descended from the stars, have been blessed to retain some part of our special abilities, and some can wield more than others. This wielding of power is what we call the *Élan Vital*. It means the life force that is used to carry out every function that is known to us."

"So only our women have these abilities?"

"Not exactly. There are men amongst our people who have been known to wield power. It is manifested differently but it is there. They are rare but usually very powerful," Sinta added.

"This is all so fascinating," Elaina mused. "My father never told me about our people or our special gifts. Maybe he was not aware that I possessed any. And what of my sister and brother? Do they have the same giftings?"

"Yes, they have their own abilities. Not quite like yours, but they do possess talents. The important thing is how they use them. Do they use them for the good of mankind or for their own selfish purposes?"

"I have so many questions," Elaina said. She was certain that she would burst any moment from the excitement of it all. She had always believed herself to be an uninteresting individual. There was nothing particularly special about her in her own eyes. Uman was smart and strong. He was his own man and he possessed a quiet strength and wisdom that surpassed men twice his age. Emona was alluring and clever. She always managed to get her way, no matter how tough the situation. Men loved her and women envied her. That was the way of it. But Elaina...she never stood out from her familiars. She was quiet and docile, bending to the will of others, trying never to overstep the limitations that had been placed upon her. Now things were different. She was different. She had stepped into a world that she never knew existed, and it was one in which she would play an important part.

Several hours had passed as they walked along the dirt road. Sinta recounted many tales of the miraculous People of the Stars to her eager pupil. A warm wind rustled through their mud-stained clothing. There was nothing refreshing about the air in Desolate Way. It was filled with the stifling stench of decay and rot. It permeated everything it touched. It soaked into their clothing and filled their lungs with the heat of death.

Andira led the party, walking only a few feet in front of the other two women. She hummed a merry tune as she strolled toward her destination. She had never been to Inglemans Plains and she was eager to see what made the town unique. Inglemans Plains was said to be just as fertile and industrious as the Upper Mantle, only it was not run by a baron. It seemed to be governed by the people. The people of that province paid homage to the lords of the Upper Mantle but they still seemed to hold a certain amount of independence. She deduced that this was due largely to Elaina's father, who was said not only to have favor with the people but favor with the late Earl as well.

The dusty dry terrain made a repetitive signature in her memory. Every sparse tuft of grass and every sun-scorched boulder looked the same until she spotted a dark huddled mass in the distance. She ran a few steps ahead, trying to get a better look at the strange dusty mound. It moved and twitched slightly, then shifted suddenly, making Andira screech with alarm. Sinta and Elaina hurried to see what had startled her.

"Andira, are you alright?" Elaina questioned. "Have you been hurt in any way?"

"Yes…no, I have not been hurt. I am quite alright. It's that thing in the road. I thought it was a dead animal at first but it just moved. Do you think it's hurt?"

"Well, let's carefully take a look, shall we?" Sinta approached the mound warily with Elaina and Andira at her heels. When they reached it they found that it was no animal at all but a man lying in the road, dirty and bruised.

"Oh my," said Andira, kneeling before him with concern. "What do you think happened?"

"I don't know," said Sinta. "But whatever it was, he got the worst of it. Let's see if he can speak to us."

Pulling him into an upright position they held a flask of water to his bruised lips, hoping to revive him. The water trickled down his chin unconsumed. After several attempts they realized it was a fruitless venture.

"Well, he's not dead," cried Andira, obviously exasperated. "I saw him move. Maybe he is hurt on the inside where we can't see. Elaina maybe you can find out."

Elaina looked about reluctantly. "I don't know about that. It is one thing to do that to a horse or even a friend, but I do not know him. And besides, it is, as Sinta said, a matter of integrity. He has not invited me to help him."

"Yes, but he can't. She did say in extreme cases you could do so anyway. Wouldn't this count as an emergency, Sinta?"

Sinta looked at her soft-hearted friend. She knew that Andira hated to see any one suffer. "Well, I guess we could try."

"Good, let's get started." Andira pulled Elaina down next to her and entreated her to begin. Elaina placed her hand on the ailing man's head, trying to connect with him. Just as she began her journey within, the man reached out and grabbed her arm. In a motion too swift to combat he leapt to his feet, grabbing Elaina around the waist with one arm and holding her by the throat with the other.

"What are you doing?" screamed Andira. "She only meant to help you."

"Who says I needed help?" the man snarled.

~ 208 ~

"I would suggest that you let my friend go. She is not the docile sort of lady that men like you prey upon." Sinta looked the man in the eye and furrowed her brow. "The game is up. You were never hurt. Of this I am sure. Tell us what you want and let us be on our way."

"It is not up to you to make the demands, mi' lady. If you are to be released, well, that is a decision left up to our choosing."

Elaina writhed and twisted, but to no avail. Her captor was strong and his hold on her was stifling. The more she wrestled the harder it was to take in air. There was no escaping him. If only she could call upon her inner strength the way she had at the maze with Manin. She did not know how the force that engulfed her came to be, she only knew it had and at just the right moment.

"There are three of us and one of you," Andira spat. "We may be women but we know violence when necessary."

The man laughed haughtily. "I never said I was alone, mi' lady."
At that, a band of hardened thieves jumped from behind the boulders that lined the road. They snarled and jeered at the women, forming a circle around them to bar their escape.

"Let us go!" Sinta demanded. "We have nothing of value with us. We are simple workers retuning to our home in Inglemans Landing."

One of the thieves pointed to the chest. "So what might that be, Madam? Maybe we should have a look and see what it is that you're carryin'." He directed two of his men to open the chest. A look of surprise and admiration spread through them.

"These seem like mighty fine things to me, mi' lady. Did you think that you would be able to trick us into believing that you were simple? You are obviously noble-born, trying to escape the noose."

"We are not!" Andira shouted. "We are on our way to Inglemans Landing."

From the back of the crowd, a voice very familiar to Elaina broke through the chaos. "If you are going to Inglemans Landing because that is your home, then I will certainly know you."

The crowd parted and through it walked a man unknown to Sinta and Andira but much-known to Elaina. He was the leader of this band of ruffians, and at once she knew that there was no longer a need to fear. At his insistence, her sinewy captor released her and she flew into his arms. After a tearful reunion, she turned to her companions. "Sinta, Andira, we have nothing to fear. We are quite safe."

The women looked at each other, baffled.

"Allow me to introduce you to my brother, Uman."

Chapter 21

     After a short rest, Rone resumed his search for the missing carriage. He had ridden through the night, stopping periodically to allow his horse to water and rest, and for him to gather his wits. The images of the slaughtered women along the road haunted him. He'd been commissioned to protect them and had failed at his mission. He had been able to see to the safe return of most of the noble families to The Citadel; however, the family deemed most important to the Upper Mantle province had been ripped to pieces by the Nanshar uprising and by Manin's insanity. He cursed inwardly. Manin managed to put his entire house in jeopardy and Rone was powerless to stop it. All he could do now was try to salvage that which remained.

     Rone was an excellent tactician. He knew and understood the workings of war better than anyone. He knew what to expect and how to act accordingly. War, at times, could be predictable. What he did not understand was the folly in the mind and heart of a man that would make him step outside of himself and embrace lunacy.

     A man such as Manin. He fully embraced the absurd ideals of greatness formulated from his own twisted mind. Now he realized that he was doing the same thing, but for a very different reason. Normally, Rone would have reported to the King first, and then formed a search party to retrieve the women. He would have ridden with his best men, stopping along the road to set up camp and allow his men to rest. But now he rode like a madman, stopping only to refresh his horse.

     He made his trek south with little care for his own safety. He had considered that there might be more Nansharian soldiers along the road. But instead of being more wary, this notion only made him push harder to find them. They might have escaped one squadron of mercenaries, but that did not mean they would escape the next one that came along.

Night was upon him by the time he found the broken carriage that had slid down the embankment. From the looks of the wreckage, it had been a dramatic descent. Finding no signs that the occupants of the carriage were still within the area, he continued down the road. It appeared that the women had taken only a few belongings with them, fearing that taking all of it would slow them down. He was able to identify the marking of some sort of pull that was apparently being dragged by the horses. He smiled to himself. They had survived thus far and were making wise choices along the way. He relaxed ever so slightly, not wanting to fully give way to relief. No, he would not do that until he found then. Until he found her.

"Elaina, where are you?" he said to himself. He imagined her as she had been that night at Warren Hall. Bathed in moonlight, standing radiant and angelic in the wind's cool embrace. She was freedom and love, and he longed for her.

At daybreak he came upon a peculiar find. There, along the road, were a dozen or more footprints. They were large and weighted, causing a deeper imprint than those of the women. There were also signs of a struggle. The tracks from the horses remained but the pull no longer made its mark in the dirt. Had they been set upon? Rone jumped astride Yelmet's saddle and resumed his search at breakneck speed.

The blooming foliage of Inglemans Plains was a refreshing change for his senses when he encountered it. It had been many years since he had first visited there. Memories of his childhood flooded his mind. He was a young lad of thirteen when his father allowed him to accompany him on a business venture for the first time. His father, Michal, had brought him to the palace after his mother, Jonelle, had died from a sweating sickness when he was eight years old. He had known very little about his father beforehand; only that he was of the royal line and his mother was not. She had been born across the waters to, from what he gathered, a meager yet proud lineage, a standing that was not acceptable for the royal family of Alionia. Michal had sought a royal wedding for the woman he loved but was denied the occasion by his parents.

They had arranged a more suitable match with a lady from an upstanding noble house, but he had refused. He had declared that if he was not allowed to marry the woman of his choice, than he would not marry at all. And thus he remained. He sired a child with Jonelle, but the child had not been readily accepted as a part of the royal house. Only when Arilian claimed the throne, did the aristocracy recognize Rone as Michal's son. Michal raised him with all the privilege that was afforded his station, but Rone never forgot the indifference that had been shown his mother by his father's family. When given the choice to follow in his father's footsteps and become a key player in Alionia's government, he declined, stating that except for his uncle, he had never really been a part of their world.

All his life he had felt separated from the place he called home. He was close to his mother until her death. She was his life and his world. When she died all that remained was the father that he barely knew. He clung to him when he went to the massive palace to live. Their ways were foreign to him and he made a great many mistakes. And while his father loved him, he found it quite difficult at times to understand him.

Rone would often overhear Michal talking to his governess, saying "He is such a bright child. At times I marvel at the things that he knows, and at such a young age." The nanny would reply, "Yes, my Lord, he is a bright child. But I must tell you, I find myself often frightened by his intensity. He has strength beyond his years, and a touch of revelation resides in him. Maybe he should be sent back to his mother's people so that he might learn their ways." His father would pace the floor, considering her words. Rone would announce himself and fall to his knees before his father and beg his patience. He did not want to be sent away. He wanted to stay with his father.

Michal would scold him for intruding and demand that he learn the proper etiquette that befits a child of the royal house. Then he would order the horses to be saddled and would take him for a ride in the country. They would ride and hunt and soon the threat of being displaced would dissipate. Rone smiled, remembering these special times with Michal. When he began to reach the age of manhood his father became more firm and demanding, expecting no less than the best from him at all times. Rone never disappointed him.

He heard the rush of water off in the distance. It was a river that ran through the heart of Inglemans Plains and spilled out into the sea. If a band of thieves had overtaken overtook Elaina and her maids, then they would no doubt want to stay out of sight. They would not take the main road, but would cut through the forest that ran the length of the river. He turned Yelmet towards the rushing water and sauntered between the shelter of the trees. He could hear the faintest echo of men's voices and the resonating sound of steel upon steel. He slid down from the great beast and tethered him to a tree. He eased his way to the camp with all the stealth and finesse of a mountain lion.

Shaded by the trees, he watched as Andira battled a man twice her size. She parried and lunged, but the man had every advantage over her. His strength and speed assured his victory every time. She ran towards him, sword raised, but he deftly moved to the side, landing a smart blow to her backside with the flat of his blade. She howled as a group of spectators cheered. He surveyed the area and found Sinta sitting by a boiling kettle surrounded by a group of burly men. He walked towards the back of the camp. He didn't see Elaina. He quietly ran back to the front of the camp where Andira was still fighting her opponent. This time when she flew at him he stuck out his foot, sending her stumbling forward while bending her elbow, relieving her of her weapon. She tumbled and landed a few feet away from him. He smiled as he stood over her, menacing and violent.

"You have lost and now you must pay the price," he snarled. Andira's eyes grew large and her face flushed red. The camp remained silent as she accepted her fate. She rose to her feet before the victor and unbuttoned her cloak. The men cheered and whistled as Andira, head down, approached the gloating man. Before she could do anything more, Rone jumped from the brush and challenged Andira's opponent.

"So, you take pleasure in besting untrained women that are half your size, do you? Well, you will collect no prize today, sir." The men parted as Rone walked through the crowd to address him face to face.

"Do I have some quarrel with you, sir?" said the man. He bristled at this interruption. He had struck a deal with the woman and he intended to see it met.

"If you have quarrel with any of the women here then you have a quarrel with me. They are under my protection."

"Your protection, aye?" the man said. "A poor protector you are to leave them helpless by the side of the road."

"I am not helpless," shot Andira, who was standing exasperated with her arms folded across her breast.

"Quiet woman, don't you see I'm busy?" She shot the man a look frightening enough to scare even the most fearless of fighters.

"I have been commissioned by the King to protect them and will do so with my life if need be. Where is Elaina? I have come to collect her."

The man looked even more enraged at this notion. "So, you are her husband, then?" he asked. His hand slowly moved to the hilt of his sword.

Rone swallowed hard. Gritting his teeth he replied, "No, I am not, but I come to claim her just the same. Where is she?" He repaid the man his action by reaching for his hilt as well.

"Rone," Andira called, "Rone, really…"

Both men scolded her this time, demanding silence. She threw her hands up and walked away, mumbling something about men and their need for blood.

"If you are not her husband, then you have no right to claim her," said the man. He struck out at Rone, who easily deflected his blow.

"Bring her to me now and I will let you live." The crowd of spectators doubled in size, the jovial mood now replaced with a palpable menace. Rone knew that he would have to fight his way through these strapping men and he was prepared to do so. He would not lose her again. "If you bring her out to me," he yelled to the surrounding soldiers, "then I will let you live. But if you do not I will kill every one of you. I have no desire to see you lose your lives and I am sure you don't either, but I will not leave here without her, or her companions. Now where is she?"

Rone's demands were met with deafening silence. The camp surrounded him, seething and uncompliant.

"Well then," he said turning to his original opponent. "I see you choose the difficult path. So be it." He raised his sword and the battle began. Rone was sure that his opponent had very little training in the way of military combat but he did marvel at the speed and dexterity with which he moved. There was something fluid and familiar in each attack. They fought matching blow for blow, each one trying to best the other.

"She's not leaving here," the man spat at him. "She is mine. My men and I will tear you limb from limb before you ever make it to your horse. However, if you go now I might leave you the use of your eyes. Makes no difference to me. Either way you will never see her again."

Rone advanced in his attack. Leaving his adversary little room to escape, he swung his blade dangerously close to his challenger's head. The blow missed his throat by an inch and hit his intended target, his forearm. As his sword flew from his wounded hand, Rone seized the opportunity to kick it as far from him as possible and land him a sharp blow with the hilt of his sword square across his nose. The man lunged forward in pain but was brought quickly upright by Rone's firm grasp.

"On your knees!" he ordered.

The man dropped to his knees, clearly defeated.

"I will let him live. Just bring me Elaina and let us go. When we have made it a safe distance away I will release him. Release the women to me and we will be on our way."

"Don't do it!" shouted the man. "Kill him."

The men surrounding him raised their swords to Rone.

"What is she to you that you would die so easily?" said the man.

Rone was quiet for a moment. He wanted to keep his composure. He could not allow himself to think of her, who she was, what she meant to him. This was not the time to give way to the imagination.

"She is more than you can understand. Now bring her to me."

Before the man could give the order, the circle parted and Elaina walked through, accompanied by Sinta and Andira.

When her eyes met his, her heart leapt with joy. "Rone!" she cried, "Oh, Rone, you came for me!" She ran to him pushing past his captive, and threw her arms around his neck. He retained a firm grasp on his sword with his right, while embracing her with his left. She was warm and smelled of flowers. Her long hair hung loosely about her shoulders. She wore a simple blue, scalloped-necked dress that accentuated her womanly figure. She was beautiful as always and she felt good in his arms.

"Rone, what is going on? Why are you fighting these good men?" Elaina looked at him, unsure what to make of the situation. She had only moments ago been summoned from the main tent by Andira. Andira was reluctant to wake her. She knew Sinta's rules and she did not want any harm to come to Elaina, but she saw that the situation was getting out of hand and knew that she must do something quickly. She found Elaina sound asleep in her tent. She'd helped to heal several men who had encountered a small Nansharian regiment. Elaina noticed that it was taking less of her energy to perform these tasks, but she knew she stilled needed to rest.

Now she stood baffled at the angry armed men around her, each with a sword pointed at Rone. She turned to see the man on his knees before them, a slight smile on his face.

"Rone, what have you done?" she shouted. Kneeling in front of the man she placed her hand on his bleeding nose and forearm and closed her eyes. After a moment, the bleeding stopped and the swelling receded, making his face handsome and stern once again.

Rone looked at Elaina and Andira and then to Sinta.

"So you are alright?" Rone queried. "You were not being held captive?"

"No, of course not," said Elaina. She was still fussing over his opponent. "This is my brother and these are his men. They have been protecting us."

The color drained from Rone's face. He could not believe what he was hearing.

"But I saw him fighting with Andira, and when questioned about you, he refused to let me see you, let alone release you. I thought you were prisoners."

"Aye, I did fight with the lady, sir. But we were having a little bit of training. I said I would teach her to fight if she promised me supper. I've been on the road for some time and miss the comforts of a good hot meal. Besides, this one has a bit of spunk in her." Uman winked at Andira, who smiled brightly, amused by his charm.

Rone turned to Andira, annoyed and speechless.

"I tried to tell you both," she shrugged. "But what do I know? I'm just a woman," she said teasingly. She took a kerchief from the folds of her skirt and proceeded to wipe the blood from Uman's newly-healed wound. He stared at her intensely as she did her work. A faint smile formed at the corners of her full lips.

Elaina rolled her eyes and turned back to Rone. "My brother picked a fight with you. I told him you might be coming. I suppose you had some purpose to this mischief," she scolded.

"Please forgive me?" Uman answered, "but I needed to test the skill and determination of the man who would be guarding my sister. I now see that you are willing to die for her. I know that I can trust you with her life."

"Thank you," said Rone. He was still a bit thrown by this turn of events, but if Elaina was alright then he would willingly accept the outcome of the situation.

"Come to my tent. We have much to discuss." Uman led the way as the others fell in line. Elaina walked beside Rone until Sinta slipped in between them, looping an arm through each one of theirs.

"It is wonderful to see you, Rone. I knew you would come, as did our Elaina here," she said, squeezing her arm slightly. "She never gave up hope that you would come for her, did you Elaina?"

Elaina looked away as her face burned bright red.

"Also, I must say," Sinta added, "I have never seen you fight as passionately as I have today. To think of what you must be like on a battlefield. Especially when you have such an… important cause to fight for."

Now it was Rone's face that turned a bright shade of red. He cleared his throat, and Sinta chuckled and walked into the tent ahead of them.

Elaina placed a hand on his arm, a silent request for a private moment. "Rone, I…thank you for coming for me, but you were up against more than a dozen men all by yourself. You didn't have to risk your life for me."

"Elaina," Rone said, his voice smooth velvet once again, "I would stand against a thousand men if it would ensure your safety."

She slipped her arm through his once more and he led her into the tent.

They did have much to talk about. Word had reached Inglemans Plains that the Nansharian invasion had overtaken much of the land, and they had not come alone.

Chapter 22

"I must say that you have ridden quite swiftly under the circumstances," Uman said, addressing Rone. "I take it that you did not cross paths with members of the rebellion. We have encountered several regiments between here and the Upper Mantle border. We have done all we can to keep them from overtaking our land, but our resources are few, and their numbers far outweigh ours." He offered Rone a goblet of cool ale.

"Aye. I rode with a purpose in mind. But I have witnessed some disturbing sights along the way. I know that the Nanshar are here and plan to remove all of the nobles from Alionia. They believe that this will leave our land defenseless, making it easy to conquer. They want to claim our land as their own." He drained the last of his ale. His thirst had not been satisfied but he thought it best to keep a clear head.

"When we encountered them on the way to the Citadel, they were only concerned with the nobles," interjected Andira. "They captured dowager Beltrane and Lily, thinking that she was noble-born."

"My men and I found them not far from the main road, along with Jothan. Their bodies were taken to the Citadel where they will be given a proper burial." Rone let the revelation of their companions' deaths settle before he continued on.

"And Chaney?" Sinta asked Rone. "Do you know what became of him?"

"I was hoping that you would be able to tell me. There was no sign of him at the camp. It was my fear that they might have taken him in an endeavor to extract information, or worse, use him against us somehow."

"Extract information? What will they do to him?" Elaina questioned. She didn't like the idea of a brave soldier like Chaney being in danger.

"They will torture him, most likely for military information. They will want to know of any secret routes that might lead into the palace or the Citadel."

"But why?" Elaina asked, a bit breathless. She already knew the answer but it did not make sense to her. In truth, she did not want to understand. The world she once knew was lost to her. Alionia was no longer the safe, fortified land that it once was.

"If the Nanshar are here to remove the nobles from the nation, dear Sis," Uman said, his tone very matter of fact, "then they will no doubt want to remove the highest noble of them all. They are going to kill the King."

"Oh no," gasped Elaina. "You think they will use Chaney to help them do this?" She leapt to her feet, not waiting for a reply. "We must go and find him. We have to help him. We cannot allow them to use him to betray his own country. He is so noble and brave...."

"I wish that we could Elaina, but it is not that simple," Rone softly replied. "We do not know what regiment captured him."

"And even if we did know where he was, most assuredly there are more of them than there are of us," Uman blurted out. "Chaney is a soldier. He understands his duty. He knows the risks that come with being in the King's army."

"How can you sit there and be so calm about this? Don't you care at all about another man's life, or are you only concerned with your own?"

"Elaina, you are not being fair," Rone said firmly. "Chaney was not only one of my men, but one of my closest friends. I care about his well-being. But your brother is right. We are soldiers. We are quite aware of the risks we take when we pledge to protect our King and our country. Chaney is a strong warrior. He would rather die than betray his people. He would see it as an honor to die for his country."

"You men and your code of honor! What good can he do for the King if he is dead?" She turned, spitting her venom at Rone and Uman. "If you will not rescue him, then I will!" As she stormed from the tent, she called for one of her brother's men to saddle Chestnut for her. Before anyone could stop her, she mounted the horse, dug her heels into his side, and bolted down the road, turning into the forest that ran the length of the river.

"She is being absolutely ridiculous. I am going to have to beat some sense into her thick little head," snapped Uman. "What does she mean, running off like that? She is going to get herself killed." He angrily stormed from the tent.

"Wait. Maybe I should go after her," Rone advised. "She is just upset. Maybe I can..."

"You have a firm handle on her, do you? If that were the case she would not be bounding down the road to her death as we speak," Uman spat.

"It is my duty to protect her. Let me do the job that I have been assigned to do."

"She is more than a job to me. She is my sister. I have more to lose than you do. Her husband is not here to protect her. That pompous son of a street dog did little to assure her safety. My father is not here and I am the only one left who can protect her properly."

"What if she refuses to return with you? Elaina can be rather stubborn when she chooses to be," said Andira.

"Then I will make her come. I am her elder brother. She must do as I say. Even if I have to tie her to her horse and lead her back myself."

Sinta placed a calm hand on Uman's shoulder. "Your sister has been through a great deal these past months. I understand that you fear for her, but in this case I think you should be wise in your actions. Send Rone to get her."

Uman opened his mouth to protest but was cut off by Sinta's curt insistence. "Rone, hurry, find her before someone else does."

Rone did not wait for further instruction. He was already navigating his way through the woods to retrieve Yelmet and find Elaina.

Uman headed towards his horse, intent on following Rone, but Sinta blocked his path.

"What are you doing, woman?" he snorted. "I will go along to make sure that he returns with her."

"I don't think that he will need assistance finding her, or convincing her to come back. You needn't worry, my Lord." Sinta flashed him a curious smile.

"Have that much faith in his abilities, do you? Well, I am not so convinced that he is as capable as you deem him to be."

"I am quite convinced, and so is Elaina. Why do you think she rode off into the woods?"

"Because she is a silly little girl who does silly little things," Uman shot back.

"She is not a little girl anymore, Uman. It is time that you recognize that. Rone certainly has." Sinta batted her eyelids in a mocking flurry until she saw the first glimmers of understanding spread across Uman's face.

He rolled his eyes and released the reins of his horse. "Women!" he snorted, walking towards his tent. "They should stick to what they are good for." As he passed Andira, he dealt her a firm smack on her backside. "Come, woman. My dinner awaits."

The men around the camp sent up cheers and roars of laughter as Andira feigned outrage but happily followed him into the tent.

Sinta smiled, turning her attention in the direction of the woods. Dusk would soon raise her sleepy head and chase the warm sunlight from the sky. She sighed, suddenly feeling her age in every bone. *"Hurry and find her, Rone,* she thought to herself. *Danger is upon us and Elaina must reach her full potential or all is lost.*

Rone took the path that lined the river. Night would soon overtake them, and though it would not be impossible to find her, the shading of the trees would add a level of difficulty with which he did not care to contend. Much to his relief, his search was a brief one. He found Elaina standing at the river bank, shivering with emotion.

"Elaina, I have come to return you to your brother's camp." He eased closer to her. "We must return before nightfall. Elaina, please come with me." He held out his hand to her, but she did not take it.

"I will not return with you, Rone. I have to find Chaney. I will not give up until I have found him." Her gaze returned to the river. The warmth of the sun peeked through the trees, warming the grass beneath her feet, yet inside she felt chilled. A shiver ran down her spine and she wrapped her arms around herself, wanting to hide from the world. If only she had not agreed to go to Warren Hall. If only she had not married Manin. If only…

But alas, she could do nothing to change her past. She felt small, helpless, and alone.

"Elaina, I understand how you feel, but there is nothing we can do for him now. He vowed to me that he would protect you with his life and he has done so. I have also taken that vow and will see it through until the end of my life if that is the price for your safety. Do not despise us for fulfilling our duties."

"Yes, but we cannot leave him to be tortured, or worse yet, die. He was captured because of me. He protected my identity. He said that Lily was the noble and not me. If he is dead it is my fault."

He pulled her close to him and she sobbed. His heart broke for her. He was a man of war. Though he was never comfortable with the notion of losing his men in combat, he was well aware of the harshness of battle. Death was not particular in picking its prey. He had come dangerously close to drawing his last breath on several missions. But this gentle creature that he now held in his arms was not accustomed to death or war. Even though the dowager and Lily had not been kind to her, he knew that her soft heart mourned them. He stroked her long hair, seeking to give her whatever brief moments of comfort he could.

"I was not sure how Lily was killed along with the dowager, but assuming things remained as they were when I left the Manor that day, I would guess she put herself in that position. It was not your fault. She looked to elevate herself through unjust means and it cost her dearly. My sympathy is for her family who have lost their kin, but Elaina, you cannot hold yourself responsible for her actions."

"It would have been me had Chaney not spoken for me. Lily looked to be a selfish woman trying to avoid her fate. The commander of that regiment only saw her to be of noble lineage. Her fate was sealed from the onset of her denial." She closed her eyes and clung to him. "Oh, Rone," she wailed, "why is all of this happening now? What does it all mean?"

"I cannot say for certain," he lifted her chin with a sturdy finger and gazed deep into the dark pools that brimmed with tears. " But I will promise you this, Elaina. We will find out who is responsible for this coup and we will stop them. And I will protect you and your family in whatever way I can. Even If I have to move all of you into the palace. You will be safe." He drew her to him once again, placing his cheek against her silky hair, his nostrils filled with the essence of her. He had managed to calm her fears by reinforcing his own. He swore to protect her and her family. He said a silent prayer to the Great One in hopes that he would be able to honor his vow.

Rone held Elaina for what seemed like an eternity. A cool breeze blew in testament to the encroaching darkness, rustling through their clothes. He knew they should be on their way, but he clung to her just a while longer, hating to see the moment end. He felt the rise and fall of her body as her deep sobs mulled into a soft purr.

"Elaina," he said gently. She lifted her eyes to his. Locked in his embrace she was aware of every part of him. His dark hair was neatly pulled into his usual ribboned mass at the nape of his neck. Several unruly curls had found their way free from their bonds and cascaded about his brow, giving him a charmingly unkept look. His wayward tendrils added to the allure of his unshaven chin. He looked rugged and wild and the intensity with which his eyes held hers rendered her incapable of doing anything other than breathing, and barely that.

In an instant his lips were covering hers. He held her tight, letting his hands roam from her waist to her shoulders and finally nesting in her silken mane. He inhaled the scent of her. Her essence was a heady mixture of moonlight and woman that thrilled his senses. Tenderly he kissed her, taking from her as much as he gave. He felt her resistance ease as she folded her arms around his neck. She pressed her body against his, melting into him. She felt the tip of his tongue tease hers into a sweet sensual dance. It told its own story, spoke volumes in silence.

It was an invitation, laced with expectation. It was a challenge.

He released her mouth but continued to hold her, resting his cheek against the crown of her head.

"Elaina," he began, "do you recall the day I found you at the maze? It was the day before your wedding. I came to visit with you and I declared myself to you. I said that if you told me you loved Manin then I would not pursue your affections." He was silent for a moment, considering his words carefully. "You have yet to answer the question."

Elaina stepped away from him. Their moment together had taken a turn she had not anticipated. She stumbled over herself, clearly taken aback.

"I do believe I answered you, sir," she retorted. She began to fuss with the stitching on her sleeve. She had indulged herself too long in his embrace. She was not a fickle woman by any standard, and did not want to give the impression that she welcomed the intentions of any man other than her husband. And yet, when Rone looked into her eyes, as if peering into her very soul, she felt the raging desire to throw her moralistic ideas right out of the window.

"Yes," Rone said, advancing toward her, "but you did not state whether you loved him. You only stated what you would seek to attain."

Elaina retreated with every forward step he took. She thought how silly she must look. She had spent a large part of her evening sobbing in his arms, soaking up the comfort that was his very essence. He was a balm to her soul and she embraced all the warmth that his heart had to offer. Now, after his inquiry, she was backing away from him, trembling under the possibility of his touch.

Her retreat was halted when the heel of her foot collided with the base of sturdy tree. There was nowhere else for her to go. She cursed inwardly.

"Rone, be kind to me." She gave him a pleading look. "You know that I am newly married. Much has happened in this past week. Allow me to retrieve what is left of the life I have known." He looked down at her hands and found that they were trembling. "I…I am just not sure of anything right now." She dropped her head letting out a slight sob. If he was aware of her true thoughts, he did not show it. He merely stared down at her, something indefinable in his expression. He soothed her cheek with the soft caress of his hand. She closed her eyes as his warm touch sent shivers through her body.

"Elaina," he breathed softly.

"Rone," she pleaded. "I don't even know if he is still alive. I must find out if I am a widow or, as you have already seen, merely an unwanted wife."

Her statement held truth. They had no knowledge of whether Manin had been dealt the same swift justice to which the dowager and Lily had fallen prey. In the event that he still held breath in his body, Rone knew that Elaina would still be considered a married woman, and therefore unobtainable. He sighed, cursing his poor luck. He looked about him. The sun had long since taken its rest and the moon shone brightly through the trees. He had not intended to stay in the woods for as long as they had. He had expected to find Elaina and return her to her brother's camp before dusk.

"We should be getting back now," he said, stepping around her. "Your brother will be worried that we have not returned and he might send out a search for us. I would not want to put any of his men in danger needlessly."

Elaina began to comment on his reference to her brother and his heavy-handed dealings with her, but thought better of it. From the expression on Rone's face, she decided that now would not be the best time to kick against reason.

He helped her settle firmly astride Chestnut. She noticed that he did not balk at the fact that she did not sit as a lady of high society would, sideways, pristine and proper, never able to endure more than a light canter. Ever since she was a child she had ridden as her father and brother did, astride and usually at break speed. She loved the smell of the quiet countryside and the feel of the wind in her face, freely flowing through her unbound hair. It was then that she felt unchained, if just for a moment. She saw that Rone seemingly took no notice of her less than graceful manner, merely admonishing her to follow him.

Unbeknownst to Elaina, Rone was actually rather impressed with the ease and steady nature of her seat. She maneuvered her horse through the trees with deft precision, keeping up with his swift pace magnificently, even in the dark. Before long they had arrived back at Uman's camp. He helped her down from her horse, grabbing her about the waist and slowly lowering her to the ground. She blushed under his strength and the redness deepened at the fact that he had not yet removed his hands from her person. They stood in a wordless exchange, hearts pounding, barely breathing. Their proximity and heavy silence felt almost as intimate to Elaina as the kiss that they had just recently shared.

"'Bout time you got here," Uman shouted from his tent. "I was considering sending a few of my men to rescue you both. What took you so long?" he asked, eyeing Rone suspiciously.

The pair quickly separated at Uman's entrance. He looked from his sister, who adverted her eyes from both men, and then to Rone. His usual regal bearing and rugged ferocity was noticeably diminished. A look of frustration darkened his countenance but flitted quickly into a jovial keenness. "Your sister is not an easy woman to dissuade when her mind is set upon something." Rone look at her solemnly. "I tried my best to reason with her but she would hear none of it."

"She is stubborn at times. It is a fatal flaw of the women in my family, I'm afraid." Uman chuckled. "My father always said that any man that took an Ingleman bride had to be a strong man indeed. How, then, did you convince her to come back?"

~ 230 ~

Rone's eyes sparkled with mischief. "I didn't convince her. She took pity on me, not wanting you or your men to think that I could not complete my mission and rescue my charge. She might well be stubborn, sir, but she has a heart of gold."

He bowed deeply to Elaina. "My Lady." He turned towards the tent, patting Uman on the shoulder as he entered.

"I almost feel sorry for the man," Uman mused as he stepped closer to his sister.

"Sorry for him. Why?'

"Because I have never seen a man so dejected in all of my life. You're a hard woman, Elaina Ingleman."

"Beltrane," she snapped. "I am Lady Beltrane, a fact everyone seems to have forgotten. I, however, am well aware of who and what I am. So forgive me if I appear to be as heartless as you claim."

Uman gazed lovingly at his sister, seeing the truth of her feelings in her eyes. "Elaina... If I were a woman, and praise be to the Great One that I am not, because you all have no mind for reason, but if I were, I would not waste my thoughts on a name or title given to me from a crazed lunatic who knew not my real value. That man rode across Alionia to find you, fought me for you, and would have stood against every one of my men if need be, to rescue you. I don't know the man personally but I have heard of his reputation. He is not given to flights of fancy. He has his heart set on you. You would be wise to take him seriously."

"But Uman, how can I? I have no knowledge of Manin's whereabouts. I am still confined to him. He is a horrible man, but I must remain true. Should I throw aside what I know to be right for the sake of passion? I think not, dear brother. In the eyes of the King and the Great One, I am still married."

"You speak true, little one. And you are right to retain your virtue, but understand this," he said as he led her towards the tent, "I know the difference between a good man, deserving of all the best that this world has to offer, and an ungrateful dog. If your dear husband is alive, darling sister, you must not fear." He stroked the hilt of his sword as his voice turned ragged with anger. "That is one problem that can be quickly resolved."

Chapter 23

Andira made a pretty picture, bustling about the grand tent, attending to the needs of everyone there. While she was used to servants' work, Andira, Elaina noticed, held a bit of color in her cheek and a liveliness in her step and action. She scurried about, pouring ale and tending to the food that she had prepared at Uman's demand. Uman seemed to be in high spirits as well. He puffed his chest and shouted orders to his guests and his men alike.

"He is no more than a peacock," Elaina chuckled to herself. She had missed her brother very much. She had not seen him since the day she departed from Inglemans Hall and embarked upon her new life amongst the elite. In that time, Uman had changed from the angry brooding youth he had been into the strong, vibrant man she saw before her. They had spoken briefly about the details of her life since she'd left Inglemans Landing, she omitting some of the more horrific moments. However, she judged by his reaction to her mention of her married status that either Sinta or Andira had filled in the details that she had chosen to leave out.

He shared his developments with her as well. With Gregor gone, Uman was forced, if such a word could be used in this matter, to take over the estate. In truth, it was an easy transition. He'd been groomed for it all of his life. He knew the business of the land and the servants responded well to his authority. After Emona settled into Ingaria with her new groom, Uman set about making adjustments to the provisional stores set up by Gregor to feed the townsfolk when times became hard or a farmer and his family fell upon bad luck. When making his rounds to check on the neighboring farms, he noticed pockets of workers, mostly men foreign to their tight-knit community, talking in groups to the farmers, speaking harsh words against the nobles and the King.

"At first I thought they were from Segnara or Marna, but they seemed different somehow. They looked to be soldiers, but they wore servant's clothes." He looked to Rone with a sly smile. "You know I can spot a man of action more quickly than a man of the soil. These were not men from Alionia."

"You are correct in your estimation of them," Rone said approvingly. "On a mission in Marna at Mallant Cove, near a cave on the coast, my men and I witnessed a meeting between soldiers dressed in livery and two cloaked figures, one of which I believe to be a woman."

"A woman? Along with the dark cloaked figure?" Uman paced the floor, lost in thought.

"Yes. She handed something to the man next to her. A pouch of some sort. They offered it to the soldier - the leader, I believe - at the cave. He inspected it and then allowed them to enter."

Uman turned to Sinta. "It is as you have said. But what can we do? How shall we prepare ourselves?"

Sinta glanced at Elaina, and then down at her own hands. Much work had been completed by her hands. Much toil and many years had passed since they were smooth and slender, eager to heal and mend the infirmities of the sick and broken. She turned them over, inspecting them. They were weathered and worn from the task she had chosen to bear. Her hands were the only sign of her burden. The rest of her person had remained smooth and supple. She was not a beautiful woman but she was attractive in her own way. Her eyes were young and vibrant and her smile warm with caring. But her hands…her hands told her true story.

"We shall do what must be done," she answered quietly.

"And what is that?" Uman queried.

"The strong will do what the weak cannot," Sinta sighed.

Rone stood warily, his aggravation building. Something was afoot and Uman and Sinta were holding their own private conversation, leaving the rest of them to scratch for understanding in the dark. The kingdom was at stake. He had little time for games.

"Out with it," he breathed, trying his best to hold on to what remained of his patience. "I have seen much destruction between the palace and your camp. If you know of some threat that we are not aware of...then be straight with it. Our time on this matter is precious." Uman and Sinta exchanged long glances. "You had better tell them," he said.

"Yes, err, Rone, please sit down. I will tell you all I know. A long time ago, on the Island of Lanier, a prophecy was given by one of the most powerful seers of all time. This is what was declared.

There will be a day when one man's folly would cost the heart of a kingdom. When the bed of one becomes the breeding place of hate, houses will fall and a nation will mourn because of its impertinence. The children of the sky will be brought low and the children of the earth will rise to overshadow them. Three houses will determine the fate of a nation. All irrevocably intertwined and yet each having its own path to follow. The House of the Red Bull will be shattered. The House of Knives, once steel, will be turned to flesh. And the House of Bronze Horns, once silent, will sound again. The one with the mighty song will come with the warrior's heart and set all aright."

"So what does that mean, exactly?" Andira was the first to break the silence. She had never been fond of riddles. She preferred to get right to the meaning of things.

"It means that what is going on right now is part of a prophecy spanning centuries. It was rumored amongst our people that one of our own would be the originator of this great rebellion. And since we are a self-governed land, it was designed by the Great One Himself that it would be one of our own who would right the wrongs of our people. Uman and I believe that the woman you saw at Mallant Cove was from Lanier Isle. There have been reports of women, mysterious and deadly, aligning themselves with the Nansharian regiments. Let me warn you now, we fight a powerful enemy, and there is only one way to stop them." Sinta stood, holding out her hands to Elaina. "My dear," she said, bringing her to her feet. "It is my pleasure to serve you. I have waited so very long for this day."

Elaina sent a questioning look about the room. "Sinta, what do you mean? I don't understand. You are frightening me."

"No need for fear, my darling," she soothed. "I am merely making you aware of your destiny. You are of the House of Bronze Horns, my dear. You are the one with the mighty sound that will set everything right."

Elaina took on an incredulous tone. "Sinta, have you gone mad? I admit that I have discovered things about myself in these past few days that I did not know were there, but...what you are saying is...is..."

"It is absolutely true. Well, at least, I believe it is," Uman offered. "There has always been a spark of something in you, little one. Sinta told me about the prophecy and the events that have happened these past months. It is hard to make sense of it all. I have never really given over to the fanciful notions that floated through the halls of our birth home. They always seemed to be a slumber tale to me. I believe in what I can see and what I

~ 236 ~

can wield in my hand," he said touching the hilt of his sword. "But I do remember amazing and impossible things happening in our home when I was but a lad. I remember mother could do things that others could not do." Uman crossed the room to sit at his sister's side.

"Do you know that once mother convinced Niethal Blown - you know, the old miser - to give half of his crops to the Dorchanders when a storm hit their farm, destroying almost everything? They would never have recovered had mother not intervened. She could get anyone to do anything she wanted. She had a way about her."

"I have seen other things, as well," he continued, turning to address Sinta. "Our sister, Emona, was gravely ill when she was a child. Elaina was much too little to remember but I do. I recall that she was ill and father was very worried. The doctors could do nothing for her. Welda, our cook, convinced father that she needed healing, real healing. She said that he must consult "our people" and do what needs to be done for the child. Father agreed. Later that evening, a strange woman came to our house to see Emona. She smelled of lavender and sea air. She was the most frighteningly beautiful woman that I have ever seen." He swallowed hard, remembering the bewitching face that had haunted his dreams often as a youth. "Emona burned like fire. She had the sweating sickness. That woman placed her hand on our sister and her body shook as if holding on to her very soul. The woman cried out and then released her. Emona's illness went away after that and so did the healer woman, but not before leaving a message with father and Welda."

Uman's eyes gleamed in remembrance. "I was sitting under the table. I…I was afraid that the woman had hurt Emona. I was afraid that she would hurt us all. I hid there, staring at my father's shoes." He was just a boy then, barely able to help his father in the fields. He had deemed his hiding a cowardly action and had convinced himself to be braver in the future. "The healer woman told father the most peculiar thing. She said, 'Guard your daughter well. Her heart is pure and good. There are those who would corrupt and bend her to their will. She is strong even now, as a child. Beauty will be her mantle, strength her crown, and kindness her banner. Be strong, man of bronze, for danger will surround her and you know not her end; but rest now, knowing her time will not come until the prophecy is fulfilled.'"

He studied his sister carefully. Everyone remained silent as his words permeated their souls. "I had once believed that she was referring to Emona. After all, she was the child that she had come to see. But...she wasn't talking about her. She was talking about you, little one. I often thought on her words growing up. I knew there was nothing pure and good about Emona. Oh, she was beautiful, but in an unjust sort of way. Even as a child, she was mean and vengeful and determined to have her way. And usually she obtained whatever it was she wanted. I admit that I am guilty of falling prey to her demands on more than one occasion." He gave Elaina a look of absolute remorse.

Emona had convinced Uncle Seth and Uman to give Elaina to Manin in her father's absence. She had convinced Uman, who was against the idea from the start, that Manin was a good man and that Elaina would be treated well. She would be a lady of high society and well taken care of. Uman thought Manin to be a sniveling brat who lived off of his father's good name. He had little time and even less patience for men like him and shuddered at the thought of giving Elaina to him, but somehow, in a manner only Emona was able to accomplish, she had convinced her brother that she was correct. And now here they were, his sister in his tent, running from unknown evils, a wretched husband, and holding scars that she would likely tend for the rest of her days. Her plight wasn't his fault alone, but he had played his part. He cursed Emona for her selfishness, and he cursed his own weakness for letting her have her way. He dropped his head in shame, only to have it lifted by Elaina's soft, caring hands.

"Brother, do not mourn your decision. Though it seemed like Emona's doing, and yes, she did use us all, it was nonetheless my destiny. Apparently my life was laid out before I entered this world, my path set from my birth.

"But why did no one tell me any of this? Father never told me of the healer's words, only that Emona was very sick as a child. I thought he was merely protective of me. I led a very sheltered life at Ingleman Hall. I had never stepped outside of Ingleman's Plains and have just now learned the origin of mother's family ancestry." She threw her hands up in exasperation. "Certainly I was not so blind that I never saw the 'mystical' essence of our people floating through our house. It is so clear to me now. Why did I not see it before?"

"You were not meant to see it, child," Sinta replied. "That is all that I can say. Some things are reserved for a special time. Your time is now."

"So where does that leave us?" Andira interjected. "We know that the nobles are being killed, there is a plot to assassinate the King, an army bigger than our own is invading our land, and powerful people that we know little about are coming for...well, everyone. What do we do now?"

Leave it to Andira to get right to the heart of the matter.

"We must fight," Rone retorted. "We have no other choice. We cannot stand by and let usurpers take the throne. I must get to my Uncle at once. He should know of their plot and any information that you can supply, Uman."

"Then I shall accompany you to see the King. I have never been to court before. It would be nice to see how the other half lives," he said with an amused snort.

"What is left of the other half, you mean," Elaina corrected.

"Yes," Uman said, sobering. "Will the King be inclined to listen to what I have to say? I am not a noble, Rone. Maybe you should speak with him yourself and-"

"My Uncle is a very open-minded man. He may be royalty, but he is a good man at heart. He will hear you, sir." Uman nodded his agreement to Rone's insistence, hoping that he was right.

"Then it is settled. We shall go to see the King. But first I need to travel to Inglemans Hall. I have some business to settle and I need to fortify our borders before we leave. It won't take long, maybe a day or so."

Rone voiced his approval and plans were made to break camp and head towards Inglemans Hall. Horses were saddled and tents were dismantled and bundled so that they could be taken with the party. Leaving a handful of men to guard the border, Uman and his entourage made their way through the sunlit countryside. Inglemans Hall stood as pristine as ever, a monument to their father's hard work and enduring nature. It was their legacy and birthright. Tears threatened as Elaina took in the sights and smells of the place she had once called home.

Rone, having not left her side since her excursion into the woods, placed a gentle hand on hers. "It is good to be home, is it not?"

"It is just as I left it," Elaina replied. Not waiting for assistance, she jumped down from her horse and ran up the stairs and into the house.

"Welda! Welda!"

She searched from room to room, starting in the kitchen and working her way to the living quarters where the family slept and washed. There was no sign of her anywhere. What if the Nansharian soldiers had already been there? What if they were able to sneak in and had taken or even killed Welda? More than a dozen possible outcomes filled her heart with fear. She ran down the hall, frantically calling her brother. The band of travelers spilled their way into the house, each one up in arms at the urgency of her summons.

"What has happened, Elaina? Are you alright?" Rone grasped her hands as she struggled to catch her breath.

"Something's wrong. I can't find Welda, or anyone, for that matter. I searched the entire house, but no one is here. Do you think the Nanshar got here before we did? What if something has happened to Welda?" They all looked about in silence. They had seen the mutilated bodies of nobles that had lined the road of each town. It was altogether possible that the Nanshar would not hesitate to commit the same horrific acts against the common servants if they remained loyal to the king and his nobility.

A shadow fell over the room as everyone held their breath. No one was quite sure what to do until the silence was broken by one lone voice.

"Uman, I told you not to bring your men into the house! I have far too many pretty girls working for me now, and I can't afford for any to be with child. And what are all of ya standing around for like you've lost something? Do something to make yourselves useful!"

"Welda!" screamed Elaina. Relief washed over her as she fell into the old woman's arms. She smelled of orchard air and sweet date bread, just as she had when Elaina was growing up. She clung to her cook's neck afraid to let her go, afraid that if she released her, she would wake up from a wonderful dream.

"Elaina, my dove, I am so very glad to see you, too. I was out in the orchard picking fruits for tonight's meal."

"Where are the rest of the servants?" asked Uman. "When we arrived here the house was empty. Finding no one, we worried the Nanshar had taken you captive, or worse."

"Nonsense," Welda chuckled. "I knew you were coming so I ordered everyone out to the fields to help me prepare for the big feast."

"Big feast? What big feast?" Elaina asked confused.

"The feast before the battle for the kingdom begins. You can't go before the King on an empty stomach."

"But how did you know they were going to see the King?" Andira inquired, clearly baffled.

Welda turned an amused eye in her direction. "My dear girl, you would be amazed by what I know!"

Welda ushered the small party of friends up to the living quarters so they could refresh themselves before the feast. Uman had taken Gregor's room in his father's absence. He felt that it brought him closer to him in some way. He recalled the morning that Gregor had left for Inglemans Landing, the sea port near their estate. His father was always a calm man with ways that could convince anyone that the sun was shining in the midst of a rain storm. Yet that morning, he was troubled and distant. His usual easygoing nature was replaced with a sense of urgency uncommon to him. He said he had business to conduct for the King and that he would return shortly. That had been nearly a year ago. There had been no word from him, and no details of his whereabouts from the inquirers that Uman had sent out to find him. Gregor, before he left, reminded Uman of his responsibility to his farm and family.

"Take special care of your sisters, Uman," Gregor told him. "Emona can no doubt care for herself - she always has," he added dryly. "But Elaina is soft and yielding. She has been sheltered, for I have maintained her as such. Take care that she remains so until such protection is no longer needed from you."

Uman had thought his father's instructions were a bit odd, seeing that he would return in a week or two to regain the reins of the house. Gregor left frequently to conduct business for the King in surrounding areas where Alionia hoped to improve trade relations. He would leave for a short time and return to resume his place as Lord of Inglemans Plains, as he had been affectionately christened by the people of the land.

But Gregor had not returned, and Uman's world was turned upside down. He tried to follow his instruction to the highest degree, but he felt that he had failed miserably where Elaina was concerned. Why had he listened to Emona's selfish pleas? Nothing but pain had come from it.

He stretched out on the bed, rehearsing his father's instructions in his mind. It was then that he realized the horrible truth. Gregor had never planned on returning to his home. He must have known that whatever the mission was, it would be his last one. Much like Warren Beltrane, there would be no warm welcome home. Without his father here to guide him he would have to stand on his own judgment in order to protect his family and his province. For the first time in his life, Uman felt alone.

Rone was placed in Uman's room. It was a large space that was handsomely furnished. The sturdy bed was made of rich brown wood, as were the chairs and the large bureau that stood in the corner. A sizable looking-glass stood by an open window.

Rone stood before the glass to study his reflection. He was a mess. He was unshaven and disheveled. His clothes were torn, and he was in great need of a bath. He had ridden for days searching for Elaina. He had slept very little and cared for his appearance even less than his growing need for food and drink. But now that he had found her and he was sure that she was safe in a room only a stretch from his, he could attend to himself once again.

A knock on the door shook him from his thoughts. Welda walked in, followed by two strong men carrying bathing accoutrements for the screened tub in the far corner of the room. Bucket after bucket of steaming water was poured into the large basin, accompanied by oils of pine and chamomile. As if reading his mind, Welda brought a cherry-wood brush and shaving supplies, along with his saddle bag, which was neatly stuffed with as many personal effects as he could manage. He had not known how long he would be on the road, and he had brought several days' clothing with him to accommodate his needs.

"Thank you," he said, truly appreciative of her kindness. "I was just thinking that I needed to bathe just before you came in."

"Yes, well, I thought you would need to refresh yourself. You traveled such a long distance and you will travel much more before you are through. Take care to enjoy what comforts you are allowed at present. You may not see them again for some time."

Rone managed a nod at her words. Welda was warm and friendly, but there was something hauntingly stern and otherworldly about her. She spoke to him as if his future was written by the words that flitted off her tongue. Everything she said to him, he felt inclined to believe.

"Is every one settling in, Welda? It has been a long journey for others, as well. I believe being here in your home will bring a joy and a peace of mind that has not been known to them of late." He did not meet her gaze as he spoke, but looked to the tub of water, playing with the tendrils of steam that rose to meet his outstretched palm.

"Yes, I believe it will bring her joy for the moment. But you and I both know that a bigger destiny awaits her than reveling in the comforts of her childhood home. Rone, listen to me," she said, crossing the room to where he stood. "Elaina is more special than she knows. She is of the same blood that flows in our veins. She is gifted, but she is so much more than that. Rone, Elaina is a Supreme Vital. You know what that is, do you not?"

Amazed, Rone replied, "I believe so, but refresh me, please. It has been a long time since I was taught the old ways."

"It means she has all the abilities that have been granted by our people. She can persuade, heal, see into the future, as well as beguile anyone with her beauty. She has the ability to be both light and dark, both good and evil. If she is protected from those who would use her for evil purposes, then she will save us all from destruction. If she is allowed to go astray…" Her words trailed off as he took in her meaning.

"You, son of the House of Knives, are the key to saving both our worlds."

"But I thought that was Elaina's destiny. I am here to help her in any way possible, but I know all too well that men do not wield the Élan Vital. She holds the power, not I."

"But that is where you are wrong, my boy. You are very wrong. Some men do wield the Élan Vital. Do you really believe that you are as skilled as you are in battle strictly by your own means? No, you have used the Élan Vital in everything you have done up to this point in your life. You are a special man. A man caught between two worlds, but fitting into neither of them. That is your path, Rone - to be a bridge between two worlds. You are the key to saving us all."

"And how do you suggest that I do that?" he asked, curiosity overriding a growing sense of foreboding.

"By saving Elaina from herself," was the reply.

Rone stood naked from the waist up, looking at Welda in disbelief. He had begun to undress, fearing that the water would turn cold while they spoke. Why would he need to save the most wonderful, gentle creature from herself? She was not an evil woman. She meant no one any harm. He could not and would not allow himself to think of her that way, and yet, there was a knot in the pit of his stomach that told him something was wrong. He always felt a knot form when trouble was at his door. This foreshadowing had saved his life on more than one occasion. He knew that he must heed its warning, but to what end? Welda, muttering about his water getting cold, exited the room, leaving him alone with his thoughts.

He had been in the King's army and under the tutelage of his father for so long that he had neglected the other half of himself...the mysterious half. The half that nobles and the social elite whispered and snickered about behind his back. His mother's half. After her death, his father rarely spoke of her. Rone held on to her memories in his young mind, tracing the outline of her face many times within his thoughts. He would not forget her face, her voice, her smile. He willed himself to remember it all, and he had.

Jonelle, his mother, had taught Rone all she knew of their homeland. When he was but a lad, in the sixth year of his life, she had given him a gift. She told him it was the Seal of Shathar. It had been in their family for generations, passed down from mother to son. She told him many times what the trinket meant. It was a silver pendant fashioned into a fierce-looking hawk. In its claws, it held a ruby heart; its eyes were rubies, as well. The hawk was surrounded by seven silver knives embellished with diamond-studded hilts. The hawk was the war bird of their clan. It represented their strength as the fiercest warrior tribe in all of Lanier Island. The heart represented the justice and honor for which their clan was known. The knives stood for the seven brothers of the clan, who banded together long ago to defend Lanier Isle from usurpers.

It was an heirloom that was given to a son by his mother when he reached the age of wisdom. He would, in turn, give the trinket to his chosen bride, and she would give it to her son. Jonelle chose to give the Seal of Shathar to Rone when he was six because he was a remarkably bright child. His actions and speech boasted more wisdom in those tender years then most lads three times his age. Also she felt that time was of the essence. He needed to learn as much as he could as quickly as he could. She taught him the precepts and regulations of the Élan Vital. She taught him to feel with his mind and not with his hands. She taught him how to use his senses, not relying on sight alone. She was a careful teacher, and he her willing pupil.

When he was eight years old his mother fell ill. Rone, realizing that her death was imminent, despaired greatly. Rone collapsed at his mother's bedside, clinging to her dying form. "Mother," he sobbed, "I wish you would not leave me. What shall I do without you? I will be alone."

"Na, child. I shall send you to your father. He will care for you."

"I do not want to go live with him. He has left us here. You are dying and he is not here to care for you. I will never live with him at the palace. The nobles there are not good people. I hate them all!"

"Hush child," she scolded. "Your father is a good and honorable man. I have loved and will always love him. He is not here with us because he cannot be. Open your heart to him, Rone. He needs you as much as you need him. What is more, there will be another woman to steal your heart. Her love will shape your future. It will either give you the strength to endure, or it will bring destruction."

Rone never really understood what his mother had told him, but he had caught a glimpse of her meaning at the age of sixteen when he accompanied his father on his first business excursion to Inglemans Plains. They visited the home of a farmer who was not only a part of the royal agricultural advisory, but also a good friend of Michal's.

While his father was attending to his business, Rone was left to his own devices. He wandered the grounds, trying his best to go unnoticed. His plans were shattered due to an unruly horse and a very unsteady hand.

Rone strode into the barn to investigate the livestock. He had always had a passion for animals, especially horses. The barn had several strong horses of good breeding safely tucked away within their stalls. As Rone moved farther into the barn, one horse caught his eye. It was a tall black mare. Her mane was braided with threads of silver ribbon coursing through it like a fresh stream of crystal water. She was a sleek, raven-haired beauty, and she beckoned for him to come to her. He approached her warily. Seeing a stranger drawing closer to the stall, she whined and bucked, voicing her displeasure. Rone reached the stall and opened it. He reached out to pet the mare and realized that she would soon foal fold. Without thinking, he touched the horse's side, and she let out a loud grunt and began to kick up her front legs. Rone, startled, and fell backwards out of the stall, maintaining his balance long enough to close the door. The mare's powerful front legs kicked the door with enough force to knock him to the ground. He was a bit stunned when he recovered himself.

"Careful, there. She is a bit feisty of late. Are you badly hurt?" He turned to see another raven-haired beauty rushing to his side. She was about his age, maybe a year or so younger, with full, pouty lips and bewitching eyes.

"I am fine. I wasn't hurt, just a bit startled," he replied.

"I'm sure you weren't. You had a week's worth of feed to break your fall," was her reply. "Father won't be happy when he sees this. The gentleman who came to see him…"

"My father…"

"Yes, your father has requested these bags of feed for the royal horses. He has already paid for them. He might think that my father has cheated him out of his money if he produces fewer bags than what was settled upon."

"I am sorry, I did not mean to cause a problem. I was merely startled and I fell. Can we not save what is left of the bag?"

"No, do you see there," she said, pointing to a puddle underneath the sack. "It is wet and therefore unsalvageable."

"Oh, no," Rone said frantically. "What shall I do? My father agreed to bring me along and I have made a mess of things. If he finds that I have made such an error surely I shall be punished." It was not the punishment that bothered Rone. It was the look of disappointment and embarrassment that would settle over his father's face. He dreaded that more than a thousand beatings. Facing what he knew was an unhappy ending he stood and walked towards the manor.

"Where are you going?" called the girl.

"To talk to my father," he replied with a grimace.

"What will you tell him?" she asked.

"The truth," he said.

The young girl followed him to the house and ran in before him. She hurried to her father's side and begged his forgiveness for the interruption.

"Father, I was just in the barn looking in on Yismer. She was unsteady and bolted upright, knocking me into bag of feed. It fell into a puddle and it is no longer useful. Please forgive me."

Rone stood in disbelief. She had just met him and she was taking the blame for something that he had done. What a terrible mistake she was making. He had to put an end to this disaster and quickly.

"No, sir, it was I who destroyed the feed. Not your daughter. She is kind to defend me but I cannot have another take the blame for my wrongdoing."

Gregor and Michal both looked to the young girl for an explanation. "Is that true?" Gregor asked.

"No," said Elaina. "I alone destroyed the feed." She remained silent for a moment, staring intently into first Gregor's, then Michal's eyes. They considered her for a moment and dismissed Rone's claims.

"Elaina, what were you thinking?" her father scolded. "Yismer will soon foal. She is uneasy right now. I have told you before to stay away from her stall. I understand your love for animals and all things nature but you must learn to obey my rules. They are only to protect you, child. I shall deal with your disobedience later. Leave me now."

Elaina gave a slight curtsey and left her father's office with Rone fast upon her heels.

"Why did you do that?" he asked. "Now you will be punished."

"I did it because you were willing to tell the truth regardless of whether you were going to be punished or not. I...I didn't want to see you shamed before your father. You have goodness about you. I don't mind being punished if I know you will be alright. Besides," she called behind her as she walked down the hall towards the stairs, "he never really punishes me. He just shakes his head and tells me that I remind him of my mother. Today will be no different."

He'd loved her from that very moment. No one had ever taken up for him, and with such sincerity and selflessness. He returned with his father to their farm often. Each time he waited for the chance to set eyes on the kind-hearted beauty that had helped him that day. He never spoke to her. There was little opportunity to do so. She would only smile and curtsy to his father, never looking into Rone's eager eyes, never giving him a sign of recognition. It was not that she was fickle, he realized, but that the older she became the more reticence her nature displayed. She was as removed and unobtainable then as she was now.

He let the warm water soothe his aching muscles. If their destinies were found in each other, then his mother's words were bound to come to pass. And that was what was troubling him. Along with his love for her, would there come a choice between life and destruction? While he was delegated to ensure she made the right decisions to fulfill her destiny, he couldn't help but wonder who would help him to do the same.

Chapter 24

    The Autumn Chamber that had once belonged to Emona now made cozy accommodations for the three women as they refreshed themselves from their long journey. Gregor, after tearing down his father's simple farmhouse years ago, built a new house, complete with spacious rooms for his new bride, and had it equipped with every comfort imaginable. One of the most coveted aspects of the lavish rooms was the large, red-veined marble bath at the far end of the privy. Beneath the apparatus, he placed a channel from the house well that allowed water to flow into the bath when a lever was pulled. By raising the silver coated lath, water would flood the tube and fill up the tub. Whenever a bath was requested, the furnace below the stone structure was heated to the correct temperature, heating the water in the tube, so that the basin walls themselves would not be scorched.

    "Ingenious," said Andira, as she slid deeper into the tub, submerging both head and body. "The water is so warm, and the view! Is that a fountain out past the orchards?"

    "Yes, it is. My father had it built for my mother when he built this house. I'm afraid I know very little about it. We weren't allowed near it as children. I believe it reminded my father too much of those happy days with her. He was seldom seen near the fountain or these chambers. Besides, this became Emona's domain a few years ago. She kept it very much to herself."

    "Well, I can certainly understand why your sister wanted this room," she said, after poking her head out from her liquid blanket. "It is a paradise in its own right. I would give anything to have a room like this."

    "I fear you would have to marry my father or my brother in order for that to happen," Elaina teased.

Andira puffed her cheeks in mock anger. "Well, seeing that your brother is completely unsuitable for marriage, I must set my devotion upon your father. I heard from the men at camp that he is quite an upstanding fellow."

"He is," agreed Elaina. "He is by far the best man I have ever known. He was a wonderful father to us all and he cared as much for his neighbors as he did for his own family."

"So there is still no word from him or his mission?" asked Sinta. "Maybe the King will be able to provide you with information as to his whereabouts when we arrive at the palace. Surely he has heard something."

Elaina struggled with her growing sense of despair. "I do hope you are correct, Sinta. I miss him so much. He was always calm and poised in the midst of chaos. We could use his wisdom and gentle guidance in the days ahead."

"True, but your brother seems capable enough to lead in your father's absence. And to have had little formal training in the art of combat, his fortitude in the matter is astounding. Yes, I think he will do nicely for the time being."

Elaina thought on Sinta's words. Uman did appear to have a handle on things. He had amassed a small army of able-bodied men, full of strength and vigor. He had begun training them some months back when the first shadows of rebellion loomed over the province. He was able to keep Inglemans Plains well protected despite his small number. He was capable after all, she concluded. Still, despite this small relief she feared for her father's life. It was not like him to be gone this long with no message or instruction for his family. He was a methodical individual, ever logical in his actions. He was not a renegade or adventurer. He was just Gregor Ingleman, widower, father, farmer. After hearing the news of Warren Beltane's death, the likelihood that her own father had met the same fate had become more reality then speculation. But still, she concluded, there was no harm in holding out hope.

Elaina rummaged through her sister's old wardrobe. Her measurements and style had always fallen short of her sister's, for Emona was a confident, voluptuous woman who did not believe in hiding her beautiful body. Though she wore modest clothing, she somehow managed to still appear seductive and alluring. Elaina chuckled inwardly as she thought to herself that Emona could wear nothing but a potato sack and still look like the most beautiful woman in the room.

After rummaging through the clothing, she settled upon a cream-colored gown with black stitching on the bodice. Black ribbon decorated the low-lying neckline, exposing her shoulders and collar bones exquisitely. At first she feared that she would have to have it taken in, and hoped it would be completed in time for the feast. But after trying it on, she found that it fit beautifully. Every curve was accentuated beneath creamed satin. Her bosom, sheathed also in cream, held taut against the fabric. She gazed at her reflection in the mirror, slightly awed. She hadn't noticed the change in her appearance since she'd left home. She looked very much like Emona, but still different somehow. The face that once reflected childlike innocence now exuded a womanly quality.

"You are the very image of your mother," Welda proclaimed as she swept through the entrance of the Autumn apartment. "She was such a beautiful woman. I could have sworn it was her standing here just now. If only your father could see you as you are at this very moment."

"She is very much like Ella," Sinta chimed in. "Not only in aspect but in character, as well. It is quite apparent that she holds her mother's spirit." Sinta rose to greet

Welda and the two women embraced. "It has been far too long, old friend. How have you been?"

"I remain in good health," Welda said with a wily smile. "And you, my young friend, how are you?"

Sinta's smile broadened. "You're the seer. You tell me how I've been."

"You always were too smart for your own good. I am certainly glad to see you. We have much to discuss."

Andira and Elaina looked to the two chattering women with confused expressions. "You two know each other," Elaina exclaimed in disbelief.

"Of course we know each other, little one. We are of the same clan. We both took care of your mother when she was a child. I was her cook and Sinta here was her nursemaid. We have both protected and cared for your family for centuries, my dear."

"Centuries...but how can that be? Surely neither of you could have lived for that long."

"And why not?" Sinta demanded. "Just because I have fewer wrinkles than my friend here," she said, pointing teasingly at Welda, "does not mean that I have not the wisdom and experience that is granted to one of my advanced age. As a matter of fact, I am three years older than she is."

"That makes you no more experienced than I am, cousin. Yes, Elaina, we have lived very long lives, and for a purpose greater than ourselves."

"What purpose is that? How can this be?"

"Come down to the main hall. The feast is about to start. We can tell you our story when it has begun."

The women descended the stairs in all of their finery. Andira was given a moss green gown with an olive border and hem to match. The dress was a fine complement to her sun-kissed complexion. Elaina had called for one of Welda's newly-hired maids to assist Andira with her hair. The young woman beamed with pride as the maid performed a masterful design, pinning it into playful cascading curls, high upon her head, and letting winsome tendrils fall where they may. Andira thanked the blushing maid profusely, remembering that she, not that long ago, had the job of servicing her mistress' hair. Though Elaina had always treated her as a friend more than a servant, Andira still felt that it was her place to serve her, noble title or not. But for one night, they would be equals. That night, she would be a lady. As she sauntered down the staircase, she was surprised to hear her name announced by the booming voice of the house herald.

"Lady Andira of Lingear Village."

She entered the hall and found it full of soldiers. They were the good-natured men that she had met at the camp on the border of Inglemans Plains and Desolate Way. Each one bowed to her as a finely-clothed footman came to escort her to her seat. A high board had been arranged at the front of the hall. Uman and Rone were already seated at their places. They were locked in some jovial conversation when Uman caught a glimpse of Andira for the first time that evening. He stood to his feet. The color drained from his face. His mouth felt dry and he immediately longed for a tall draught of wine to quench his thirst. He quickly left the high board and, dismissing the footman, offered his arm to Andira.

"My Lady, may I escort you to your seat?"

Andira blushed demurely and took his arm. "Thank you, my Lord," she managed to squeeze out.

Uman led her to the high board and placed her in the seat right next to his. As he sat down, he could not resist the urge to steal several sidelong glances at her. Rone made no attempt to hide his amusement. Uman struck him as a man of the world. He was rough and rustic; a man of the land who seemed unmoved by much of what went on around him. He had found him to be a robust and good-natured man, not given to flights of fancy. But to see him now in the presence of Andira was a sight wondrous to behold.

"My word," Rone leaned in to whisper, "the mighty Uman, tongue-tied at the sight of a beautiful woman. Is it good that your men see you so humbled by a pretty face?" he teased.

A red-faced Uman, annoyed by Rone's clear amusement on the matter, quickly whispered, "Careful, my Lord. You have not yet turned your attention to the entryway." He stood to his feet. "I believe it is now your turn to be laid low." He motioned to the herald who was introducing the next attendee.

"The Countess Elaina Beltrane."

Rone and the soldiers in the hall joined Uman on their feet. The room went silent as Elaina glided through the entryway. The soldiers bowed reverently to their hostess. She greeted them with kind words, welcoming them to her home and calling the servants forth to begin the feast. Rone heard none of it. All he could hear was the beating of his heart fill his eardrums and crescendo to a deafening pitch. He was sure that the entire room was aware of it.

Uman shook him slightly, "Rone, Rone. By the Great One, collect yourself and escort her to her seat." He shoved him to the edge of the high board. Rone nodded mindlessly, grateful for the assistance. His legs had momentarily lost their ability to function; any help he received from outside forces, he deemed extremely useful. He struggled to control himself. Why did he react to her this way? If the mere sight of her rendered him useless how would he be able to effectively perform his duty? He was sent by the King to protect her, and by fate to save her from herself. How could he fulfill his destiny when he could not control his emotions when he was around her? He vowed to remove himself from her at that very moment. He would bury his feelings for her deep inside so that they would not be a hindrance to him any longer. Regaining his composure, he pressed forward to a table of adulating soldiers, intent on gaining Elaina's attention and affection.

"You are a vision, Countess."

Elaina turned to face him. His declaration had been spoken in truth, for he immediately realized that never had he laid eyes on a more striking woman. She was exquisite in her flowing cream gown with black trim. In her ears, she wore drop earrings of onyx that matched the neckline of the gown. Her hair fell loosely about her shoulders like a silken cape. He remembered what it felt like to run his fingers through her sultry mane, to experience the feel of it, the scent of each raven tendril. His hands burned with the desire to experience it again. He lifted his hand out of impulse but ran his fingers through his own hair instead. *Control yourself*, he scolded. *You made a vow and you must keep it.*

"Thank you, my Lord," she said with a gentle curtsey. She held his eyes with every move she made. "I take it your room is to your comfort. Whatever you desire you need only ask. I will see to it personally that you are accommodated."

Rone bowed deeply. *What I desire I cannot have at the moment*, he thought bitterly. "My room is quite comfortable and your servants have been very accommodating. Thank you, my Lady. Shall we?" He offered his arm and together they climbed the high board.

Uman hugged his sister's neck, being careful not to mess her adornment, and they all took to their seats. "You have certainly changed from the knobby-kneed tree branch that you used to be," he teased. "You are quite fetching, sister. I believe that I am not the only one to think so," he said, winking at Rone. "But then again, you are not the only fetching woman in the room," he said, stealing a glance at Andira, who pressed her slender fingers to her plump lips, suppressing a giggle.

~ 258 ~

Welda had not lied when she promised them a feast. The table was laden with delicious fare, pheasant stuffed with onions, bread, and apples, trout in a lemon-butter sauce, a vegetable pottage with loaves of crusty bread, and a flaky-crusted meat pie consisting of wild hare, vegetables and brown gravy. A roasted pig was presented to the high board, along with an assortment of hard cheeses and stewed fruits. Golden spiced pears with sweet cream and a variety of delicious tarts capped off the sumptuous meal. Several of the servants took to their instruments, filling the hall with song and gaiety. Stories and laughter were shared over endless goblets of ale and wine. Dancing was suggested, and when the meal was completed and much appreciation and praise was lavished upon Welda and her fellow cooks, the tables were removed to make room for the dancers and musicians.

Sinta, who had not eaten with the rest of her companions on the high board but in the kitchen with Welda, joined the merriment by dancing with several of the men in Uman's company. Welda even joined in by clapping and singing, encouraging the maids and service men to dance. Uman hovered protectively about Andira. He scowled shamefully when anyone asked her to dance and by the end of the night, he no longer allowed her to dance with anyone but himself. Andira appeared to be quite content with the arrangement and danced gingerly with her jealous partner. As the evening drew to a close, Welda and Sinta stood on the high board and addressed the crowd.

"I dare say that we have enjoyed ourselves this evening," Welda called out. A cry of agreement came from the jovial mob below.
"I am glad to hear it. But now we must turn our attentions to the matter at hand. There is trouble in our land. Trouble that threatens your lives, your families' lives, and that of your neighbors and friends. It is a darkness we must fight.

Tomorrow when you leave this place to go do what must be done, remember the joy and laughter that you shared this night with your brothers and neighbors. Remember the faces of your wives and children. They are who you fight for. I am sure you are aware that it is not just the Nanshar we face. They, in an effort to insure their victory, have enlisted the aid of traitors from Lanier Isles. They are a powerful foe, but all is not lost. We have been given a catalyst to stop this rebellion. The young companions that you have dined with, they that sat upon the high board this night, have been born into this world, at this time, to bring change and save this kingdom. Guard them with your lives. Follow their instructions, and by all means do not let them fail."

Sinta looked into the faces that lined the crowed. There was a mixture of emotions floating among them. Some were filled with determination, others anger at the intrusion upon their land by usurpers. But on most there was despair. Despair of the unknown. Despair of battling an enemy that they only knew in their childhood dreams. It was as if a dreadful slumber tale had awakened and they knew not how to fight against it. She felt the need to assuage their fears.

"I implore you, friends, to take heart. Though the task is a heavy one, the One God is on our side. Your victory has been destined for centuries. Hundreds of years ago on the Isle of Lanier, one of the most powerful seers of all time gave a prophecy stating that a rebellion would threaten the peace of two nations. But there would be one who would stand against the evil of that day and right would prevail. Several women were assigned to care for that individual, waiting patiently for centuries for her to be born. The women of my clan were chosen to carry out this task. We have lived long and difficult lives, but we have done so for the good of our nation. We will prevail."

"The night is at an end. This will be our final dance. Enjoy it now, for tough times are ahead of us and I fear that days of celebration are far off."

It was then that Sinta sprang into action, ordering the servants to snuff out the candles on the wrought iron light fixtures that loomed above them. Once the lights were dimmed, leaving only the candles around the walls to illuminate the room, a slow, romantic tune was played, accompanied by the melodious voices of Welda and Sinta.

Rone hadn't danced with Elaina all night. He had watched as soldier after soldier offered her invitation. She kindly accepted them all and was quickly spirited away by numerous eager partners.

Elaina searched the room for Rone. She had hoped to dance with him, but he had disappeared in the midst of the merriment. Her heart sank, for the evening would soon draw to a close and she would have missed her opportunity to be in his arms. As the music began its low, seductive lilt, she heard a smooth voice behind her.

"May I have the honor of this dance, Madam?"

It was Rone, looking as handsome as ever. Her heart skipped several beats as she attempted to calmly reply, "Yes, my lord. As you wish."

The melodic music continued to play, accompanied by two voices singing in the old tongue. It was a song of love and heartache, a tale older than time itself. Elaina felt dizzy, euphoric even. She laid her head on Rone's chest, breathing in his essence. She could feel his heart beating through his linen shirt and vest. It was a rapid cadence that matched her own.

Rone rested his cheek on her silken mane and sighed at the smell of jasmine and summer breeze that tickled his nose. They twirled to the music, clinging to each other, barely breathing. As the music faded, they became aware of the crowd once again. Some of the men hurried home to spend what might be their last night with their loved ones; others found companionship with a lonely maid for the remainder of the evening. A few men retreated to the tents that were set up near the newly-built servants' quarters, intent on getting a good night's sleep so they would be refreshed in the morning. As the crowd thinned, Rone willed himself to release Elaina. If these men were under his charge, he would have ordered them all to the camp for rest hours ago. But he reminded himself that these were not his Tumults, nor were they part of the King's army. They were farmers and tradesmen, with a few choice house guards among them. They were Uman's men, and he could command them as he saw fit.

Rone glanced around the room and with a wily smile, noticed that Uman was nowhere to be found. He had disappeared with his dancing partner some time before the dance ended. "Lucky fellow," Rone smirked.

"Hmmm?" Elaina asked dreamily. She was intoxicated by the candlelight and the other-worldly aura that permeated the room.

Rone knew he should soon retreat to his room so he could solidify the plan of action that he would present to the King when they arrived. He looked down at Elaina, who was now looking up at him with a childlike innocence. Before he could stop himself he asked her to accompany him on a moonlit walk of the grounds.

Elaina breathlessly accepted, relieved that she would not lose his company as quickly as she had feared. Rone had been very aloof the entire evening and she was beginning to think that he might not feel for her as much as she had thought he did. She had pushed him aside to fulfill her duty to her family. It was a regrettable action that she was forced to take. But seeing Uman and Welda moving forward with their lives and having the knowledge that her father could not be punished for breach of contract, she considered her options. It was true that she did not know if Manin was alive or dead, but she was quite sure that if he was alive, he would be brought up on charges of treason and rebellion towards the King. He had disobeyed a direct order from Arilian and caused the loss of innocent lives. He had committed an unpardonable sin punishable by death. *If I am still married, I will not be for long.*

Besides, it was her life that had been turned upside down at the hand of another. *Why should I be held accountable for my sister's* actions? she thought as they strolled hand in hand through the orchard. The moon playfully danced off the leaves, giving the appearance of tiny reflective mirrors hanging from crystallized branches.

Rone was a lovely man. He was handsome and strong, ready to defend her at a moment's notice. He had pledged his life to her, and she was moved by his passion and intensity. She never quite understood why he felt so strongly for her. At this moment she didn't care. All she wanted was to be wrapped in his arms once more and to feel the consuming heat of his kiss upon her lips.

"The moon is full tonight," Elaina said, breaking the silence. "She paints a pretty picture of her servant stars. Do you know the story of the Island of Lanier?" she asked. "When the One God created the world, all was peaceful, until the ruler of them wanted a wife hewn from the stars. The One God obliged him and made him the most beautiful bride the world had ever seen. Seeing that she was beautiful, he hid her away in his house, afraid that another man would take her from him. But one night…"

"…One night," Rone interjected, "the maiden woke up and left her house, wanting to see the world. Every man that saw her fell in love with her. The women of the land became so jealous that they killed her, chopping her into little pieces. When the Great One saw what they had done, he cursed them all, and taking the broken pieces of his beautiful creation, turned them to dust and sprinkled them over an uninhabited island. Thus the people of Lanier came to be."

"I see you know your Lanierian history, my Lord."

"I should. My mother made sure to instill as much of it into me as she could before she died. She wanted to know that I would continue in the old ways, like my ancestors before me."

Elaina was stunned by this revelation. "So your mother was from Lanier Isle like mine. I never knew that. So you and I have more in common then I once believed." She was delighted by her own words. They did seem to have a common bond between them. The attraction they felt towards each other was immediate that day, not so very long ago, at the feast in Warren Hall. Hearing the news of his ancestry solidified her thoughts all the more.

"Isn't it wonderful?" she gushed.

"What?" he retorted, staring out into the darkness. The moonlight danced across her face, giving her a celestial appeal. He averted his eyes to keep from being laid low under her spell.

"Isn't it wonderful to be a part of two such rich heritages? I am quite amazed at all I have learned these last few days. I realize now that I never knew who I was or what I wanted. But now I know." She stood in front of him, open and hopeful. He need only ask, only say the words her heart longed to hear, and she would be his.

"I am not sure I would say it is wonderful. It is only now that you have had to deal with the notion of belonging to two worlds. I have dealt with it all my life. I know what it is like to belong to a world that is without borders and full of life, and then have it taken away to follow another that is foreign, and sterile. When my mother died, I was taken to live with my father. Though he loved my mother, his family did not. He was not allowed to bring her into his world. We lived in a cottage on the outskirts of the palace in a little village where the servants resided. We had no one there to help us when she fell ill. My father would send a maid to bring us food and clothing, but he did little else for us."

Elaina saw the pain in his eyes. She had lived a sheltered but comfortable life at Inglemans Hall. It was true that she had little control over much of what went on there, but she was still cared for and loved by her father. And though she never knew her mother, she felt a strange connection with her, almost as if she was with her, watching over her. How dreadful it must have been for one so young to lose the only person that cared for him.

"I am sorry," she offered truthfully. "I had no idea that life was so difficult for you as a child. I believed you to be a man content with your situation. You are well received by your uncle, are you not? Certainly you must derive some affection from him."

"I love my uncle. He was one of the few people who accepted me when I came to live at the palace. He was never against my father marrying my mother. And I was never just Michal's bastard son to him. I have always been his nephew and will continue to be." He paced the orchard grounds, stopping to pull a ripe apple from a nearby branch. "Though I was young, I heard the whispers and saw the disapproving stares from those at court. My father never hid me and I loved him for it, but I couldn't help but feel that my uncle accepted me more than even he did. My father was a good man but not as strong in character as my uncle. And that is what concerns me."

"But how could your uncle's love give you cause for alarm? Certainly no harm can come of it."

"It is not his love that concerns me, but my father's weakness. If he loved my mother, then they should have lived their lives together. My mother left the land she knew to be with a man who chose his family's wishes over the woman that he supposedly loved. When she fell ill she had no one to care for her. If he had been there maybe she would have gotten treatment for her infirmity. She might have lived." Bitterness filled his mouth as he spat out the words.

All his life, he had sought to please his father. He wanted to make him proud of the son that he appeared to be so ashamed of before his family. Why couldn't Michal have been stronger, loving him and his mother out in the open? He turned toward the shadows of the night so that she could not see the anguish on his face. She would pity him and he didn't want her pity, only her love. But even that was a desire that he might never see satisfied. He knew that with her love would come choices, and he feared what they might be.

"Rone, I am sure your father wanted to marry your mother, but surely he felt he had no choice in the matter. Sometimes we have to do what must be done for the good of the whole. Your father was a part of the royal family. He believed that he had a responsibility to them as well as to you and your mother. Certainly it was not easy to divide his allegiance between two houses," she soothed. She reached out to caress his face with her palm. It was warm and soft and he enjoyed the gesture thoroughly. "We can choose our families no more than we can help who we fall in love with. I once believed that I had no choice in my decision to marry Manin. But now I see that I was wrong. I cannot help who I love, Rone. And I do not love Manin."

"So in your heart you are free to choose another," he said, more to himself then to her. This is what he had been waiting for. This was his chance to claim her forever.

"Yes, I will make my own choice, and Rone, I choose…"

Before she could finish his mouth was covering hers in a sweltering kiss. She surrendered completely to him, wrapping her arms around his neck. His kiss was different from the one they had shared before at the maze, or even in the forest. It was sweet and gentle at first, swelling into a fever pitch of passion. He kissed her urgently, wanting to taste every part of her. He released her mouth to kiss her eyelids, her cheeks, her forehead, and her chin. Everywhere his lips landed, the flesh burned with heat on Elaina's body. She gasped with delight when he found her lips again, bestowing upon them all the passion he felt inside.

He wanted, no, he needed to tell her how much he felt for her. How he lived for her and would die for her. He wanted to claim her as his love right then and there. But just as he prepared to fulfill his dream, he heard the untimely words that Welda had spoken to him earlier that evening.

"....*You and I both know that a bigger destiny awaits her,*" he heard her say. "*Elaina is more special then she thinks. She is Supreme Vital.*"

He pushed her voice out of his head for a moment. He delved deeper into their embrace, wanting to lose himself totally, but Welda's voice penetrated the walls of their passion.

"....*She has the ability to be both light and dark, both good and evil. If she is protected from those who would use her for evil purposes, then she will save us all from destruction...You, son of the House of Knives, are the key to saving both our worlds...Save her from herself.*"

Rone jerked back from Elaina, releasing her rather abruptly.

"Elaina, I...I am sorry. I am not sure what came over me. You are still a married woman, at least until you hear news of your husband's fate. You asked me to be kind to you and I am afraid that I have dishonored your request."

"But Rone, you have done no such thing. I wanted..."

"Also, my Lady," Rone interrupted before she could say more, "we should be turning in for the night. Morning will soon be upon us and we have much to accomplish. War is hard on even a trained soldier such as myself. I do not wish to detain you any longer and keep you from your rest," he lied. "Please allow me to escort you back to the Hall." He offered her his arm and she reluctantly took it. They walked back to the house in silence. When they reached the dining hall, Rone bowed deeply to Elaina and bid her good night. She returned a deep curtsey with a look of absolute confusion. *What just happened between us*, she wondered. *What went so terribly wrong?*

He left her there, in the entryway of the dining hall. He walked erect and with purpose to his room, and it wasn't until he reached it that he allowed himself to breathe. It was for the best, he told himself, but he couldn't shake the sick feeling that he felt when he saw the confused and slightly crushed expression she wore as he turned to walk away. He was behaving like an unmitigated arse. She would no doubt hate him for it, but he had no other choice. It was settled. In order for his plan to work he would have to be unyielding.

Her destiny was bigger than him, bigger than his love for her. He had to protect her in her endeavor to fulfill it. So...he would protect her...even if that meant protecting her from himself.

Elaina climbed the stairs to the Autumn apartment, and was greeted by Andira's friendly smile. "Wasn't it a wonderful evening?" she prattled. "With all of the food and laughter and dancing, I don't believe that I have had a grander time. You know, that brother of yours is quite a dancer, amongst other things," she blushed. "So, how was your walk with Rone?"

"Hmm?"

"Your walk? Uman and I were walking the grounds when we spied the two of you stealing away to the orchard."

"Anything eventful?" she asked with girlish excitement.

Elaina glanced at Andira long enough to see the ruddy color of her cheeks and the flakes of crushed leaves tangled in her tussled mane. She raised an eyebrow at her friend but dismissed her thoughts of interrogation.

"Eventful, yes," she groaned. "He covered me in kisses and then rejected me."

"How odd. Did he explain himself? I believed him to be completely taken with you," said Andira.

"As did I, but apparently he is more concerned with the state of our nation then than his feelings for me, if he truly has any that is."

Elaina collapsed on her bed with a sigh. Rone's behavior was confusing, to say the least. Had she said something to turn him away from her so harshly? She reviewed their conversation and found nothing that could have been deemed offensive. The only option available to her at this point was to get some sleep and hope that the morning brought clarity to both her and Rone.

Chapter 25

The morning began with a crisp start. The soldiers rose at dawn to prepare for the journey before them. Welda and her maids rose early as well to prepare a hearty breakfast. The men filed into the hall in a somber mood, every heart fixed upon its duty. Protect the chosen; protect the King; save the nation. It was a tall order, but they were ready to face the challenge, come what may.

Welda had prepared sliced pork, coddled eggs, oats with apples and cream, and fresh milk. The saddlebags were filled with a hefty supply of fruits, nuts, dried meats, and a vessel containing cool ale.

Rone and Uman did not sit at the high board. Instead they chose to sit with the men that they would fight next to in battle, as was custom in Alionia. When Andira and Elaina descended the stairs that led to the dining hall, they looked about, seeing the grim faces of the soldiers that would escort them to the palace.

"These are good men," Elaina said to her friend. "Good men willing to give their lives for us, for me. I shall not let them down."

Andira placed a reassuring hand on Elaina's shoulder. "Of course you won't. You are a most determined individual. If anyone can accomplish a task such as this, it is you. But first let's put some food in you so that you may have strength to save all of our necks." Andira led her to the table where Rone and Uman sat, and they were immediately served. A sweet-faced maid poured fresh milk for the two women. She smiled brightly as she left them, but not before filling Rone's cup with another serving of the rich, cool liquid. As she poured, she leaned over the table just enough for the fullness of her chest to spill out of the opening of her blouse.

"Milk to give ya strength for your journey." Her smile brightened when he uttered a word of thanks. "Is there anything else I can do for ya, mi Lord?"

"No…uh, your name miss?"

She blushed at his acknowledgement. He was the King's nephew and a nobleman in his own right, not to mention one of the most handsome men in all of Alionia. She was overjoyed to think that he would even care to know her name.

"Lula. Mi name is Lula, mi Lord."

"Well then, Lula, the only thing that I require from you is prayer every night that we are able to accomplish that which we set out to do. Nothing more. Can you promise me that you will do that for us?"

"Aye," she said breathlessly. Her milky white bosom rose and fell with abandon. "I will beseech the Great One on ya behalf every night and day as well, mi Lord. Nere one night shall pass when ya are not on mi heart with prayer," she vowed holding her hands over her ample chest.

"Thank you, Lula. I know you shall keep your promise." Rone flashed her a winning smile and the bosomy maid melted in her shoes. She attempted a dignified curtsey and turned on her heels to return to the kitchen. With her head held high she slowly sauntered back to her duty, swaying her hips in a grand fashion as she went.

"I am certainly glad that our fate does not rest on her prayers alone," Uman chuckled.

"You doubt the power of intercession, my friend?" Rone inquired.

"No, not at all. I just doubt that she will remember to pray for the rest of us." Laughter exploded from the table as the other men nodded their agreement.

"There is nothing wrong with giving a pretty young maid a task to set her heart upon," Rone said wryly.

"Pretty young maid, indeed," Elaina interjected. Her tone was low and curt and she did not remove her eyes from the plate before her. "Maybe you should go to the kitchen and give all of the pretty young maids the same speech. From where I sit, you are going to need as much prayer on this journey as you can get!" She stood from the table, having suddenly lost her appetite, and stormed from the room.

Uman laughed as he patted Rone, who sat surprised and feeling a bit beaten, on his shoulder.

"I told you, Ingleman women are a tough lot. It takes a firm hand to hold them, a strong mind to understand them, and an open heart to love 'em. I pray you have double your normal due to deal with that one." He resumed his conversation with a fellow soldier seated across from him, leaving Rone to his thoughts. She was angry with him. He had spurned her affections last night in the orchard and then openly flirted with another woman in front of her. He deserved whatever punishment her wrath produced. He wished that he could go to her and tell her that no other woman existed in his world but her, but he could not. He could not tell her his true feelings, not yet. He would wait until there were no dangerous choices to make and no future to risk. If they survived the destinies that fate had laid out for them, he would bare his soul. But until that time he would resign himself to her anger, and love her in silence.

Within the hour, they set out for the palace. Rone indicated the need to utilize as much day light as possible. They did not want to risk ambush or capture in the moonlight. His Tumult knights might have been able to fight their way out of such a predicament. He had trained them to do so himself, using the darkness to their advantage, but then again, they were the King's special army. They were made to work under extreme conditions and still come out victorious. Uman's men, though some of them good fighters, were not so skilled in the war arts. He would need to be careful not to lose many of them along the way.

They waved goodbye to Welda and the rest of the servants and headed north, staying clear of the main roads. They took the less-traveled dirt roads through the heavier parts of town, crossing farms and wide pastures. Uman sent several men ahead of them to scout the area. Reports of Nansharian regiments between Inglemans Plains and the Upper Mantle had doubled in recent days. They needed to be alerted quickly if the opposing army was spotted.

The trip to the palace would usually take no more than a day's time by carriage on the main road. But they had taken an alternate route so they would not call as much attention to themselves. Who knew if there were spies from the Nansharian army stationed in town, reporting every move they made? After all, movement from such a large party of riders was sure to raise eyebrows. The trek to the palace would take several days now. Great One be with them.

The first stretch of the journey was uneventful. They rode in the heat of the sun, thankful for every cool breeze that blew their way. Elaina noticed that Rone had kept his distance from her since they had left Inglemans Hall. He rode at the head of the party alongside Uman. From time to time he would circle the riders, taking visual inventory of all of the men, making sure everyone was well and accounted for. As he rode by, his eyes would meet hers for a brief moment, and then he would quickly turn away and continue with his task. She wondered if he could see the longing that was masked by her fury. If he recognized it, he made no sign to show it.

It was late afternoon when they stopped to rest and to take a light lunch. The horses were watered and fed and the men took to honing their combat skills. Elaina watched as Andira sparred with a man named Leland. He was burly and dark, with arms the size of tree trunks. He was a guard for a respectable House in the Upper Mantle before the Nanshar had invaded. He snarled at Andira, weaving in and out of each attack she threw at him.

Elaina could not help but cheer her friend on in her futile attempt to best Leland. He was swift for his size and his power was unmistakable. From the looks of it, he would certainly be a fierce opponent in battle.

"Be careful. Watch out. Faster, Andira. Use your shoulder more."

Leland smiled at Elaina, a look of mischief on his tanned face. "You offer your friend good advice, but I wonder how you would fare in her place? Come, she is tired. Why don't you try your hand at practice?"

"Oh, I…I couldn't. I haven't done that since I was a child. And I wasn't very good at it then."

"Please?" said Andira, collapsing beside her. "Avenge my honor. Besides, I am withering. I will certainly feel this tonight. Go on," she said, giving her a gentle shove, "try your hand at it. You might find it exhilarating."

Elaina took hold of her practice sword and met the burly man in the center of the training area. He nodded his consent to begin and she lunged at him, ready to strike. Before she could land a blow, she felt the wind being knocked out of her as she landed hard on her backside. Leland had landed a mighty blow to her midsection with the flat of his practice blade. She went down instantly.

"Good, come at me again," he said, offering her a hand up. "This time, do not leave yourself open." They practiced for several minutes before her strokes started becoming more fluid. After a while Leland was no longer able to predict what moves would follow his calculated assaults. A crowd began to form around them. Leland was said to be one of Uman's best men, and he used him often to train new recruits. No one was able to upend him save Uman himself, who was an excellent swordsman.

Gregor was a peaceable man, but he believed in being able to defend himself and those he loved. He had had all of his children learn to wield a sword from the time they were able to adequately hold one. Emona had not cared much for the lessons, and refused to continue them after only a few sessions, stating that men were meant for fighting, not women. Women, she insisted, were meant to rule those who fought.

Elaina continued with her training because her father wished it to be so. She wanted so much to please him, even though she doubted that she would ever have need of such a skill. She considered herself neither expert nor even adequate in swordplay. She had never beaten her instructor, or her brother, with whom she would spar with on occasion. They were her only opponents for as long as she could remember, and she lost to them every time. How am I besting Leland now? she wondered.

Leland put a bit more force into each blow. He didn't mean to hurt her, but he was surprised by her level of skill, and wanted to see how far he could drive her. Silence grew as their dance continued. All Elaina heard was the slice of her practice sword cutting the air, meeting Leland's weapon with solid strength.

"Good, good," rang an amused voice amongst the crowd. "You have improved greatly. I think you might even stand a sporting chance against me." Uman's words sent ripples throughout the crowd. Surely this delicate flower was no match for him.

"I have never bested you before, brother, and I don't ever believe I will. What happened just now was pure luck. And to tell you the truth, I had forgotten that I even knew how to hold a sword." She glanced at the practice sword. It was grooved where the force of her blows had met Leland's. "I guess it was a good idea for

Father to insist that I learn swordplay. In the coming days I may need it."

"I thought this was a battle of magical abilities. Well, for you anyway. Shouldn't you be sharpening your...uh...mystical weapons for whatever it is that you are destined to do?"

"I am sure you are right, brother, but I am not sure what it is I shall do, or with whom I shall be fighting. All I know is that there is a great evil, far stronger than a sword, ready to destroy the world we know." She sighed, looking up into the cloudless sky. "But it felt good to spar with Leland. Perhaps I shall do it again someday."

She bowed to the burly man, who lifted his sword in a gesture of salute and then left her to find other opponents to conquer.

"Maybe it is best that you continue to hone both skills." Rone had been standing on the outside of the training circle, watching in amazement as Elaina held her own against a skilled fighter. He would eventually wear her down by brute strength and stamina, but for the moment, she fought better than many of the men that Uman had recruited to defend their province. He thought back on Welda's words, informing him that he was touched by the Élan Vital himself. If warriors wielded the power and Elaina was a Supreme Vital...then perhaps...

He called for Sinta and entered the training circle. The crowd had thinned considerably after Leland's departure. Now, seeing Rone and Elaina in the circle, and Sinta approaching with her ever-commanding presence, they gathered quickly, not wanting to miss what talents might be displayed.

Sinta took a seat next to Andira on the soft grass outside of the training area. A sense of understanding flashed in her eyes, and she nodded for Rone to continue.

"Elaina, I believe that your father had more reason for you learning to wield a sword than you understood at the time. You will have great need of that skill now."

He held her in his bold gaze. She returned with just as much intensity. They had avoided each other for most of the journey, and hadn't spoken even after they had stopped to rest.

"It is said that Lanierian men who are warriors wield the Élan Vital. That is how they are able to be fierce and unmatched on the battlefield. It is possible that you have some of those abilities as well. You already know the basic rules of swordplay; now it is time for you to couple it with the inner strength that you possess. Will you trust me to teach you?"

She watched his lips as he spoke to her. His perfectly formed lips that dripped words of wisdom in honey form. Those lips could tell her to jump into the sea and she would be inclined to listen. She longed to have his lips meet hers. She needed his kiss. His lips called to her.

"Yes,'" she said, stepping closer to him. "Yes," she nodded in agreement. Yes she would kiss him and melt into him. She floated towards him until his chin nearly touched the crown of her head. Looking up into his handsome face, she whispered, "Yes." His jaw hardened as something indefinable flashed in his eyes.

"Good," he said, stepping away from her. "Pick up your sword and let's begin."

Anger coursed through her. He obviously had not changed his view of her or their relationship while they journeyed. He was not interested in her advances and would make no further display of affection towards her. Elaina took up her position opposite Rone and planted her feet in her beginning stance. It was all she could do not to launch at him at that very moment and run him through with her wooden sword.

How dare he seduce her with every fiber of his being and then expect her not to act upon her desires! Wasn't it he who had pursued her, wooing her with his passionate promises? He had all but declared his undying love for her and now he was treating her as if she was just another soldier. A weapon to command. He was intent on making a fool of her and she would not stand for it!

"Now Elaina, it is very important that you listen to your instincts. Anyone can land a blow on a stationary target, but in the heat of battle, there is a great deal going on around you. You must concentrate on the opponent that you are facing, while being aware of possible attacks from every direction." Rone held his sword at the ready. "Come," he commanded.

Elaina burst at him, slashing and cutting from every possible angle. Rone swept to the side and raised his sword to block a blow that was obviously meant for his head. Good idea to use practice swords, he thought. She is so angry that she might actually remove my head from my body.

Moving in much too close, Rone risked his head and locked his arm through hers, bringing them face to face, swords crossed. Elaina tried with all her strength but was not able to break the hold. She looked at the position of his arm. How had he immobilized her so quickly?

Flustered by his effortless victory, she looked up to find him smiling down at her. "It would seem that I have you, lovely," he said, his voice barely a whisper.

"So you have," she managed to squeak out. Her breath was ragged more from the closeness of their faces than from the hard work she had just performed. By the Great One, he was handsome. "That is, until I escape."

"Escape," he chuckled. "I think not. This is a highly effective hold. You will not be released unless I say so. I could hold you all day."

Something in his words sent a tingle down her spine. He was taunting her yet again! She looked at him with dreamy eyes. "Rone," she said sweetly.

"Yes, my dove," he whispered.

Her answer was a searing pain in his right foot as Elaina stomped on it as hard as she could. He released her more from the surprise of her attack than from the pain itself. He limped away quickly in case she decided to inflict some other kind of discomfort on his already injured person.

"Never underestimate the mind of a woman," laughed Sinta.

"And an angry one at that," he mumbled.

Despite his injury, Rone continued to practice with her. Sinta assisted by instructing her in the use of her powers in conjunction with her sword.

"Close your eyes. Concentrate on the energy inside of you. Circle that energy into one mass and then release it."

Elaina envisioned a swirling white light ebbing though her body. She collected the light and brought it to the center of her mind. Forming it into a little ball in her hands, she released it with as much force as she could muster. Hearing a crackling sound, she opened her eyes to see smoke rising from a partially smoldering tree at the far side of the camp. The trunk held a hole the size of a man's head.

"Oh my," she gasped.
"Amazing! I've heard stories of the fascinating feats that our people are capable of, but I've never witnessed it firsthand." Rone, truly astonished by her ability, looked at Elaina in awe. She at one time appeared to be a docile little angel in need of rescuing and constant protection. But the more her story unfolded before him the more he realized that she was special. Not just to him, but to the world.

"Do you think you can push that energy out through your sword next time?" Rone asked.

"I don't know, but I can try."

"Wait. You can attempt that later. Right now we should be going. We need to cover more ground," suggested Uman. "We have camped here for much too long."

They all agreed that it was time to move on. They needed to make it through much of Desolate Way before nightfall. They would be easy prey for not only the opposing army, but also for the inhabitants of the desert. Many fierce animals called the dusty, barren land their home. And since the land itself produced little sustenance, they were always prowling for fresh meat.

The small unit journeyed faster than before, covering much of the dry terrain. When night fell, they drove the horses harder. Veering west, they made camp just below a hill that overlooked the remainder of the desolate land. Far off in the distance, lights from the city entrance, the gateway to the Upper Mantle, could be seen.

"Maybe half a day more and we will be in the heart of the city," said Leland thoughtfully. A small party had scaled the hill to scout the area ahead of them. Leland was chosen to lead the excursion, a duty, like every one that he was assigned to, which he took seriously. "It will be easier if we cut through the west city entrance. There is no gate there and it is overgrown with shrubbery. We will be better concealed from enemy scouts."

"Very well. We should settle down for the night," Uman said. "We leave at first light."

Several men stood guard, Uman being among them. They would change shifts every two hours so that every man would get an equal amount of sleep. The night wind blew threads of warm breeze through the camp, teasing every parched tongue. Though they had flasks of ale, it was little relief from the thick dust and putrid smell of rot that lingered in the air.

Elaina lay awake in the tent that she shared with Andira and Sinta. She assured herself that it was the oppressive heat that made her restless, but she knew better of it. She thought of the training lessons and the tree and the faceless enemy waiting to destroy her. It was coming to destroy Alionia. This unknown force would break up the fabric of the world she knew and throw   Alionia's people, her people, into a life of darkness. She must save them, from the nobles in their pristine estates to the lowly serving maids in the kitchen, working for their bread. Her jaw clenched tighter when she remembered the maid that served them breakfast that morning. The way she had smiled at Rone. How he had flirted with her openly. He had pushed Elaina aside the night before, and then accepted the advances of another woman, and openly at that. Wasn't that just what Manin had done with Lily?

"How dare he handle me in this way," she growled. Throwing aside her cape that she used as a crude blanket, she eased off her pallet and tiptoed out of the tent. The camp was quiet. The only footsteps that stirred were those of the guards who stood watching their companions sleep safely through the night.

She edged herself around the perimeter of the tents, trying to stay within the shadows. She spotted Rone's tent across the clearing that separated her and the moonlight. Was this really necessary? Should she really be in her bedshift in the middle of the night wandering towards a man's tent when she was a married woman? She scolded herself for being so sensible. "I have seen little in the way of proper etiquette since all of this began," she reassured herself. "This will be no different." Scurrying in the moonlight, she crossed the path and pulled back the flap of the warrior's tent. He was lying on his pallet naked from the waist up. His body glistened with the perspiration of a warm summer night. His unbound black hair made a handsome contrast against the bronze muscled arm that he used as a makeshift pillow. By the Great One, he is beautiful, she mused.

Gathering up her courage, she eased down next to him on his pallet. Her breath caught for a moment when he reached out and pulled her into a strong embrace. Eyes closed, he inhaled the scent of her, tussling his fingers through her hair.

"….mmm Elaina," he breathed.

"Yes, Rone," she whispered.

"Elaina, I lo…" His eyes flew open, a look of sheer surprise touching them before recognition took its place. "Elaina, what are you doing here? Why are you not in your tent?" he demanded.

"I was cold," she replied flatly.

"In the desert?" he growled.

"I…I wanted to see you. I behaved badly at breakfast and I wanted to make amends," she pleaded. "Please do not be angry with me."

Realizing that he was still holding her, he released his grasp and jumped to his feet. "Yes, I can forgive you that. Emotions run high during war. It is easy for the best of friends to fall out of favor with each other at such times."

Friends, Elaina rehearsed. She loathed the word. "Yes, well, by the time I made it to your tent, I was so tired that I didn't know if I had the strength to make it back to mine. Would you accompany me?"

She looked up at him through drooped lashes. She was ethereal with her unbound hair and her billowy night shift. It was all he could do to contain himself.

"Yes, I shall accompany you. We should hurry before they change the guard. If someone were to see you leaving my tent dressed as you are, your brother might succeed in killing me this time."

Elaina blushed at the memory of Rone's daring rescue attempt several days earlier. "I would not want that."

"Nor would I," he said pulling her into his arms once again. She braced herself against his chest, letting soft skin caress hard naked muscle. For a moment they stood transfixed, oblivious to the world around them. Tenderly he grazed her cheek with his. He was clean shaven, unlike most of the Alionian nobles, and smelled of wood spice. Pulling her closer still, he traced the outline of her face, brushing over eyebrows, grazing her nose and ending at her lips. She grabbed his wrist and turned his hand over to reveal his warm palm and planted a soft kiss in the center of it. The simple act of such a chaste gesture rocked him to his core.

She reached up to him as he met her lips with eager force, bending her into a heated embrace.

Focus, Elaina, she chided. *Remember why you came here. Kiss him until he loses his wits and then leave him. Throw him away as he did you.* But the longer Rone kissed her, the more she lost the battle with her mind. She had come to seek revenge on him for his behavior since the orchard incident, but instead she stood trapped in his arms, enthralled by his passion. She pushed away from him, intent on seeing her plan brought to fruition. She would have her revenge. But as she swung way from him and headed towards the safety of the tent flap, she was halted by Rone's smooth voice and his arms guiding her back to him.

"Elaina, please don't leave just yet," he pleaded. Holding her once again, he resumed his inspection of her soul with his lips, delving deeper into her with every passing moment. The tent itself seemed to exude the passion between them. Elaina could almost hear a crackle of flames surround them as they held each other. The tent grew hotter and Elaina found it hard to breathe.

She opened her eyes to see the horror on Rone's face. It was not passion itself that had consumed the tent, but actual flames. Shouts of men mingled with the clash of steel brought the swift realization that they were being attacked. Pulling her away from the flames, Rone gathered his belongings, slipped on his jerkin, and grabbed his sword. The entrance was blocked by a wall of flames. There would be no escape for them there. Smoked filled the tent, burning their eyes and lungs.

"Here, cover yourself with this. We are going to have to make our own exit." Throwing her his riding cape, he ran to the back of the tent. He chose a spot that was less dense with flames and made a long tear in the fabric.

"Come on," he ordered. "While we still have a chance." Covering herself with the cape, she rushed through the opening. When Rone sprang forth behind her, they found themselves in the midst of combat.

They ran through the chaos, dodging skirmishes that came near them. The women's tent was still standing, and he directed her towards it. Andira and Sinta were waiting inside, swords in hand. "Where have you been?" Sinta snapped, running to take the singed cape from Elaina's shoulders. "We were worried when the alarm sounded and we awoke to find you missing."

"Well..." Elaina stumbled. "It's a long story," she said, color rising in her cheeks.

"Indeed," Andira said, raising an eyebrow at Rone. "But it is one that will have to wait for another time. Right now you must get dressed and prepare to defend yourself. I'm afraid that tonight might be our first real lesson in true combat."

Rone stood outside the tent, guarding it against would-be attackers. The Nansharian soldiers, though not as skilled as the Tumults, were fierce in their own right. It was a small band that had attacked the camp, but they made quick work of the townsmen, herding them towards the center of the camp. If they could circle the entire troop, then they could easily slaughter many of Uman's men merely by hedging them in. Suddenly, he heard a cry come from the inside of the tent. The rear panel was cut open and several soldiers spilled into the shelter, intent on capturing the women. Rone entered the tent in enough time to see Andira fell the first soldier. Elaina grabbed a sword from a chest beside her and slashed her way through a growing crowd of Nansharian men. Sinta stood to the side, observing the fight, as Rone joined the fray. The battle continued outside in the light of dawn. Soldiers from the Ingleman rebellion were left to regroup as more and more Nansharians turned their attention to the small group of fighters to the south of the camp. Elaina was afraid that they might be outmatched until she saw Uman and Leland fighting their way through the crowd. Soon they joined Rone as he felled one soldier after another. Elaina was set upon by a large fighter. He sneered at her, baring crooked yellow teeth.

"Hello, my pretty," he spat. "How's bout ya give up now and come wit me. After I've 'ad a bit o' fun with ya I'll turn ya ova to mi master and 'is Lady. They've great plans for ye."

He lunged at her, clashing his steel upon hers. Returning each blow as swiftly as she could, Elaina swung in and out of the man's reach. Her agility, though great, was no match for his strength. He pushed her back towards the crest of the hill. She fought him steadily, giving everything she had into each blow. As they fought their way up the rocky incline, the man reached out and landed her a blow to the jaw. The pink and purple sky swirled about her as she lost her footing and fell to the ground.

When she came to, she saw the burly, yellow-toothed man standing over her, a look of mad hunger on his ugly face.

"Now poppet," he said, bending down to straddle her. "I shall 'ave a little fun with ye." He grabbed her and kissed her roughly. His breath was foul and she gagged and sputtered as his tongue probed its way into her mouth.

"Aye! What are ya doing there?" shouted another voice from the bottom of the hill. Her captor sprang to his feet, pulling her up with him. "Mind your own business. I captured her. She is mine to take in."

"We were ordered to bring 'er to the master. He said nothin' 'bout this, Norland."

"Aye, that is true, but he said nothin' agin' it, either." The man called Norland looked about nervously. "Look, Mallow, they're still fightin' down there. Let's you and me 'ave a bit o' fun with this pretty lil one. No one will know the wiser. She's no different from the others we've taken. I don't care what she's supposed to do. I still captured 'er, didn't I?"

Mallow considered the man's words for a moment and found them to be sound enough for him. "She is a comely lass, isn't she?" he leered. He grabbed her backside, pulling her to him. "'er skin is so soft," he said, grinning mischievously. "Are you that soft everywhere, mi little wanton wench?" He reached for her tunic, seeking to tear the fabric right off of her trembling body.

"Ah' look at 'er Norland. She's shaking with anticipation. The little slut wants it! Don't worry mi lovely," he said. "You'll have enough between the both of us." He clutched her face in a smelly unwashed hand. Leaning forward he licked the side of her cheek where a lump was now beginning to swell from the hit from Norland's fist. She struggled away from him and slapped him as hard as she could with a free hand.

"This un 'as spirit," he sang to his friend. "I advise ye not do that again," he threatened. "I'm inclined not to be so gentle." He began pulling at his britches, eager to begin his deed.

"Now wait a minute, Mallow. I captured 'er. I go first," Norland stepped up. "Tis only fair."

"If you want me to keep it to mi self, then maybe ye should think otherwise," Mallow shot back.

As the men argued, Elaina eased her way back slowly. If she could get clear of her captors enough to put some distance between them, she might be able to run back to camp, sounding the alarm along the way. She edged back further, careful not to disturb the growing argument between the two men. She was ten steps away and on the path to freedom when she stepped on a cracked, dry, bristlewood twig. Its roots were far beneath the earth, but the plant itself had long since died due to lack of moisture. Her foot crushed the twig that had coiled itself around a fruit-sized rock. The rock dislodged, causing a cascading effect on the surrounding rocky ground. Hearing the movement of the terrain, the men turned around to see their prize edging way.

Realizing that she was caught, she threw caution to the wind and ran. To her dismay, she did not get far. Before she could call for help, they had her by the arms dragging her back up the hill.

"I told you not to try nothin' funny, poppet. Now you're in for it."

"No, you are," she said, her voice ragged with anger. In that instant, in that horrible moment of realization that her womanhood, her life in general, was once again being threatened, a tidal wave of rage broke free inside of her. She had grown tired of the selfish, callous, depravity of mankind. She directed all the anger that she felt against those whom she'd witnessed commit abominable acts within the last year at her two captors.

It was men like these that brought shame to war. It wasn't the carnage on the field or the need to fight for a worthy cause or even the loss of life, Elaina decided. It was the deplorable and depraved atrocities that evil men committed against those they felt were weaker than them.

Their victims were usually women and children. Elaina felt the anger burn white-hot in her veins. They would not hurt another helpless soul, she vowed. Elaina called all the power she could find inside herself and pooled it into the core of her being. As her anger rose, the bright morning sky began to darken, alarming even the fighters on the field below. A howling wind stirred from the east and blew through the camp, tossing tents and fighters about as it passed.

Mallow was too set upon his task to notice the dark swirling cloud that had formed above them. Norland, on the other hand, stood frozen in his tracks. He motioned to Mallow, but was unable to speak. He looked at Elaina and found her eyes had turned from black to an eerie translucent white. He waved his hands in front of her face but received no reaction. Mallow still struggled with his britches. He had laced them quickly in an attempt to run after his prey when she tried to escape. But he had her now and he would have his fill. He smiled to himself as he released the last loop and let his pants pool around his ankles.

"It's time now lovely," he said with a greedy laugh.

Elaina turned slowly to him, thunder pealing over her head. "Yes, it is your turn," she hissed. She raised her arms and the wind whipped around her, spiraling currents of power from her to the swirling mass above her. Lightning scattered across the darkened sky. Everyone, even the fighters at the camp, stood transfixed, amazed at what they were witnessing.

Mallow's smile faded into tears as he realized his fate. "I should 'ave followed mi first mind and reported Norland to the Master. I should 'ave walked away. No," he thought. "I should 'ave knocked 'er out when I 'ad the chance. I should 'ave…" Lightening cracked through the sky and burst down through the swirling cloud and straight into Mallow, engulfing him in white light.

Elaina slowly turned to Norland and raised a hand in his direction.

"Now wait a minute," Norland pleaded. "I wasn't gonna hurt ya none. I was just playing with ya." He backed away slowly. "After all, it's not a lowly servant like me ya be wantin'. It's the master and his lady. They are the ones that sent us for ya. I'm…just a simple soldier following orders."

Elaina sent her mind across the currents of the wind and probed his thoughts.

"Were you following orders when you burned down four houses with the families still in them on your last raid?" She probed further into his heart, seeing the depraved acts that he had committed. "Were you following orders when you killed the young girl you assaulted, defiling her right in front of her family?" Her voice rang out over the hill and down through the camp. Everyone, even the rebellion fighters, trembled in fear.

"Ye…Yes," he lied. "My master told me to do such things. He said he would kill me if I didn't wreak as much havoc as I possibly could. I'm a victim of 'is rage." He looked as distraught as he could muster and pleaded for his life.

"Then I shall deal your master the same justice that I now send upon you." At those words a blinding bolt of lightning shot from her hand and hit Norland in the chest. He looked at her, mouth open, amazed to see such a thing come from so docile an individual. Surprise turned to pain as the lightning consumed him from the inside out, leaving only a smoldering heap of ash in his place.

Elaina turned her attention to the camp. There were more evil men down there, trying to hurt and kill those she cared about. They must be stopped. She glided down the hill effortlessly, barely touching the ground. The lightening cloud floated with her, sending down rays of white light as it went. At the sight of such horrid beauty, the Nansharian soldiers dropped their swords and ran. Steel was no match for such power. Hers was a magic that they could not fight and did not want to try.

Chapter 26

The roar of the wind dissipated over the camp as the stench of rot and decay returned to fill their lungs. Dust flew about wildly, covering everything like a dingy blanket. Broken bodies of fallen soldiers lay strewn across the disheveled camp, giving credence to the barren land's namesake. The resistance fighters watched as the opposition fled in fear, not stopping to view the terror that floated behind them.

The sun's rays bit at the dark clouds that loomed overhead. Daylight came in an instant, illuminating the aftermath of the storm. The men set to dividing the fallen into groups of friend or foe. Though the number of the dead Nansharians far outweighed their own, any loss to their ranks was too high a price to pay. Every death was mourned. A tent that had been spared in the battle was adopted as a makeshift infirmary, sheltering the dying and wounded.

Rone stood with Sinta and Andira at the base of the hill where they had witnessed Elaina's display of power. After the Nanshar fled, Elaina, in all her ethereal splendor, glided back to the top of the hill and planted her feet firmly in the ashen sod that was burnt by the bolts of lightning that she had used to do her bidding. Her back was towards them but they could still see that she had not yet returned to herself. The power within her surged through and around her, sending ripples of wind swirling about, stirring her hair and clothing. Everything around them that belonged to nature's arms was silent, save the wind she controlled and the buzzards that perched nearby, ready to feed on dead flesh.

Uman busied himself with the regrouping of his soldiers. The attack had been unexpected, but they had fought bravely. They had lost five men and several were left wounded. He would take better care to deliver all that remained safely to the palace. When he had finished directing Leland in matters of recovery, he joined the others at the bottom of the hill.

"She's been like that for some time now. Should we not see if she is alright? What if…something has happened to her?"

"That is my concern, as well," Sinta said, addressing Uman. "She has been in Waté for some time. I hope she can get back."

"Waté? What is that?" Andira asked fearfully. "It is the state in which a seasoned Vital explores their powers. In this stage they begin to merge with the Élan Vital itself," Rone explained. He was obviously concerned, and that scared Andira even more. "It is not the finale stage in power wielding, but it is close." Turning to Sinta he asked, "Are you sure she's in Waté? And if she is…how do we get her out?"

"I'm not sure," Sinta said, wringing her hands nervously. "I have never seen anyone stay in this stage for this long." Shaking her head in frustration she added, "I do know that it must be done carefully. Elaina is young in the use of her abilities and yet her growth in the arts are astounding. If she is brought out of Waté too quickly, there might be irrevocable consequences."

"What kind of consequences?" Rone questioned.

Sinta looked pale with worry. "Well, for starters, she can be separated permanently from her reality. Her mind is partially one with the Vital right now. If she digs deeper into that power, it is not likely that she can come back to us. We must reach her before that happens, but we must ease her out of it. It is possible that part of her could be left in the Waté state."

"So that means…?" Andira began.

"That means she would return to us as a shell of her former self, or worse, a clean slate with no life in her at all," Uman finished.

"Yes. I'm afraid that she would be much like an infant, learning life for the very first time."

Their worried attention once again returned to the woman on the hill. She was a confined storm waiting to unleash her fury.

The small company of friends approached the apex of the hill warily. Sinta broke from them and inched her way steadily towards Elaina, careful to make no sudden moves. Elaina's body stiffened. She did not turn around to face them, but kept her gaze directed at the town below. Her only acknowledgement of their presence was the slight shifting of her head, as if straining to hear.

"Elaina," Sinta's voice rose above the swirling winds that enveloped her. "You are in the Waté state. We have to bring you out. Come to the sound of my voice. Can you do that?" She moved forward, but found the force around the entranced woman to be so great that she could barely keep her footing. Her small frame was to her discredit. Despite her meager stature, she pressed further into the tempest, clawing at the wind.

"Elaina," she called. "Elaina, can you hear me?" She reached out to place a hand on her shoulder, but was thrust back by the wind's current. Uman rushed forward and caught her before she hit the ground.

"I can't reach her. It's like she has some sort of energy barrier around her. I have to try to break through it."

Sinta made another attempt at breaking through the barrier of her defenses, but only found the same result as before.

"I fear I am too slight of figure," she said breathlessly. "We need someone stronger."

"Can you try to touch her mind from here? If I do recall, my mother spoke of a technique that could be used to touch the mind of another to combine power." Rone ran his fingers through his mane. "Maybe you could do that now."

Sinta shook her head. "I could manage it if I could get near her. I could touch her mind now, but she is not there. She is on a plane that is different from the one on which we exist. For me to follow her…it would require physical contact."

"Then let me try," offered Rone.

"Are you insane?" Uman protested. "Look, I know you feel for my sister, but this is a dangerous thing. How do we know where she is in this…this plane that she has retreated to?" He shuffled his feet nervously. "Besides, from where I'm standing, she doesn't seem to be too fond of men right now," he offered as he motioned to the smoldering dirt where her assailants once stood. "And to that matter, it is only women who hold this power. You are of no use here."

"That is not so," demanded Rone. "Men are also able to wield the Élan Vital. It is not widely known, but it is so. That is how we fight so well," he added wryly. "Haven't you ever noticed a stirring of something inside of you every time you have entered a battle? Some special insight stored inside from an unnameable source?"

Uman thought for a moment. "Like slowing down time or walking through a waking dream."

"Yes," said Sinta. "That's how I've heard it described before. But Rone," she said facing him, "Uman is right. This could hold just as much danger for you as it does for her. When you enter into the abyss of the mind, there is no telling what you will face there. Your mind will be joined with hers. There could be defenses that have been set up by both of you to protect against intruders. If you are not able to overcome them, then you may not be able to find her or recover yourself."

"But I must try. Welda told me that I was the key to saving Elaina. Do you not see? It is my destiny."

"If you are intent on saving her, I will prepare you," Sinta resolved. She placed her palms on Rone's temples and searched his mind for signs of decay. An unstable mind would never be able to withstand the journey he was about to take. Finding nothing wayward, she moved to the center of his being and found a peculiar-looking object much like a sword, only its blade was a shaft of blinding light. The hilt of the sword was a silver perched hawk with its wings outspread. The pommel was its head, where two fiery rubies blazed to represent its eyes. It twirled slowly, sending shards of light out to pierce the darkness. "Fascinating," she declared. She had explored the souls of others before but never a Lanierian male. There were many questions that rose in her mind, but they would have to be answered later. Time was of the essence. They needed to reach Elaina as quickly as possible. Releasing his mind, she gave him final instructions.

"Remember, Rone, once you touch her you must delve deep into the Élan Vital. I saw the source inside of you. You must find it and tap into its power to help you reach Elaina. You will face much to reach your core. You must overcome it. You must embrace it. You must conquer your own mind before you can transverse the planes of hers.

Nodding his agreement, he turned to face Elaina. The winds had grown stronger, as if she was aware of what was to come. Braving the brewing storm, he pushed forward until he reached her. He spoke her name, but the sound was muffled by the torrent around him. He was startled to see that her usual rosy warmth was replaced by a cold, stony gray. Elaina, he thought to himself. I am coming, my love. He embraced her as tightly as his arms would allow. The force around her pulled at him, cautioning him away, but he did not release her. He could hear the rush of the wind around him rise to a deafening burr. The world he knew ebbed away, fading from daylight to the black of night. Reality became nonexistent. Elaina, the hill, his friends, were all a distant memory, a shadow on the edge of his conscious.

Rone waded through the darkness, measuring each step with care. There was no light to illuminate his way, no sound to urge him forward. The atmosphere around him thickened and became so thick and heavy it felt like a cape draped about his shoulders. Breathing became a laborious task. He grappled for air, feeling lightheaded and weak. Though shrouded in darkness, more from habit than hope, he looked down at his feet to discover why he could no longer walk, and realized that he was falling. The disorienting darkness had hidden his plight and altered his reality. He flailed madly, reaching for something to steady himself, but quickly accepted that it was a fruitless notion. There was nothing solid in this dark pit. With his heart pounding wildly in his chest, he closed his eyes and embraced the darkness that swallowed him into a deep abyss. He fell in silence for a time. There was nothing but the whirling of the wind in his ears and the black void that trapped him in a spiraling descent into madness and fear. But eventually, a sickening voice, like the sound of crows calling in the winter morn, pierced through the thick cloak of silence, grating his senses through to the bone.

"You will be lost forever to the darkness," it screamed. It resounded in his ears like a funeral dirge. "You will never be able to return." He shook at the thought, the agony of eternal captivity in darkness. Like a vulture it thrust its talons into the cavity of his chest, and pulled at the fibers of his soul. "You will never reach Elaina," he heard it say. "She is lost to you forever."

Sinta had warned him that he would face his greatest fear in the abyss. Were these hope-shattering words his deepest fears? Could it be possible that he was afraid, not only of losing Elaina, but also of losing himself?

Thud.

His bones shuddered as he made contact with the ground beneath him. He was still shrouded in shadows, but he could feel firm sod beneath his feet. As he stood in the darkness, he heard an approaching rustle, like the sound of footsteps on cracked leaves.

"Hello," his words echoed. The rustle was his reply. "Hello. Is someone there? Show yourself."

"Why have you come?" a voice bellowed in the distance.

"Who are you?" he answered.

"Why have you come?" the voice rang out again.

"I am Rone Mosenvelt. I have come seeking assistance. I must know how to free my...friend, Elaina, from the Waté stage. I believe her to be trapped here. Will you help me?"

The air around him crackled with excitement. Several flashes of light streaked across the darkness. There was a rumbling of thunder, causing the ground to shudder when they landed before him. The lights turned to red flames the height of oak trees. Rone shielded his face from the heat of the flame.

"Rone, it was not by accident that you have come to us. It was predestined before your time that you would do so," said one of the flames.

"But who are you," he inquired.

"We are the Seven Sons of Shathar." As they spoke, the flames receded, leaving seven men dressed in ancient attire before Rone's astonished eyes. Their silver armor gleamed with the shimmer of stars against a black velvet sky, and their eyes pulsed red with flames. They were fearsome to behold, and Rone dropped to his knees in respect. "We are the keepers of the Seal. You, son of Jonelle, hold the Seal, do you not?"

"Yes. I have it. As it was given to me by my mother, so shall my wife give it to my son, as is custom amongst our people."

"The Seal will not exchange hands much longer. The secrets that it holds will be revealed in time, but for now you must guard it well. Give it to us," said one of the warriors.

Rone removed the Seal from his pocket. He usually did not carry the Seal with him when he traveled, but for some reason he felt it necessary to bring it with him on this journey. Great One be praised, he thought to himself. He always knows.

Approaching the brothers in reverenced awe, he handed over the Seal. Once in the warrior's hand, the silver charm began to glow. The hawk sprang to life, spreading its wings over the seven knives, and released a piercing cry. The heart in its talons began to beat as the knives that were surrounding it began to rotate.

"Rone, son of Jonelle, protector of mankind. You have lingered between two worlds and found no place in either, or so you thought. Nevertheless, you have fought bravely to preserve both heritages from the ravages of deceitful men. You have proved yourself worthy of the task that we now bestow upon you." The warrior held up the Seal.

"The Seal of Shathar was forged to protect the secrets of our people. A time will come when those secrets must be made known. Lanier Isle has been disgraced and brought to shame by those seeking to serve themselves. From you will our race be restored to its former glory." Another warrior stepped forward. He held a diamond-shaped shield adorned with a red hawk. He held it out to Rone. "Take this to protect yourself. You will need it in the days ahead."

Another stepped forward and held out a sword. "You have won many battles, my son. But your greatest victory is yet to be known." He held out the sword and bid him take it. "It cannot be broken or defeated. It will not tarnish or decay. It is the defender of mankind and it is now yours to wield."

Rone took the sword and examined it. Its blade was made from an unknown metal that gleamed with blinding light. The hilt of the sword was a silver perched hawk with its wings outspread. The pommel was the bird's head, where two fiery rubies blazed to represent its eyes. It fit his grasp as if made for him alone. The balance of the sword was perfect. Energy flowed from it and engulfed him.

"Can you feel it?" asked the warrior. "You are connected to the sword. The only way that you will not find victory with this weapon is if your heart is not pure. It's a weapon of justice. Not destruction."

The warrior with whom he had first spoken stepped forward yet again. "It is a precious thing, your task. One not to be taken lightly. From the beginning of time, when Lanier was first called into existence, and the ashes of our mother were sprinkled like grains of sand over the Land, men have wielded the Élan Vital. They have long since left the old ways, leaving the rights given to them by the Great One himself to the women of the clan. You are commissioned to bring back the order of the Shathar. From your house will come the greatest wielder of the Élan Vital that this world will ever know. Teach your descendants to remember the old ways." He held out the Seal. "This has been worn as a chain about your neck. Now it will be branded upon your heart, that you may hold the glory of our people deep within you."

He placed the glowing Seal upon Rone's chest and pushed the burning object into his heart. Rone gasped in pain as fire ripped through his body. He fell to the ground, clawing at his chest, searching for relief that he feared might never come.

"What you feel is the anguish of your ancestors, due to a wayward people. That pain is now yours, as is the joy in seeing it restored."

The pain began to subside, and Rone was able to once again regain his feet.

"Our time in this place has come to an end," said another. "We will leave this plane, but not your heart." The warriors turned to depart. Rone raised his hand in salute and instantly remembered why he had ventured onto this plane in the first place.

"Wait," he called. "I am grateful for the gifts that you have given me. I pray your favor in assisting me with one more matter."

"Ah, yes," said the warrior. "You seek the She-thar. She is quite safe." He tilted his head in a questioning manner. "You care much for her?" It was a statement more than a question. "Take care to follow your heart on this matter. It has been destined before time began. But know this, my Son. In choosing what is in your heart, you will pay a heavy price. But do not despair. It must be done. Go now. She is waiting for you."

With a wave of the hand they were gone. With their flames extinguished, Rone found himself in darkness once again. How would he find Elaina if he could not see what lay before him? He walked, yet again, for an undetermined amount of time. Frustration threatened to free itself from his keen control, but he fought hard to master the gnawing irritation that was growing inside of him.

"Where is she?" he demanded. Just then, the sword at his hip began to vibrate. He removed it from its hold in his belt and watched as its silver luster grew strong enough to illuminate his path. In the distance, he could see the faint outline of a shadowy figure. As he drew "closer, he could see that it was Elaina. He mouthed her name as a lump rose in his throat. He ran to her but stopped short, not sure of what he should expect.

"Elaina," he said, resting a hand gently on her arm. She turned to face him. The recognition and joy that she displayed upon seeing him was enough to send his heart soaring.

"Rone, I am happy to see you. May we go now?"

"Yes, of course," he said warily. "Elaina, are you not surprised to see me?"

"Not really. They told me you were coming."

"Who?"

"The chosen of the Vital. They said that you would be here soon and to wait for you until you had completed that which you came for."

"So you saw them? They spoke to you?" Elaina merely nodded and shrugged as if it was a normal occurrence.

"Great One be praised," he muttered. "So how do we leave this place?"

"It is simple. We remove ourselves from the plane." His puzzlement induced more explanation. "We are here only in mind, not in body. We have to search out our natural selves to leave here. The same way we came is the way we will leave. Hold my hands." He obediently gripped her slender fingers. "Now concentrate and ease your mind back from where it came." Swirling into the abyss once more, Rone could hear the sound of elemental fury drawing closer. When his feet found solid ground once again, he opened his eyes to find Elaina standing before him. Her eyes were closed, lips slightly parted. There was a flush of color in her cheeks, and if Rone had not been aware of what had previously taken place, he would have thought her simply asleep.

"Elaina. Elaina do you hear me? We've made it back." When there was no answer, he drew her in closer, enveloping her in his arms.

"Elaina. Don't do this. Don't leave me here to fight alone. Our destinies are intertwined. I have no purpose without you. Please return."

He held her for a while longer, not sure what he should do. Suddenly there was a rumble and the ground shook under their feet. He heard the shrieks of those nearby, but did not release her. When the rumbling subsided, Elaina gasped for air and collapsed in his arms.

"Elaina," Rone said wearily. "Elaina, are you alright?"

The wind around them swirled into a mere tussle and then melted away. Shaking her head, she clung to him. There was no strength left in her and she felt as if she might retch. Cheers and adulation went up as their friends approached.

Sinta was the first to reach them. "Elaina, you are well?" she asked. "Have you returned to us whole?"

"Quite," was her breathless whisper. "I am a little tired, but no worse for the wear."

"Good. And what of you, my lord?" she said, turning to Rone.

"I am well," he lied. It was all he could do to remain standing. Every muscle in his body screamed for relief.

"No matter, I will help you anyway," Sinta offered with a wily grin. "You are a strong man, no doubt, but everyone needs assistance now and again. Besides, a journey of that difficulty would leave a normal man on his back for days. You are a remarkable fellow, Master Mosenvelt." He peered into her eyes and he found understanding in them. Having no answer for what she already knew to be true, he put his head down and allowed her to place her palms on his temples. After only a few moments he felt the strength returning to his body.

"Thank you."

"It is my pleasure, my lord."

Uman had picked Elaina up and was already carrying her down the hill. She was set in a tent away from the infirmary in order to give her privacy. Andira, Uman, and Sinta crowded around the two "travelers" to hear their rendition of the story.

"There isn't much to tell," Rone said, turning away from Sinta's perceptive gaze. He wasn't sure that he wanted to divulge his newfound knowledge just yet. He was still digesting everything that had occurred in the Waté plane. He could share his news with them when he had it all figured out. "It was dark and hard to maneuver. After much searching I found her and here we are."

Apparently, Uman and Andira were too overjoyed to contradict his short answer. Uman clasped his shoulder. "Thank you for returning my sister safely to us. I am forever in your debt."

"Well, Elaina, what is your side of this fascinating adventure? We were worried that you would not return to us."

"I know. I could hear you calling me, but...there was something that I had to do."
You could hear us? Why did you not respond?" demanded Uman. "You had us scared out of our wits."

"I am sorry to worry you. It was not my intention. In fact, I believe that I had very little control over what happened to me there. It's as if the plane itself guided me to...well, to another land.

"Fascinating." Sinta sat down beside her, taking Elaina's hands in hers. "Was it the same land that you visited in your vision when you collapsed at the fountain?"

"No. It was a different place altogether. I have seen nothing like it in my life. It felt....powerful and fearful and terrible and, all the while, safe. Almost like being at home. I entered a cavern where smoldering rock littered the ground and fire flowed from the walls, forming rivers and lakes that glowed red and angry." She shuddered at her own description. "Is it shameful to have an attraction to such a dark place? I felt a strange desire to stay in that cavern, to be a part of the chaos that was growing there."

"What kind of chaos?" Rone asked.

"Truthfully, I'm not sure. There was a soft hum that steadily grew into a large bellow, almost like the sound of a...a horn." She looked to Sinta, her wide eyes filled with fear. "It was then, after the horn blew, that I saw them."

"Saw who?" Even Andira was on the edge of her seat, riveted by Elaina's tale.

"It was a great army that was preparing for battle. They are ready to be led by the general appointed to them. They are strong and fierce, and they are waiting to be called into action."

"We know they are preparing for war. The Nanshar have made that very clear," Uman said, exasperated.

"I do not speak of the Nanshar, brother."

"So we have another foe to fight? What land would rise against use now?"

"They are not against us, Uman. At least I do not believe that they are. I think I've been to the other side of the world...where they are waiting. We cannot win this war without them, but they will not come without being bidden by their leader."

"So who is their leader?" asked Andira. "How do we find him?"

Sinta watched Rone from across the room. She'd said nothing and yet, as she rose from her seat and walked the perimeter of the tent, he felt a growing sense of discomfort all the same. He turned his back to her, hoping to avoid her piercing gaze.

"Rone," she said softly, putting a comforting hand on his shoulder. "Where did you get that sword?"

He was so pleased to have Elaina back that he had forgotten the gifts that were given to him by the Shathar.

"Where did you get them?"

"They were given to me when I went into the abyss. I was greeted by the Seven Sons of Shathar. They gave me this sword and shield and then took the seal I bore and placed it in my heart. He reached for his chest and felt something beneath his tunic. Pulling it out, he was astounded to find the Seal hanging on a chain around his neck.

He looked at Sinta questioningly. "But it really did happen. I felt the pain of it. And I have the sword and shield as proof." Feeling a little unsure, he looked to Sinta for answers. Sinta said nothing. She stepped away from him, covering her mouth in surprise and fear.

"Sinta, I am not insane," he demanded. "I swear to you it happened."

"Never in all of my years did I believe that I would see this day." She dropped to her knees before him, causing everyone in the room to take notice.

"What's this, then?" Uman asked. "What is going on?"

"Uman, son of Lanier, bow before the King of Shathar."

"What?" the men said in unison. When the declaration was made, the hawk on Rone's pendant came to life. It let out a piercing cry as it leapt from the Seal and flew a course around the tent, coming to rest once again on its perch.

Uman knelt beside Sinta and Andira followed suit. "I thought the Shathar was a myth, but I see now, my lord, that it is not. Forgive my ignorance. I swear my life and allegiance to you."

"As do I," said Sinta.

"As do I," echoed Elaina from her cot.

"Hey, you can count me in, too," Andira added.

"That's all well and good," Rone said, the color rising in his cheeks. "But would someone mind telling me what all of this is about?"

Chapter 27

The torches burned brightly among the tents as dusk settled over the camp. They had decided to bunk down for the night and make their way to the palace in the morning. They had much to tell the king.

King.

The word alone sent a shiver of trepidation through Rone. His uncle was king of Alionia and by his character, the title suited him. A king cared for his subjects. He sorted out the problems of a nation and wore the weight of his world upon his shoulders. It was a responsibility that Rone had never asked for.

As a child growing up amongst the court, he vowed never to become like the nobles in Alionia. They were haughty and snide, lording themselves over those who were born to a lower station in life. They often took credit for what their servants worked hard to accomplish, while never lifting a finger to complete the task themselves. They could be insipid, deplorable creatures, drunk on power and affluence.

Of course, not every noble could be labeled as such. Warren Beltrane had worked hard to gain the respect and good name bestowed upon him. His deeds alone made him worthy of his title. Arilian was the head monarch of their great nation, and he displayed such compassion and sincerity that, to him, there was no equal. Even his father, Michal, though he could never call him a man of great warmth towards others, had loved his mother, a commoner by Alionian standards, and sired a son by her. It was that same son who, when his mother died, was brought to the palace at his father's insistence to be brought up at court amongst the elite.

To these great men, the barrier between noble and common was still a fixed gulf. Warren Beltrane's household certainly could not boast of its ideals of equality. And Rone's own father never married his mother because of his family's disapproval of a common bride, and a foreigner to boot.

Even the strong convictions of King Arilian were not enough to change the attitude of a nation. He had worked tirelessly to unify the classes, and yet his efforts- albeit through outside influences- had still led to civil war. Would he fare any better?

Rone walked away from the camp and up a nearby hill. He needed a quiet place to be alone with his thoughts. Sinta and Uman believed that he was a king of the Shathar order. He knew that he was of their clan, but he could not accept this role to be his destiny. Every king had his court, his advisors, and his enemies. Power produced unscrupulous men who would smile in one's face while controlling matters of state behind one's back. He had witnessed it too many times to count. He would never allow a gaggle of self-serving nobles to dictate his every move.

If he were to be king, he would change things somehow, make them better than before. He understood that Lanier Isle did not at present have a ruling monarch. How would the people feel about a half-breed bastard assuming the throne? He laughed bitterly. Sinta and Uman had to be wrong. He could no more rule in Lanier Isle than he could in Alionia. If the people did not deny him the right, then he would do so himself!

Rone sighed, bracing himself against the inevitable. He could no more run from his destiny than Elaina could hers. He looked down the hill to the tents below to see Elaina assisting Sinta in the task of revitalizing the health and strength of their small army. Welda and the Sons of Shathar had alluded that his love for her would lead to a fateful decision. He had already vowed to keep his distance from her, and yet when he thought he had lost her in the Waté plane, he realized that he could not live without her.

As if sensing his eyes on her, Elaina turned to him and smiled, and the radiance of it stole his breath. She made her way through the camp until she was at his side. Wordlessly she gazed into his eyes and slipped her hand into his.

The sun reflected its last flecks of pink and gold light against billowy clouds. Night was falling, casting shadows across the unlit corners of the camp. Rone watched as torchlight and moonlight fought for a chance to dance in Elaina's hair. He stood transfixed by her. She was a delicate flower, and yet, in the same respect, she was an instrument of destruction. She was beauty and terror. Order and chaos. Compassion and…malevolence?

He pulled her into his arms and held her close to his heart. No, he thought. There was no evil in her. He would not let there be. He would do whatever was necessary to shield her from the ills fate had in store for her. He would conquer every trial, and surrender every luxury. He would give up anything for her…even a kingdom!